"Sarcasm, violence, blood, w reader engaged and the story another wonderful addition t urban fantasy cliché of cloa atmosphere. In the Sandman Slim novels the reader can feel the heat of L.A., smell the smog, taste the carnitas and tamales, and know the joy of finally sliding into the AC and onto that barstool at the end of a brutal, bloody hard day of searching, fighting, killing, and just plain old surviving."   —*New York Journal of Books*

"Kadrey's done amazing work keeping one of literature's great anti-heroes in adventures this long, and *Killing Pretty* proves that he isn't slowing down."                    —Cory Doctorow

"If your tastes trend to noir grit and L.A. cool, Slim is your man."
                        —Barnes & Noble Sci-Fi & Fantasy Blog

"Kadrey's fantastic seventh Sandman Slim installment rivals the first."                    —*RT Book Reviews* (top pick)

"Six years after stumbling into Sandman Slim's seedy, seamy world, I'm still hungry to go back every time. To get lost in it. I have yet to be disappointed. But if this is escapism, it's the most masochistic kind I can imagine."                    —NPR Books

PRAISE FOR Richard Kadrey's Bestselling
Sandman Slim Series

"We can savor every insight from a grand master of the blunt exposition."                    —*Locus*

"Profane, intensely metaphoric language somehow makes self-tortured monster Stark sympathetic and turns a simple story into a powerful noir thriller."                    —*Publishers Weekly*

# KILLING
# PRETTY

## ALSO BY RICHARD KADREY

*Metrophage*

*Dead Set*

### Sandman Slim Novels

*The Perdition Score* (Summer 2016)

*Killing Pretty*

*The Getaway God*

*Kill City Blues*

*Devil Said Bang*

*Aloha from Hell*

*Kill the Dead*

*Sandman Slim*

# KILLING
# PRETTY

A SANDMAN SLIM NOVEL

RICHARD KADREY

**HARPER Voyager**
*An Imprint of* HarperCollins *Publishers*

KILLING PRETTY. Copyright © 2015 by Richard Kadrey. Excerpt from *The
Perdition Score* © 2016 by Richard Kadrey. All rights reserved. Printed in
the United States of America. No part of this book may be used or repro-
duced in any manner whatsoever without written permission except in the
case of brief quotations embodied in critical articles and reviews. For information address HarperCollins Publishers, 195 Broadway, New York, NY
10007.

HarperCollins books may be purchased for educational, business, or sales
promotional use. For information please e-mail the Special Markets Department at SPsales@harpercollins.com.

A hardcover edition of this book was published in 2015 by Harper Voyager,
an imprint of HarperCollins Publishers.

FIRST HARPER VOYAGER PAPERBACK EDITION PUBLISHED 2016.

Harper Voyager and design is a trademark of the HarperCollins Publishers
L.L.C.

*Designed by Paula Russell Szafranski*

Library of Congress Cataloging-in-Publication Data has been applied for.

ISBN 978-0-06-237325-0

HB 05.04.2022

*To all the writing teachers who told me to quit.*

*I'm still not listening.*

# ACKNOWLEDGMENTS

Thanks to my agent, Ginger Clark, and my editor, David Pomerico. Thanks also to Pamela Spengler-Jaffe, Jennifer Brehl, Rebecca Lucash, Kelly O'Connor, Caroline Perny, Shawn Nicholls, Dana Trombley, Jessie Edwards, and the rest of the team at Harper Voyager. Thanks also to Jonathan Lyons, Sarah Perillo, and Holly Frederick. Big thanks to Martha and Lorenzo in L.A. and Diana Gill in New York. As always, thanks to Nicola for everything else.

"I had noticed that both in the very poor and very rich extremes of society the mad were often allowed to mingle freely."

—CHARLES BUKOWSKI, *Ham on Rye*

"This isn't America, Jack. This is L.A."

—LT. MAX HOOVER, *Mulholland Drive*

# KILLING
# PRETTY

I BREAK HIS wrists so I don't have to break his neck.

He falls to his knees, but I don't think it's the pain, though I make sure there's plenty of that. It's the sound. The crack of bones as they shatter. A sound that lets you know they're never going to heal quite right and you're going to spend the rest of eternity drinking your ambrosia slushies with two hands.

I'm surprised to see an angel down here right now, considering all the cleanup going on in Heaven after the recent unpleasantness. Still, there are sore losers and bad winners in every bunch. I don't know which one this guy is, but I caught him spray-painting GODKILLER on the front of Maximum Overdrive, the video store where I live. I might have let him off easy if all he wanted to do was kill me. I'm used to that by now. But this fucker was ruining my windows. Do these winged pricks think I'm made of money? I'm about broke, and here's this high-and-mighty halo polisher setting me up for a trip to the hardware store to buy paint remover. I give his wrists an extra twist for that. He gulps in air and makes a gagging sound like he might throw up. I take a couple of steps back and look around. No one on the street. It's just after New Year's, the floods have receded, and people are just beginning to drift back into L.A.

"What exactly is your problem?" I ask the angel. "Why come down here and fuck with me?"

He rests his crippled hands on his thighs and shifts around on his knees until he's facing me.

"You had no right. You killed him."

"I didn't kill God and you know it. He's Uptown right now putting out new lace doilies in Heaven."

What really happened is a long story. Truth is, I did fuck over Chaya, a weasely fragment of God who, if he'd lived, would have ruined the universe. But I also left one good God part, Mr. Muninn, fat and happy and back in Heaven. But that's the problem with angels. They're absolutists. I clipped a tiny bit off their boss and now I'm the bad guy. Once angels get an idea in their head, there's no arguing with them.

Like cops and people who listen to reggae.

The angel narrows his eyes at me.

"Yes, a part of the father yet remains. But you didn't have the right to kill *any* of him, Abomination."

Damn. This old song.

"See, when you start calling me names, it really undercuts your argument. You're not mad because I got rid of Chaya. You're mad because you know *you* should have done it, but you didn't. And what happened was a mangy nephilim had to step up and do the deed for you."

The angel staggers to his feet and sticks his hands out in front of him, pressing his mangled wrists together.

"You must pay for what you've done, unclean thing."

"Go home, angel. My store is a mess, and looking at the big picture, I'm more afraid of Netflix than I am of you."

To my surprise, the crippled creep is able to manifest his Gladius, an angelic sword of fire. He has to hold it with both hands, but he can move it around by swinging his shoulders back and forth. Maybe this guy is more trouble than I gave him credit for. A badass will try to break your bones, but someone crazy, who knows what they'll do? Mostly, though, I'm glad the neighbors aren't around so I have to explain the gimp with the lightsaber in my driveway.

The angel comes at me hard and fast, all *Seven Samurai*, ready to send me to asshole Heaven. In his present condition, he's still quick, but far off his game. I sidestep the Gladius and punch him in the throat. He falls. The Gladius turns the pavement molten where it touches. As the angel goes down, I snap up a knee and break his nose. He falls over backward and the Gladius goes out.

I walk around behind him and push him upright. His eyes have rolled back in his head. He's completely out. I take out a flask full of Aqua Regia, everyone's favorite drink in Hell, and pour some down his throat. The angel gasps and his eyes snap open. He looks up at me and sputters.

"You're trying to poison me."

"You were unconscious. If I wanted you dead, I could have drilled a hole in your skull and tea-bagged your brain. Now shut up and go home."

The angel crawls away and lurches to his feet. He's covered in blood and booze and his hands are sticking out at funny angles, like he just fell out of a Picasso. He takes a breath and hauls himself upright, trying for a last little bit of dignity. I walk away.

"This isn't over," he yells.

I open the door to Max Overdrive.

"Yeah it is. See? I'm going inside. Bye."

I close the door and wait a second. When I open it again, the angel is gone. But he left blood and mucus all over the front steps. Something else to clean up.

Inside, Kasabian is behind the counter. He looks at me as I come in.

"What was that? I heard shouting."

I wave it away with my hand.

"Nothing. Some idiot rented *Bio-Dome* and wanted his money back."

Kasabian shakes his head.

"Fuck him. We're not paying for some schmuck's bad taste."

"That's pretty much what I said."

"Did you say it with your knees? You've got blood on them."

I look down. He's right. I'm hard on clothes.

"I'm going upstairs to change."

Here's the thing. Most angels aren't like the idiot outside. They're annoying, but a necessary evil, like black holes or vegans. Most angels are gray-suit-yes-sir-no-sir-fill-it-out-in-triplicate company men. Someone you wouldn't remember if they shot themselves out of a cannon dressed like Glinda, the good witch. A few angels, not many, go rogue and have to be put down like dogs. No tears shed for them. Still, as annoying as angels are, they keep air in the tires and gas in the tank so the universe can go on dumbly spinning. The only angels anyone is happy to see take a powder are Death and the Devil, one of whom is currently asleep in the storage room at Max Overdrive.

But I'll get to that later.

So, the angels are fucking off and God's away on business. What do the mice do when the cat's not looking? They drink. And if they're smart they do it at Bamboo House of Dolls. Candy and me, we're mice with PhDs. I'll meet up with her at the bar.

Chihiro, I mean. Not Candy. I have to remember that. *Chihiro.* Candy is dead. So to speak. Dead enough that the feds and the cops aren't looking for her, and that's all that counts. Now she's Chihiro, with a different face and name and, well, everything. Everything we can think of. I just hope it's enough. I'm sure we've missed a few things. I hope not so many that anyone is going to notice. I might have to kill them.

I change and go back downstairs, my na'at, knife, and Colt under my coat.

"I'm going to Bamboo House. Want to get a drink?"

Kasabian shakes his head, carefully putting discs in clear plastic cases with the tips of his mechanical fingers.

"Nah. I'm waiting for Maria. She's coming by with a new delivery."

"Anything good?"

He looks up and shakes his head.

"Don't know. She said it's a western."

"Fingers crossed it brings some goddamn customers into this tomb."

"Patience, grasshopper. This new deal with Maria is our stairway to Heaven."

"It better be. There won't be room for you, me, and Candy in a refrigerator box if this place closes."

"Chihiro," he says.

"Fuck. Chihiro."

"Later, Mr. Wizard," he says.

"Yeah. Later."

Outside, I wonder if I can scrape GODKILLER off the windows with the black blade instead of spending money on paint remover.

A week ago I saved the whole goddamn universe from extinction and now I can't afford the hardware store. I need to have a serious talk with my life coach.

I LIGHT A Malediction, the number one cigarette Downtown, and walk the few blocks to Bamboo House of Dolls, the best punk tiki bar in L.A. People are hanging around outside, talking and smoking. I get a few "Happy New Years" on the way in. I give the crowd a nod, not in the mood for chitchat.

Carlos, the owner of the place, is behind the bar in a Hawaiian shirt covered in snowmen and wreaths. The little plastic hula girls by the liquor bottles on the wall still wear doll-size Santa hats. There's a lot of this going on in L.A. I feel it a little myself. Hanging on to the last few shreds of holiday spirit after a flood-soaked, apocalyptic Christmas.

What did I get under the tree? A fugitive girlfriend. An LAPD beatdown. A last dirty trick from Mason Faim. And one more thing: I lost the Room of Thirteen Doors. It's not gone, but I can't use it anymore to move through shadows. Now I'm just like all these other slobs. I have to walk or drive everywhere. That's not such a bad thing considering L.A. is still half ghost town, but what happens when it fills up again? I don't deal well with things like traffic and other people.

Inside Bamboo House, I head straight for the bar. Martin Denny is on the jukebox playing "Exotic Night," a kind of gamelan and piano version of "Greensleeves," like we're on some mutant holly jolly tropical island.

"*Feliz Navidad*," says Carlos.

"Same to you, man."

I look around the place. It's a nice crowd. A mix of civilians, Lurkers, and even a few brave tourists.

"What do you think? How long do you figure you can get away with the Father Christmas thing?"

Carlos adjusts a piece of holly on a coconut carved like a monkey's head.

"As long as I want. My bar. My rules. Maybe I'll do it all year-round. Crank up the a/c. Rent customers scarves and gloves. It'll be the holidays twenty-four/seven."

"I think you shouldn't put so much acid in your eggnog."

He raises his eyebrows and points at me.

"That could be the house drink. 'El Santo Loco.' "

"You and Kasabian, always looking for new business plans."

"That reminds me. You get anything good over the holidays?"

"Maria is supposed to be coming by today with something. A western."

"Cool. I'll stop by."

I'm not sure I want visitors. Not with the strange guy asleep in the storage room.

"Don't worry about it. If it's any good, I'll burn you a copy and bring it by."

"*De nada*," says Carlos and clears away some empty glasses. He slides a shot of Aqua Regia across the bar to me.

"Can I have some black coffee instead?"

He looks at me, surprised.

"A New Year's resolution?"

He goes to the pot and pours me some coffee. Brings it back to the bar.

I say, "I don't know. Just after all the shit that went down at Christmas, I thought I'd start off the new year with a clear head."

"So, you're a teetotaler now?"

I reach in my pocket and pull out the flask. Carlos nods approvingly.

"Thank you, Papa Noel. For a minute I thought we'd lost you to the angels."

"Not much chance of that."

Carlos leans over and looks past me.

"I believe you're being summoned."

I turn and spot Julie Sola at a table in the back corner of the place. I guess she's sort of my boss now at the PI firm she started when she quit the Golden Vigil. I nod to her and look back at Carlos.

"You don't mind us using your place for an office?"

"It's fine with me, but when I turn the place into Christmas all year-round, you'll have to pay for your mittens just like anybody else."

"Always a new business plan. Talk to you later."

"Adios."

I take my coffee and head over to where Julie is sitting. There are papers scattered on the table. Photocopies of newspaper articles and printouts of what look like police reports and hospital records. How the hell did she get those? She used to be a U.S. marshal and it looks like she's still got some of those connections.

She smiles and moves some of the papers out of my way so I can set down my cup.

"Afternoon," she says. "How are you today?"

"I just went three rounds with an angel Ebenezer Scrooge. Do you know any cheap ways to get spray paint off glass?"

"Turpentine? Acetone?"

"No. Those cost money."

She glances at the coffee in front of me like she's wondering how much of it is whiskey.

"I thought you could do magic," she says. "Can't you just wave a wand and make it disappear?"

"First off, only hillbillies and Harry Potter use wands anymore. Second, I mostly know Hellion magic. Melting faces and killing things. If I try hoodoo at home I'm afraid I'll just blow out the windows."

"You really can't afford paint remover?"

I sip my coffee.

"We have a little money, just not enough to blow on luxuries like cleaning products and food."

"You know, you could have asked me for an advance on your salary."

"People do that?"

"Normal people, all the time. I'll write you a check right now. Will five hundred dollars do?"

"It would do great, but you know I'm legally dead, right? I don't have a bank account, a passport, or a library card."

Julie puts down her pen. I can tell she's rethinking the wisdom of offering me a job.

"Fine, man of mystery. I'll bring you some cash tomorrow."

"Appreciate it. I was one day from hanging around with one of those signs. You know, 'Will Save the World for Food.'"

"Panhandling is illegal. I saved you from a life of crime."

"Yeah. I wouldn't want to get a bad reputation or anything."

Here I am again, scrambling for pocket change. Getting screwed out of half a million dollars by the Golden Vigil has left me a little touchy about money. I'm lucky Julie offered me a job. I owe her a lot, more than Candy—Chihiro—and I can ever repay.

"So, how's our guest?" says Julie.

"Our guest? You mean the bum in my storage room? He's still asleep."

She frowns.

"Is that good? Maybe we should take him to a doctor."

"And tell him what when he sees the guy's heart is gone, but he's still alive?"

"Touché. So what do you think we should do?"

"I had Allegra and Vidocq patch him up, but he *is* Death. Give him a couple of more days. If he doesn't come around, we'll figure out a plan B."

"I thought Death would be better at, well . . ."

She shrugs. I pick up my coffee.

"Being dead? Look, we don't even know if he is who he says he is. He could be a lunatic angel gone off his meds, or some mad scientist's Christmas present gone wrong. The real point is, I don't like him and I want him out of my place as soon as possible."

Julie ignores the remark and picks through some of the printouts on the table.

"You're the magic man, so you're in charge of him for the time being. But there's something I wanted to show you."

She pushes some of the papers across the desk to me. I pick them up.

"What is all this?"

"Articles. Police and accident reports. Patient records from the last week."

"Okay. Why do I care?"

"Because they all say the same thing: no one has died since right after Christmas. There are the same number of people with terminal illnesses, gunshot wounds, car accidents as always, and most of them should have died. But they haven't."

"Then what's happening with them?"

"They're in deep comas, with their vitals hovering just above death. Hospitals are full of them. Thousands. All over the world. No one is dying anywhere."

"And you think this proves that the hobo I'm babysitting is Death."

"You have another explanation?"

"Yeah. God is doing construction jobs in Heaven and Hell. Maybe He doesn't want a busload of new kids getting in the way."

"Then you think it's a coincidence that at exactly the same time an injured man calling himself Death came to us—"

"Came to *me*."

"Came to you, that people around the world stopped dying?"

I gulp my coffee, thinking. Trying to poke holes in her argument.

"I admit, the timing seems a little weird."

"You've dealt with God and the Devil. Why is it so hard to admit that when Death has a problem he might come to you?"

I look back at the bar, wishing I'd taken that drink Carlos offered.

"Because I thought I was done with that stuff. The Angra Om Ya are gone. Mason Faim is gone. The Room of Thirteen Doors is gone. I hoped that part of my life might be over for a while and I could just be a boring PI. Hunt down insurance fraud and lost cats."

Julie leans forward, her elbows on the table.

"And we'll do those things, but we're going to solve Death's murder first."

"You're not getting it."

"What am I not getting?"

I push the papers back across the table.

"This thing you want to get into, you're screwing around with bad angelic hoodoo. And if this guy really is Death, whoever dragged him into a human body and cut his fucking heart out is into some of the heaviest, darkest baleful magic I've ever seen."

Julie brightens, like a kid just remembering it's her birthday.

"And that's why it's perfect for us. Look, it can take years for an investigations firm to build the kind of reputation it takes to bring in the big jobs. We might bypass all that with a single case."

"Years? I should have stayed in the arena."

"I guarantee if we solve this case, the kind of clients we'll have, there'll be plenty of money for you and Max Overdrive."

I try to come up with an argument, but I can't because she's right. This is exactly the kind of case that would get the attention of every Sub Rosa, wealthy Lurker, and Beverly Hills magic groupie in California. Besides, Julie is ready to hand me money right now.

And there's the other debt . . .

"All right. I'm in. Let's do your Mike Hammer thing."

She raises a bottle of light beer I missed behind all the papers. I click it with my coffee cup. There's just one more question.

"So, we're partners?"

She shakes her head.

"No way. I'm taking all the financial risks. It's my company. You're an employee."

"But I get stock options and you'll match my 401(k)."

"Tell yourself whatever story you need to get yourself out of bed, but as of now, you're on the clock. Which means sticking to coffee during daylight hours."

"You know how to suck all the fun out of being sober."

"That's a boss's job."

My coffee is getting cold, but I sip it anyway. It tastes lousy. I mean, it doesn't taste any different than it did a minute ago, but knowing it's my only drink of choice all day, every day . . . Let's just say that the romance is over.

"I thought Chihiro would be here with you," says Julie.

I turn and scan the room for familiar faces, but don't find any.

"She's out getting some new clothes and things. Since she got her new face, she's been doing this bleach-blond kogal look. You know, Japanese schoolgirl drag. She was having fun, but I went through the plaid-skirt thing back with my old magic circle. A woman named Cherry Moon. She wanted to look like a junior high princess forever. After that, I don't want anything to do with that Lolita stuff. So, she said she'd figure out something else."

"Sounds like she likes you."

"She just likes my movie collection."

"I'm sure that's what it is."

A new song comes on the jukebox, a fifties cha-cha version of "Jingle Bells." I'm going to have to speak to Carlos about how his Santa fetish is curdling his taste in music.

"I have some good news," Julie says. "I think I found a real office. On Sunset, near Sanborn. It's a little two-story building that used to have a dentist on the first floor and a telemarketing company on the second. The woman who owns it left when the floods started. There's some water damage in the lobby, but it's not bad and she has insurance. Best of all, after all the craziness, she doesn't want to come back to L.A. and will sell me the whole place for a song."

"That's great. Congratulations."

Julie smiles.

"I mean, it's not much to look at. It's between an El Pollo Loco and an empty garage, and across the street from a used car lot."

"A car lot? That's convenient. I'm going to need to steal a lot more cars now that I can't shadow-walk anymore."

"Don't even think about it," says Julie, suddenly serious.

"Fine. I'll get around on a Vespa. See how much your clients like that."

"Can't you ride your motorcycle?"

"I brought it back from Hell. There's no way it's street legal and I'm not looking for any more run-ins with LAPD."

"And you think stealing cars will help you avoid that?"

I'm not a huge fan of other people's logic.

"Don't worry," she says, "we'll figure out something. Just no stealing anything in the neighborhood."

"Cross my heart."

"With luck I'll sign the papers next week. I'm putting my condo up for sale. That will cover most of the costs."

"I'll cross my fingers and toes too."

"Thanks."

Julie shuffles the printouts until they're straight. She riffles through them one more time and puts them in a soft-sided leather attaché case.

"I really think we're onto something," she says.

"I hope so."

I look at the last dregs of cold coffee in my cup.

"I need another drink. You?"

She drains the last of her beer. Shakes her head.

"I'm good. You're sticking with coffee, right?"

"While you drink beer?"

"I don't have a drinking problem."

"You think I do?"

She starts to say something, but stops, like she doesn't want to get into it.

"Just stick to coffee for now."

"Yes, boss."

I head back to the bar. Carlos sees me coming and has the coffeepot ready.

"How's the sober life treating you so far?"

"It's been ten minutes of sheer hell."

"I hear it gets better."

"Really?"

"No."

"Fuck you."

Carlos puts a hand to his ear.

"Sorry. I can't hear you over the music."

I give him the finger as he moves on to other customers.

"You heard me just fine."

Someone says, "Drink up, cowboy. I'll get the next round."

It's a woman's voice, but when I look there's no one there. Someone taps me on the shoulder. I have to turn to see her.

She's wearing shades. Round and deep black, so her eyes are invisible. Her hair is buzzed to maybe an inch long and dyed cotton-candy pink. Black lipstick and a bomber jacket over a "Kill la Kill" T-shirt. Black tights with thigh and shinbones printed in white down the sides. Shiny black boots with pointed studs on the toes and heels.

"So," Candy says. "Different enough?"

"Plenty. Perfect. Still got your knife?"

She opens her jacket and shows me where she's had someone at Lollipop Dolls sew in a leather sheath.

"Think my lunch-box gun will go with the ensemble?"

"I think you'd look naked without it."

She grins and gets a little closer.

"Naked. I like the sound of that. I checked out my reflection on the way in. I'd do me. How about you?"

I shake my head.

"Careful. Out here in the world we're still getting to know each other."

She purses her lips and pulls the jacket around her.

"You're goddamn paranoid. You should see someone about that."

"I tried, but she kept writing things down. It made me more paranoid."

Candy looks away at the bottles behind the bar.

"I went to all this trouble and I can't even kiss you."

"Grab a drink and come back into the corner. Julie and I are just about done with our meeting."

"Fine," she says.

I can hear the disappointment in her voice. She went way out of her way to change her look and all I can do is nod and smile like a tourist admiring the view. Truth is, even before Candy became Chihiro I'd been feeling funny about the two of us. When she was locked up in a Golden Vigil jail cell for attacking a civilian, she said some things. Like I was using her. Like I thought she was sick. Later, she said it was just poison talking after someone spiked her anti-Jade potion. She said it made her crazy and suspicious. Maybe. Because some of what she said hit close to home and I've been wondering about it ever since. There's a lot of unspoken stuff between us. I used to think that was a good thing. Now I'm not so sure.

When I get back to the table, Julie says, "Who was that?"

"Guess."

"You're kidding me."

"You'll see for yourself in a minute."

Candy comes over with a shot of whiskey. I swear I can smell it all the way across the bar.

She takes off her sunglasses and hooks them over her shirt. Grabs a chair and sits down at our table.

"What do you think?" she asks Julie.

"I can't believe you're the same person."

"That's the idea," I say.

"Admit it, I look like a superhero, don't I?" she says.

"I don't know many pink-haired superheroes," said Julie. "But if there are any, you'll be stiff competition."

Candy looks at me.

"See? She likes it."

"I told you. I like it fine. We just have to be cool."

Candy rolls her eyes.

"He thinks if I stand too close to him we're going to get nuked."

"He might have a point," says Julie. "About playing down your relationship."

Candy sits back in her chair.

"You two should start a band. The Buzzkill Twins."

"Julie is going to have a new office soon," I say, trying to change the subject.

That gets Candy's attention. She sits up.

"Cool. If you're hiring this scaredy cat, can I have a job too?"

"What are your skills?" says Julie.

"I was afraid you'd ask that."

I say, "You used to run the office for Doc Kinski."

"Yeah. I did."

"I might need a receptionist at some point," Julie says.

"Swell."

I look at Candy.

"You really want to be a receptionist?"

"No," she says. "I want to kick down doors like you, but apparently I'm not allowed."

"I never said that."

I want a drink and a cigarette. I want zombies, dinosaurs, and flaming giraffes to come crashing through the door so I don't have to talk anymore.

"Look," I say. "Maybe I *am* being a little paranoid. It's just, we faked your death once. I'm not sure we can get away with it again. What do you think, Julie?"

"I think the U.S. Marshals Service isn't dumb," she says.

Candy sips her drink.

"So, I should hide out at Brigitte's forever and learn to knit?"

I take her shot glass, drink half, and hand it back.

"It would probably be okay if we partner up, but you have to do it as Chihiro, not Candy. Pretend it's the first season of *X-Files*."

Candy leans back and smiles. The black lipstick with the short pink hair looks good. But I'm not sure she gets that I'm as frustrated by all this clandestine crap as she is.

"A Scully and Mulder thing? Yeah. I can handle that," she says. "Does that mean I get to move back home?"

Julie gets her bag and stands up.

"This is getting a bit personal. I think I'll go."

"So, can I have a job?" says Candy.

Julie thinks for a minute.

"You can work with him as an unpaid intern. We'll see from there."

"Awesome."

Julie slips the bag over her shoulder and looks at me.

"I'll call you. Keep an eye on our guest."

"My guest."

"Call me if anything changes."

"Bye. Thanks," says Candy as Julie weaves her way through the crowd.

When she's gone, Candy finishes her drink.

"Seriously," she says. "We have to talk about some kind of timetable for me coming back to Max Overdrive. I love Brigitte, but I can't live without a plan."

"Trust me. I know how you feel."

"Do you?"

"Yeah."

"Okay. I wasn't sure for a while there."

She pushes her leg against mine under the table. I look around, making sure no one can see. I think we're okay and she feels good, so I don't try to stop her.

"Look," I say. "If we work together we'll see each other all the time. Aside from that, give it until the later part of the month before you come back. Okay? Maybe by then I'll have Sleeping Beauty out of the store."

"Can I come over now?" she says. "Seeing as how we're colleagues, I should have a look at the dead man."

"I don't see why not. But we can't leave at the same time. I'll go. You go and order another drink. Take off in, say, twenty minutes."

She picks up the shot glass and rolls it between her palms.

"Twenty minutes is a long time to be all on my own. What if someone asks me for a date?"

"Do what you think is best, but remember that your guitar amp is still at Max Overdrive."

"What do I have to do to get it back?" she says.

"Awful things. Depraved things."

"You bad man."

I get up from the table.

"Forget twenty minutes. Make it ten."

"That's the first sensible thing you've said all day."

She heads back to the bar. I go out the door.

LOS ANGELES IS a busted jukebox in a forgotten bar at the ass end of the high desert. The city only exists between the pops, skips, and scratches of the old 45s. Snatches of ancient songs. Lost voices. The jagged artifacts of a few demented geniuses, one-hit wonders, and lip-synching frauds. Charlie Manson thought he was going to be the next Beatles and we know how that turned out. This city is built on a bedrock of high crimes and rotten death. The Black Dahlia. Bugsy Siegel. The Night Stalker. We've buried and forgotten more bodies than all the cemeteries of Europe. Someday the water is going to run out and the desert will strip this town down to its Technicolor bones. Even the buzzards won't want it and the city knows it. Maybe that's why I like it.

It's not a long walk back to Max Overdrive and I can let my mind wander.

It's funny to be thinking about the desert when there's still so much water around, cutting off streets with blocked sewer drains. Signs of the weird floods that nearly drowned the city at Christmas are fading fast, but not completely gone. L.A. doesn't have the luxury of hundred-year flood warnings. We don't have that kind of relationship with water or the past. And this flood wasn't anything to do with global warming or El Niños. It wasn't real weather. It was the symptom of a disease. An organism worming its way into our world from another.

The Angra Om Ya were old gods. Older than the God most good little girls and boys think about. That God, sneaky bastard, stole the universe from the Angra and walled them off in another dimension. When they broke out and headed back into our space-time, they brought the floods with them. One long golden shower of hate. I fought the Angra, if *fight's* the right word. I danced around until I foxed them into the Room of Thirteen Doors and locked them in forever. If you live in this universe, you're welcome, and could you spare some change for a fellow American who's down on his luck? Okay, Bogart said it better than I did, but you get the idea.

The city was still underwater when we killed Candy. No choice. The feds were trucking Lurkers out into the Mojave to a hoodoo Manzanar. So, Julie helped us out. We staged a scene where it looked like she shot and killed Candy. What was another Lurker stiff to the Vigil jackboots? And now I owe Julie and will be working off the debt until she dies or I die or the oceans turn to Jell-O and Atlantis rises.

You'd think after that, things might smooth out a little. What could be worse than your city underwater, pissed-off elder gods, and killing your girlfriend? Nothing, you'd say, but if you bet me the farm on it, I'd be asshole-deep in cotton. You see, a bum wandered into my life around New Year's. He called himself Death, and who was I to argue? Someone had ripped out his heart and he was still walking around. He wasn't a zombie because I destroyed all of them (seriously, how about that spare change?) and he definitely wasn't an ordinary angel. The fucker, who or whatever he is, came to me specifically and asked me to find out who killed him. *Me.* Like I need more bullshit in my life. Between BitTorrent and video streaming, Maximum Overdrive is about dead. Now I have to drop all that to wet nurse another supernatural shit heel because why?

Because I'm a freak. A nephilim. Half human and half angel. Heaven hates me because I shouldn't exist and the world hates me because, well, I'm really good at killing things. Yet for some reason, the schmuck asleep in my storeroom thinks I'm a Good Samaritan. When he wakes up, despite what Julie wants, I'm going to skate his ass out the door as fast as I can. I simply do not need crap like this in my life.

What I need is a drink, a week in Mexico with Candy, and tickets for Skull Valley Sheep Kill when they reopen the Whisky a Go Go. I'm not betting on the last two, but I can magically conjure up the first by reaching into my pocket and taking out my flask.

Which is almost empty.

Story of my life. Thanks for listening. Be sure to tip your waitresses on the way out.

PAUL NEWMAN AND Steve McQueen are jumping off a cliff when I get back to Max Overdrive. I recognize the movie immediately. It's *Butch Cassidy and the Sundance Kid,* but not any version I've seen. Robert Redford is nowhere in sight.

"You like it?" says Maria. Her voice cracks a little, like she only takes it out on special occasions.

Maria is about my height, her skin darker than Allegra's. She reminds me of a young Angela Bassett if she'd grown up with alley-cat gutter punks. She's got a heavy-gauge ring through her nose and a smaller one in her lower lip. A muscular neck with tattoos of the four elements—air, earth, fire, and water. Her hair is about shoulder length, dyed sky blue, but with black roots showing, and pulled back in a couple of ragged pigtails. Each of her fingernails is painted a different color.

"It's great, right?" says Kasabian. He's drumming on the front counter like a beatnik with a pair of new bongos, his metal hand bouncing like silver spiders.

"McQueen was originally supposed to play the Sundance Kid, but the deal fell through," he says. "Get it? This is the future for the store. Movies that never happened. *Dirty Harry* with Frank Sinatra instead of Eastwood. David Lynch's *Return of the Jedi*. Brando in *Rebel Without a Cause*. The right people will pay a fortune to see this stuff."

I watch Newman and McQueen trading quips for a couple of minutes.

"It's not the worst idea you ever had."

"It's goddamn genius and you know it," he says. "The next one Maria is getting for us is Alejandro Jodorowsky's version of *Dune*."

I look at Maria.

"Was this his idea or yours?"

She rubs her throat nervously, like she's not used to being the center of attention.

"Neither," she says. "It was Dash. Want to meet him?"

"Now we've got another partner? How many people are we bringing in to this thing? I don't like surprise guests."

Kasabian stops drumming and gives me a look.

"Calm down, Frank Booth. Tell him who Dash is before he needs smelling salts."

Maria reaches into a small clutch bag and pulls something out.

"It's okay, Stark. He doesn't want money. He just likes to keep busy. He's a ghost."

Christ. I hate ghosts. They're nothing but trouble.

"I need a drink."

"Good," says Maria. "He likes liquor. Bring down a shot for him."

"Your ghost is a drunk? Fuck me with all this good news."

I go upstairs and find the Aqua Regia. I refill my flask, pour a shot into a glass, and down it. I fill the glass again and take it downstairs.

"Right there is fine," says Maria, indicating the counter. I set the shot glass down.

"You don't have anything to eat, do you?" she says. "Something sweet."

Kasabian takes a Donut Universe bag from under the counter, removes an éclair, and sets it next to the shot.

I watch as Maria unfolds a black plastic clamshell. An old-fashioned makeup compact.

"If we're doing dead-people makeovers, the guy in the storeroom can use one."

"Give it a rest, man," says Kasabian. "Show an artist a little respect."

Maria sets the open compact on the counter with the mirror facing the glass and donut. She blows on the mirror and draws a symbol I don't recognize on the misted glass.

"Are you home, Dash?" she says.

Nothing happens.

But then the mist fades, and a face drifts into view behind the drink and donut. I can't get a good look at him. A lot of his face is hidden behind the food. He's a kid, maybe sixteen, with messy blond hair streaked with bright red. He closes his eyes and sniffs. He's getting high off the food offerings.

"Dash, this is Stark," says Maria. She moves her hand, letting me know I need to get closer to the mirror so the kid can see me. I don't really want to get too close. I don't trust ghosts.

I lean over, but stay on the far side of the food.

"Hey, kid. Thanks for the movie. You have good taste."

Dash mouths something, but I can't hear him.

Maria, standing behind me, has been watching the whole thing.

"He says you're welcome and he hopes to bring more with him next time you meet."

Next time. Great.

"You read lips," I say.

Maria nods.

"I learned when I was a girl. Like Dash, some ghosts are shy and will only appear through a looking glass."

Kasabian shoulders me out of the way and practically sticks his mug in the mirror.

"Hey, Dash. How's it going?"

The kid's grin widens. They've talked before.

"You working on getting us *Dune*?"

Dash nods and gives a thumbs-up.

"Swell. Do it and next time you come by I'll have a steak dinner waiting."

Dash shakes his head.

"He's vegetarian," says Maria.

"Okay," says Kasabian. "How about a big salad with croutons and edible flowers?"

Dash nods.

I look at Kasabian.

"Edible flowers?"

"Yeah. Fairuza uses them when she cooks. They're not bad."

"If you say so."

I lean over to the mirror.

"Keep the movies coming and I'll get you a whole damned wedding cake next time."

Dash mouths "thanks."

"Thanks, Dash," says Maria. "Now everybody knows everybody. Isn't that nice? I'll talk to you tonight."

Dash gives a little wave and drifts out past the edge of the mirror. Maria snaps the compact shut.

"That's Dash," she says.

I pick up the shot glass.

"Seems like a nice kid. Thanks for hooking us up."

Maria puts out a hand as I raise the glass to my lips.

"I wouldn't do that if I were you."

"Why? What's wrong with it?"

"Nothing. It's just that when we present food to Dash, any looking-glass ghost, he eats the essence of the offering. Don't worry. The food isn't poison or anything like that. It's just a bit empty."

I look at the glass. Ghost leftovers. Why not? I open up and toss the Aqua Regia back.

Maria was right. It isn't awful, but it's not booze anymore. The taste is thin and slightly sour, like the memory of a drink. I take a bite of the éclair. It's worse. Like Play-Doh and chalk. I go behind the counter and spit it into the wastebasket.

"Classy," says Kasabian. "You really know how to impress the ladies."

"I don't need etiquette tips from you, Tin Man."

Maria is tugging on the loose threads of her jacket sleeves again. She's used to nicer people than us.

"What do we owe you for the movie, Maria? We aren't exactly rolling in cash, you know."

"Oh, no. It's not like that," she says. "I was just hoping you could show me some magic."

"You're a witch. What do you think you can learn from me?"

"That's it. Kasabian said you know different kinds of magic. And that you're good at improvising spells and hexes."

"Yeah, I can improvise things. But that's not what you're after, are you?"

She looks up from her sleeves.

"No. I want to see Hellion magic."

"Why?"

"It's different. I'm curious."

Her pupils contract almost imperceptibly. She's lying.

"Maria? What's this really about?"

She takes a breath and lets it out.

"Some ghosts are angrier than others. They want to get out of where they are. Some are scared. Some are vicious.

I'll want to talk to one like Dash and one of the others will appear. It's getting worse."

"Did you ever think about not talking to ghosts? You're not a Dead Head necromancer. Why bother?"

Her brow furrows.

"They're my friends. I can't abandon them. Would you refuse to see a friend because she lived in a bad neighborhood?"

"No. I guess not. But I'm not a ghost expert. Mostly I deal with things I can punch. For ghosts, I'd have to think about it."

"That's okay," she says. "I'd rather have the right answer than a quick wrong one."

"Okay. But I just started a new job and I kind of have my hands full right now. Let's maybe talk the next time you come by."

"Great. Thanks."

"No. Thank you," says Kasabian. "I'll make sure he doesn't forget."

Maria puts her handbag under one arm.

"I appreciate it. I'll come by when Dash gives me your movie."

"Thanks. You're always welcome to come by," says Kasabian, suddenly a fucking diplomat. He and Fairuza broke up a few days ago. Is he already on the prowl? Does Maria know he's 90 percent machine?

"See you around, Maria," I say.

She smiles and starts out. Stops.

"Did you know there's something sprayed on the front of your store?"

"Yeah. I'll take care of it tomorrow."

"Okay. Bye."

Kasabian and I watch the big-screen monitor bolted to the ceiling for a few more minutes. He was right, of course. The movie has a completely different feel with McQueen playing the Sundance Kid. We could make a mint if we can get more never-mades like this.

Candy comes in during the closing credits.

"Chihiro?" Kasabian says. "Holy shit."

She smiles and does a turn.

"You like the new me?"

"You look great. I mean you always looked great, but I think you nailed it this time."

I take out a Malediction.

"She doesn't look like Candy. That's the important thing."

"Don't light that cigarette," she says.

"Why?"

She comes over to me.

"Why this?"

She leans in and kisses me. I kiss her back. It's been long enough that we've been even somewhere safe together that it feels strange and new to hold her. And I'm not used to her being Chihiro yet. It feels a little like I'm cheating on Candy. But she is Candy. This whole thing is going to take a while longer to get used to.

When she lets go of me she steps back and laughs.

"What?" I say.

"You have lipstick all over yourself. Hold it."

She gets a napkin from the Donut Universe bag and wipes my lips. Which, with perfectly lousy timing, is when Fairuza decides to walk in. She's a Lurker. A Ludere. Blue-skinned, blond, and sporting a small pair of Devil horns. She knew

Candy for a long time. She played drums in Candy's band back before she "died."

Fairuza takes a DVD from her bag and slams it down on the counter. Walks over and slaps me hard enough it feels like hornets are having a hoedown on my cheek.

"Candy's barely gone you're already with this little bitch? Fuck you."

She starts to hit me again, but I get my arm up and her hand glances off.

"Fairuza," says Kasabian.

She turns and stabs a finger at him.

"And fuck you too for hanging around with this asshole. Is this the bitch he gave Candy's guitar to? Yeah, I heard about that. Fuck all of you."

She heads for the door and slams it hard enough I half expect the glass to crack.

Candy takes a step back and hands me the napkin. I wipe the last of the lipstick off my face myself.

"I've got to tell her," says Candy.

"No, you don't. The more people that know, the more dangerous this gets. Let her hate me. I can live with that."

"Goody for you," says Kasabian. "What about me? She's never going to speak to me again as long as I'm here with you two."

"What are you worried about? I thought you broke up."

"We did," he says. "But at least we were friends and . . . I don't know. Maybe there was some chance of getting back together. Now, though . . ."

I put my hands out like a goddamn preacher.

"No one tells Fairuza or anybody else. We are on thin

fucking ice. One mistake and Candy ends up in a federal pen. It's too much of a risk."

"What about me?" says Candy. "Okay, some people are going to think you're an asshole for being around Chihiro, but you still get to be you. I'm no one."

I hadn't really thought of that.

"Look, I'm still trying to get my brain around all this too. Maybe down the line it would be safe to let a couple of more people know. But we've got to play this out for a while. Chihiro didn't even exist a couple of weeks ago. You stick out. Let people get used to you. Then maybe we can think about letting other people in."

Candy thinks for a minute.

"I'll give it till the end of January. Then I'm talking to Fairuza. I'm not asking you. I'm telling you."

"Fine. But she's the only one for the time being."

"I guess."

"Listen. If this thing falls apart, it's not just on you and me. There's other people too. Julie. Brigitte. Allegra and Vidocq."

"Aren't you maybe leaving someone out?" says Kasabian.

"I was getting to you, Iron Man."

"I thought we discussed no more nicknames."

I ignore that.

"I know you think I'm a drag sometimes, but there's a lot at stake here."

"I know," Candy says quietly.

"I saw you dead once. I don't want to see that again."

"I wasn't really dead, dumb-ass."

"You sure looked like you were."

"That's 'cause I'm such a good actress. Me and Brigitte are going to star in a remake of *Thelma & Louise*."

"As I recall, that didn't end well."

"In our version the car is a Delorean time machine, so we just drive off and have adventures with pirates and robots."

"Or *Lethal Weapon*," says Kasabian. "You could do a girl-girl remake."

"Or *Bill and Ted*," she says.

She looks at me.

"I need another drink. You have supplies upstairs?"

"You know it."

I step aside and let her lead the way.

"Hello? Is anyone there?"

It's a man's voice coming from the storage room.

I look at Kasabian.

"Lock the front door."

"Sure. It's not like we're a place of business or anything."

As he does it, Candy and I knock on the storage room door.

"You all right in there?"

"Where am I?"

I open the door. He squints and pushes himself back to the farthest corner of the cot I set up for him, huddling there like a bug.

He says, "It's too bright."

Candy and I go inside and close the door. It's ripe in here. The guy wasn't clean when I met him. Add an extra week to that. We're in a cheese factory.

Candy hits the overhead light. It's only a sixty-watt. Candy liked the room dim when the band rehearsed.

I take a step closer, getting between the guy on the cot and Candy in case he's as unhinged as he looks.

"Is that better?"

Slowly, he opens his eyes. He keeps a hand up, blocking the bulb. When he can focus he stares at me.

"Where am I?"

"At Max Overdrive. Do you remember coming to me at Bamboo House of Dolls?"

He sits up and leans against the wall. Candy steps around me, fiddling with her phone. Who the fuck is she calling right now?

"Who's that?" he says.

"A friend. What do you remember?"

He looks at the blanket, his hands, and the room like he's never seen any of it before. When he looks at me I can see the gears starting to turn in his head.

"You're Stark."

"That's right. And this is Chihiro. You met her the other night too."

He stares at Candy for a little too long.

"That's not her real face," he says. "Or her name."

Candy shoots me a worried look. I hold up a hand to say "be cool."

"You can see through the glamour," I say. "So, you really are an angel."

He nods.

"The oldest, known to mortals as the Angel of Death."

"Yeah. You said that the other night."

"And you don't believe me."

"I'm not saying I don't believe you, but I've met my share of, let's say, unstable angels."

"You mean Aelita."

"There were others but, yeah, she was the worst."

"I'm not mad and I have no desire to be here or to be a burden."

"Then why are you here? And why come to me?"

Death touches the gauze bandages over the hole in his chest.

"You closed the wound."

"Not me. It was friends. And you haven't answered my question."

"It hurts," he says, rubbing his chest. "Everything hurts. I'd forgotten what pain is. Do you have anything for it?"

I take out my flask, unscrew the top, and hand it to him. He takes a swig and coughs, practically spitting the Aqua Regia all over himself.

"This is Hellion brew," he says.

"That's right. Drink up. It tastes like gasoline, but it'll help with the pain."

"I'm not sure it's permitted."

"I don't think anyone would hold it against you," says Candy. "It's not like you're here to party."

He looks at Candy for a few seconds, then drinks. He keeps it down better this time, but he'd probably be happier with an aspirin. Fuck him. I drank Aqua Regia for eleven years in Hell because there weren't any angels to help me. Death can choke down a couple of mouthfuls.

He hands me back the flask.

"Feeling better?"

He wipes his mouth with the back of his hand.

"No."

"You will."

"The brew smells interesting."

"Huh. I never thought of that. I guess it does."

Candy gets in closer to him.

"Why did you come here?"

"I was looking for Sandman Slim."

"Why?" says Candy.

"I need help."

"Because you're in a body."

He nods.

"And someone has murdered it. Murdered me."

I say, "Why not call one of your angel pals?"

He closes his eyes again.

"I don't know who to trust."

"But you trust Stark," says Candy. "Why?"

"Because Father trusted him."

Father. Mr. Muninn. God.

The bloody, dirt-streaked trench coat he had on when I met him is in a pile on the floor. I pick it up and go through the pockets. He doesn't object.

I say, "Why not go to Mr. Muninn if you need help?"

He shrugs.

"I've called and called to him, but all I get is silence."

There's a knife in one of his coat pockets. I've never seen one quite like it. It's over a foot long, double-bladed, with a black wooden grip. Sort of like an oversize athame ritual blade, but with a silver eagle on the grip. There's what looks like a glob of tar by the pommel, maybe to hold it in place.

I hold it out to him.

"What's this?"

"That, I believe, was what killed me."

"How do you know?"

"Because someone pulled it out of my chest and I awoke."

"Who pulled it out?"

He holds up a hand and gestures vaguely.

"I don't know. I get the impression they were teenagers having some kind of party. By their startled reaction when I awoke, I don't think they were looking for me."

"Okay," I say. "It's New Year's and some kids are out partying. They find you and pull the sword out of the stone like King Arthur. Then you came and found me. Is that pretty much it?"

"I think so," he says.

"And you've never seen this knife before?"

"Not before I woke up."

"How did you find me?"

He's closed his eyes again. We're losing him.

"I'm an angel. I reached out and there you were, so I walked to where I found you."

"Where did you walk from?" says Candy.

"I don't know. There was a concrete structure. Not quite a building, but like it once was. It was covered with painted words and images. There were trees and scrub. It was dry and warm there. And stone stairs. Yes. I had to walk up a long stairway. After that, I walked for a long time down a highway and then through the city. That's where I found you."

He's looking at me and I don't want to believe any of it, but he's such a whipped dog I can't throw him out yet.

"I'm tired again. You are right about the brew. It took the pain away," he says.

"Okay. You get some more rest. But we're going to talk again later."

"Yes."

"And you're going to take a goddamn shower. Today."

"Yes. Thank you," he says, and lies down. "Would you turn the light off, please?"

"There's just one more thing before we go."

"Yes?"

"I'd appreciate it if you never mentioned anything about Candy's face or name again."

"As you wish."

Candy turns off the light and we go back outside. It's good to be out of the room and the dead man's stink. I turn the knife over in my hands.

"You ever see anything like it?"

Candy shakes her head.

"Never."

I take it over to Kasabian.

"How about you? You recognize it?"

"No, but I can look around online if it'll get him out of here quicker. He gives me the creeps."

"I'm with you there."

"I think he's kind of sad," says Candy.

"Shit."

"What?"

"I should have taken notes or something. I'm never going to remember everything he said."

Candy holds up her phone.

"Welcome to the twenty-first century, Huck Finn. I recorded the whole thing."

"Nice job."

"I know."

"Why don't you forward that to Julie? You'll make her day."

"I'm on it," she says, punching numbers into her phone.

I heft the knife in my hand. It has good weight and balance. With enough strength you could easily ram this through someone's ribs and pull out whatever the hell you wanted.

"I'm going to put this away upstairs. You still want that drink?"

"Hell yes, Agent Scully."

"Wait. I thought Scully was the woman."

"Stop being so heteronormative. You'd look good in a dress."

"I don't know what one of those words means, but okay."

"I really do have to drag you into this century."

"Drag away. I'm not going anywhere."

"Not without me."

"I wouldn't dream of it."

"Will you two please go the fuck away?" says Kasabian. "You're giving me diabetes over here."

We go upstairs and don't come down for a long time. My phone rings. It's Julie. I let her go to voice mail. Who's Huck Finn now?

I CALL JULIE back an hour later. We set up a time for the next day when she'll come by and see Sleeping Beauty. She says she might already have a line on another case and will call me when she's sure. I guess this is how things are from now on. Business calls and meetings with clients. Jobs we get and jobs we lose. Time to shine my shoes and carry my lunch in a brown paper bag. Soon it will be heart-healthy egg salad on vitamin-enriched organic free-range whole-wheat bread.

I'm so doomed.

Here's the thing: once upon a time I ran Hell. I didn't break the place, but I didn't exactly spruce it up. I don't have a good track record with nine-to-five responsibilities.

I wonder how long it will take for me to fuck up so badly that Julie gives my job to a guy selling oranges by the side of the freeway? Maybe I can swap gigs with him. He can do the surveillance and the paperwork and I'll stand by the off-ramp sucking fumes and selling oranges all day. It doesn't sound like such a bad life. A little repetitive, but so was fighting in the arena. The freeway job would have less stabbing and more vitamin C, and that's a step up in the world by anyone's standards.

I'm on my way to the big leagues one Satsuma at a time.

KASABIAN HAS REOPENED the place when I come downstairs and a few customers are browsing our very specialized movies. Before Maria and Dash, Max Overdrive was doomed. Kasabian made a deal with them to find us copies of lost movies. The uncut *Metropolis*. Orson Welles's cut of *The Magnificent Ambersons*. *London After Midnight*. Things like that. The problem was that a lot of the best of the bunch were silent movies, and in L.A. we like our gab, so those movies had a limited audience. They brought in enough money to keep the lights burning, but not enough to live on. The new, never-made movie scheme makes a lot more sense. Maybe we'll be able to sleep at night without worrying that the next day we'll be running the store out of the trunk of a stolen car. It's this possibility that makes me even more pissed about the angel tagging the front windows.

Fuck waiting for paint remover tomorrow. I get the black blade, go outside, and start scraping.

I'm at it for maybe ten minutes when I see someone's reflection in the glass. A tall guy in a brown leather blazer.

Someone is watching me from the street. I managed to get GOD off the glass, but now it reads KILLER, which really isn't much of an improvement.

I turn around and give the guy a "move along, pilgrim" look. He gives me an irritatingly polished smile and comes over to where I'm working.

This day just keeps getting better.

"Someone really did a number on your windows," he says. "Any significance to the word?"

"Some to him, I guess. None to me. What do you want?"

He looks around like he's checking to see it's just us chickens.

"You're James Stark, aren't you?"

"Who's asking?"

He reaches around his back. I make sure he can see the knife in my hand. For a second he looks nervous, but he recovers quickly and flashes me that shit-eating grin.

He holds up his wallet and shows me an ID card from the *L.A. Times*. The name on the card is David Moore. I nod and he puts it away.

"Impressive. I bet you own a dictionary *and* a thesaurus."

"Paper too," Moore says. "Lots of blank printer paper."

"And you want to print something about me. Why?"

He takes a step closer. He smells of adrenaline with a hint of fear sweat.

"We're doing a feature—maybe a series—on the people who stayed here during the flood. The pioneers and eccentrics."

"It sounds like you think I escaped from the Donner expedition."

"Nothing like that," he says.

He pulls out a pack of cigarettes. Taps out one for himself and holds the pack out to me like he's throwing a bone to a ragamuffin refugee in a World War II movie. I don't like the guy, but I take the cigarette. He lights it and then his own. It's not bad. A foreign brand that burns the back of my throat pleasantly.

"Thanks."

I go back to scraping the window.

He doesn't say anything for a minute, then, "How about it? Can I ask you a few questions?"

"Let me ask you one. Why me? Lots of people who stayed behind, including some of my customers. Why not interview them?"

He comes around where I'm scraping, so I get a clear view of his mug. Trying to establish eye contact and intimacy. Letting me know that even though he's from the press I shouldn't hold it against him. He's one of the good guys. But he's too eager to be convincing.

"You're the only celebrity around here," he says.

"And here I thought I was just another small businessman. Tell me, do all celebrities scrape their own goddamn windows clean?"

"We can start there. Why would someone paint 'killer' on your store?"

"Maybe they thought I was Jerry Lee Lewis. Look, I don't like talking to strangers. Next thing, you'll try to lure me into your van with promises of candy and puppies."

He doesn't react to the dig, so I keep on scraping. He watches me for a while before he speaks again.

"Maybe it said something else before. Maybe it said 'God-killer.'"

This time when I face him, I put the knife to his throat. There's nothing behind him, so there's plenty of room to move if he can get his brain and feet to function, but he can't. That means he's probably not one of Audsley Isshii's crew, an assassin sent to settle a score. I don't think he's Sub Rosa either. That's the first thing that would be coming out of his smug face if he was. He's just a ridiculous civilian looking for a story or an autograph.

"Why would you say 'Godkiller'?"

He puffs his smoke, trying to look like he's rolling with the scene, but his hand is shaking. Not enough for most people to see, but I can.

"There are a lot of rumors about you. About your past. And what you did during the flood."

"What do *you* think I did?"

"Some people say you saved the world and that it wasn't the first time. Other people say you lost your mind and killed God, which is a big surprise to some of us."

"You're an atheist."

"I guess you're not."

"I wish I had the luxury."

A couple of people come out of Max Overdrive. A civilian guy and a female Lyph. Lyphs are generally a friendly bunch, but they freak out a lot of regular citizens because they look like what kids draw when they imagine the Devil. Horns and hooves. A tail. This one has rented from us for a while, but I can't think of her name.

"What's the matter, Stark?" the Lyph says. "He return a movie late?"

I take the knife from his throat, but keep it by my side.

"See? My customers are a lot more interesting than me."

"Everyone's more interesting than Stark," says the Lyph. "He's just a Mr. Grumpypants."

"This guy is a reporter from the *Times*. He's looking to interview people who stayed in town when it was underwater. Want to talk to him?"

The Lyph and her friend come over.

"It was awful," says the guy. "Our whole place flooded, but our pet rats are good swimmers, so it turned out okay."

I take a drag off the cigarette and look at Moore.

"See? Human interest. That's what your readers want. Real stuff. Not hocus-pocus rumors."

"Hi," says the Lyph, holding out her hand. "I'm Courtney and this is Jeremy."

Moore shakes Courtney's hand. I'm not sure he can see her for what she is. When they're in the street, Lyphs usually use cloaking hoodoo to blend in with the civilians. I try to read the sour look on Moore's face. It's hard to tell if he doesn't want to touch the devil lady's hand or if he's pissed that we have an audience.

"Nice to meet you," he says, and tosses his cigarette into

the street. "Maybe you can give me your number and I can get back to you later for an interview."

"Meow," says Courtney. "I haven't been brushed off like that since fourth grade and Father Barker realized I had a tail."

"Really, Mr. Stark. I was hoping to talk to you specially about something besides the flood," says Moore.

"What's that?"

"Your wild-blue-yonder contract."

"Why do you think I have one of those?"

He pats me on the shoulder and I consider cutting off his hand.

"Because you're famous and L.A.'s famous always have a backup plan."

"What's a wild-blue-yonder contract?" says Jeremy.

What do I tell him? Just because he dates a Lyph doesn't mean he knows how things are. How people with enough pull, fame, or infamy can get contracts that bind their souls to Earth so that when they die they don't have to go on to the afterlife. And let's face it, for people in L.A. that usually means Hell and they know it, and want to put if off for as long as possible. I really can't blame them. The contracts are handled by talent agencies specializing in ghosts. You want Jim Morrison or Marilyn Monroe to croon "Happy Birthday" at your next party? Come up with the cash and they can do a duet with James Dean or Jayne Mansfield. It's not just show-biz types, though. Plenty of bankers, politicians, crooks, and cops don't want to head Downtown too soon. A wild-blue-yonder contract is Heaven for mama's boys.

Moore looks at me, waiting to see if I'm going to answer the question. I'm not sure what to tell Jeremy.

"It's a death deal for chickenshits. When you die, you stay here and the company that sold you the contract can send you anywhere they want to be a performing monkey. Mostly, the contracts go to the famous so rich assholes can mingle with them over finger sandwiches."

"Cool," says Jeremy. "Can I get one?"

"Anyone can get one," says Moore.

I tuck the black blade in my waistband. I'm not going to need it with this band of cutthroats.

"Yeah, but if you're not an A-list celebrity, you'll probably end up being Mickey Cohen's towel boy. Not all ghosts are born equal, are they, Moore?"

"Oh," Jeremy says. "Wait—who's Mickey Cohen?"

"A notorious ventriloquist. His dummy worked for Murder Incorporated."

Jeremy and Courtney look at each other.

"This doesn't sound like something for us."

Moore looks a little uncomfortable confronted by actual people who see the scam for what it is.

"Smart," I say. "Don't let anyone talk you into one."

"We won't," says Courtney. Then to Moore, "What did I tell you? A big sack of grump."

She and Jeremy take their movie and head off, leaving me alone with Moore.

"You're not really a reporter, are you?"

He looks away and back and does the grin again. I wonder what he'd look like with no lips?

"That's not entirely true. I have friends at the *Times*. Sometimes I bring them stories and they slip me a little something."

"But that's not what you're really about."

"I work with a talent group. One of the biggest postlife artist agencies in the world."

"And you want to offer me a contract."

"Why not? A lot of Sub Rosas have them. And you're right about A-listers versus everybody else. But I can guarantee you that you'd be on the A-list of A-lists. I mean, everyone wants to meet Lucifer . . . even an ex-Lucifer."

I move faster than he can react, dragging him around the side of the building and shoving him up against the Dumpster. I tap the black blade against the crotch of his jeans, right under his balls.

"Listen up. If you really knew anything about me, you'd know that I wouldn't sign a blue yonder if you promised me chicken and waffles with Veronica Lake. I don't know how you know all that Trivial Pursuit stuff about me, but forget it. It's ancient history and nothing you should be talking about. Understand?"

"I understand."

"Do you? I know threatening to kill you won't matter because you have a blue yonder and you think you're safe. But think about this: I know how to cut off your head so you won't die. Who knows how long I can keep you alive? You can be my lab rat. How's that sound?"

"I'd rather not," says Moore.

"Then don't ever bother me, my friends, or my customers again. If you do, I'm going to use your head for kindling."

"I understand."

"Now shoo."

I take the knife away and he sidles past, not turning his

back on me until he's on the sidewalk, running down the street and across Hollywood Boulevard. I listen for the sound of squealing brakes in case he does the polite thing and scampers in front of a semi. But the sound is all just normal traffic. It's disappointing.

When I come around to the front of the store, Candy is standing there. She's looking off in the direction of Moore's sudden exit.

"What was that all about?" she says.

"A man tried to sell me some magic beans."

"Was there a giant with treasure at the top of a beanstalk?"

"No. Just old movie stars and dead gangsters."

"You know the most interesting people."

"You're more interesting than any of those bums."

"Aw. I'm better than a bum. You say the sweetest things."

She leans over and kisses me on the cheek, uses her thumb to wipe off the lipstick.

"Listen," I say. "I have to go see Vidocq and Allegra. Do me a favor and babysit our guest until I get back?"

She nods. Sighs.

"Sure. It's not like I have anything better to do tonight."

"Thanks."

She looks at me.

"You know, I know what you're doing."

"About what, in particular?"

"You're trying to keep me out of sight, trying to keep me at arm's length at Brigitte's. This is still about what happened when I was in jail, isn't it?"

Candy is quick when it comes to people. It's one of the things I like about her. I give her a slow nod.

"Some. You said I was using you. I didn't like that. I still don't. Later, when you said you didn't remember, I always wondered if that was true."

"The poison Mason gave me made me crazy and paranoid."

"See, Mason said the drug was like liquor. It loosened people up so they said things they wouldn't normally say. Truths they were afraid of."

"Mason was a monster and a liar."

"Not about everything. That's why he was so good at it."

She crosses her arms.

"So, you believe him more than me? Why don't you just shut up and listen when I say I'm fine. I'm here 'cause I want to be."

I shrug.

"Okay. Maybe I'm pushing things a little harder than I should. But another woman I cared about got killed because of me. I'm not letting anything like that ever happen again."

She pats me on the arm.

"You need to calm down, drink some tea, and hug a teddy bear."

"I'm serious. No one else gets hurt."

"Everyone gets hurt around you, but we stay anyway."

"And sometimes I wonder if that's a mistake."

She puts up a finger and aims it at my chest.

"You know, there's a fine line between caring and pissing people off. If I say I'm okay, I'm goddamn okay. Stop playing Mr. Sensitive and trust me. You want to see things get fucked up between us? Keep not listening to how I feel."

I look away, then back at her.

"I see your point."

"Smart boy. Stop worrying about all this relationship stuff. You're really bad at it."

"You've got to give me points for thinking about things."

"You've got to give me points for kicking your ass if you don't believe me again."

"Done."

She rubs her chin with her index finger.

"One thing. Your friend in the closet, he could see me through the glamour. What do you see when you look at me? Candy or Chihiro?"

"Don't tell me you're jealous of yourself."

"Put a sock in it, Jack Benny. Can you see me?"

"I see both of you. Sort of a ghost hovering over another ghost. Chihiro is in the foreground, but I can see you just fine."

That seems to satisfy her, but she's still frowning.

"You know what I'm really afraid of? Meeting new people. You and Brigitte and our friends know who I am under all this magic, but when I meet someone new I'll just be Chihiro. That means the first thing that person knows about me, the first thing I tell them, will be a lie."

"I thought about that. But consider the alternative."

She taps her round sunglasses against her knuckles.

"Yeah. I wonder if there's a statute of limitations or anything on assault. Maybe I don't have to hide forever."

"I don't know. I'll ask Julie. But, you know, the law might not be the same for Lurkers. The government was already throwing you in internment camps. I don't think forgiveness is high on their agenda."

She slips on the glasses. Does an unhappy half smile.

"Then, I'm Chihiro forever."

"We don't know that. I'll see what I can find out."

"Okay."

"I should get going. I don't want to leave you alone with that guy any longer than I have to."

"Don't rush. The way he looks, if I speak harshly he'll faint."

"I won't be long. I've just got to find a car."

"Don't steal anything boring," she says as I start away.

"I just need to find something with an engine that didn't die in the flood."

She points to Hollywood Boulevard.

"There's a Range Rover around the corner. It might work."

"Thanks. I'll look for it."

"I'm going to get drunk with Kasabian."

"I'll join you when I get back."

I head down the street, but she yells after me.

"Where can I get brass knuckles?"

"Why?"

"I want a set."

"Why? You don't need them."

She runs a hand through her short hair.

"Candy doesn't need them. I think Chihiro would look fetching with a pair."

"Christmas is over, you know."

"It's the first I'm hearing of it. Maybe they should be pink to match my hair."

"No. They'll be brass or black."

She opens the door to Max Overdrive.

"If you love me you'll find me a pair."

"I think regular people refer to this as emotional blackmail."

She starts inside.

"I can't hear you. I'm going now."

"You're a horrible person."

"Find me a pair or learn to love fucking your hand."

I walk down to the boulevard, and sure enough, there's a Range Rover Defender near the end of the block. I slip the black blade into the driver's-side lock and the door pops open. When I jam the blade into the ignition, the Rover starts on the first try. I pull out into the sparse traffic wondering who I know who deals in knuckle-dusters.

I GET ON the 101 south to the 10, get off and head north on Crenshaw to Venice Boulevard, and pull up by an old battleship of a building. They used to manufacture safes inside, back when there were only three TV channels and everyone dreamed of L.A. in black and white.

I go inside and take the battered industrial elevator up to the third floor. I lived here twelve years ago, before Mason sent me Downtown and Alice was still alive. Vidocq took over the apartment after I disappeared. Used some of his alchemical tricks to make the door invisible and, better yet, make everyone in the building forget there was ever an apartment here. He's lived in the place rent free ever since.

I knock on the door and Allegra opens it, hugs me, and invites me inside. Vidocq smiles from his worktable. He's in a stained lab coat, boiling red gunk in a beaker so that it condenses and trickles down a glass tube and drips into another beaker, clear now and full of what look like small spiny fish swimming around in slow circles. It looks like he's either just created life or is making dinner. He's well preserved for two hundred (though he doesn't like to admit to being over a hundred and fifty). Close-cropped salt-and-pepper hair, nice clothes, and a trimmed beard. A mad scientist by way of GQ.

"How's life without whooshing in and out of shadows?" says Allegra.

"Slow. Terrifying. I'm more like regular people every day. I'm going to end up wearing Costco suits and going to cup-cake stores."

Allegra's hair is jet black and shorter than Chihiro's. Her café au lait skin is paler than when we first met. She's spent a lot of the last year indoors at the clinic looking after sick and injured assholes like me.

"You could do with a little more real life in your life," Allegra says.

"As long as I don't need an accountant or a résumé."

Vidocq leaves his hoodoo table and goes into the kitchen.

"Your scars are your résumé," he says. "What sensible employer would ask you for more?"

It's the truth. After eleven years in the arena in Hell my body looks like it was run through a wood chipper and put back together with a hot glue gun.

"Would you like some coffee?" Vidocq says. "I just made it."

"It doesn't have little fish swimming around inside, does it?"

He glances back at his worktable.

"That's an interesting project. I'm experimenting with blood and blue amber to reanimate fossilized animals."

"Whose blood?"

"Mine, of course."

"Why?"

"To understand life, why else?"

"I'm not sure it's working that well."

Allegra goes over and stares into the beaker.

"He's right. Your critters have refossilized."

Vidocq sighs.

"We learn as much from our failures as our success."

"Then I'm a goddamn Rhodes scholar."

I take the coffee he offers. He hands the other cup to Allegra.

"You inspired the experiment, you know. Or your guest did," she says. "Ever since he showed up it's life this and the nature-of-death that."

"What about you? He set off any new thoughts for you?"

She blows on her brew.

"You're the only angel I've treated extensively, and you're only part angel. I'm curious about what a full angel might be like."

I sip Vidocq's coffee. It's good and strong.

"Which brings me to the subject at hand: How do you know he's an angel?"

The day after Candy and I brought the guest home, Vidocq and Allegra came over and took hair, sweat, and saliva samples while he was asleep.

Allegra taps the side of her mug with her index finger.

"Technically, we don't. I'm just hoping."

Vidocq comes in with his own cup and sits on their sagging couch.

"The body we examined is that of an ordinary man," he says. "Nothing more and nothing less."

"Except that he's missing his heart and, I'm guessing, most of his blood," I say.

"Yes. Whatever is in the body is clearly not human."

"Could he be a new kind of zombie?" says Allegra.

"I doubt it, but maybe I should have Brigitte look him over. She's the Drifter expert."

"He could be exactly who he says he is. I mean, no one has died since he appeared."

I nod and lean against the kitchen counter.

"Julie mentioned that. Okay, let's say he's the real thing. What am I supposed to do with him?"

"What would you do if he was just an ordinary man who came to you for help?" says Allegra.

"Buy him a drink and give him cab fare to the next bar. I almost died wrestling the Angra Om Ya. Don't I get a day off?"

"Maybe not."

"Maybe time off is not your fate, Mr. Sandman Slim," says Vidocq.

He smiles like he's being goddamn witty. Maybe from his point of view he is.

And maybe what he said hits too close to home.

"Fate is what happens when you don't run fast enough. Keep moving and fate gets dizzy."

"Looks like you didn't run fast enough this time," says Allegra. "So what would you do if someone came to you for help and you *did* decide to give it to them?"

I look at the coffee. Sip it, but suddenly don't want it anymore and set it down.

"I'd find out who he was."

"You're already doing that. What else?"

"I'd find out where he came from and backtrack from there. Maybe look for some physical evidence. All Mr. D had on him was a coat and a knife."

"What did the knife look like?" says Vidocq.

I take it from my pocket wrapped in a red utility rag I found in the Rover and hand it to him. He carefully unwraps it. Picks it up with his fingertips and turns it over.

"Do you recognize it?"

"I'm afraid not," says Vidocq.

"Me neither," Allegra says.

"Do you mind if I run some tests?" says Vidocq.

"Please do."

He takes the knife to his worktable, sets it on an iron disc the size of a dinner plate, selects a green bottle from a jumble of similar bottles at the back of his table. He gives it a shake and unstoppers it. I leave my coffee and go over.

"What is that?"

Allegra stands on his other side.

"My own invention. A personal amalgam of quicksilver, sulfur, and other rarer elements I've gathered in my travels."

"What's it going to do?"

"It reveals the history and composition of any object. Its true nature. Let's see what it tells us about your knife."

He puts an eyedropper into the bottle and suctions up a small potion of shimmering silvery metal. Holding the tip over the knife, he lets three drops fall.

The mercury slides down the length of the blade, making it look soft and liquid. A few seconds later, it begins to sizzle like someone frying an egg with a blowtorch.

I lean in for a better look.

"Is it supposed to do that?"

"Not necessarily," says Vidocq.

Smoke rises from the boiling metal. It shudders. Turns yellow, then deepens to black. The mercury cracks like a broken roadbed, silver veins of the knife blade visible beneath the charred metal crust. A few seconds later, the black fades and the mercury turns back to its original shimmering form, flowing off the tip of the blade. When it falls on the worktable, it spreads and burns a poker-chip-size hole in the wooden surface, sending up a ribbon of gray smoke.

Like me, Allegra leans in to watch.

Vidocq pushes us both back.

"Don't inhale the vapors," he says.

The smoke stinks. I go to a window and open it.

"I'm guessing that hasn't happened before."

"What did we just see?" says Allegra.

Vidocq rubs his chin with the knuckle of his thumb.

"I don't know. It's never reacted so violently before."

I reach for the knife and Vidocq pushes my hand away.

"I wouldn't do that," he says.

He takes a dark, ragged chamois from a drawer and wipes down the whole knife, holding it in a set of heavy pliers that look like they came from a yard sale at Hannibal Lecter's. I point at the chamois.

"What is that?"

"You don't want to know."

"I might need one later."

Vidocq wipes every inch of the blade, not looking at me.

"It's the skin from a Hand of Glory, purified and loosened from the bones by soaking it in holy water."

A Hand of Glory is the left hand of a hanged man. Powerful hoodoo. Not something you find at Pier 1.

"I thought you got rid of that thing," says Allegra.

"As you see, I need it for my work."

Vidocq wraps the knife back in the red utility rag and hands it to me.

"Where does a person get something like that? I could use it to clean up after Kasabian."

Allegra shakes her head.

"Bad people," she says. "Dangerous people."

Vidocq picks up his coffee.

"What safe life is worth living?" he says.

"What are you going to do with that knife?" says Allegra. "You can't take it home with you."

"I'm not letting that thing out of my sight. I want to know exactly what kind of power is in there."

"As do I," Vidocq says. "Perhaps we should take it to a Fiddler."

A Fiddler is a nice resource when you have a troublesome toy, like a nerve-gas-pissing knife. Their hoodoo lets them tell you about an object just by touching it. Not all Fiddlers are on the up-and-up, but I think I can tell the grifters from the real ones by now.

I put the knife in my pocket.

"You sure you want to do that?" says Allegra.

"I have other coats. Besides, I always have you if it sets me on fire."

Allegra pushes a test tube back from the edge of Vidocq's worktable.

"I could use the distraction. I've been going a little stir-crazy since the clinic closed."

A clusterfuck of cops and vigilantes torched Allegra's clinic right before Christmas. The fire took down the whole mall, killing off a nail salon and a pizza joint too. Some people have no respect for the finer things in life.

"Have you had a chance to treat any patients?"

"I've done a few house calls. Ever since the Lurker roundup, things have gotten progressively quieter. I suppose if the clinic was open and empty I'd be even more depressed."

"We're looking for somewhere she can open a new clinic," says Vidocq. "But it's a slow process."

"I don't know if it's any help or not, but I'll pay you for running the tests."

Vidocq rubs the chamois over the burned spot on his table.

"We have no use for your money."

"It's not mine. It's the PI agency's."

"In that case," says Allegra, "we're happy to accept."

"I'll probably have more work for you as business ramps up."

"Good. It will be nice to be working again."

"Speaking of which, do you have any painkillers for the guest? Whatever he is, I don't think he's used to having a body, and it hurts."

Allegra goes to a kitchen cabinet and comes back with a plastic aspirin bottle with the label scratched off. The pills inside are small black ovals.

"These should help. I've used them on both Lurkers and humans for pain."

"Thanks."

I put the pills in the pocket with the knife.

"Bill me for these, too. One more thing: Does either of you know where I can find some brass knuckles?"

"That's more your thing than ours," Allegra says.

"I know. I just thought I'd ask. I'll bring these pills back to Sleeping Beauty."

"He has a name, you know."

"I'm sure he does. I'm just not sure we know it yet."

I GET IN the Rover, head back up the Hollywood Freeway, and end up getting caught in a traffic jam while trying to get onto Sunset. This is my future. Brake lights, angry lowriders, stoned jocks in a party van, frustrated soccer moms, and sweating salarymen fumbling for their heart pills slow-rolling on and off freeway ramps until one of us snaps and opens fire on the rest. Even dead we'll be stuck in traffic, our corpses pickled in fumes and lit by the glare of light bars on squad cars. We'll make the evening news, and be talked about at work the next day. Cars, guns, cops, and gossip. Reality-TV immortality. Show biz and murder. That would be a good name for a drink. I'll have to remember to tell Carlos about it.

I ditch the Rover by Roscoe's Chicken and Waffles, where Candy and I tried to have a sort of first date. Naturally, it all went wrong. A phone call from a demon got in the way. I promised to take her back. Did I ever do it? So much has happened in the last year, a lot of it is a blur. Shuttling between Earth and Hell, cutting off heads, getting shot, playing Lucifer, dying a couple of times. Even if I did take her back, it's time we went again. Just a couple of monsters out for dinner, clogging our arteries with gravy and not giving a damn because this is California, where everyone lives forever.

I go down Sunset, cut up Ivar, and walk into Bamboo House of Dolls a few minutes later.

When Carlos sees me he holds up a shot glass and a coffee cup.

"You on or off the clock?"

"A little bit of both, but I'll take a drink."

"Thank you, Jesus. I don't need you in here sober and sad. It bad-vibes the room."

"Then give me a double and let's spread the Christmas cheer."

"Ho ho ho," Carlos says as he sets down a double Aqua Regia.

"I can't remember, are you married?"

Carlos smiles.

"Happily divorced five years now."

"Mind if I ask why?"

"It just happens sometimes, you know? You start out young and a certain kind of person, then you grow up and you're not that person anymore. Sometimes the people you become just shouldn't be together. You stick around that shit long enough, you end up hating each other. My ex and me, we stuck it out too long. By the end, our differences got damned irreconcilable, so instead of torturing each other anymore, we finally called it quits. Why are you asking?"

"I don't know exactly. I'm just trying to figure some things out."

"Losing someone is never easy," he says. "If it was, I'd be out of business."

"I don't think there's much chance of that happening."

"Drink up," he says, pours us another round, and holds up his.

"To other people's misery."

We clink glasses and drink.

He pours us one more.

"To Candy. A great girl."

I look at him. He waits for me. After a few seconds of thinking, I drink and he does too. Carlos knows that Candy is Chihiro, but he's right about losing people. I didn't really lose Candy, but she's still gone.

I look around the bar for familiar faces among the twinkling Christmas lights. I find one at a nearby table: Brigitte is drinking wine with a handsome trio—two men and a woman—laughing and talking loudly, having a fine old time. She spots me and I invite her to the bar by pointing to my drink. She excuses herself from the table and walks over.

She kisses me on both cheeks and I say, "At least someone's having a good time tonight."

"Yes. They're from Prague. From the old days, when I was still a killer like you. It's good to see old friends."

"That must be nice."

"It is. And I so seldom get to speak Czech anymore. It makes me feel more at home here."

"I felt the same way speaking English when I was Downtown."

"Did it make things better?"

"A little. Sometimes during the holidays I feel very far from the things that made me happy."

"Like hunting Drifters?"

She smiles.

"I came here to destroy revenants and become a real live Hollywood actress. The first is done, but no matter what I do, the second feels as if it's barely begun."

Brigitte used to do artsy porn flicks back in Europe. I never saw any, but Kasabian worships her as a goddess. A producer brought her to L.A. with promises of big roles in big movies. He croaked and Brigitte has been trying to get a foothold in the business every since.

"All our apocalypses keep getting in the way of work."

She slowly shakes her head.

"You'd think someone was conspiring against our happiness."

"The universe hates happy people, that much I'm sure of. You need to cultivate a taste for colorful misery."

"Like you and your Aqua Regia."

We both drink. I finish mine, but don't ask for a refill this time.

"Maybe things will settle down awhile, end-of-the-world-wise. Once the movie moguls slink back into town, you'll be rolling in work."

She pushes a stray strand of hair out of her face.

"You haven't said anything about my voice. I've been taking lessons, trying to lose my accent. How do I sound?"

"Like the queen of the county fair. What do you think?" I say to Carlos.

"You sound like Angelina Jolie. Kind of husky. Kind of silky."

"You'd think I was American?"

"*Absolutamente*," he says.

"I think you're both being kind. Nevertheless, I'll take the compliment."

I take her arm to pull her in closer so we can talk quietly.

"You haven't heard any talk about High Plains Drifters, have you?"

"No. Nothing. Is this about the man Chihiro talks about? Do you think he's a revenant?"

"To tell the truth, no. I just don't want him to be who he says he is."

"You're afraid of another apocalypse."

"No. Just a lot of goddamn trouble. If this guy is Death, the people who killed him aren't going to be hard to find, and I guarantee they're going to be unsympathetic."

"How do you know it's more than one person?" says Carlos.

"I don't, but I also don't see someone pulling off this kind of hoodoo all on his lonesome. You're talking about capturing an angel in a human body . . . and that's after you find the right body. Then you need to know the hexes and magicians who can pull them off. Then you need a weapon that can kill him. On top of that, you need a motive. *Why* kill Death? There are potions that will keep you going for a hundred years. Yeah, they're expensive, but it's easier to rob a bank than shanghai an angel."

"How does one kill an angel?" says Brigitte.

"With this."

I take the knife from my coat and unwrap it on the bar.

"It looks quite ordinary," she says.

"It's not. It was thinking seriously of burning down Vidocq's place."

"It looks Roman," says Carlos. "Like an antique Roman

dagger. See the silver eagle? Legions used to have those on their standards."

"How the hell do you know all that?"

He clears away some glasses and pours Brigitte more wine.

"My brother-in-law. Ex-brother-in-law. He's crazy for old weapons. He has something like that. I can send him a picture if you want and see what he knows."

"This brother-in-law of yours, is he the person who's been slipping you potions?"

Carlos tries to suppress a smile, shrugs.

"He dabbles in a lot of things."

"He's a magician, isn't he? You married into a Sub Rosa family."

He nods.

"She kept it from me most of the time we were together. Her family thought I wasn't worthy and I think maybe she did a little too. You were the first person I met who did real magic right out in the open. After seeing that, I knew I'd been right to leave."

"If she hid it, was she into baleful magic?"

"Baleful?"

"Black magic," says Brigitte.

Carlos carefully arranges a Santa hat on a small plastic hula girl.

"I don't know if her magic was black, but her soul turned dark. That's what I meant about people changing. First figuring out that she was a real *bruja*. Then finding out she wasn't the only one. Then seeing her go to darker places. I didn't know what she was looking for, but I knew I didn't want any part of it."

I say, "You knew about our funny little world, but played innocent this whole time."

He shakes his head.

"This? Lurkers and zombies and shit? I didn't know any of that. And it's cool at the bar. But home I like boring. The only magic I want there is in games and bad movies."

"It was cruel of your wife not to tell you who she really was," Brigitte says.

Carlos cocks his head.

"We had some good times. And anyway, my brother-in-law and me get along fine. Want me to send him a picture?"

"Go ahead."

Carlos takes out his phone, clicks a picture, and thumbs in a message.

"I'll let you know what he says."

"Thanks."

Carlos moves on to other customers.

Brigitte looks at me.

"Stark."

"What?"

"Chihiro needs to come home."

"It's not the right time."

"She said you said that, but I'm here to tell you that caution be damned. You'll lose her if you keep pushing her away."

"I told her we can do something around the end of the month."

"She's a dead woman. She lost her identity. She needs to be around the things that matter most to her."

"We're going to be working together for the agency."

"And you'll send her home alone every night. Your time

in Hell might have taught you to plot strategy and when to strike, but it hasn't helped you understand how people work. Chihiro isn't a strategy and she isn't someone who makes plans. She's spontaneous and intuitive and more easily hurt than you might understand."

That go-for-broke quality is one of the things I always liked about Candy. She went all in when she got into something, whether it was anime, being Doc Kinski's assistant, or hooking up with me. I never thought of myself as a brain person, but maybe I'm turning into one. Like I said, it's been a funny year.

"Let me think about it."

"Don't lie to me or her, and especially don't lie to yourself. If you're going to think, do it fully and soon."

I want to change the subject, but I can't ask Brigitte about her love life. Her lover, Father Traven, is dead.

"Has either of you seen a Fiddler in here tonight?"

Carlos looks around.

"How about Christopher Marlowe over there?"

Marlowe is by the jukebox chattering at one of Brigitte's friends. The lady doesn't seem interested.

Brigitte shakes her head.

"He's wasting his time," she says. "She doesn't like men and she doesn't speak English. I'll rescue her and send him to you."

She squeezes my hand.

"Think about what I said. What's more important: Chihiro or one more little apocalypse?"

She goes over and says something to her friend. The woman goes back to the table, and when Marlowe turns his attention to Brigitte, she points at me. All the fun goes out of his face. He's not scoring with any of the Euro girls tonight.

Marlowe comes over and puts his hands up like a robbery in a cowboy movie.

"I swear, Sheriff, I didn't lay a hand on her."

He's boyishly handsome, wearing a green-striped shirt and khaki pants, looking a lot more J.Crew than Elizabethan. He's not the real Christopher Marlowe, of course. At least I don't think so. Last I heard, the real Marlowe is a vampire living happily in Tangiers. Still, I bet this Marlowe has a screenplay. There are more unproduced scripts in L.A. than rats.

"Relax. I'm not playing chaperone. Besides, Brigitte carries a gun, so she doesn't need my help."

Marlowe glances at her, back at the table with her friends.

"Thanks for the warning."

"It was more friendly advice, but you're welcome."

He leans against the bar and orders a dirty martini. When Carlos goes off to make it, he turns to me.

"So, if you're not minding the beauty's business, why have you summoned me? Fashion advice? First, ditch the Johnny Cash coat. This is L.A., not the Grand Ole Opry."

"Thanks. When I want advice from a Banana Republic catalog, I'll come to you."

Carlos brings him his drink and he pays.

"Carlos says you're a Fiddler. Is that right?"

"Are you asking because you're famous and want a favor?"

"Not at all. I'm a small businessman myself. I can pay."

"Cash?"

"You can bill the agency."

He looks at Carlos.

"Is this guy for real?"

"Yeah. He's a regular Derek Flint these days. His boss comes in here all the time."

"Fine," he says. "Show me what you have."

I hand him the knife.

"You looking for anything in particular? I'm good with dates and original owners."

I put the utility cloth in my pocket.

"Just tell me anything you can tell me about it."

Marlowe runs his fingers around the hilt, over and around the blade. He sniffs it. Presses the blade to his forehead.

"That's weird."

"What's wrong?"

"There's nothing on here, and I mean nothing. You're not even on here and you just handed it to me."

"Can you tell me how old it is or where it came from?"

He takes a gulp of his drink.

"What did I just say? There's *nothing* here. I've never felt that before. It's a complete blank."

"Could someone do that with hoodoo?"

"Of course, but I've always been able to read through magic. This thing is wild. I might know buyers for something this special. I do consulting and appraising for some of the auction houses."

I take back the knife.

"It's not for sale."

"Your loss," he says, and finishes his drink. "Even though I didn't find anything, it still counts as a reading, you know."

"Sure. Bill me."

He puts down his glass.

"This is pissing me off. Let me try it one more time."

I hand him the knife.

"I want to try something."

"Whatever you need to do, Kreskin."

He holds the knife with the tip straight up and just stares at it for a minute. Then puts the blade to his mouth, licking it from the hilt to the tip in one motion.

Carlos looks at me. I don't know if I'm getting my money's worth out of Marlowe or just feeding some secret knife fetish.

"If you're going to popsicle that knife, it better be for business reasons."

"Fuck," he says, and hands me back the knife. I take it using the utility rag and wrap it up without touching it. I'll have Vidocq chamois it off again later.

"There's nothing on there," he says. "I get the slightest trace of you, but nothing else. It's like that thing is a black hole, sucking everything in. You've got to tell me where you got it. Are there any more like it?"

"No, I don't, and I don't know. Just bill me for your time."

"Where should I send it?"

"Bring it to Max Overdrive."

"Or he can leave it here," says Carlos.

"I think I'd be more comfortable here. That friend of yours with the metal hands creeps me the fuck out."

"He was even worse when he didn't have a body."

"What?"

"Nothing."

Marlowe holds up his glass for another drink.

"Listen, I know buyers with way too much money on their

hands. I won't charge for the reading if you tell me where you got the knife."

"Sure. From a murder scene."

He shakes his head.

"It doesn't make sense. That's the first thing I would have felt."

"But you didn't and that's all I need to know for now."

"If you find out who hexed the knife, I'll pay you for the name."

"Maybe. I do enjoy the company of money."

Carlos sets the martini down in front of Marlowe.

When he reaches for it, his hand goes limp. He knocks the glass over. It falls to the floor and he goes down with it, his body rigid and convulsing.

I remember something about turning choking people on their sides, so I roll him over. Carlos comes around the bar and hands me a small blue bottle.

"Get that down his throat," he says.

I roll Marlowe onto his back and pry his jaws apart enough to pour in a syrupy orange potion that smells like cat piss and bubble gum.

It takes a minute for the convulsing to stop. I roll him back onto his side and soon he's breathing normally.

He opens his eyes and looks around, realizes he's on the floor, and sits up.

"What happened?"

"You dosed yourself, jackass, when you licked the knife."

"I take back the offer. Keep that thing away from me."

I get his shoulders and wrestle him to his feet. There's a crowd around us, but Carlos gets them back to their tables and drinking again. I set Marlowe on a bar stool. Carlos gives him a glass of water and he gulps it down. I wait for him to finish.

"Did you see anything when you were unconscious?"

He takes a long breath and lets it out.

"Yeah," he says. "It felt like I was dying and someone was coming for me."

"You mean, like Death?"

He rolls the glass between his hands.

"That's the weird part. I knew it should be, I felt like it, but it wasn't Death. It was someone else."

"You mean 'something.'"

"No. Some*one*."

I take the glass out of his hands and set it on the bar.

"You should go home."

He looks at me, still woozy.

"I'm billing you for a cab, too."

"Fine. But you owe Carlos for the potion that brought you around."

He takes out his wallet and slaps it on the bar. The leather is so expensive it looks like it came off an angel's backside.

"Take what you want," he tells Carlos.

He turns to me.

"And you, get the fuck away from me. Don't talk to me and don't ever bring me any of your poison shit again."

Carlos already has his phone out. He pushes Marlowe's wallet back at him. I reach over to get it, but knock it off the bar. I pick it up from the floor and hand it to him.

"There's a cab on the way," Carlos says. "Keep your

money. The potion is a business expense. Better that than dead people piled up in the bar."

Marlowe pushes himself up and starts to go outside to wait for the cab. He stops by the door.

"I saw one other thing, Stark."

"What's that?"

He steadies himself with a hand on the wall.

"It knows you're looking for it. Whatever that knife is, it knows about you."

Marlowe gives me the finger and goes outside.

Carlos wipes the spilled drink off the bar. I sit down and Brigitte comes over.

She says, "This is exactly what I was talking about. What just happened isn't something Chihiro should have to hear from me."

She goes back to her friends and I take out my phone.

"Hi," Candy says after a couple of rings.

"How's our friend?"

"What do you think? Still asleep. And Kasabian's gone out to buy beer."

"Sounds boring."

"It is. Where are you?"

"At Bamboo House. Why don't you come over."

"What, be seen in public like a real person?"

"Just like one. I'll buy you too many drinks. Later, we can order Chinese food from bed."

"Thai."

"Demanding harlot."

"Watch that mouth, boy. You're going to need it later."

"Hurry. I'm at least three drinks up on you."

"Then order me three drinks and stand by."

"See you soon."

She doesn't say anything for a beat.

"Hey, why did you suddenly get smart?"

"I'll tell you a funny story when you get here."

"It better have clowns and Sailor Moon in a bikini in it."

"And ponies."

"I'm swooning."

"See you soon."

I order a drink for myself and three extras. Carlos sets the glasses down and I arrange them in a pyramid just like a clown would.

WE WEAVE BACK to Max Overdrive after an hour or so of drinking. The first three drinks pretty much did Candy in. I don't know how many more she ordered, but Carlos cut her off at two. I got cut off too, but more, I think, to encourage me to take Candy home. It was time anyway. I'd told her about Vidocq, Marlowe, and the knife by then, so there wasn't much more to say. I didn't mention what Marlowe said about a bogeyman waiting for me in the great beyond because I was 90 percent sure he was fucking with me. If he wasn't, I figured I'd know soon enough.

We go in through the side door because I don't want to look at KILLER on the front windows. I'm in too good a mood for that. It doesn't last long. The moment we get inside, Kasabian comes clanking up on his Tin Woodsman legs.

"He's awake," he says. "He woke up just a little while after you left."

He gives Candy a look that's half accusing and half scared shitless. I wave a hand in his face to get his attention.

"Where is he?"

"Right the fuck inside."

We go around the counter and there he is, the Angel of Death, stark damned naked in the middle of the empty store watching *The Cabinet of Dr. Caligari* on the big screen. He's got this goofy grin on his face, like an ankle biter seeing a mobile for the first time.

I walk over and stand next to him, watching the movie. *Caligari* is a silent film. Cesare, the somnambulist, is carrying Jane across rooftops that look like they were designed by Dalí and drawn with crayons on blotter acid.

"Is this old?" he says.

"Yeah. From 1920."

He points at the big screen.

"I remember all of them. When each passed on, I remember taking them."

Candy comes over. Kasabian stays back by the counter.

"How are you feeling?" she says.

He looks at her, then back at the screen.

"I still hurt, but watching helps take my mind off it."

"You just described the entire twentieth century," I say.

I take the pills out of my pocket and put them in his hand.

"Try these. They should help with the pain."

"Thank you."

He pours some out and looks at them.

"How many does someone take?"

I shrug.

"Try two."

I look at Kasabian.

"You have anything to drink?"

He takes an open beer from under the counter and hands it to me with his fingertips, keeping as much distance as he can between himself and our naked guest. I hand Death the beer.

"Wash them down with this."

He sniffs the beer. Makes a puzzled face and puts the pills in his mouth. Then raises the beer can, draining it.

"This tastes familiar," he says. "I think whoever this body belonged to liked it."

"That narrows the suspects to about three million in L.A. County."

He stares at the can like he doesn't know what to do with it. I take it from him and toss it to Kasabian. Death looks at me.

"I'm sorry, but I don't know what else to tell you. I'm as confused as you must be. But I appreciate you giving me a place to stay."

Candy says, "Stark knows what it's like being lost somewhere you don't want to be. Isn't that right?"

"Sure. I've been to Fresno."

He pulls away the bandages over the hole where his heart should be. The wound has closed. There's just an ugly scar the size of a man's hand. He touches it and winces.

"You don't believe me, do you? When I say that I'm Death."

"How do you know that?"

"I know you. We've met before. More than once."

Candy puts a hand on my arm. I take Death's bandages and toss them, like the can, to Kasabian. He pulls his hands away like I tossed him dirty diapers.

"I don't remember you. If you're Death, why didn't you take me?"

"There's dying and there's dead," he says. "You were on the cusp, so I let you decide, angel."

"Half angel."

"That's why I came to you. I don't trust other angels right now."

"You finally said something I understand."

He turns and looks around the store like he's seeing it for the first time.

"I'm cold."

"I have some things that might fit you."

I turn to Kasabian.

"You want to bring him down some stuff? You know where the closet is."

"Sure," he says, overjoyed for an excuse to leave.

Death watches him go upstairs. He looks at the floor, wiggles his toes like he's not sure if they're attached to his body.

"How can I prove to you that I am who I say I am?"

"That's the problem. I *do* believe you. I've been trying to figure out a way around it, but I can't. The real trick is figuring out what to do with you."

"What do you propose?"

"You can stay here for as long as you need," says Candy.

"Thank you."

I take the pack of Maledictions from my pocket and light one. Death sniffs the smoke and sneezes. I don't put it out. When things get weird, sometimes you just have to smoke.

"Our boss, Julie, is going to want to talk to you. She's the brains. We'll figure out what to do after you've talked. That okay with you?"

"That sounds fine."

Death gets distracted by the movie again. Kasabian creeps down the stairs with a pile of clothes in his arms.

"I didn't know what he'd like."

"So you brought everything I own? Just set it down on the counter."

I point at Death.

"You. Come here."

He walks over. I hold up one of the few Max Overdrive T-shirts left that doesn't have bullet holes or my blood on it.

"That looks like it'll fit. Try it on."

He slips the shirt over his head. And gets tangled in it. Candy has to help him get it on.

I toss him some pants. He looks them over and starts to put them on backward.

"The other way around," I tell him.

He navigates the pants better than the shirt. I toss him a pair of socks and he figures those out right away. Boy genius will be ready for *Jeopardy!* any day now.

"Is that better?" says Candy.

"Yes. Thank you for these."

"Just don't get cut open again. Those shirts are rare."

"I'll try."

"Maybe he's hungry," says Kasabian.

"You hungry?"

"I don't know," he says. "My stomach hurts."

"You shouldn't take pills on an empty stomach. Let's order some food," says Candy.

I toss Death a black hoodie to wear over the T-shirt. Candy helps him put it on. I look at her looking at him. She's not scared of him. Another one of the things I like about her. I put out the Malediction. No reason to torment the poor slob.

I say, "You like Thai food?"

"I don't know," he says.

"Let's find out."

"Don't worry. We'll get everything mild," says Candy.

He looks up at the big screen.

"Can I watch something else? Something where people speak?"

"We might have one or two of those. What do you think, Kas?"

"No action movies. Nothing with guns or explosions. I don't want him getting ideas."

Death zips the hoodie, then looks at Kasabian.

"We've met before," says Death.

I smile in Kasabian's direction.

"That's right. He blew his dumb ass up."

"Lucifer was the one who brought you back, wasn't he? I like him. He has a funny sense of humor."

"Tell me about it," Kasabian says.

"Maybe cartoons?" says Candy.

Kas raises his eyebrows.

"Some of your fucking anime with monsters and robots? I don't think so."

"What about a musical?" Candy says.

Death looks from her to me.

"You like music?" I ask.

"Oh, yes."

Kasabian says, "Okay. Fred Astaire or Gene Kelly?"

"Definitely Gene Kelly," Candy says. "He's the sexy one."

"*Singin' in the Rain*?"

I pick up the rest of my clothes.

"Can't go wrong with a classic. We're going upstairs to call for food. You need anything?"

Death shakes his head.

"No. Thank you."

Candy and I head to our place. Kasabian follows us halfway up the stairs.

"Don't leave me alone with him."

"Relax," I tell him. "Get him a chair. Give him a donut or whatever else you have stashed behind the counter. Put the movie on and play nice. We'll be in earshot."

"How are you going to pay for the food? We haven't rented much since Mr. Charisma got here."

"As it happens, I helped a guy with his wallet and some of his cash fell into my pocket. He's a whiner and he'll overbill the agency, so it will all balance out in the end."

"What do you want when we order?" says Candy.

"Green curry with pork. Extra spicy. None of the baby food you're feeding him."

We start up again.

Kasabian stares downstairs and says, "Stark. What if you help this guy and he, you know, calls us in? I mean, we were dead. What if he wants to make it permanent?"

"Then I'll kill *him* and we can all go to Hell together."

"That's a fucking comfort," he says. Then, "I want some of those fried shrimp rolls too."

We go upstairs. A minute later the overture to the movie starts.

When we're alone, Candy laughs.

"You finally bring me back here and there's Death waiting for us with his cock hanging out. You know how to make a girl feel at home."

"Did you really expect a normal homecoming?"

She flops onto the sofa.

"Never. I'm drunk and hungry. Order me some food, garçon."

"Hold your horses, Calamity Jane."

She leans her head back on the sofa and says, "Shit. Should we call Julie now that he's awake?"

I drop my clothes in a pile on the closet floor. There's an envelope lying on the bed. I bring it with me back to the living room.

"Let the man eat. Between the pills and the food, my guess is he'll pass out again. Julie can wait until tomorrow."

"Good. All I want to do is eat and fuck and go to sleep."

"I have that on my business card."

"Find the menu. Dial quickly. I'm going to pass out here for a minute."

She curls up on the sofa and I toss a blanket over her.

The menus are in a drawer by the sink. I call in the order and open the envelope. Crisp paper falls out onto the floor. Heavy, expensive stationery—Sub Rosa–grade stuff. Sure enough, it's from the Augur's office. Looks like I'm invited to tea with the grand high lord and master of the whole California tribe. Thing is, I'm done with the Sub Rosa and don't have any interest in who's running the show now.

I wad up the note and envelope and toss them in the trash.

DEATH IS WATCHING another movie when we go down in the morning. *Duck Soup* starring the Marx Brothers. Kasabian comes over as quietly as he can.

"He's been at it all night. I'm fucking beat. It's your turn to babysit."

"What have you been showing him?"

"More musicals. *Mary Poppins. My Fair Lady.* Some Disney cartoons."

"Shiny happy people stuff."

"Like I said, I don't want him getting ideas."

"Go to bed. We'll take the morning shift."

Kasabian slinks back to his room, right next to the storage room where our guest sleeps.

"Good night, Kasabian," he says. "Thank you for sitting up with me."

"Sure. Glad to. Anytime."

He closes and locks his door.

"Are you hungry?" says Candy.

Death turns away from the movie long enough to look at her.

"Yes, I am."

"I'll bring down the leftovers."

I head back upstairs.

Julie calls while I'm in the kitchen. I tell her Death is awake and she should come over if she wants Thai food.

"For breakfast?"

"It's this or the last of Kasabian's donuts, and those have been around since 'Steamboat Willie.'"

"I'll pass on the food, but I'll be right over."

I thumb off the phone, get the food out of the microwave,

and head downstairs with some plates. Candy clears all the crap from the top of the rental counter and puts it underneath. I set down the cartons and Candy digs in.

Death sticks his fork in each dish and sniffs. Touches the food to the tip of his tongue. I don't think he's gotten the hang of having human senses.

I pick at a couple of things, wanting coffee and a smoke more than curry. Julie arrives about twenty minutes later with a large messenger bag over her shoulder. Death straightens up and puts out his hand when he sees her.

"Hello. I'm Death," he says.

Julie gives her best professional smile and shakes his hand.

"Yes. We met briefly at the bar where you found Stark. You look a lot better now than you did then."

"I feel a lot better. Stark and his friends have been taking good care of me."

He looks at Candy.

"I'm still not sure what I should call you. You have two faces and apparently two names. Which do you prefer?"

"Look at either face you want, but please, call me Chihiro."

"Then Chihiro it is."

"Thanks for recording the interview," Julie says to Candy. "It was a good start."

"Glad to be part of the team, chief," Candy says.

Julie opens her bag, then looks at me.

"You were interested in the knife. Did you find out anything about it?"

I fill her in on what happened with Vidocq's experiment and Marlowe's reading.

"Have you ever seen that happen before?"

"Never."

"All right. We'll set the knife aside for now and concentrate on other areas. At least we have a starting point with our visitor's identity."

"We do?" says Candy.

"People still aren't dying. Religious groups are up in arms, some calling it the end of days. There have been runs on grocery stores and banks. Hell, the president gave an address about it last night, saying the government is conferring with our allies to make sure this isn't a terrorist act. This has been all over the Web and TV since it started happening."

She frowns at me.

"You don't pay much attention to the news, do you?"

"I make a point to avoid it."

"Start watching TV, at least. It's part of your job to have a clue what's going on in the world."

"I'll take care of it," says Candy.

"At least one of you is a grown-up."

I take out a Malediction.

"I make a point to avoid that too."

I open the side door, blowing the smoke outside so Death doesn't choke and I won't look bad in front of the boss. This is worse than Hell. I can't even kill anyone to get on her good side.

"Where are your other clothes?" says Julie to Death. "The ones you woke up in."

"There. In the room where I was sleeping."

"I'll show you," I say, tossing the cigarette into the alley. Good-bye, old friend.

We go into the storage room and I flip on the light. Julie pushes past me, slipping nitrile gloves on over her hands.

"Have either of you handled the clothes?" she says.

"We both helped him undress," says Candy.

I step deeper into the room, out of Julie's way.

"And I searched his gear."

Julie hands us each a pair of gloves.

"In the future, don't touch any potential evidence bare-handed."

"Got it," says Candy. Teacher's pet.

Julie holds up Death's coat, then his pants. There's pale dirt or dust on the bottom of each, and more on the floor. She checks his shoes and finds more dust. From a padded compartment in her bag she takes out a gizmo that looks like an iPad crossed with a game controller.

A small tray pops opens on the side of the tablet and she carefully drips in a sample of the dust, then pushes the tray shut. The screen lights up, showing some kind of multicolor readout.

"What is that?" says Candy.

"It's the chemical composition of whatever is on his pants and shoes. It doesn't look like city dirt. Something drier and desert-like. I'll collate the numbers with USGS maps of the area."

"Awesome," says Candy.

I angle for a better look at the tablet.

"That's Vigil tech. How did you end up with it?"

Julie puts the tablet away and collects more of the dust in a paper envelope.

She says, "We have an understanding. Now that I'm a

civilian, I can do things, go places, and ask questions the government can't. In exchange, I get access to certain Vigil equipment and information."

"Can you use your toy to tell you anything about the knife?"

"I doubt it," she says, sealing the envelope and putting it in the bag. "I wonder if we loaned it to the Vigil they'd be able to come up with anything?"

I pick up an empty DVD case and toss it back on a pile of others.

"Forget it. Boss or not, there's no way I'm handing over our only serious piece of physical evidence to those Pinkertons. We'd never see it again."

She stops working, her hands still in the bag.

"I hate to say it, but you might be right. They wouldn't want civilians to have access to a magical artifact that powerful."

She turns to Death.

"Have you showered since you've been here?"

He shakes his head.

"Good. I'd like to take some samples of the dirt under your nails. Also, if you don't mind, I'd like to take your fingerprints and do a quick physical exam. Is that all right with you?"

Death frowns slightly, looks from Julie to me.

"She wants your clothes off so she can make sure everything is where it's supposed to be."

"If it will help," he says.

"He's not the shy type," says Candy.

Julie doesn't ask what that means. She just pulls another device from her bag, this one like a large cell phone.

"Good," she says. "That will make things go faster."

To Death I say, "After this, you're cleaning up. This place is starting to smell like the reptile room at the zoo."

"Smells are interesting," he says.

"Some less than others."

Julie sets one of his hands on the device. It lights up for a second. When she takes his hand away, his finger and palm prints glow pale blue on the screen. She does the same thing with the other hand and puts the device away.

"Can I take your picture?" she says.

Death nods.

She uses her phone to take full-face shots and each profile.

"Stand up," I tell him. "It's 'Nick the Stripper' time."

I mime taking off a shirt. He starts undressing.

"What are you looking for?" says Candy.

"Identifying marks. Scars. Birthmarks. Tattoos. That kind of thing."

Death looks down at his naked body, as interested in it as they are, but baffled at being surrounded by his own flesh.

Julie goes over his front, legs, and back.

"Lift up your arms, please," she says.

The moment he does, Candy says, "What's that? A tattoo?"

Julie and I look where Candy is pointing, near his left armpit. Death cranes his head around trying to see.

"It's not a tattoo," says Julie.

I put my finger on the design. The skin is slightly raised and pinker than the surrounding flesh.

"It's a brand."

"Do either of you recognize it?"

Candy and I both say no.

Julie touches the brand with her gloved fingers. She glances at Death.

"Do you know where it came from?"

"No."

She photographs it, stops when she checks the shot.

"There's something else."

She fits a zoom lens to the phone's camera—more Vigil tech by the look—and takes another shot.

A pattern on Death's skin glows a bright green.

"It looks like a tattoo that's been lasered off," she says.

She shows the design to Candy and me. Neither of us recognizes it. The marks look like letters, heavily stylized, in a circle.

"It's not a word. Maybe it's his initials," I say.

"Why would he remove his initials?" says Julie.

"People lose their names all the time," says Candy. "When they're scared and want to hide from something."

No one says anything for a minute.

"Is this the body of a good man?" says Death.

Julie takes the lens off her phone and puts it in the messenger bag.

She says, "It's too early to tell. You can put your clothes back on."

This time, Death dresses himself. Just like a big boy.

"I've gone over the recording Chihiro made of your first talk, so I know you woke up in an isolated area near a deserted concrete building, right around Christmas. There were people nearby. Teenagers, you said. Did you get a look at any of them? Would you recognize one if you saw them again?"

Death picks at a sleeve cuff.

"No. I didn't see any of them well and they ran away so quickly."

"Is there anything else you can tell us about your awakening? Anything else you saw?"

"One of the men had horns."

I say, "What do you mean horns?"

"On his forehead. Above his eyebrows. I suppose they could have been markings."

"Tattoos. Okay. Anything else?"

"The same man had a drawing on his cheek. A number fourteen in a circle of letters."

"That's it?"

"I'm afraid so."

"Approximately, how long did you walk?" says Julie.

"Five hours," he says.

"You sound very certain."

"I am. I found a watch. One of the teenagers must have dropped it."

"We looked through your things. There wasn't any watch," says Candy.

"It stopped working, so I threw it away."

I say, "Do you remember where?"

"Of course."

He points to a trash can by the head of his cot.

Julie reaches in and fishes out a gold pocket watch attached to a broken fob chain. She presses the winder on top and the cover pops open. The watch shines, but it's just cheap plastic in a metallic coating.

Julie holds it up.

"There's something stamped on the cover, but I can't make it out."

She hands me the watch.

I study it while Candy looks over my shoulder.

On the inside of the cover is a skull with candles in the eye sockets and an open book in its mouth.

"It's a necromancer's mark," I say.

"Then maybe the kids weren't partying," says Candy. "Maybe they were part of the resurrection."

"Maybe, but this thing is a piece of shit. No professional Dead Head would carry something like this."

I hand Julie the watch. She looks it over.

"They sell things like this at flea markets and goth shops, don't they?"

"You can buy them all over Hollywood Boulevard. Good luck tracking it down," I say.

"Maybe they weren't professionals, but that doesn't mean they weren't necromancers," says Candy.

"It's possible," says Julie. "May I keep this?"

"Of course," says Death.

"Maybe I can pull some prints or DNA off it."

She puts it in a small container and places it in her bag.

"I'm wondering something," says Candy. "Could we use a spell to track where Death walked from? Maria, who gets the store videos, is a witch. She might be able to help us."

"That's not a bad idea," says Julie.

"Yeah, it is," I say. "If you backtrack Death, then you're backtracking the knife, and I've seen what happens when you aim hoodoo at that thing. Let's see what Julie comes up with before we get too Tinker Bell."

Julie arranges things in her bag.

"All right. I have plenty to work with right now. We'll hold off on any spell work until I see what the physical evidence shows us. Do you have the knife with you?"

"You sure you want to take it?"

"I'd like to examine it myself."

"But no hoodoo and no Vigil?"

"That's right."

"I'll get it."

I go upstairs, dig the knife out of my coat, and bring it back down. Julie slips it in an evidence bag.

"Just be careful," I say.

"I always am," she says. There's a note of irritation in her voice. I shut up.

Julie puts the knife in her bag and takes out a plain white business envelope.

Handing it to me, she says, "Here's the five-hundred-dollar advance I promised you."

I open the envelope and look inside. It's full of crisp, new twenties.

"Thanks," I say, then to Candy, "It's lobsters and Twinkies tonight, baby."

She takes the envelope and riffles through the bills.

"May I say something?" Death asks.

"Shoot," Candy says, rolling up one of the bills like she's smoking a cigar.

"There's something else to consider. Trapped in this body, I can't do my job of escorting souls from Earth. Essentially, I am no longer Death. But there must be a Death. It's one of the fundamental laws of the universe."

"But no one is dying," says Julie.

Death nods.

"Exactly. And yet there must be a Death. This leaves the question: Who has usurped my role and why isn't he or she taking souls?"

I think back to Marlowe and his bogeyman for a second, but let the thought drop.

I give Death a look.

"You had to wait till now to bring this up. You just took a massive shit all over our feel-good moment."

"I know," says Death. "I'm somewhat famous for that."

"You can fucking say that again," yells Kasabian through the storage room wall. "Now, will you people fuck off so I can get some sleep?"

JULIE GOES HOME soon after the interview, but calls back a few hours later. She needs Candy and me on a quick one-night job that has nothing to do with the guy in my storage room. I like the sound of that. Maybe *like* is too strong a word. The job is a stakeout. Sitting in a car for hours without a break, so I don't actually like it, but I do like the chance to walk away from Death's case for a few hours.

"While I have you on the line, I need to know something. Is there a statute of limitations for a Lurker with an assault charge?"

She doesn't say anything right away.

"As far as I know, there isn't a statute of limitations for Lurkers at all."

"Thanks. I had to know."

"I'm sorry, for both you and Chihiro."

"One more thing. Do you know where I can get some brass knuckles?"

"Those are illegal in California, you know."

"And yet I need them. Years ago, a friend bought a set off an ex-cop. He was selling them as novelty paperweights."

"They could have both gone to jail for that."

"Sounds like you don't have those connections."

"No. I don't. And you shouldn't be asking questions like that. In the current climate, they can get you in trouble."

"Understood. I'm going to need a car for tomorrow night."

"Swing by the office later today. I bought one just to keep you out of trouble. You'll love it. It's a big, comfy Crown Vic. Retired just a couple of years ago."

"A retired Crown Vic. You're talking about a cop car."

"Indeed I am. It's in great shape."

"You're going to make me drive around L.A. in a cop car?"

"It's this or you can get a Vespa."

"Don't say that to Chihiro. If she ever got her hands on a scooter, we'd never see her again."

"Then it's the Vic?"

"You've got me cornered."

"We should see about getting you a driver's license."

"I told you. I can't get docs like that."

"I didn't say it would be real. I'm sure the Vigil can put some papers together for you. Maybe you can even open a checking account."

"Yes, that's what I came back from Hell for. Overdraft fees."

"I'll see you this afternoon."

SHE'S RIGHT ABOUT the Crown Vic. It's big and it's comfortable, painted a highly forgettable gray. With its cop suspension, it even handles well.

It's after dark. Candy and I are sitting in the eight-thousand block of Wonderland Avenue in Laurel Canyon not doing a goddamn thing. I want to play a new off-the-board bootleg of Skull Valley Sheep Kill's last show at the Whisky a Go Go on the stereo, but Candy got there ahead of me and we're listening to migraine-inducing noise from Tokyo. It's a band called Babymetal. A trio of chirpy girl singers cheerleading their way over razor fast metal riffs. They sound like Britney Spears on helium backed by Slayer.

I reach for the volume knob.

"Touch that and you're a dead man," says Candy.

"I just want to check in with Kasabian."

"Fine. You have my permission to turn down the stereo for the duration of your call. Then it goes right back up again."

"You're just torturing me. It's the singing robot sunglasses all over again."

She frowns.

"I'd forgotten about those. They were fun to play with when you had a hangover. I wonder whatever happened to them?"

"If there's justice in the universe, they're in Tartarus."

"Just make your call, Pinkie Pie. The best song is coming up."

I dial Kasabian and he answers with his usual charm.

"What?"

"I wanted to know how things are going with our guest. You keeping an eye on him?"

"He's right here talking to Maria, our friendly neighborhood witch."

"You opened the store?"

"Don't whine. We've been open so little people are lined up. We're making brisk money."

"What's Death doing?"

"He's helping behind the counter."

"Are you crazy?"

"He's putting DVDs in little plastic cases so customers can take them home. I think even an angel can handle that. Besides, I'm sick of being alone with him watching kiddie movies."

"Okay, but the first sign of anything weird, the first unfamiliar face that tries to get in, you lock the place down and call me, understand?"

"I can't hear you. I'm doing actual work. Have fun sitting on your fat ass all night."

He hangs up.

Candy is snapping pictures of the street through the windshield.

"How are the kids?" she says.

"I should have bound and gagged them before we left."

"You're such a good dad."

I watch her with the camera, playing with the angles, popping the zoom in and out. She's having too much fun, like she thinks she's David Hemmings in *Blow-Up*.

"Since when are you a photographer?"

She snaps away.

"Since today. Julie gave me a Vigil point-and-shoot. It does the work and I make the art."

"Why didn't I get one?"

She moves the camera just low enough that I can see her eyes.

"Julie says you break things."

I don't reply, just let her shoot. It's distracting her from turning the music up again.

"So, some old lady thinks her neighbors are dealers," Candy says.

"That's what Julie told me. We're supposed to get hard photographic proof of their evil ways."

"I've hardly seen anyone go by. They must be lousy dealers."

"Ours isn't to judge. Ours is to show up and collect a paycheck for the night."

"Why didn't the old lady just call the cops?"

"Apparently, she did. They sent a couple of patrol cars to do roll-bys, but they didn't see anything. I guess she wants proof before she calls back again."

Candy rolls down her window and takes some shots of a coyote running up the winding street.

"She must have money to throw around to pay for an all-nighter."

"God favors the wellborn and the well connected."

"That sounds like something Vidocq would say."

"I stole it from him."

A couple in matching tracksuits strolls by, walking their dog.

"Julie says there's no statute of limitations on Lurkers."

Candy nods, checks some of her shots in the LED screen on the back of the camera.

"Yeah," she says. "I really blew it, didn't I?"

"You didn't blow it. Mason blew things up when he dosed you. He could have killed you, but he knew ruining your life would be more fun."

"I didn't even know the guy."

"That made it even more fun. Dragging you into his random craziness."

"But it wasn't random, was it? Before, he fucked with Alice because she was with you, and then he came after me."

"He liked to get to me through people I cared about."

She takes shots of the other cars and a lone cat sitting on the trunk of a nearby Lexus.

"Too bad he's dead. I wouldn't mind hurting him."

"It sounds kind of lame to say, but I'm sorry for everything that's happened."

She shrugs.

" 'Course there's another way of looking at things. I mean, making me crazy, making you angry and paranoid. If we were smart, we'd have broken up by now. But we didn't," says Candy. "The way I see it, we won."

"Me too."

"I'm hungry. Did you bring snacks?"

"I forgot them."

"Moron."

"Yeah."

A door slams somewhere up the street. Maybe a second later, three men in identical clothes come running down Wonderland Avenue. In the pale light from the surrounding houses, it's easy to see the bats and pipes in their hands. Two of the men look scared. I can't see the third because he's facedown in the street. The idiot tripped over the low brick boundary around a small garden in front of one of the houses. His buddies start back for him, but he gets to his feet and breaks into a stumbling run.

"You shooting?" I say, but it's unnecessary. When I hear Candy clicking away with the camera, I hit the headlights to give her a better view of the street.

The Three Stooges freeze. They're dressed in matching desert camo shirts and black slacks tucked into what look like paratrooper boots. Their shirts are soaked in blood I'm pretty certain isn't theirs. With light on them, I see something else. An insignia on their shirts. Like a capital W in a white circle, and something else I can't identify.

Their brains reconnect with their bodies and they take off. I jump from the car and run after them. Two are dead ahead, but the third one is gone.

There's a thudding blow against my right shoulder, then a stinging sensation that spreads across my back and right up my neck. One of the Stooges was hiding behind a car and clocked me good on the back with a length of pipe. I turn just as he swings for my head and duck out of the way, letting the metal sail by, barely missing me. I'm still getting my balance when I hear footsteps moving up behind me. There's nothing I can do but turn because I know from the sound that both of the other Stooges are back there.

I swing around, staying low, hoping Stooge Three behind me holds back, waiting for his buddies. That might give me time to hurt them just enough that I can get back to him, even with numbness spreading from my shoulder down my right arm.

I should have known better than to worry, but, you know,

it's embarrassing and distracting getting hurt that early in a fight.

The two guys coming at me don't ever connect because they're too distracted by their friend's screaming. I don't have to look to know that Candy's back there, gone completely Jade. Red pupils sunk in black eyes. Shark teeth in a pretty mouth and claws like scythes. She's shredding Stooge number three's shirt and skin. One of the other Stooges, a beanpole with a baseball bat, pulls a Glock from a holster on his hip. I turn and dive, not heading for the beanpole, but going for Candy, knocking her down just as the first shot goes off. Beanpole pops off a couple of more rounds before he and the Stooges leg it into the shadows, disappearing between a couple of houses down the street. It's too dark to know which ones.

When I let Candy up, she's already changing back into Chihiro. By now a dozen people are all dialing 911, but I want to know what the hell just happened. We run up the block and spot a boxy two-story stucco place with a blood trail all the way down the side stairs. We follow the red up, careful not to step in any, and come to an open door on the first floor. There's just enough light reflected inside to see a sizable pool of blood and four bodies laid out like sausages in a frying pan. The weird thing is, the way their bodies are angled, it looks like they're making a W. Candy might have called me the brains the other day, but she's the smart one. She pulls the Vigil's camera from her pocket and starts taking pictures. I have to pull her back down the stairs.

We sprint for the car. Once in, I gun it, heading back down the hill with the lights off so no one can get our license plate.

When we hit Laurel Canyon Boulevard, our lights are on and I've settled in at the speed limit as the first cop cars blow by.

Still, I take the long way back to Max Overdrive and leave the Crown Vic parked down by Hollywood High. If someone did see us up on Wonderland tonight, maybe the cops will blame the cheerleading squad.

While we walk home Candy rubs my shoulder.

It would be sweet if she weren't laughing at me for getting hit.

ONCE WE'RE HOME, I get out my phone. It takes all of ten minutes to fill Julie in on what happened in the canyon.

"And you're both all right?" she says.

"We're fine. I'll have a bruise tomorrow, but my pride will hurt more."

"Have Candy bring the camera by in the morning so I can download the photos. And when I say morning, I mean morning. Not two o'clock or even noon. I want you in by nine."

"What's the big deal? We didn't see anything that looked like a drug den, unless they're using cats to carry their smack. The other thing we saw, the cops will handle."

Julie curses quietly.

"I wish you hadn't gone to the crime scene, but since you did, I want to see what you have."

"I think Candy got some good shots of the three assholes. If you give them to the cops or the Vigil or whoever, just leave our names out of it."

"Don't worry. You're the last person I'm bringing in as a witness."

I take the phone outside so I can light up. It feels good to have the smoke in my lungs, burning out the smell of all that blood in the apartment. The stink reminds me of the arena Downtown. Of course, there the blood was usually mine.

"Something bothered me all the way home. The address you gave us. The eight-thousand block of Wonderland Avenue. Does that sound familiar to you?"

"Should it?"

I puff the Malediction and scrape at the KILLER paint job on the windows with my thumb.

"The Four on the Floor murders, way back in '81. It was big news at the time. Four people beaten to death with bats and pipes."

"And you're saying the murders took place nearby?"

"On the same block. Those murders were drug-related and we were there on a drug case."

"But you said you didn't see any dealing going on."

"Fine. Alleged drug case. But you see the similarities, right?"

"It *is* a funny coincidence, I'll give you that," she says. Then, "Are you talking about the murders where they arrested some big porn star?"

"John Holmes. Ex–porn star by then. He was on a long downhill slide. The cops were certain he was one of the killers, put up to it by a big L.A. dealer named Eddie Nash. They put Holmes and some other losers on trial. Everyone walked."

"It's an interesting story, but a hell of a stretch. Where's the connection after all this time?"

I turn around and there's a wino watching me from across the street. I can practically smell him from fifty feet. He makes finger guns and yells, "Bang! Bang!" Then, "Have a nice night, killer!"

I really have to get rid of this paint job.

"I don't know the connection. Look, maybe, at worst, it's a copycat crime. But those guys in uniforms, they stank of crazy. And not just any crazy. L.A. crazy."

"What does that mean?"

"L.A. crazy is when you don't just kill someone, you turn it into a cheap made-for-TV movie. The Wonderland killings, starring Laurel Canyon money, dope, and porn. B-horror-movie killers like the Hillside Strangler and the Night Stalker. It's Charlie Manson hanging out with the Beach Boys because he thinks they're going to make him a rock star. It's the Black Dahlia, a murder so strange a lot of people didn't believe it at first. Hell, I'm babysitting Death. That's what I'm talking about. L.A. crazy."

"I'm not going to tell you this often, Stark, but I'm going to tell you now," says Julie. "Go and have a drink. Have two or three. Calm down and bring me the pictures in the morning."

I drop the Malediction and grind it out with my boot. Feel around in my pocket for the flask, unscrew it, and take a pull.

"I wonder if what happened is going to make the news?"

"Why do you care?" says Julie.

"Maybe someone else saw the Three Stooges."

"Let it go for tonight. We'll talk tomorrow."

"Okay. See you then."

I hang up, but don't go inside right away. I have a couple of more drinks. Boss's orders. Besides, something else is bothering me.

Tonight is the first time Candy's gone Jade since becoming

Chihiro. It was a beautiful thing to see, but it brings up a problem I hadn't thought of before. What if down the line someone sees her change and starts calculating the odds of me hooking up with two Jades in a row? Maybe I can just pass it off as having a thing for shark-toothed berserker girls. I've heard of worse fetishes. Still, it's one more thing to worry about.

WE DROP THE photos with Julie and head back to Max Overdrive with a bag full of cleaning supplies and paint thinner.

Kasabian and Death stay inside, having sort of elected themselves the new store staff. It's too early for customers, but they've already opened. I get the feeling now that he's healed, Death doesn't sleep much, and Kasabian is trying to keep up. I give it until tomorrow before he collapses on a pillow of Bavarian creams and empty beer cans. I think Death is kind of fascinated by Kasabian and his mechanical body, a yappy sideshow attraction not quite dead or alive. Kasabian must be feeling better around Death. When Candy and I came down this morning, they were watching *This Island Earth* together. It's not exactly *Friday the 13th,* but people do die.

Candy and I are still experimenting with the paint thinner, trying it on a couple of different spots, when Maria comes up the block. She waves when she sees us. Candy waves back.

"Hi, Candy. Hi, Stark," she says in that halting "I don't talk to live people that much" way she has.

"Morning," says Candy.

I wipe paint thinner off my hands.

"Hi. If you're looking for Kasabian, he's inside with his friend from Narnia."

She shakes her head tensely.

"That's all right. I was looking for you."

"Why's that?"

"Dash is missing."

"Dash is your ghost pal, right? The one you talk to through the mirror."

The morning is warm, but she keeps her arms wrapped around herself like it's ten below.

"Yes, that's him. I haven't been able to contact him in a couple of days."

"Why are you coming to me with this? Aren't there other witches who can help you track down a lost ghost?"

"That's the problem," she says. "We've been trying, but he's just not there. I was hoping . . ." She trails off.

"What?"

"People say you can go places. Hell. Heaven. The Tenebrae. I was hoping that maybe you could look for him for me."

Candy and I exchange a look. I walk over to Maria.

"I'd like to help you, but I can't shadow-walk anymore, which means I'm stuck on Earth like everybody else."

I don't want to tell her that I *might* be able to go to the Tenebrae, a kind of wasted, lonely, hangout for souls not ready to move on to the afterlife, but I don't want to. To go there, I'd have to perform the Metatron's Cube Communion ritual. Slit my wrists and bleed out in a magic circle, letting my half-dead ass drift to Tenebrae Station. It isn't as much fun as a naked brunch with Candy, but back when I had access to the Room of Thirteen Doors I was always sure I could get back and into my body. Without the Room, I'm afraid I could get stuck in the Tenebrae with a bunch of manic-depressive spooks forever.

"Oh," she says. "I didn't know."

"Whatever rumors you've heard, they're probably wrong or out-of-date."

Candy comes over.

"Isn't there something else we can do?"

No, I want to tell her, but Maria looks too miserable to hear it.

"I can pay," Maria says. "I mean, I don't have money, but I'll give you movies. Your next three movies, four movies are free."

"Listen, I have another job these days and I'm working on a case right now."

Maria furrows her brows like she doesn't believe me.

"We'll talk to some people," says Candy. "Maybe our new boss can help. She finds things for people."

Maria smiles a little.

"That would be great. Dash isn't just my spirit guide. He's my friend."

"We understand," says Candy. "And we'll do what we can to find him for you."

"But no guarantees," I say.

Maria loosens her arms a bit and lets them drop to her sides.

"I understand. And thanks. I really appreciate it."

"I'll talk to Julie today," Candy says.

Maria nods.

"That would be great. Well, I don't want to keep you from your work. I'm sorry someone wrote on your store."

I look at the lettering. We haven't made much progress getting it off yet.

"Thanks. I broke the guy's wrists, so, you know, that was fun."

Maria starts away. She gives us the same little wave she gave us before.

"Bye," she says, and heads back down to Hollywood Boulevard.

I look at Candy.

"Exactly, how are we supposed to help her? Julie doesn't know anything about ghost hunting. And I can't do it anymore."

"Maybe the Vigil has a machine or ghost surveillance cameras or something," she says. "Or maybe Death could help."

"Death lives in a closet and sleeps on a cot. If Death could help anyone, he would have helped himself by now."

Candy pats me on the shoulder.

"You're clever. You'll think of something."

"Thank you for your misplaced confidence."

Our phones go off at almost the same time. I pull it out and look at the number. The screen doesn't show a number or BLOCKED. It reads ANSWER ME. I've never seen that before. I figure anyone who can do that must be at least a little interesting, so I answer.

"Who is this?"

"Stark?" comes a woman's voice. "It's Tuatha Fortune. How are you?"

"Hi. I'm fine," I say, wanting to hang up but sober enough to know that it would be a bad idea.

Tuatha Fortune is the wife of the previous Augur, Saragossa Blackburn. Widow actually. He died while in office. I have it on good authority he was dismembered and flushed out the pipes with the garbage. Not a pretty way to go.

"How are you, Ms. Fortune?"

"Lovely, my dear. Let me guess. You received the current Augur's invitation, but decided to ignore it?"

"Not exactly. I threw it away. I was sure the name was a misprint."

She laughs quietly.

"He said you'd do that. Tommy is a fine scryer."

*Scryer* is a fancy word for fortune-teller. They use their hoodoo to get glimpses of the future. All Augurs are scryers. It makes the Sub Rosa rabble feel more secure.

"Did he see that you'd call me and I'd come?"

"Yes, he did."

"Why does he think that would work?"

"Because it's me asking you. Not him. This is an anxious time for everyone, and Saragossa was always sorry that you were so estranged from the Sub Rosa family. He would have wanted you to give the new Augur a chance. I'd like that too. And remember: you're responsible for me."

"How's that?"

"You saved my life. Remember? That makes you responsible for me. Isn't that how the old saying goes?"

"And if I say no, he'll send someone less pleasant to ask next time."

"That's not how he works," she says. "But it would do you and everyone else a great favor if you met him."

"You're very sweet, Ms. Fortune, but however you put it, this is still an order from on high, isn't it?"

"Yes, dear. I'm afraid it is."

I want to tell her to fuck off. I want to tell the Augur too. But I don't need trouble right now. I have a new job and the store is just getting back on its feet. And I'm not as strong as I once was. Just a few weeks ago, I could walk anywhere I wanted, to Lucifer's palace or the Augur's office, and put a knife to their throat. I can't do that anymore. I'm vulnerable, which makes Candy and everyone else vulnerable. I need to figure out how to get around without the Room. I don't like feeling weak and I don't like driving a Crown Vic.

"All right. When does he want to see me?"

"Right now, dear."

"Give me the address."

She does. I put it into a map app. The address is all the way across town. It will take an hour to get there driving.

"It was a nasty trick, him sending you to talk me into seeing him."

"Not really. It was how things were always going to happen. Just as it was fated that you'd say yes."

"How did you know?"

"Tommy told me you'd agree. As I said, he's a clever Augur. See you soon, my dear."

"Not that soon. I'm stuck in a car these days."

"How charming for you," she says, and hangs up.

I look at Candy—she's deep in her own phone conversation. After another minute, she finishes and hangs up.

"Who was your call?" she says.

"The Augur. Who was yours?"

"How fancy. Julie called. She wants me to come in and go

over some of the photos with her. She thinks I caught some interesting stuff."

"When does she want you?"

"Now. How about the Augur?"

"Now."

"We're like a couple of school kids being summoned home."

"For an egg-salad lunch."

"I like egg salad."

"You could have kept that ugly secret to yourself."

"I know, but I don't want any secrets between us. I love egg salad. It's my boyfriend."

"Stop. I have to go see fucking Sauron. I don't need images of you with egg-salad teeth swimming in my head."

"Where are my brass knuckles?"

"Carried away by flying monkeys."

"Then you better get working on that banana gun."

We gather up the paint thinner, rags, and cleaning supplies.

All we got off the windows is ER. Now the front of the store reads KILL. That ought to really bring in the customers.


THE 405 FREEWAY is the yellow brick road after the apocalypse. A winding stretch of paved bullshit choked with bumper-to-bumper demon drivers and banshee kids wailing away for the SpongeBob juice box Mommy and Daddy left on the kitchen counter. Road rage was invented along this cursed road. Murders and suicides are planned in the stinking miasma of stalled trucks and overheating Hondas, enough to fill all the graveyards in California and more. The 405 is one breakdown away from turning into the Donner Party. Starvation and cannibalism. Movie producers gnawing on starlets' severed legs. School-bus Little League teams crunching on the coach's skull. All I want to do is get to Marina del fucking Rey. Or die quick right here and now. I don't really care which anymore.

A century or two later, I dump the Crown Vic in a parking lot near the Basin E harbor. The dock number Tuatha gave me isn't hard to find, but it's behind a locked gate. I jam the black blade into the lock and it pops right open. The walkway is lined with pristine boats like floating palaces. I don't have to look for a slip number to find the boat Tuatha described. It stands out like a rotting pig carcass in a butcher-shop window. It just goes to show you how much pull the Sub Rosa has, parking this junk heap among the seafaring mansions.

You have to understand something about Sub Rosa aesthetics. While civilian blue bloods flaunt their inheritances buying the biggest, gaudiest Xanadus they can afford, the Sub Rosa go the other way. Their wealth and status get displayed by fronting their estates with hovels. Collapsed warehouses. Ransacked crack dens. Abandoned hotels. The current Augur has taken things a step further. His manor looks like the only things that are keeping it afloat are strong ropes and good wishes.

I don't know shit about boats, but this looks like it was once a nice one, and fast. Maybe it was a fishing boat that took tourists out to catch whatever kind of fish sporty types like to kill and varnish for the den. It looks like it could hold a dozen people easy. Main deck, lower deck, and a raised area where the captain could pilot the thing like Ahab on coke and

Red Bull. It was clearly very pretty at one point. Very sunny and merry. I can almost smell the white wine and gourmet box lunches. Just being here makes me miserable.

It looks like an engine fire took the boat out of commission. The lower deck and captain's area are black, wood-charred, and plastic-melted into long brittle ribbons. I put one foot on the deck, not sure if the french-fried shit box will hold my weight. It does. Too bad. Now I don't have an excuse to leave.

I look around for any nosy neighbors, don't see any, so I duck down and climb into the burned-out lower deck.

And come out on the deck of a ship that would make Howard Hughes blush.

A spotless deck. Polished oak and gold fixtures. Also, a group of bodyguards. Big boys, puffed up on steroids and protein powder. I wonder why the Sub Rosa's King Tut is working with civilian muscle and what kind of charms they're carrying that would stop any self-respecting magician with ill intent from blasting them to charcoal briquettes? They're probably part of an addled outreach program. The Augur's office throwing a bone to a local security company, sealing some kind of mutual aid pact between the Sub Rosa and civilian worlds. Hey, we're not better than you. We'll let you into the Augur's place, as long as you make sure the riffraff don't drop any cigarette butts on the deck. They're glorified hall monitors. Still, I'm not here to hassle anyone, so when one of the meatballs gets up, I stay calm and cool. Instead of coming for me, the flank steak slides open a glass door to an even lower deck.

"Welcome, Mr. Stark. Mr. Abbot is expecting you," he says.

I wait a second to see if it's a gag and someone is going to laugh. When no one does, I head for the open door. But I keep a hand in my pocket where I've stashed my na'at, my favorite weapon from when I was in the arena in Hell.

Tuatha is in a leather easy chair across from an annoyingly handsome guy. Sandy-blond hair, all-American-boy face with a movie-star nose idiots in Beverly Hills would pay a small fortune for. He looks young. The youngest Augur I've ever seen. He's wearing jeans and a yellow polo shirt with expensive-looking deck shoes. Captain America at the yacht club. He jumps up when he sees me and puts out his hand.

"Stark—that's what you go by, right?—it's great to finally meet you."

I shake Abbot's hand and he hits me with a high-watt Cary Grant smile that could melt the polar ice cap.

"Nice to meet you too," I lie.

When he lets go, I put my hand out to Tuatha. She takes it in a more placid way. Not ladylike really, but in a "there's nothing you can do about the situation, so sit back and enjoy the show" kind of way. She's still wearing mourning black.

"Hi, Ms. Fortune. Good to see you."

"And you. I'm glad we could finally get you boys together."

"Me too," says Abbot.

"Then let me make it official," she says. "Mr. James Stark, I'm happy to introduce you to our new Augur, Mr. Thomas Abbot."

"Ta-da," he says, holding up his hands.

They both laugh lightly. I don't.

"Please sit down, Stark."

He points to another leather chair that's probably worth more than most of the boats in the harbor.

"Would you like a drink?"

I debate getting out my flask and asking for a glass or being polite. I'm in unknown territory, so polite wins.

"I'll have what you're having," I say.

"We're having margaritas," he says.

"In that case, I'll have a whiskey, if you have it."

He gets up.

"Jack Daniel's, right? I got in some Gentleman Jack just yesterday."

I'm not surprised when he pours me the drink himself. It's the perfect move in whatever man-of-the-people charm offensive he has planned. Only one question bothers me. What if the fucker is on the level? Tuatha seems to trust him and she's far from stupid. That's something I hadn't considered until now. Charles Foster Kane I can fight. I'm not so sure about Mr. Rogers.

"Ice?" he says.

"No thanks. I'll have it neat."

"Of course."

He brings me the glass, then settles back down in his seat.

"I understand you knew Saragossa Blackburn pretty well," he says.

I look at Tuatha.

"I don't know. Did I?"

"In your own way," she says. "You helped him in ways others couldn't or wouldn't. He liked that you were so straightforward. He trusted you and it upset him that he could never get you to trust him."

"I always respected the fact he didn't have me bumped off. On that account, he was my favorite king ever."

"Is that how you see the Augur? As a king?" says Abbot.

"How else should I see him? I don't know any other Sub Rosa who could, say, hex the governor out of office, take over, and no one would bat an eye."

"That's the kind of misperception I want to clear up. You see this relationship as one side holding all the cards and the other—"

"Holding shit and high hopes he lives another day."

Abbot sets down his glass and leans forward with his hands on his knees, going for deep sincerity.

"That's exactly what I want to change. This antagonistic attitude. We shouldn't be adversaries. I know what you've done for the city. Hell, the world. When others ran, you stayed behind and fought the Angra Om Ya on your own. If you ask me, those are the actions of a hero."

"You admire me for that? Let me ask you a question . . ."

"Call me Tommy. That's what my friends call me."

"Okay, Tommy. If you admire what I did so much, where were you when it all went down? I could have used some help, if not fighting the Angra then in getting LAPD off my fucking back."

He nods.

"For one thing, I knew you'd win. I foresaw it and didn't want to get in the way."

"That's a bullshit answer and you know it."

He leans back, steepling his fingers.

"You're right, it is. As far as the police are concerned, I wasn't Augur yet, so I didn't have the power to deal with them. And as for the fight, I'll admit it in front of both of you. I was scared. Mad gods. Other dimensions. It's a bit out of my experience. But not yours, and when it came time to stand up, you did. I want to acknowledge that. I want to *reward* that."

"How?"

"I want to offer you a seat on my advisory council. You'd have an important voice in shaping policy where it comes to both the Sub Rosa world and how we interface with the civilian population."

Okay. He got that punch by me. I was looking for a right cross and he hit me with a body shot. The nicer this guy gets, the less I want to trust him. He oozes sincerity, but so do cave birds Downtown. They look like cute little sparrows. They'll perch in your hand and cuddle right up. Then the stinger comes out and they get you with one of the most noxious poisons in Hell. Lucifer kept a cageful of cave birds in his palace. He'd dip his royal dagger in their poison every morning before staff meetings. Everyone knew it and no one caused trouble. So the question is: Is Abbot the old Lucifer or Samael, the reformed and less homicidal Devil? What if I guess wrong? I want to get out of here, but the whiskey is good. Trust isn't my greatest virtue, but it might be interesting to see how the other half lives. I might be able to get something out of it.

"Does it pay anything?"

"It could. I know you've had some financial problems. I could authorize you a stipend. Say, a hundred thousand a year? It would be steady money to give you breathing room. You wouldn't have to give up the store or your other job."

So he has been keeping tabs on me. At least he's honest about it.

All this honesty is giving me a migraine.

"What do you know about my job?"

"I know you're working with a respected ex-member of the Golden Vigil. If she can trust you I think I can too."

"What if she's wrong?"

"I told you he'd say something like that," says Tuatha.

Abbot nods at her and looks back at me.

"She's not wrong, Stark, and all three of us in here know it. You come on like you're still the monster you were when you came back from Hell. And I don't use the word 'monster' lightly. You were a menace. Out of control. But you're not that person anymore, just as I'm not the person I was when I hid from the Angra Om Ya when I should have been right there beside you."

"What's changed?"

"You. The idea that you might work with us. With your experience and knowledge of the dangers plaguing both civilians and the Sub Rosa, I think we could accomplish great things together."

"You know, Audsley Isshii still has a hit out on me."

Isshii had been Blackburn's security chief. When Blackburn was murdered, Isshii decided I did it. He's been after me ever since.

"I do know about that and I want you to know that we're dealing with it. I guarantee you we will find him. In fact, if you wanted, I could assign you and your friends their own security teams."

"That's very generous of you."

"It's just partial payment for all you've done for us."

I look down at my glass and finish the drink.

"I like your whiskey," I tell him, trying to deflect his bruising sincerity with some of my own.

Abbot gets up, goes to the liquor cabinet, and comes back with an unopened bottle of Gentleman Jack.

"Take it. Please."

"Thanks."

I take the bottle and set it on the floor next to my chair. If it's a bomb, I want it out in the open where it will kill all of us when it goes off.

Abbot settles back down into his chair.

"I don't expect you to decide right now. But at least tell me you'll think about it."

I tap the bottle with my boot. It doesn't explode.

"Sure. Why not?"

Abbot flashes me a Mount Rushmore–size smile.

"That's terrific news."

He gets a business card from his pocket and hands it to me.

"This has my private number on it. You can call anytime. If you need anything or just want to talk."

I put the card in an inner pocket of my coat.

It feels like the end of the audience, so I get up. Abbot and Tuatha stand too. It's handshakes all around, a little awkward and self-conscious, like the end of a mediocre job interview.

"Don't forget your bottle," Abbot says.

I pick up the Jack and cradle it in my arms like a newborn.

Tuatha says, "I'll see him out, Tommy."

He nods and sits back down.

"It was great meeting you, Stark."

"Yeah. You too."

With a light touch on my arm, Tuatha steers me outside. We walk to the far end of the boat.

"Thank you for coming and for listening. I know this kind of thing is hard for you."

"Let me ask you something straight. Do you trust this guy? He seems too good to be true."

"I thought so too when we first met. He does work hard to make a good impression, doesn't he? But over the years I've learned that a few people are what they appear to be. Especially the ones with good hearts."

I look back the way we came.

"But he'd still have a troublemaker killed if he thought it was for the greater good."

"Of course. Don't take his good manners for weakness. He is the Augur, after all. But I don't think you have to worry. I can tell he likes you."

"Maybe you're right. I wouldn't give Gentleman Jack to an enemy."

Tuatha looks at me more seriously than she ever has before.

"Think about the offer. Really think about it. I think you two could do wonderful things together."

"Thanks, Ms. Fortune. Take care of yourself."

She goes back to the cabin and Abbot to talk about me. If I could still shadow-walk, I'd come out behind the drapes and listen to what they really think. As it is, all I can do is speculate. Like, are they setting me up for something or is this a chance to get some real money?

I walk past the bodyguards. They don't show the slightest interest in me.

Back on the deck of the burned-out boat, I stand and look out to sea, playing the last few minutes over in my head.

I don't know what to think. I want to tell Abbot to fuck off and walk away, but I've played that game so many times before and where has it gotten me? Broke. Almost homeless. With no real prospects and less power than I've had since I went Downtown. Being an Abomination is one thing, but being a loser Abomination is really not acceptable. Still, I can't get past the fact that the James Dean pretty-boy prick was just too good to be true.

I weigh the bottle in my hand. Cock my arm to throw it out into the harbor. I'm halfway through my swing when I stop.

On the other hand, he could have poisoned me on the boat and dumped my body in the ocean where no one would ever find it. Even if Abbot is a snake, it doesn't mean I have to take it out on an innocent bottle of good whiskey. And being on the outside so long is starting to lose its charm. What's the saying? Keep your friends close and your enemies closer? I don't know who Tommy is, but maybe I should be the cave bird in his hand, just for a while. It's something to think about.

As I wander back to the Crown Vic, a stretch limo pulls up a few yards away. Four goons climb out of the back, two from each side of the car. They eye me like a Gucci SWAT team. Unlike the meat pies on the boat, these are Sub Rosa heavies, second-rate magicians, but with big balls and a lot of dark, baleful magic tricks.

I act like I don't see them, open the car door, toss in the Jack, and slide inside the Vic like any good civilian heading home after a day at the marina. With my left hand, I adjust the rearview mirror so I can see them. I keep my right hand on the key in the ignition just in case. Once the wolves have decided the coast is clear, a squat, older man with a cane climbs out of the car.

His clothes are so out of style, for a second I think he must be a vampire. Some of the slow ones lose track of the decades and fail to notice that not everyone wears zoot suits anymore. It makes them easy to hunt. This guy, however, is out in broad daylight, so he's no shroud eater, meaning his look is deliberate.

He has on a bright red leisure suit, white patent-leather shoes, with a white belt, like the regional manager of a carpet-cleaning company in 1974. I only get a glimpse of his face before the goons close in around him, but it's enough.

It's Tamerlan Radescu, the necromancer. He's not just a Dead Head, he's the McDonald's of Dead Heads, the only magician I've ever heard of who's licensed his name to other magicians. Any competent but mediocre necromancer can buy a franchise, use Tamerlan's name and "techniques," and instantly double his or her income, all while kicking back a percentage to the home office. People say Tamerlan himself hasn't done a lick of hoodoo in years. He just collects the checks and buys bad suits.

Tamerlan lets himself through the gate I had to break into and heads down the dock for the Augur's boat. Where else would he be going? Looks like Tommy is still getting acquainted with the local Sub Rosa heavy hitters. Have fun staring at that grisly suit for an hour.

As I start the car I stare at all that money, feeling sorry

for myself. Because I have to drive another hour back across town. If I end up taking Abbot's offer, I don't want a stipend.

I want a jet pack.

I'M BACK ON the 405, stuck behind a vegan bakery truck with a flat tire. It's not their fault, but now I'm hungry for a plate of *carnitas*. As the traffic in our lane slowly merges into the next to get around the carrot huggers, my phone rings. I answer it and hit the speaker button so I don't have to hold it.

"Stark? It's Julie. Where are you?"

"Stuck in traffic on the dark side of the moon. Where are you?"

"At the office. Can you get over here? I have some information."

"Me too. I just met the new Augur."

"Really? Wow. You'll have to tell me about it."

"Not anytime soon. Seriously, nothing is moving. I'm going to be here for a while."

"Fine. We'll do it this way. I have an ID on Death. Death's body."

"Who is it?"

"His name is Eric Townsend. A commodities trader at a boutique company called Yaa and Sons." She spells it out. "It sounds like it might be China-based. I'm going to check them out."

The guy behind me honks, an existential bleat in a concrete river of despair. I give him the finger. Fuck you, Jeff Gordon.

"Yaa isn't Chinese. It's an old Indian name for Los Angeles. And I mean old. Like five thousand years old."

"How do you know that?"

"I'm a magician. We know lots of funny things. And sometimes Kasabian watches *Jeopardy!*"

"Anyway, that's an interesting name for an investment company."

"No shit. You have anything else?"

"A lot. From all accounts, Eric Townsend was a very upstanding businessman, one of his company's best. That's before he disappeared six months ago."

"Any idea what he's been doing for all that time?"

Brake lights flash like fireflies up ahead.

"Listen to this," says Julie. "That tattoo he had lasered off? It's the same emblem that was on the shirts of the three men you and Candy saw on Wonderland Avenue."

"What does it mean?"

"It's the insignia of the White Light Legion. Ever heard of them?"

"Aren't they some freaky skinhead group? Like religious Nazi assholes?"

"You're partly right, but they're much stranger than that. The Vigil has a whole library on the White Lights and the Silver Shirts."

"Now, the Silver Legion I've heard of. Local Hitler groupies back in the thirties. They were kind of a big deal at one point."

"Their leader was a disgruntled screenwriter named William Dudley Pelley."

"Leave it to a writer to go nuts and think he can take over the world with his Dungeons and Dragons crew."

"It goes much deeper than that. Pelley didn't want to take

over the country. He wanted to pave the way for the Führer in the U.S. when he won the war in Europe. Pelley started the Silver Shirts on January first, 1933, the day Hitler became chancellor of Germany. But he wasn't a run-of-the-mill fascist. Yes, his group attracted the usual bullies and thugs you find in those groups, but Pelley saw himself as a spiritual leader. Call it New Age fascism."

"What does that mean?"

A Caddy cuts off a plumbing truck to move farther left, so I cut off a Prius to do the same.

"In 1928, Pelley had a 'clairaudient' event. A kind of out-of-body experience that later, in an article, he called 'My Seven Minutes in Eternity.' He said he was hit by a shaft of bright white light that took him to another plane of existence where he heard voices. He talked with the souls of the dead, even God and Jesus. Along the way, he gained special psychic powers."

"This guy is starting to sound like every snake-oil salesman I've ever heard of."

"Not quite. Pelley was special. The Silver Legion had fifteen thousand members at one point, three thousand in California alone. But Pelley didn't want to just be a fascist. He saw himself as a great religious leader and that the beings he met on his out-of-body journeys had picked him to bring about a spiritual revolution in America."

"What kind?"

"Pelley had psychic experiences for four years after the first one in '28. According to him, they unlocked his mental powers. Some accounts say he claimed he could levitate. He could speak to 'secret masters' that lived on other planes, and it was his job to teach others what they taught him. He even had his own metaphysical magazine, the *New Liberator,* where he published general spiritualist articles and his own teachings."

We come to a complete stop again. A pickup truck and a Maserati almost sideswipe each other as they wrestle for an exit ramp.

"What does any of this have to do with Townsend? He wasn't a Silver Shirt. You said he was in another group."

"Yes, the White Light Legion. They were split off from the Silver Legion in the late thirties over some kind of metaphysical dispute. They didn't think Pelley's teachings went far enough. They weren't practical enough. If Pelley could levitate and communicate with dead souls, they wanted to do the same. Their leader, Edison Elijah McCarthy, thought Pelley was holding out on them."

"A Nazi must have loved having a name like Elijah."

"By the time he legally changed his middle name to Monroe, it was too late. Enough people knew his real name. He spent years trying to cover it up."

"What are you saying? Those White Lights guys slaughtered a whole houseful of people on Wonderland because someone knew their leader's real name?"

"I doubt it, but it's hard to say exactly what the White Lights want. We know they demanded access to Pelley's most esoteric teachings, but there's no way of knowing if they got it. They had their own publications, but they destroyed them all in the early sixties when an FBI agent briefly infiltrated the group. Since then, all their teachings have been by word of mouth and no other plants have gotten close enough to the inner circle to learn their most important beliefs."

Julie is on a roll. I don't want to stop her, but I'm going crazy sitting here. I dig the Maledictions out of my pocket and light one up. It's a small victory.

She says, "We know that Edison kept in touch with some of Pelley's contacts in German fascist and metaphysical organizations. But we don't have much information about that either. What reports we have say he did have dealings with the Thule Society."

"I've heard of them. Dark-magic dilettantes and trying to prove Aryans were the master race, tracing them back to earlier made-up civilizations. Atlantis and other cheap fantasies."

"Right. Apparently he was in touch with other groups too, but there are no records of which ones."

"So really, all you know is that this Townsend, a straight-arrow banker type, was a member of a group that wanted to ascend to higher planes and turn themselves into Nazi X-Men. Do I have that right?"

"Essentially."

"Guess he didn't ascend fast enough. But why is Death walking around in his skin? And what happened that made him burn his association with the White Lights off his body?"

"I'm sure the two are connected, but I don't know how. Maybe killing and mutilating Townsend was punishment for leaving the group."

"Sounds right for bully boys like that. They don't like quitters and they'd probably see anyone who wanted out as a potential rat."

"This is all assuming that the White Lights have anything to do with this at all. We don't even know if the White Lights are the ones who killed him. And even if they did, it could have been another group that used him as a vessel for Death."

"Like Dead Heads?"

"Exactly."

"I saw Tamerlan Radescu headed to the Augur's place when I left just now."

"That's interesting, but again, we don't have any concrete connections."

"Maybe we should look for them."

"Maybe. We need to talk to Death about this. He might have heard or remembered something."

"Have you found anything about the abandoned building where he said he woke up? Sub Rosa like trashed buildings where they can hide their mansions inside."

Like a miracle, traffic begins to open up. I can touch the accelerator without feeling like a storefront preacher praying for rain.

"I'm working on that now. I have some ideas, but I need to do more research."

"This is all too strange. I like my Nazis young, bald, and dumb. I don't like clever fascists. I knew one once. His name was Josef. He did a lot of bad things to nice people."

"Is he still around? Maybe I could talk to him."

"Good luck. I cut off his head."

The line goes silent and I wonder if the call dropped. Then I hear Julie's voice.

"Sometimes it's hard to tell when you're kidding."

"Of course I'm kidding," I say, but I'm not. I burned Josef

and his skinhead dogs out of their clubhouse, and when he came for me, I took the fucker's head off with the black blade. It wasn't a hard choice. Josef was a Kissi. But Julie would never understand that, and sometimes a little white lie saves a lot of time. So I just say, "Josef really is dead. There was a fire at his group's compound and I heard he went down with the ship. Besides, he was smart. He'd smell the cop on you and laugh in your face."

"You're probably right. Stop by the office when you get back to the city. I want to hear about the Augur and Radescu."

"I should be there in less than an hour. We're finally moving. Cross your fingers it stays that way or you're going to be there till the Rapture."

"I'll light a candle for you. Get here as soon as you can."

"You got it."

As the road opens up more, it occurs to me that I'm an idiot. I had the perfect opportunity a few minutes ago. I mean, if anyone could get me brass knuckles it would be the Augur. Now I'm going to have to ask for knuckles *and* a jet pack.

It's past one when I get back to Julie's office. She didn't have anything new on Death's case, but she was plenty interested in the Augur and his floating mansion. I couldn't tell if it was professional curiosity or if she's just fascinated by the idea of the Sub Rosa world because she's never been quite so close to it before.

It's two before I can pry myself loose and head home. The whiskey at Tommy's place is coming down on me. I'm out of practice morning drinking. I need coffee and food and bed, not necessarily in that order.

But things never quite turn out the way you want, do they?

I find a spot across the street from Max Overdrive and park the car. Waiting in front of the store, in a pressed suit probably hand-stitched by archangels, is Samael.

Samael has his back to me as I cross the street. He's staring at the word KILL painted on the window. I go over, take out a Malediction, and light it with Mason's lighter.

Samael makes a rectangle with his fingers and looks at the paint job through it like a pretend movie director.

"Your work?" he says.

"No. It was one of your creeps."

"And what did you do to him?"

"Just spanked him a little. No more than he deserved."

"I'm sure."

Samael gestures at the store.

"How is the little lost lamb?"

"Stick your head inside and see. He's right there."

He waves a hand dismissively.

"No thanks. Frankly, he gives me the willies."

"When did you get so sensitive?"

"Death isn't any more popular with angels than he is with mortals."

"That must make company picnics awkward."

"You have no idea."

"What's the story with Mr. Muninn? Why is Death still here? Why hasn't he sent an army down here to bring him home?"

"Can't. Politics," he says, nods at my cigarette. "May I have one of those? I forgot mine."

I take out the pack and offer him one. Light it for him.

"You were saying politics."

He nods.

"Many angels object to Father opening the gates of Hell the way he did. They don't want to allow those damned souls into Heaven. Some, the younger, angrier ones, want to expel the souls already there."

Unfortunately, shutting down Hell and opening the gates for both souls and Hellions was my idea.

"You're saying I made everything worse."

Samael leans against the wall. I bet his suit doesn't even get dirty. It wouldn't dare.

"No. Father made it worse by following your advice. But yes, it was your idea. Still, you aren't the daddy of this particular rebellion."

"But I'm its uncle."

Samael smiles.

"No good deed goes unpunished. You should know that by now."

"I don't do good deeds. I do pragmatic."

"You keep telling yourself that."

We just smoke for a minute while I think. How could things be even worse than before? There was a civil war in Heaven, and Hell was coming apart faster than a gelatin Harley.

"Who do you think could have put Death in a body?"

"No angel is that stupid. Even Hellions. It had to be a human magician."

"What about all the people who are half dead?"

Samael checks his watch.

"They're not going anywhere until Death can lead their souls away again."

"A guy I know almost died. He said instead of Death he saw something else. Any ideas what that might be?"

"Possibly. There's something moving on the outskirts of the Tenebrae. A shadow. Imagine an immense dust devil made of lightning and emptiness. Whatever it is, it's trying to will itself into being, but it doesn't have the strength yet. That's why no one is dying. The shadow is struggling. If it's trying to take Death's place it's doing a piss-poor job. I don't think it knows what it's doing."

"That's good."

Samael waggles his hand.

"Not really. It has all eternity to figure out how things work. If it got this far, it isn't stupid."

"Angels die as easy as people if you know what you're doing. You and the other halo polishers have a dog in this fight."

He raises his eyebrows.

"Very much. Once it figures out how to dispose of human souls, there's no reason to think it will stop there."

"It could go after Muninn."

"It's possible."

"And you don't have any ideas on how to stop it?"

Samael blows smoke rings.

"I don't even know what it is yet."

"You'll let me know when you do?"

"Of course," he says. "How is it these days, not being able to walk between worlds?"

"Hell. So to speak."

"Do you regret what you did?"

I look up and down the street, wondering why he checked his watch.

"No. I just wish I was smart enough to figure out a way that didn't cost me the Room."

"There wasn't any other way. As I said, no good deed etcetera etcetera."

"Yeah, but how can you keep getting your teeth kicked in when you don't have any teeth left?"

"Then they'll kick your ribs. There's always something left to kick. Trust me. It used to be my specialty."

"Trust me. I remember."

A stretch Lincoln Town Car rolls slowly down Las Palmas. Samael drops his Malediction, stubs it out with the toe of one exquisite shoe.

"I should get going before the winged pests discover I'm on Earth. They'll know I've been talking to you and I won't be able to get a decent seat at any of the good restaurants."

"Know any tricks to get me out of having to drive everywhere?"

Samael walks to the curb, turns around, and looks at me.

"Grow wings, little angel."

"I'm only half an angel."

"Then grow one and learn to glide. Squirrels do it. Surely, you can figure it out."

The limo pulls up. A driver gets out and comes around to the passenger side of the car, opens the door for Samael. I toss my cigarette into the alley beside the store.

"Nice to see how modest you're living in these uncertain times."

Samael stops halfway into the car. He puts his hands together like he's praying.

"Lord, grant me chastity . . . but not yet."

"See you around, Augustine."

He drives away and the car disappears into traffic.

I was hoping Marlowe's threat, saying something knew I was coming, was just a line. Now it sounds like it might be true. But I can't do anything about it right now. Given a choice between worrying about Death and having breakfast, I'll take breakfast.

I head inside.

THE STORE IS empty of customers. It's just Kasabian and Death in a cozy little homespun scene. Kasabian labeling discs. Death putting them in cases and shelving them, sometimes stopping to sniff them. They smile at me as I come in. Domestic bliss. There's a movie playing on the big screen. An operating room lit up like something on the Discovery Channel, only there are a few too many neat stacks of wet, random organs and body parts laid out like a cannibal buffet to be TV-friendly.

"David Cronenberg's version of *Frankenstein*," says Kasabian, catching me watching. "He tried to make it in the eighties, but couldn't get the cash. Now we have it. Maria brought it by after you left."

I nod, remembering what Maria said.

"That ought to bring in some cash."

"Damn right. People will pay blood money for this one."

I look at Death. He's happy with his discs, but ignores the screen. Guess he's seen plenty of stuff like this before. I scratch the palm of one hand with the top of the Gentleman Jack bottle.

"Cherish it. We might not be getting any more movies for a while."

Kasabian looks stricken.

"What do you mean?"

"Dash, Maria's movie hound, took a powder. She asked me to find him."

"You're going to do it, right? I mean, this is our livelihood."

I hold up the bottle to point at Death.

"No. *He's* my livelihood right now and he's the job I'm working on. Dash will have to wait. We must have enough inventory to keep the yokels happy for a while."

Kasabian thinks.

"Maria's brought by a few things I haven't put out yet. I've got the *Buckaroo Banzai* sequel and Pasolini's Saint Paul movie. I guess I can hold them for a while and bring them out one at a time."

"There you go. Keep the public hungry."

" 'I'm waiting for my man. Twenty-six dollars in my hand,' " says Death.

Kasabian and I both look at him.

"How do you know that song?" I ask him.

"It's just something I've heard somewhere. It's about hunger, isn't it? About trying to buy drugs?"

"That's right. The Velvet Underground's first album. Nineteen sixty-seven," Kasabian says.

I go over to where Death is working. He stops when he sees me approach.

"You remember that, but you can't remember how you got here."

He nods.

"I like music," he says. "Everyone thinks I like chess because of that movie."

Kasabian turns down the sound on the big screen.

He says, *"The Seventh Seal.* Ingmar Bergman. Nineteen fifty-seven."

I shoot him a look . . .

"Thank you, Rain Man."

. . . then turn to Death.

"You want to have a drink with me? Maybe it'll shake something loose."

"You really want to get him liquored up?" says Kasabian.

I shrug.

"I figure it's that or electroshock. What do you say?"

I put down the bottle on the counter. Death looks it over, his forehead creased.

"I don't know. But if you think it will help."

"You liked beer the other day. Maybe you're a whiskey man too. Let's explore that possibility."

"All right. When?"

"Give me an hour. I'll let you sniff the cork and everything."

Kasabian doesn't look happy. I'm stealing his help. And keeping him from buttering up the Grim Reaper.

"I'm going to see Candy. When I come back down, we'll start the party. You know any party songs?"

Death thinks for a moment, then sings, " 'Happy birthday to you . . .' "

I start upstairs.

"You two have fun. I'll be back in a little while."

CANDY IS ON the sofa. A laptop sits on the coffee table, photos scattered around it. I recognize some as the Three Stooges from the other night. Others are new. There's one of a dour-faced, doughy guy with dark, wavy hair and the White Light insignia on his crisp white shirt. I pick it up.

"Don't lose that," says Candy without looking up.

"Who is it?"

"Edison Elijah McCarthy."

"Our favorite fascist."

"That's him at the height of the White Light Legion's popularity, in the early fifties. Julie gave me this laptop to do some research for her."

I sit down next to her on the sofa.

"What happened to kicking down doors with me?"

"I like that, but I like this too. It's different. I'm learning a lot."

"Promise you'll come out and break things with me sometime. I don't want to be jealous of a machine."

"I promise," she says.

I move more of the photos around and she gives my hand a smack.

"Don't mess those up," she says. "I need them. Julie has access to all kinds of crazy law enforcement intel."

"What are you looking at now?"

"A few minutes ago I was in NamUs, the National Missing and Unidentified Persons System. Now I'm in the NCIC. National Crime Information Center. It's an FBI site, but Julie can get into crazy Golden Vigil sites too. Not just DNA and fingerprints, but auras, drone Lurker surveillance, Power Spot monitoring. Congregations of ghosts. There's even a huge database called 'Soul Viability.'"

"That one's easy to figure out."

"What do you think it is?"

"Some kind of computer program that runs odds on if you're going to Heaven or Hell. Like guys at racetracks set the odds for horses."

"Cool," she says. "Who should we look for?"

"Am I in one of those databases?"

She laughs at the screen.

"Yeah. You could say that."

"Meaning?"

"In Homeland Security's Extranatural Cryptologic Register—sort of their fanboy Pokémon card collection—there's two files with a million times more security than the others. Guess who."

"Karl Marx and Patty Duke."

"Lucifer and Sandman Slim."

"Does mine have pictures? I need new head shots for my movie auditions."

She shakes her head.

"No. But don't you think it's just a little cool?"

"I'm not sure if I'd say cool. More like you've confirmed all my worst fears."

"Don't worry. It says some nice things too. They know how you saved the world and things."

"They just don't know why and don't trust me that I'm not doing it for some nefarious reasons all my own."

"Yeah," she says. "Something like that."

Thank you, Marshal Wells.

"Do we have any food around here?"

"I got burritos on the way home. Yours is in the fridge."

"You are a goddess."

"I know."

While the burrito heats up in the microwave, I get out my phone and call Vidocq.

"*Bonjour*, James. How are you today?"

"Up to my eyeballs in Nazis and burritos. I had a quick question for you."

"And what is that?"

"Death is awake, walking around. Want to come over and meet him while he's conscious?"

"I thought you'd never ask."

"Get over here ASAP."

I sit down next to Candy again.

"What does Julie have you looking for?"

"Where the White Light Legion used to hang out, and places they might have used as a base of operations."

"Sounds exciting."

"Shut up and eat your burrito."

"If you get bored, you want to do something for me?"

"What?"

"See what you can find on Tamerlan Radescu."

"The Dead Head?"

"That's the one."

"What do you want to know?"

"I'm not sure. Just general background stuff for now. Who he hangs out with. Where he came from. Is he just a snappy dresser or is he into anything shady?"

"If I have time," Candy says.

"Sure. I'm not bothering you, am I?"

"Of course not, dear. But why don't you take your food

into the bedroom and watch cartoons until your little friend comes over and you can go out and play?"

"This is a really good burrito."

"Get out," she says, so I do. Vidocq gets to the store a half hour after I finish eating.

DEATH, VIDOCQ, AND I go into the storage room. I bring three glasses.

It's introductions all around, then it's drinks all around. Vidocq and I down some of the Jack. Death sniffs his, sips, and makes a face.

"I don't know if this body likes it."

"You're not supposed to like it. You're just supposed to absorb it into your tissues."

"I think you're making fun of me."

I shake my head.

"I wouldn't do that."

"What he means," says Vidocq, "is that whiskey, like many of the more interesting things in this world, is an acquired taste."

"Why acquire a taste for something you don't like?"

I set the bottle down by my chair leg.

"Do you hate it?"

"I don't know."

"Well, there you go. You try it. Then try it again until you know. Sometimes you find the thing you didn't like the first time becomes one of your favorite things."

Death sips his whiskey again.

"I don't think this is going to be a favorite thing."

"That's all right. It just means more for Vidocq and me."

Death sets down his glass on a box that stands in for a bedside table.

"So here's the thing: no one is coming for you," I say. "There's no cavalry. No golden chariot full of angels. Trust me. I checked."

Death sighs, unconsciously rubs his chest and the scar over his missing heart.

"I'm not surprised. Someone would have come for me already if they could."

"For now, you're just one of us chickens."

"That might be preferable to being a human."

"I hear humans taste lousy deep-fried."

Vidocq clears his throat.

"What is the process of death like? From your perspective, as a being not subject to its laws."

Death stares at him for a minute.

"That's an interesting question. You're not entirely subject to its laws yourself, are you?"

"That's right. I've been, as far as I can tell, rendered immortal. It was an accident, a slip of the hand while performing an experiment in Paris in 1856."

"Why is it that you want to know? You've had ample time to observe the process of death. You must have learned something."

"Not enough," Vidocq says. He finishes his drink. "I've only seen it from the outside. I want to know what it's like. The transition from life to unlife. Is it something felt? Is it a journey or the blink of an eye?"

"You're not asking for yourself, are you?"

Vidocq leans back against the storeroom wall.

"There was a woman I knew in Paris. Liliane. I loved her very much. I want to know what she experienced when she died and went from our world to yours."

"Oh yes. I know who you're talking about. She didn't."

"Die? Of course she did. I saw it with my own eyes."

"I'm afraid your eyes were wrong."

"Her heart stopped. Her breathing. How is this possible?"

"It's not my place to say."

"All right. I was wrong and she didn't die then. When did she die?"

Death keeps his mouth shut.

Vidocq says, "Is she not dead?"

Death looks away.

"Can we talk about something else?"

Vidocq stares down at his hands. I pour him another drink and look at Death.

"I know your name. Your body's name. It's Eric Townsend. He was some kind of stockbroker. Does any of that sound familiar?"

"No."

"He was part of a group called the White Light Legion. That's what the tattoo on your arm is. Their sigil. I didn't think about it until this morning, but I wonder if he could have been a necromancer in his spare time."

"I wouldn't know. Necromancy has never interested me. And most magicians involved in death magic want to speak to the souls of the departed, not me."

"But some must have tried to contact you."

"Of course."

"What happened?"

"None was powerful enough to compel me and I didn't have any interest in the weak ones. As you might have guessed, my job is a busy one."

Vidocq says, "How is it you're able to be all places at once and carry away a thousand souls all dying at the same time?"

Death drums his fingers on his knee.

"It's my nature."

"Who is more powerful, Death or God?"

"All gods die. I do too when each universe dies and I resurrect with the birth of each new universe. But there's no guarantee it will happen. Who knows what the next universe will bring? Maybe there will be no death there. Can you imagine?"

I sit down on a box of old *Mannix* VHS tapes. How the hell do we still have these?

"You've seen other universes before this one?"

"Dozens. But this one is my favorite. I've touched parts of human lives—each soul leaves a tiny echo of itself with me—but I've never been flesh before. All these senses are interesting. Except for the pain."

"That pretty much sums up what we like to call the human condition."

"How do you live with it?"

I hold out the bottle.

"This helps."

"I'm not sure I believe that."

"Well, we like to think it does."

"Wishful thinking is also part of the human condition," Vidocq says.

I sip some Jack, say, "What's the last thing you remember before you woke up here? When you were still yourself?"

"I was gathering souls to the Tenebrae."

"See anyone unusual? Did anything funny happen?"

"No."

"Then what?"

"Nothing."

"It just went blank?"

"Yes. It was like I was sucked out of myself. Like a seed from a husk."

I feel the Colt against my back.

"You're one unhelpful dead man."

Death looks at Vidocq and then back to me.

"I'm sorry."

I stare up at the ceiling, thinking.

"Maybe we're looking at this thing all wrong, making it more complicated than it really is."

"What do you mean?" says Vidocq.

"What I mean is, Death is stuck in a human body, right?"

"Right," says Death.

I take out the pistol.

"What if we unstick him?"

Death's eyes widen and his pupils turn into dinner plates. I wonder if Eric Townsend ever looked that freaked out, like maybe when the market tanked. I doubt it. I get the feeling that Death has found a whole new expression in an otherwise ordinary face.

"I don't think I like your idea," he says.

"I think that perhaps you're getting frustrated and are looking for a quick answer," says Vidocq.

He puts his hand on the barrel of the gun and points it at the floor.

"You don't think it's even worth considering? Maybe we can fix things right here and now."

"Not all of life's answers are in guns and na'ats. It just isn't that simple," Vidocq says. "Besides, we don't know what might happen if we damage Death's body too badly. He might be lost to us forever."

"I can think of worse things than no death in the world."

"To spend eternity in a coma like all those poor people?" says Vidocq. "That sounds like Hell to me."

Very quietly, Death says, "Everyone hates me or is afraid of me or both. Angels, Hellions, humans, Gods. It gets lonely."

"Then there's no Mrs. Death, I take it?"

"That's not funny," he snaps, and for a second Death isn't just a sad sack in dead skin. There's a flash of cosmic fury in his eyes. A power that hasn't been there before. Then it's gone.

"Hey, I know what hated feels like, so we're in the same club," I say.

Death does a small nod, but I don't think he's convinced.

Vidocq finishes his drink and motions for the bottle. I give it to him.

He says, "Some texts claim that death is just a way station on a journey to somewhere else. That to die again in Heaven is a gateway to other planes. Is that true?"

"Ah, that. You people have a lot of ideas about what death is."

"You ever hear the name Edison Elijah McCarthy?" I say.

"No."

"What about Tamerlan Radescu?"

"It's not familiar."

"Give me your arm."

He does it, but slowly, like he thinks I'm going to tear it off and use it for an ashtray.

"We know about the tattoo. I want to know what that brand is."

Maybe to distract himself, Death turns to Vidocq.

"Why have you been looking for me for so long?"

"Becoming immortal was never my choice. Now I would like to be like other men."

I look at him.

"You want to die? What about Allegra?"

"I didn't say I wanted to die now. But I would like to know that it's a possibility."

"Of course it is," says Death.

"How would I go about it?"

"You were changed with a potion. The right potion will return to a normal human life."

"Potions. I've tried an endless parade of godforsaken potions."

"Try more."

Vidocq frowns and stares at the far wall. I guess that wasn't the answer he was looking for. I let go of Death's arm.

"Samael, an angel, says something is trying to take your place."

Death nods.

"Of course. There must be a Death, therefore there will be one."

"You don't seem too concerned."

"I'm very concerned, but what can I do in my current state?"

"I wonder what would happen if we got you two together."

"I suspect one of us would destroy the other."

"You think so?"

"I doubt the universe could survive or would permit more than one Death."

"Too many yous does sound like a drag."

Death twists his arm around, looking at the underside.

"I think I do remember something," he says. "I've been thinking about the brand."

"What about it?"

"I don't know what it is. But I'm sure I've seen it on some souls. Ones that didn't want to move on."

"You mean ghosts."

"Yes."

"A branded soul?" says Vidocq.

Death nods.

"The mark was only on a few, but it was there."

Vidocq and I look at each other, neither sure what to make of that information.

Death starts looking uncomfortable. I want a cigarette, but I have a drink instead.

"So, you know any funny jokes or stories?" I say. "Something you and the other angels giggle about around the water-cooler."

Death looks at the floor, then at me.

"Knock knock."

"Who's there?"

"Doorbell repairman."

Vidocq chuckles. I slap Death's knee.

"Hey, that was funny. I didn't think you had it in you."

"Now it's your turn," he says.

"No. I forgot my jokes during my vacation Downtown."

"You're always making jokes. You must remember one."

"Yes," say Vidocq. "You must remember one."

I shoot him a quick "fuck you" with my eyes.

"Okay," I say. "Here's one. There's this old preacher home in bed. He's dying and doesn't have much longer to go. So he sends a note to a banker and a lawyer that go to his church. They come over and sit in chairs he's set out, one on each side of the bed. The only thing is, when they get there the preacher doesn't say a word. He just lies there. Finally, the lawyer speaks up. 'Excuse me, sir. We don't seem to be talking about anything. Why did you ask us here?' 'Well,' says the preacher, 'Jesus died between two thieves and I figure if it was good enough for him, it's good enough for me.' "

Death stares at me for a second like I was speaking Urdu. Then his face changes, relaxes, and he laughs.

Vidocq holds out his glass and clinks it against the bottle as I pick it up. What do you know? We had kind of a normal moment there. I look at Death smiling. Guess I'm glad I didn't shoot him after all.

VIDOCQ LEAVES NOT long after that, still shaken by what Death said about Liliane. Figuring someone to be dead, then finding out they're still alive and kicking, can be a shock. It happened to me with Mason. Before Christmas I thought I'd gotten rid of him so many times, but the fucker always scuttled out from under the floorboards like an armor-plated cockroach.

Vidocq is luckier than me. At least his nondead pal is someone he liked. Didn't he? Or did I read it all wrong? Was he upset because he didn't know someone he loved was still around and lost to him, or did he melt down because he thought he was done with her, but now knows she might be waiting around the next corner? I'll have to ask him, but not now. He needs to calm down and remember how to breathe. He was so pale when he left he looked like he'd been huffing paint thinner all afternoon.

I guess the movie is over. Kasabian has the news on the big screen, so Death and I go over and watch with him.

What do you know? The world is still a big ball of shimmering shit. But before the usual parade of misery detailing all the wars, famines, and atrocities people enjoy so much, we lead in with a long story about the nondead piling up all over the world. In the U.S., they say that civilian and military hospitals are full, so they're setting up temporary wards in school gyms and empty stadiums. The dreaming dead lie motionless under sheets, like bugs in spider silk, between goalposts and filling the outfields of baseball diamonds. The news hack describing all this says the one bright spot is that suicides are down, since the poor saps know that killing themselves is a ticket to nowhere. I look over at Death. I can't read his expression. He's staring at the monitor, big-eyed. He takes long, deep breaths.

I say, "I can't keep calling you Death. It's beginning to creep me out. You have any other names we could try?"

"Many," says Death. "Thanatos. Azriel. Mrityu. Yan Luo. Malak al-Maut—"

I hold up a hand.

"Stop. Most of those are more depressing than Death. But I need something to call you when civilians are around. How about Vincent?"

"Why Vincent?"

*"The Masque of the Red Death,"* says Kasabian.

I nod.

"Vincent for Vincent Price. Death himself, as directed by Roger Corman."

Vincent looks back at the news.

"I suppose it's as good a name as any."

Kasabian says, "It's better than Sandman Slim."

I look at him.

"Hush, Gort."

Everyone quiets down as the news goes local. There was another massacre in Laurel Canyon. Five dead. All beaten to death. No one saw anything.

What the fuck is wrong with that place?

I should have seen it coming with the Three Stooges the other night. A massacre is nothing new out there. You could fertilize all the farms in the Central Valley with the bodies buried in Laurel Canyon.

In the sixties, when the young and the beautiful from music and movies ruled the roost, they dumped hapless shit-heads who OD'd at parties there when it was too risky to call an ambulance. In earlier, classier days—the twenties through the forties—well-connected stars could call a manager or agent who'd arrange a discreet disposal of human waste by studio security. Not that they'd necessarily need it. There was always been plenty of room to bury an unruly spouse with the help of a lover or two.

The Army Air Corps even built a base at the top of Wonderland Park Avenue in 1941. It was transformed from an air defense site into a military movie production house, but rumors still persist that they ran experiments on some of the hippie locals. Mostly MKUltra-style acid tests. Dose enough innocents and you're bound to end up with a few bodies, and who knows how to get rid of bodies better than the army?

Cops have always loved the canyon. In the old days, they'd drive mobsters high up into the hills and dump them into the ravines. Let the coyotes have them. A lot of gangland hits went down out there too. For a while it was Bugsy Siegel pulling the triggers, then, after a sniper splattered his brains all over his Beverly Hills mansion, it was Mickey Cohen's turn. He was a professional boxer in his youth and knew how to use his hands. After him, Johnny Stompanato got to run a little mayhem through the Sunset and the canyon. Of course, no one could prove anything. There were accusations of murder, but nothing came of them. In the end, Siegel got shot for his Las Vegas sins. Johnny Stomp was knifed to death by Lana Turner's daughter. And Cohen was put away for tax evasion.

Laurel Canyon hosted a thousand random deaths over the years. The still unidentified Jane Doe number 59 was found with 157 stab wounds. Aging star Ramón Novarro—"Ravishing Ramón" in happier times—was murdered by a couple of not very bright rent boys. In the late twenties, Samantha Bach, a rising MGM starlet, was wasted by her producer/lover Irvine Lansdale. The killing was a kind of proto–Black Dahlia affair. Like the B movie before the big feature. Bach was found propped up in bed, pale and lovely, not a drop of blood on her, but with her heart and eyes resting on a bedside table.

Laurel Canyon still beckons generation after generation to its promise of the good life, its movie-star frisson, and faux-rural splendor. Most of the current show-business creeps and money-shuffling assholes who roam its hills and trails smile down at the suckers below in Hollywood, never knowing or caring that they're gazing out over one big graveyard.

And now some New Age Nazis were beating the shit out of the locals. Anywhere else I'd be surprised. But not there.

From outside the store comes a series of pops, like a string of firecrackers, only the sound is too low and flat. I shove Vincent and Kasabian to the floor and yell, "Candy, get down!" before taking a dive myself.

Bullets tear up Max Overdrive's front wall. One shatters the edge of the big screen. Kasabian squeals "No!," more afraid of losing his screening room than catching a slug in the face. Vincent is flat on the floor spread eagle, like a pinned butterfly. Not too dignified, but he's new at the duck and cover game and doesn't grasp the necessity of keeping some shred of dignity while hunkered down, scared shitless. For example: you don't want to be found dead, say, head down and ass in the air, ostrich-style. That's guaranteed to give the crime-scene squad the giggles as they zip you into a body bag, and who wants to leave the world a funny corpse?

Finally, the shooting stops, but not before the last bullet blows apart the Gentleman Jack, an innocent bystander.

When the room goes quiet, I jump up and head to the door. A blue Honda Civic is idling at the curb. I head outside. Reaching behind my back for the Colt, I realize it fell out of my waistband when I hit the floor. Still, I'm mad enough that when the Honda pulls away, I run after it, hoping to catch it before it reaches the corner. I can't recommend this method of chasing down bad guys. It's not subtle or a good use of your adrenaline.

Plus, when the banditos decide to back up and run you over—like they seem to be doing right now—you're standing in the street like a side of beef with a glow-in-the-dark target painted on your brisket. I take a few steps back toward the store, but the car keeps gaining speed.

Gunfire pops over my shoulder and the Honda's back window explodes. Candy runs up with her 9mm blazing. The Honda squeals to a stop, then takes off in the opposite direction. I grab Candy and pull her into the shadows at the side of the store, hoping the neighbors haven't moved back to town so they can call the cops on our little O.K. Corral.

I hold Candy in the dark for a couple of minutes. She's vibrating with animal rage, her body in the transition state between regular Candy and her Jade form. I've never seen a full-on Jade with a gun, and I'm not sure I want to. Soon she calms down and folds up the pistol. I let go of her and we walk around to the front of the store. There are more than a dozen bullet holes in the walls, but not a single shot through the glass.

"Here's why," Candy says.

Some clever boots has painted ED on the window, so the angel's tag now reads KILLED. Next to that is a squiggle that looks like a left-handed monkey painted it with his right hand. But if I squint at it hard enough, I can make out the emblem of the White Light Legion. Turns out these guys might be murderous Nazi shitheads, but they'll need some community-college art classes before they take over the world.

The paint is still wet, so Candy leans on my arm and smears out the letters and emblem with the sole of her boot.

When we get inside, Vincent, always the good guest, is soaking up the spilled whiskey with paper towels. The Colt is lying by the edge of the counter. I pick it up and put it back in my waistband.

Vincent stops wiping the floor and looks up.

"Was all that because of me?"

I look at him on the floor on his hands and knees, wet towels in one hand and a confused look on his face. I've never seen an angel so out of his element.

"I don't know. We ran into them the other night. It could be you, or it could be on us."

"How did they find you?" says Kasabian. "I mean, am I going to have to crawl around the store like a goddamn schnauzer waiting for round two?"

"That's a good question," says Candy. "How did they find us?"

"I turned on the car lights the other night. Maybe one of them saw the license plate."

"That would lead them to Julie, not us."

"Yeah, but they wouldn't be looking for her. They'd stake out her place and look for the two idiots that went after them."

"Still, if they know where to find Julie, that's bad."

"Call her," I say. "And tell her to get out of there."

"What are you going to be doing?"

"Nothing. I just want you to call. She'll be nicer to you when you tell her about her maybe getting shot."

"She knows you attract trouble."

"*We* do, sweetheart. We. It was a doubles act the other night, so you get to give her the good news."

"Lucky me."

Vincent pops a couple of his pain pills and dry-swallows them. I can't say I blame him.


CANDY IS STILL doing more computer research in the morning, so I go over to the office alone. Julie is pouring coffee when I get upstairs. She brings both mugs over to her desk. I sit down across from her and take the cup she pushes my way.

"Thanks."

"Of course," she says. "I thanked Chihiro for the call about the shooters. I slept with my Glock under my pillow last night."

"You might make a habit of it for a while."

"Trust me, I will."

She takes a couple of sugar packets out of a desk drawer, shakes them, and dumps the contents into the mug.

"You sticking to coffee during working hours?" she says.

"Pretty much. The Augur offered me a drink on his boat. It seemed unwise to turn him down."

She nods. Sips. Sets down the cup.

"That makes sense. This morning, Chihiro told me more about what happened last night."

I pick up a paper clip from her desk. It's an odd shape. Round, the metal spiraling down to a point. I start unwinding it.

"I wish I could have gotten my hands on those White Light pricks."

Julie says, "Has anyone ever talked to you about PTSD?"

"No. What's that?"

"Don't play coy. You know exactly what it is. In this case, it's you running after a carful of people with guns."

I stop fiddling with the clip.

"At the time, I didn't know I was unarmed."

"The point still stands. Your reactions aren't always those of a normal person."

What the hell did Candy tell her? I go back to tormenting the paper clip.

"Exactly which normal part of my life are you talking about? The normal part where I spent eleven years in Hell? Or the normal part where my father told me I wasn't even a human being, right before he was murdered by an angel. Maybe it's the part where I live with a dead man's head and I have to beg for my cigarettes from the Devil. Or maybe it's how I can't even look at my girlfriend without seeing a stranger's face. Which of these normal things in my life are you referring to?"

Julie takes her coffee cup in her hands and leans on the desk.

"All I'm saying is that your fight-or-flight response is dialed up a little high and it's something you might want to look into."

"You mean I need a shrink. No thanks."

She takes a sip of her coffee.

"Aren't you going to drink yours? It'll get cold."

I set down the paper clip and pick up the mug, but I don't drink.

"Consider this," Julie says. "If you'd finished your psych evaluation forms when you worked for the Golden Vigil, they would have paid you what they owed and you'd be a wealthy man right now. But you didn't do it. I wonder why?"

"I don't know. Maybe I was busy saving the fucking world."

"You're always saving something or killing something or chasing cars. You scare people, Stark. You scare your friends. You scare me sometimes. You scare Chihiro."

I thought the two of them were talking about the case this morning. Is this what's going on behind my back?

I set down the mug.

"Thanks for your concern, and don't take this the wrong way, but there are two things in this world I don't respond well to: threats and interventions."

"This is a conversation over coffee, not an intervention. And don't go looking for threats where there aren't any. That's exactly the kind of thing I'm talking about."

The only thing worse than being threatened is being told you're not being threatened. No way I'm drinking my coffee. There could be Prozac in there or an evil Vigil feel-good powder. I don't want some psych poison telling me how to think.

When I stay quiet, Julie says, "You're going to burn out and you won't be good for anyone, including yourself."

"I handled the arena. I can handle this."

"What about Chihiro? Do you think she's all right with you just handling things?"

"Did she say something to you or is this just coming out of your own skull?"

"Human beings are capable of doing more than just existing. They can be happy."

I pick up the mangled paper clip from her desk and toss it in the trash can.

"But I'm not human, am I? I'm not a Hellion or an angel or a person. I'm not anything except maybe, as angels like to remind me, an Abomination. Try explaining that to a shrink."

Julie picks up her mug, starts to take a sip, but sets it aside.

"All right. Let's forget this for now. I didn't mean to upset you. But you need to know that there are people worried about you and that they have your best interests at heart."

"Noted. Now can we get back to work?"

"Of course."

"You know all about these White Light clowns. Where are they and how are we going after them?"

Julie shakes her head.

"We're not going to, and when we do, I'll be the one doing the legwork. I don't want you running in cutting off any heads."

"It gets people's attention."

"Chihiro is doing some background work on the Legion for me. Right now that's more important than you skulking around, looking for revenge."

"Just to be clear, as my boss, you're officially telling me not to go after them."

"Yes."

"Then what exactly am I supposed to do?"

Julie picks up a pen from a pad sitting next to her laptop. She taps it on the paper.

"I agree with you about looking into Tamerlan Radescu, but we have a problem. You're too well known to do it discreetly."

"I'd say let Candy—Chihiro—do it, but people will have seen us together. If they know me, they'll know her."

Julie looks away, thinking.

"I suppose I could call some old colleagues from the Vigil and see if they want any after-hours work."

"I have a better idea. Brigitte Bardo can do it. She's an actress, so she can look and sound like anything you want. Plus, she's a trained zombie hunter, so she can handle herself if there's any problems."

Julie sits back in her chair.

"I don't know her that well. I'd have to interview her before I can agree to anything."

"I'll call and get her over here today."

"All right. Do that."

"You know, one thing I could do is talk to some Cold Cases. They keep tabs on the dying and the recent dead. Maybe one of them has heard about some necromancer badassery."

"That could be a good idea, but don't you have a history with the Cold Cases. Didn't one try to have you killed?"

I wave it off.

"Who hasn't tried to have me killed? We'll have a chat over tea and cakes. It will be fine."

"Keep it civil. No fighting. No guns. At the first sign of trouble, you excuse yourself and report back to me."

"Got it. I wonder if I should talk to some ghosts."

Julie frowns.

"You can do that?"

"I don't see why not. I saw a witch do it at Max Overdrive. It didn't look all that hard."

"Once again, I don't know if you're joking. But if that's something you can do, hearing from the dead might be helpful."

"I know a couple that will probably talk to me. All it'll cost is some coffee and donuts. Maybe a sandwich."

"Don't forget to get receipts."

"Right. Receipts. Sure."

"I'm serious—if you want to get paid back I need paperwork."

"No problem. I'm on it."

Julie picks up her mug and takes a swig of coffee.

"Are we going to be all right working together?" she says. "You were pretty upset earlier and I need to know that it's not going to affect things."

I touch the cigarettes in my pocket, wanting to get outside and have a smoke.

"We're fine. I'm sorry I flew off the handle. I know you were trying to help, and I'll take what you said under advisement."

"Good."

"I can head over to Bamboo House later and see if there are any Cold Cases around. And I'll call Brigitte."

"Good. Chihiro and I have a meeting later. She's doing a great job."

"She's a smart girl. Smarter than me."

"I'll have to tell her you said so."

"She already knows."

I take off, stopping in the stairwell to light a Malediction.

Outside, I draw the smoke in and let it out slowly, pacing up and down the block, checking the parked cars. I don't see any Honda Civics, blue or otherwise. Anyway, most of the what's happening is on the sidewalk or in the street. Not many people hanging out in parked cars or loitering on the block. No one obviously casing Julie's office. I check the door to her building, making sure it locked behind me.

I think about Candy, but I call Brigitte and tell her to make time between auditions to come by the office. She sounds happy. I think I made her day.

At least someone in L.A. is happy.

"A LITTLE BIRD told me you've been talking to Julie about me."

Candy glances up, then back to the laptop. She reaches out and half closes it.

"Just about the other night."

I dumped the Crown Vic a few blocks away on Hollywood Boulevard so I could walk off some anger.

"But you did it in secret. I thought we weren't supposed to have secrets."

She shifts around on the sofa.

"Everyone has secrets."

"You think there's something you can't tell me? You think I'm that shockable?"

She looks up at me, two sets of eyes—Candy's and Chihiro's—nervous and wounded.

"Don't make this into a bigger thing than it is. I only talked to her because she can say things to you I can't."

"Like PTSD. Because you probably have it too after Doc Kinski and all the shit that went down at Christmas. Are there other things you haven't told me about?" I don't want to sound angry, but I am even if I'm not sure it's fair.

She shakes her head, the expression on her face changing.

"Nothing I want to talk about now."

"But sometime."

She puts her hands together and nods.

"Probably sometime."

"I guess that's the best we can hope for in this life."

"Don't be mad."

"I'm not. Just defensively curious."

"You still trust me?"

"Who else am I going to trust? Kasabian? He'd sell me for a dozen glazed if he thought he'd get his body back."

"No, he wouldn't."

"You don't know him like I do."

"And you don't know him like *I* do."

Downstairs, Kasabian and Vincent are watching *A Hard Day's Night*. Vincent was singing along when I came in through the store. The sound comes up through the floor. I want to choke him.

"This stuff you can't tell me . . . is it Jade stuff?"

"Some is. Some isn't."

"So there's that much. Does this have anything to do with Rinko? She came by the other day, didn't she?"

"Yes."

"Are you still in love with her?"

Candy leans back on the couch, crosses her arms.

"I was never in love with her. But if you're asking me the bigger question, yes, sometimes I miss dating women."

"That's not something you have to hide from me."

"There's just been so much craziness and now I'm not even me anymore. I don't know what I want."

"I'm not about to stop you if you want to be with Rinko or anybody else. Just be honest with me."

She frowns.

"Hey, why is this only about me? This was about you trying to get shot the other night."

"I've been shot plenty of times. I'm not that afraid of it. Not when it's important."

"What about me? I'm afraid. Do I get a say in you putting yourself out as a target all the time?"

The back of my neck itches. Can't tell if it's real or just nerves. I rub it with the palm of my hand, thinking.

"Okay. Point taken. I was just mad then."

"You're always mad and then you can't think. That's what I mean. Maybe you should talk to Allegra about it."

"Not now. Not when I'm being pushed. I won't push you about your secrets and you won't push me on this. All right?"

"Yeah. Okay," she says quietly. "You *are* mad at me."

"A little. Don't talk about me behind my back anymore, even if it's for my own good."

"I can do that."

Candy opens the laptop again and bookmarks the page on the screen, keeping her eyes down.

"Are you going to go out now?" she says.

"Why would I do that?"

"I don't know. This just seems like when you'd leave and go to Bamboo House for a drink."

"We have booze here. I can drink fine at home."

"You want to have a drink with me?" she says.

"Sure. I'll have a drink with you. But make it coffee. I'm on duty."

She gets up and goes to the sink, takes a couple of cups from the drainer, and turns on the coffeemaker. She talks without turning around.

"You're always so ready to run away. It's like you still have one foot in Hell and you're ready to go back there forever. Just don't ditch me, okay?"

I walk up close behind her.

"I'm not going anywhere."

She leans back against me as the coffeemaker gurgles, the noise mixing with the music coming from below. I put my arms around her. We stay that way for a few minutes, no one talking, just letting the sound hang around us in the air.

WHEN I GET to Bamboo House of Dolls, there isn't a single Cold Case inside, which is lousy. I was hoping to see them on my turf. Now I have to go to theirs.

When the young ones aren't slumming it at Bamboo House, there's only one Cold Case hangout in L.A. It's a West Hollywood club called simply Ibis . . . but not the word. On the front of the place is a skinny, stylized long-legged bird in an Egyptian cartouche. You either recognize it or fuck you. It's funny. With their sharkskin-suit aesthetics, I never thought about the Cold Cases as giving much of a damn about ancient mythology. Maybe they don't. The ibis and other glyphs on the façade are always a hot sell to spiritual tourists. Egyptians believed in five parts of the soul. I wonder how many Cold Case drinking games have been invented around that?

There's a line outside Ibis, even in the crushing afternoon heat. But it isn't like most L.A. club crowds. It's quiet and orderly. No pushing or shoving. No one harassing the doorman. Everyone is on their best Miss Manners behavior because no one wants to get bounced. These sorry suckers are all looking to buy a clean soul or to sell theirs, hoping it's untainted enough to be worth some filthy lucre. Most of the sellers will be turned away. The buyers, on the other hand, are always welcome. Metaphysical capitalism at its finest.

I park the car on La Cienega, facing south. In case things go sideways, I can jump in and hit the freeway. If there's a problem getting on, I can always keep heading down toward to LAX, all the way to the La Cienega oil fields. Maybe lure whoever is following me out among the derricks. Sure, there's a lot of traffic nearby, but no one ever goes into the fields themselves. It wouldn't be hard to hide a body behind the big pumps sucking dirty crude from the ground. But we're far from that right now, and anyway, I'm trying to play nice with others now that I'm a working stiff.

I walk back along Sunset and turn up a side street that lets me circle around behind the club.

From the back, the Ibis looks like any other drink factory. A blank back wall. Locked delivery door. A line of Dumpsters. Floodlights, turned off during the day. A fire escape leading to the second floor. The whole back area is covered by a couple of security cameras. The good news for me is that I only have to take out one.

I run down the alley next to the club. I'm fast when I have to be. Fast enough, I hope, to be not much more than a blur on the club's low-res cameras. When I'm under the fire escape, I get out the black blade and throw it, aiming high up on the wall. I wait around the side of the building for a minute to see what happens.

When nothing does, I go back around the club and push a Dumpster under the fire escape. It's just tall enough that I can jump, grab the bottom of the ladder, and pull it down, all the while hoping that my aim was good and the knife sliced through the cable of the nearest security cam. No one tries to stop me as I climb, so I guess I got it. On my way up, I grab the knife out of the wall and climb onto the roof.

There's not much up here. Vents for the air-conditioning. Some abandoned furniture and fixtures baking in the sun. A small satellite-TV dish held in place with a couple of cinder blocks. On the side of the roof is a closet-size structure with a metal door. My way inside.

None of this *Man from U.N.C.L.E.* cat-burglar bullshit would be necessary if the Cold Cases didn't hate me quite so much. It almost makes me want to be nicer to them in the future. Almost, but not enough.

I try the knob on the door. It rattles in its collar but the damned thing is locked. It's not much of a lock, though. Who's stupid enough to climb up here when all the action is downstairs? I slide the black blade between the door and the frame and cut straight through the latch. Abracadabra, it opens, nice and quiet.

I walk carefully down a steep wooden staircase, trying not to make noise. I'm doing a pretty good job of it too, until some asshole comes around the corner carrying a case of champagne.

He's your typical pro bouncer/bodyguard type. A mountain of meat and muscle. The idea of a guy like this isn't to protect you or your property. It's to scare people stupid so they don't even think about getting out of line in the first place.

The beefsteak is wearing a parka, which seems a little odd until a breeze hits me coming up from the club below. Guess that means the stories are true. If I'm going to find out for sure, I'll have to get past Gorilla Monsoon here.

I reach for my na'at. He drops the champagne and pulls a goddamn machete out from under his parka. This fucker thinks I'm a baby seal. He smiles at me, but I can tell there's something wrong with him. It's all on his face. The guy acts normal enough, but his eyes are dead and glassy. He reminds me of some of the more pathetic souls I met Downtown. As he raises the machete I know that's kind of what he is.

This double meat patty is one of the truly desperate or epically stupid who've sold off their souls to the Cold Cases. I'd bet you a dollar he's working here cheap to get in good with the bosses, hoping they'll cut him a deal on a new soul. Not quite a person, not a zombie—or a ghost or anything else you'll ever see on a normal day—he's almost a living jabber. A sad husk clinging to a body because he has nowhere else to go. I'd feel sorry for him, except he's waving a machete for his masters down below, bastards every one of them, living off people's desperation and misery worse than any smack dealer or pimp in town. I'd like to cut this fucker down just on general principles, but a fight would be noisy and draw more chuck steaks up here.

He swings the machete hard at my head. I step back and bark some Hellion hoodoo. It freezes him in place, the empty-headed creep. I take him by the arms and lower him to the floor, pull his parka off, and drag him and his blade behind the stairs. Stack a couple of boxes in front of him and leave him there to sleep off the hex. The parka fits fine over my coat. I shove the crate of champagne against a wall and head downstairs.

THERE ARE DARK clubs and there are dark clubs, but this one is goddamn dark. I stand in the back of the place for a minute, letting my eyes adjust to the nonlight.

There's a good reason the Ibis is so cold and dim. Ever hear about those ice hotels in the winter in Sweden? This is an ice club. The bar, the chairs, the tables, the glasses, the low walls around the VIP booths—all glass-clear ice. And the only light in the place comes from glowing test tubes suspended in the frozen blocks.

Each of those shimmering tubes contains a piece of a person.

What I mean is, they're using human souls to light their love shack. I didn't think I could hate these assholes more, but they just hit a level of disgust a notch below where I'd consider locking all the doors and setting the Ibis on fire. But this isn't the time or place for a lecture on Buddha-like compassion for all living things, and I'm not the person to give it. My meditation mantra for the next few minutes is "Ask some questions. Get some answers. And get out before I'm surrounded by a mountain of ground chuck and have to fight my way out."

I zip up the parka and walk around, looking for any familiar faces. Of course, the only ones I spot are the Rat Pack that used to go slumming at Bamboo House. "Used to" because we had a disagreement and I sent them home from the club naked and broke. I also used a little hoodoo to make one of them think I was pulling his skin off. Like Candy said, sometimes I get mad and don't think. Anyway, the kid got a little bit of revenge. Turns out, he was the nephew of Nasrudin Hodja, grand CEO of all the Cold Cases on the planet. That's why I ended up with a hit out on me. Saragossa Blackburn calmed Hodja down, but I never formally made up with the nephew. I suppose now's as good a time as any.

I head over to their table near, but not in, one of the roped-off VIP areas. I don't want to surprise the nephew and make him bolt. I get into his line of sight so he sees me coming. He starts to get up and his friends look around. I talk fast.

"Relax, boys. I'm not here looking for trouble. I just want to talk. I might even be able to do you a favor."

"We don't want any favors from you," says the nephew.

"Sure you do. You can't be moving many souls these days, not with people refusing to die. Inventory must be stacking up. I'm trying to change that. Come on, admit it. You love dead people. That's all I'm looking to do. Help people die again."

"What do you think we have to do with that?"

"I don't know. That's why I'm here. Mind if I join you?"

I don't wait for anyone to answer. I pull up an ice chair and sit down. Even through the parka my ass starts freezing.

"So," I say. "What have you heard? What do you know? Any ideas who's fucking with the dead? You have to have some theories."

The nephew pours himself a glass of champagne I've never heard of. I'm guessing that puts it out of my price range.

He says, "Isn't it obvious? It's an attack on us. On our business. Hell, our whole way of life."

"You think tens of thousands of people aren't dying just to spite you?"

"Think about it. When people aren't afraid of dying, they don't need new souls. Meanwhile, idiots come to us wanting to sell, but what are we going to do with the merchandise? We have souls going bad on the shelves."

"Souls have an expiration date?"

"Everything has an expiration date."

"What happens to a soul when it gets moldy?"

"I couldn't care less. All I know is it costs us money."

"You think that's what this is all about? Money?"

"What else?"

"Revenge, maybe," says one of the nephew's idiot friends. He's a creepy kid with a million-dollar pompadour and a little John Waters pencil-thin mustache. What works on an eccentric movie director just makes the kid look like an Arkansas pedophile.

I say, "What kind of revenge?," reach across the table, and take the kid's champagne.

"What I mean is *you*. Some of us thought you were using your angel bullshit to get back at us for . . . you know."

"Trying to shoot me and almost killing a friend of mine?"

"Yeah."

The champagne is good, but, oops, what a clod I am. I splash some on the table and set the glass on top of it.

"Don't be stupid. If I was looking for revenge, I wouldn't involve thousands of innocent morons. Plus, I'd have cut all your throats by now."

"Don't threaten us," says the nephew. "My uncle would still like your balls on his wall."

"Let him know that I'd be happy to come by and tea-bag any furniture he wants, but that's a little off topic. Let's all concentrate on the real question. What's going on and who's doing it?"

The nephew opens and closes his fingers around the champagne glass.

"I don't believe you. You come in here claiming to want to fix things. So know what? Fuck you. The only one who's offered any real help is Tamerlan Radescu."

"Radescu's been around? What did he want?"

"Like I said. To help."

"The bastard," mutters the pompadour.

"Shut up," says the nephew.

"Why's he a bastard?" I say.

No one says anything.

"Boys, I have nowhere to be, so if you want to get rid of me, tell me something."

"What Eddie means is Tamerlan drives a hard bargain," the nephew says. "He wants a piece of our business."

"A big piece," says the pompadour.

The nephew throws the last of his champagne at the kid.

"Don't go telling this fucker our business."

"Let me get this straight. Tamerlan Radescu told you he knows what's going on and can maybe make people start dying again?"

The pompadour uses a thumbnail to scrape at a flaw in the ice on the edge of the table. The nephew shakes his head back and forth like he can't believe this is his life. I can see that he's had about enough. Scared or not, he's close to making a scene to get security over here.

"One last question. Did Tamerlan say anything about the Angel of Death?"

The nephew says, "He said the last thing he wants is

what's going on. Both of our businesses rely on complete death. These loafers in comas are hitting business hard."

The nephew's eyes go hard. Time to stop pressing my luck. I get up. The pompadour reaches to retrieve his glass, but it's frozen solid to the table where I spilled the champagne.

"Thanks, boys. Come around the Bamboo House sometime. I'll buy you all milk shakes."

"Don't think just 'cause we talked to you we believe you, Stark," says the nephew. "We know you're part of this, and when we get proof, my uncle is going to the Augur and he'll put a hit out on you himself."

Out of the corner of my eye I see a woman sit up straight, like she's startled. I turn and find Tykho, head of L.A.'s more powerful vampire gang, having drinks with a cluster of business creeps in one of the VIP areas. She smiles and nods when she sees me. She's the only one in the club not wearing a parka. Being a shroud eater has its advantages.

I turn back to the boys.

"You don't know where I could get some brass knuckles, do you?"

"Get out," says the nephew.

I head for the front door, tossing the parka and ten dollars to a coat-check girl on the way out.

"Thanks for the loan," I say.

She looks at me funny, but doesn't say anything. Just pockets the money. Smart kid. One day she'll be a millionaire.

When I get back to the car I almost call Julie, then think twice about it on the off chance she asks me how I got into the club. Instead, I'll write down the meeting when I get home. I figure I can remember the important parts because they were so few and far between. From what the nephew and the pompadour said, it sounds like Tamerlan might be flat-out blackmailing the Cold Cases. I wonder who else he's muscling? And how did he get a line on Death? What's changed that he has that kind of power? I can't wait to hear what Brigitte comes up with.

I START THE Crown Vic and head south on the 101. Get off in Little Tokyo, pick up a few things from a bakery, then swing the car west to Beverly Hills. I leave it in a lot on Wilshire and head up Rodeo Drive on foot.

I hate this place. You can't get a cup of coffee unless it has a backstory and a pedigree so the café can charge you as much for the cup as a normal human pays for dinner. Women drive by in cute little sports cars with more power under the hood than a Saturn V, but the speedometer will never top twenty because then they might not be seen and admired. Men window-shop in silk jackets made by indentured servants in countries they've never heard of while their sons all imagine they're Tupac because they bought their thousand-dollar designer jeans a couple of sizes too big.

Up near Santa Monica Boulevard is my destination: the Lollipop Dolls boutique. The Dolls are a strange kind of girl gang, a coven of middle-aged women who've used their hoodoo to remake themselves into prepubescent anime girls. When they're together, they look like someone left the *Sailor Moon* cloning machine on all night. They used to be run by Cherry Moon. She was in my old magic circle and was one of the people I came back from Hell to kill, but someone got to her first. Cherry was neurotic before she died, and being a ghost hasn't improved that.

The Lollipop Dolls store is every bit as pricy as the nearby Prada and Gucci shops. They just cater to a different clientele—ones who can afford couture gothic Lolita tutus that costs as much as a blimp, or a custom hand-stitched Hello Kitty wearing a real diamond collar. And that stuff isn't even in the case with the really expensive merch, the one where everything looks vaguely blue because it's behind bulletproof glass.

I only spot two Lollipops when I go in the store, Kitty Chan and Noriko. Neither one of them looks older than sixteen. How did they even get a business license for this place?

Kitty sees me first. Stops by a display of plastic Godzillas taller than me and probably with better manners.

She calls to Noriko.

"Look what just crawled in."

Noriko rolls her eyes extravagantly and goes behind the counter, making a big show of stacking bags and arranging pens, taking great pains to ignore me.

Kitty says, "What do you want, Stark? You're on the wrong end of town. There aren't any Kmarts out here."

"Nice to see you too, Kitty. The plastic surgery turned out nice. I can hardly see the crow's-feet from over here."

Noriko slams the drawer of the cash register shut.

"I'm only asking one more time, then I'm calling the cops and telling them a vagrant came in and exposed himself to us poor working girls. What do you want?"

"I'm here to talk to Cherry."

"What makes you think Cherry wants to talk to you?" says Noriko.

I look over at her.

"She's a big girl. Why don't we let her decide for herself?"

"I'm pretty sure she's busy," says Kitty.

"And I'm pretty sure if she knew I came all this way and put up with you two, she'd at least want to tell me to go away herself."

Kitty walks to Noriko. They whisper back and forth for a minute, glancing at me every now and then.

"Okay," says Kitty. "She's in the back. The room behind the office."

"Thanks."

I start back when Noriko yells, "Hey!"

I stop by a pile of stuffed unicorns that are really plush cell phones. She points to a credit-card slide.

"This is a place of business, you know. Gas, grass, or ass. Nobody rides for free. Buy something or get out."

I look around, grab a Hello Kitty hand mirror from a pile in the kids' department and head for the back of the store.

"You going to pay for that, sport?" says Kitty.

"I'll pay on the way out if Cherry talks to me."

In the back is a pretty ordinary-looking business office. There are a few too many polka dots and a peppermint-striped desk, but the place looks functional. I go through a door in the back.

I don't know what the hell this new room is for. Actually, I have a pretty good idea, which means I don't want to sit on anything or touch the bedspread.

The place is decked out like a girl's bedroom decorated by a cartoon princess. Pinks and lace everywhere. White furniture and a makeup table. Big posters of Idoru bands on the walls. Anime-character pillows stacked on a frilly canopied bed. The big *Ultraman* video monitor on the wall has octopus *hentai* playing on a loop.

Cherry Moon's dream home.

The last time I saw Cherry was in the Tenebrae. Now that I can't go there and I can't depend on her coming to me, I'll have to try Maria's trick. I set the Hello Kitty mirror on the makeup table and whisper some off-the-cuff ghost-conjuring hoodoo. I've always been good at improvising spells, but this one might be a bust. Nothing appears in the mirror. I open the bag I picked up from the bakery and lay out some mochi and a bun filled with sweet red bean paste. A few seconds later, Cherry's face drifts into focus in the mirror. She looks over the edge and crinkles her nose.

"Why did you bring that garbage?" she says.

"They're Japanese desserts. I thought you'd be clicking your ruby slippers and wishing you were home when you saw them."

She shakes her head.

"I hate that stuff. If you want to talk to me in the future, bring ice cream or pie."

"Cherry, right?"

"Who's my smart boy?"

Cherry hasn't changed. She looks around twelve, but she's really in her midthirties. She wears a schoolgirl uniform and pigtails. Seeing her face in the mirror reminds me of Maria's lost ghost, Dash. Some ghosts don't like the limelight and some can't get enough. Cherry, for instance. I glance at the TV when something makes a weird squishing sound, wish I hadn't, and look back at the mirror. Cherry is gone.

Over to my right someone says, "Where did you learn the mirror trick?"

I turn.

"A witch named Maria. When did you learn to manifest yourself?"

She tosses her head, making her pigtails bounce.

"Like it? I thought if I was going to be a real ghost, I might as well be able to haunt the store properly." Cherry nods at the mirror. "If your friend has to use that trick, she must know some shy spooks."

"The one I've met seems a bit reserved."

"Well, I'm not, so put that silly thing away."

I set the mirror on the table and put the pastries back in the bag. When I start to drop it in the trash, Cherry says, "Leave it for the girls. Kitty has a gentleman caller who'll grunt like a pig and eat it off her ass. It's hysterical. You should stick around."

I tap my wrist.

"I'm a working man these days. I have a schedule and a boss and everything, but thanks."

Cherry presses her fingertips to her chest in mock horror.

"How the mighty have fallen."

"We can both probably say that."

"Touché. Now, why are you here, Jimmy?"

"Now that no one is dying anymore, I'm trying to find out what's going on with people who are already dead. Has anything changed for you? Is there anything new in the Tenebrae?"

"New? Nothing. Oh, unless you mean the humongous

black twister that's blowing all over the desert on the out-skirts of town. Aside from that, it's a mellow scene. How are you doing?"

"Swell as always. What does the twister look like?"

"Like something out of the Bible. Wrathful God stuff, you know? It's a tower of swirling black as far up as you can see, and every now and then there's sort of a guy's face."

"Can you tell me what he looks like?"

"He doesn't stick around long. I guess he's a WASPy-looking white guy. Sometimes he talks. Sometimes he screams. Maybe being a big tower of farts and lightning isn't as much fun as it looks. What do I know?"

"He talks? What does he say?"

"That he's Death. The true Death comes to us at last. Hal-lelujah."

I pick up a tube of lipstick off the makeup table and open it. There's a knife inside. I put it back where it was.

"I can guarantee you that's not Death. The real Death stubbed his toe and is staying with me right now."

Cherry gives me a crooked grin.

"You scared Chihiro off already? That was fast."

"She's still there, don't worry. By the way, thanks for help-ing outfit her. I owe you."

"We Japanese girls have to stick together in this big cruel world," she says. "Tell me, when did you turn into such a rice queen?"

"The Japanese look was her idea. She always wanted to be in *Spirited Away*."

"Don't lie to me. You love it," she says.

I don't say anything or change my expression. Just give her

a minute to settle down. Then I say, "How are you doing? Do you feel any different? Is there anything else strange going on besides the twister?"

Cherry turns and watches the TV.

"I don't want to talk about death and dying. You don't know what it's like."

"In fact, I do. I've died. A couple of times."

She laughs quietly.

"You're a fucking angel. What do you know? I mean dying like a person, with no power, no say, no nothing. Just a cold hand on your arm and everything you ever were slipping away. It's horrible. He's horrible."

She turns back to me. Gives me a big smile.

"But all that's over with and everything's peachy now."

"Have you felt anything else? Any tugs or nudges from necromancers trying to wheedle secrets from you?"

"All the time. A lot of them, they sound desperate. Hysterical. I guess the half dead are sucking up all the bandwidth and it's hard to get through. Who cares? I never bothered with them. Some of the duller spirits love to chat away with them. Not me. I have my girls and my store. And you, of course."

"I'm flattered."

"Except today you're being boring," says Cherry.

She goes and sits on the bed. Her feet don't touch the floor. She swings them back and forth.

"Bad desserts and dumb questions," she says. "You should work more on your patter before you come around. You used to be a real player before you went away. Remember? You were a looker back then. But you've got no game these days."

"I didn't come here to hit on you. Or get hit on."

She shakes her head gravely.

"You should have fucked me when you had the chance."

"You looked like you were twelve. That isn't exactly my thing."

She moves her legs apart.

"You really missed out."

"Why do we have to do this every time we meet?"

She pulls her legs back together.

"Because it's fun to watch you squirm."

"Now who's being boring? See you around."

I open the door to the office.

"No, Jimmy. Don't go away mad. I promise I'll be good."

I come back in and she points to the small chair by the makeup table. I sit down, feeling like a giant in a dollhouse.

"Have you ever watched any ghost porn?" she says. "I bet that girl of yours has. It's quite the thing among discerning perverts and L.A.'s jaded royalty."

"What the fuck is ghost porn?"

She sighs and drops her shoulders like a little kid about to have a tantrum.

"Fine. Never mind. What were we talking about?"

"Where are all the souls of the half dead? Anywhere in the Tenebrae?"

"The new souls are suspended in the sky like rotten fruit on sick trees. You'd love it, you morbid thing, you. Sometimes the twister reaches out like he's trying to pluck them. He gets closer each time. You think it's scary having people not die? Wait until this new Death gets going. He's going to be a wild one."

"I told you. He's not Death. Maybe he thinks he is. Maybe he just wants to be, but he's not the real thing."

"I know he's not really Death," Cherry says. "He's the Devil, finally coming to eat us, sins, bad dreams, and all."

"That's not true either. Listen to me. Lucifer isn't like he was before. I know him and that isn't him."

Cherry crosses her arms and leans forward on her legs.

"I'm scared, Jimmy. I don't know what to do. I'm scared all the time."

Her face turns a pale red. She brushes some tears from her eyes.

"None of this would be happening if I'd listened to Mason and gotten myself a blue-yonder contract. If you love that girl of yours, you'll get her one. You don't want us to end up roomies here in the middle of this nowhere, do you?"

"Trust me, Cherry. Hell isn't what you think it is anymore. It's opening up to Heaven. You won't have to stay down there. Soon you'll be able to walk straight Upstairs."

"If that's true, come to the Tenebrae and go there with me."

"I can't. I've lost the Room. I can't go anywhere anymore."

"If you won't go, then I'm sure not going alone."

"I'm going to work it out. I can't stand being stuck here on Earth all the time. When I fix things, I'll see what I can do about you."

"Sure. Later. When you're not busy," she says, and disappears.

I look around and find her in the mirror. I pick it up. She wipes away more tears.

"I'll just wait right here, shall I, while you go save everybody else but me? Go away, Jimmy. You always let me down."

I go out through the office and head for the front door.

"Wait a minute, Stark," says Kitty. "You owe us for the mirror."

"The mirror is in the back. I'm not paying for it. Cherry said it was a freebie."

"Liar. I'll call the police."

"Leave him alone," says Cherry.

I see her, blurry and distorted, in the side of a polished metal display case.

"The police won't come. He's too dull to arrest," she says.

"Thanks, Cherry. I'll take you on a tour of Downtown sometime."

"Of course you will. Remember to bring ice cream the next time you come by."

"Right. And mochi for Kitty's ass."

"Excuse me?" Kitty shouts.

"Get out, Stark," says Cherry.

This is the second time today someone's thrown me out. A few more times and my feelings are going to get hurt.

DON'T TALK TO ghosts.

Don't talk to ghosts.

Don't ever talk to fucking ghosts. They're carrying more baggage than the *Hindenburg* and are just as likely to burst into flames.

Still, through all her bullshit, Cherry coughed up something useful. The new Death—wannabe Death, this year's model Death—is slowly pulling himself together, accreting form and power. It's not a new story in the mystical transformation game. Hell, I went through something like it myself after a Drifter bit me. I died a little. The human part of me. Just enough that the angel half began to take over. I could feel it happening. Layers of me stripped away, like someone skinning a dead deer, until the human part of me was gone and all that was left was the red raw meat of a bouncing baby angel. Only with this neo-Death the effect is the opposite. I was un-becoming. New Death is getting stronger, growing in power and position. What's he going to do when he manifests himself completely? No one joins the Death game as a retirement plan. This is an active boy who'll soon have plenty of plans, tricks, and toys. I hope I have the chance to put many, many holes in his face before he gets to play with any of them.

It's another hour home from Beverly Hills, but the traffic doesn't make me angry this time. It just reminds me of the freeways Downtown. Lined with damned souls twisted into lane dividers and guardrails, and other souls trapped in rusting hulks of barely functional cars stuck in bumper-to-bumper traffic on the endless loops, sucking fumes and exhaust heat for the rest of eternity. That's all over now in Hell, but I have to admire L.A. for its dedication to this primal form of Hellion humor.

KASABIAN IS BEHIND the counter explaining to a couple of new customers about how our movies don't really exist in this world and that's why the discs rent for $100 a night. You'd think that all they had to do was turn around and watch a few minutes of the *Mulholland Drive* TV series David Lynch never got off the ground, or maybe acknowledge that they're haggling with a dead man on a mechanical body. Either of those things should give them a hint to our business model, but no. Some people's brains can only handle so much weirdness. So, they pretend this is a regular video store and they should get a discount on the *Die Hard 2* someone threw in the bargain bin (which is where it always belonged). Me? I would have shot both of them by now and burned their bodies in the Dumpster, but that's why Kasabian is the businessman and I'm the silent partner who lurks upstairs, which is where I head before I get drawn into the debate society.

Candy is on her lunch break, picking at a baguette and watching an episode of *Yakitate!! Japan*. She looks up when I come in and pauses the cartoon.

"How did it go, Nick Charles? Did you crack the case?"

"Yeah. Death is really a crooked shoe magnate from Minneapolis on the run from loan sharks in the Wisconsin cheese Mob."

"I'd run too. There's a lot of cannibals in Wisconsin."

"Hey, Ed Gein spent his golden years as the asylum barber, a decent and noble profession. Don't slander the man for a few bad dinner choices."

"What about Dahmer?"

"Dahmer was a drunk with power tools who watched *Return of the Jedi* one too many times. I know I've thought about murder when people won't shut up about *Star Wars*."

"Guess I won't be sending for those *Millennium Falcon* sheets after all."

"Please don't."

I want a drink, but I go to the kitchen and pour myself a cup of coffee. Just what I need: a three-hundred-degree drink on a scorching L.A. afternoon. I once considered learning to love iced coffee, but then I remembered I'd have to kill myself, so I gave up the idea.

"Have you seen Vincent? He wasn't downstairs."

Candy restarts the anime.

"I think he's on the roof."

"Why is he up there?"

"I think he's feeling cooped up, but is too afraid to go out."

"You don't think it's dangerous, him on the roof by himself?"

"He's a smart boy. He understands gravity."

"I wonder."

I go through the door in the back of the closet and climb the stairs to the roof. Vincent is crouched on the edge like a black-clad pigeon.

"If you're thinking about jumping, we're not high enough. You'd just break your legs and ruin the pants I loaned you."

He glances over his shoulder, shielding his eyes with his hand. When he sees who it is, he turns back to the street.

I walk over and sit down beside him.

"What are you doing up here?"

"Just looking at the city. All the lives. They used to form a floating web of sound and heat that I could follow to any individual. It was like a symphony in a furnace. Now . . ." he says, and shrugs. "Everything seems so much more fragile since I've had this body."

"Yeah, we break easy, but we fix ourselves too."

"Not all of you."

"You mean suicides? Yeah. That whole thing sucks. It doesn't seem right for anyone to get pushed that far."

Vincent half turns to me.

"When you were imprisoned in Hell, did you consider it?"

"Why bother? I was already in the belly of the beast. What were they going to do? Send me to Super Hell?"

That makes him smile. He takes out his bottle of pills, taps out a couple, and dry-swallows them.

"You're getting good at that. You're not turning into a pill head, are you?"

"Being human never stops hurting."

"You learn to roll with it. And seriously, don't get hooked on those things. It's hard getting off."

He nods, but I don't think he's listening. We sit together, neither of us talking.

A couple of minutes later, I say, "You ever have any second thoughts about your job?"

"No. Do you?"

"Sometimes. We're both sort of in the same game. Death."

"You can choose to change."

"That's easy to say. My father, the archangel Uriel, called me a warrior, a natural-born killer. He said that's what I was good at, what I was made for, so I should get on with it."

"I wonder if all the nephilim were killers like you. Maybe that's why they were so hated."

"You don't know?"

He shakes his head.

"The affairs of angels don't interest me."

Then he looks at me.

"You're still human too. You don't have to listen to your father."

"Yeah, but he was right. Killing and hoodoo are the only things I've ever been good at. They're sure the only things that have ever helped anyone else. Why should I quit? Shouldn't I just get better at it?"

"That's not for me to say. But I do appreciate the steady

stream of work you've sent me over the years. I like keeping busy."

"Glad to oblige."

I take out a Malediction, light it. I'm downwind, so the breeze blows the smoke away from Vincent. If he's annoyed he doesn't say it.

He says, "When I was younger, there was a time when I didn't want to be Death. I wanted to be one of the guardian angels, protecting life, not taking it. For a while I pretended to be one."

"Wait. This isn't the first time people stopped dying?"

"People? No? There weren't any people back then. Most of the life in the universe was teeming swarms of microscopic organisms. I liked them. I didn't want to see them go."

"Why did you change your mind?"

"Life stagnated. Things were born, but nothing ever changed. After evolving from almost nothing, the universe filled with copies of copies of copies of the same organisms for millennia. It felt wrong. So, I went back to work."

"And along came us."

"Eventually."

"Well, thanks for that. Understand, that's my answer today. If you'd told me that story last Christmas, I might have punched you for letting humans, gods, and angels live at all."

"It will all be over soon enough."

I look at him.

"That's by immortal standards, right?"

Vincent nods.

"Don't worry. I'm talking about billions of years from now."

"Good, because I haven't even seen that Sergio Leone *The Godfather* we got."

"It must be nice to have things to look forward to."

"I hadn't thought of that before. I guess your job is kind of production-line work. The same thing over and over."

He looks up, tracking a seagull as it flies over us.

"When I took Henry Ford's soul, he made some suggestions about how I could operate more efficiently."

"Did you take any?"

"No. I have few enough surprises that turning death into a true assembly line would make existence unbearable. I might have to end things early."

"Then by all means, be as inefficient as you can."

I smoke and Vincent looks down at his hands.

"What if I never get back to myself again? I can feel myself getting weaker. My spirit is settling into this body. I feel like I'm losing all connection to the eternal."

"From what I hear, the guy who's taken your place is getting stronger. That's probably what you're feeling. Don't worry. We'll stop him."

"Thank you."

"Why don't we go back inside. I'll introduce you to some annoying customers downstairs. They deserve a good scare."

"All right."

VINCENT HEADS DOWN to see Kasabian and I stay upstairs with Candy. She ignores me, wrapped up in her cartoon. I walk around the table and take a peek at her laptop. The screen saver is running, blocking my view of whatever she's been working on.

"You researching the White Light Legion?"

"Yeah," she says. "They're interesting. Why?"

"Just curious. Wikipedia says they used to publish books and pamphlets. Do they still do that? Maybe I could go over and get some."

Candy pauses *Yakitate!! Japan* and looks at me like I just lied about eating the last cookie.

"Do you have my brass knuckles?"

"I'm working on it."

"Then forget it. Julie said not to tell you anything, and she's right. We need to understand them, not clunk their heads together like coconuts."

Damn. Candy has gone reasonable on me.

"Listen to you, Nancy Drew. I thought we could pay them a visit together, like old times. Put a nice scare into them."

She looks back at the frozen image on the screen.

"You struck out with the Cold Cases and Cherry?"

I sit down on a stool by the kitchen counter.

"No. I got some information. Little scraps. I think Tamerlan is up to his ass in this thing. But I'm sick of tiptoeing around. Come on. Let's go break things."

"As much fun as that sounds, you should just sit down and write your report for Julie. You're the one always saying how much we need the money."

"Can I use your laptop?"

"Sure. All my work files are password protected, so don't bother snooping for the White Light's address."

"That's a hurtful thing to say."

She puts out her lower lip in a mock pout.

"Poor dear. Want me to run you a bubble bath?"

"Fine. If you insist on being no fun, I'll do it your way. But you're going to regret walking away from hilarious mayhem."

"I'm trying to watch my show," says Candy.

I sit down at her laptop, open a blank text file, and start typing. I'm pretty much a two-finger typist. With a good tail wind, I can sometimes work in a third finger. Let her listen to me hunt and peck my way through this report. By the time I'm done, she'll be begging to kick someone's ass.

Candy picks up the remote and cranks up the volume on the TV, drowning out the sound of my crude key smashing. Outsmarted again.

Around six, Julie calls. She thanks me for the report, says, "That's fine work, except for the part where you roughed up the security guard."

"I didn't have any choice."

"You could have found a different way into the club."

"Where's the fun in that?"

"And that's what I mean about most of your day being good work, but not all."

"I got some useful stuff on Tamerlan."

"Maybe," Julie says. "You're more convinced of his involvement than I am. Clearly, he's connected, but I don't know that he's at the center of things."

"He's up to his eyeballs in this. All roads will lead to him."

"I think you have a problem with necromancers and it might color your work. Don't let your prejudices lead the investigation."

"Got it. But I'm not wrong about Tamerlan."

"I don't know why I bother talking to you sometimes."

"Hey, I'm listening, but sleuthing isn't my style. You're going to have to cut me some slack while I ease into it."

"I'm doing my best. Anyway, get to bed early tonight. I have a surprise for you in the morning. Come by the office tomorrow about nine, and bring your guest. You'll enjoy this. We're all going on a little field trip."

"Where?"

"You'll see."

"It sounds like fun."

No. It doesn't.

"Oh, and one more thing. You and Candy should be sure to bring your guns."

"Now it sounds like fun."

"Do you have anything else to tell me? Anything that didn't make it into your report?"

"Yes. His name is Vincent."

"Whose name?"

"The guest. He's going by Vincent these days."

"Charming. Was that his idea?"

"Not entirely. But he likes it."

"How's he holding up?"

"Not so good. We need to speed things up. If this is going to be a prestige job, we don't want to solve the mystery but lose the client."

"Nine o'clock tomorrow, on the dot."

"Got it."

"And, Stark . . ."

"Yes?"

"You don't touch your gun unless I tell you to."

"Whatever you say, boss."

"I mean it. And don't call me boss."

"Whatever you say."

"Let me speak to Candy for a minute."

"Don't worry. She hasn't told me anything about the White Lights."

"At least one of you understands orders."

"I understand them. I just don't like them."

"I'll see you in the morning."

"Wait, don't you want to talk to Candy?"

"No. I just wanted to know if you'd been trying to get information out of her. Now I know."

"All roads leads to Tamerlan and they're going to detour through the White Lights."

"Good night, Stark."

"Good night, boss."

"Stark."

"Sorry."

THE ALARM ON my phone goes off at eight the next morning. I shake Candy and she kicks me with her heel.

"Go away," she says.

"Rise and shine, Miss Marple."

She sits up and blinks.

"Fuck. Julie is great, but this early-bird thing is for the birds."

"I'll put on some coffee."

She drops back down onto the bed.

"I'll just lie here and make sure the blankets don't run away."

"If you say so, but you won't be teacher's pet anymore if you make us late."

She sits up and throws a pillow at me.

"I don't like you when you don't drink. Without a hangover, you're too chipper in the morning."

"You think I like it? I feel like Andy Hardy."

"Come back to bed. We'll tell Julie we were captured by pirates."

"She'll never believe that. Tell her killer robots."

"Robots are sexy. You're not right now. I'll get up when I smell coffee."

"You're a morning pest."

"I'm a goddamn princess. Now go and make me coffee."

I start up the coffeemaker and go downstairs to roust Vincent. When I knock on his door, he opens it on the second knock. He's fully dressed and bright-eyed.

"Shit, man. Did you even go to bed last night?"

"For a while," he says. "Now that I've healed I don't need much sleep. Where are we going?"

"You've got me. But it better be goddamn outstanding. I mean Disneyland with dancing girls and a bourbon Slip and Slide."

"Sounds wonderful."

"If it's not, Candy's going to hate me for getting her up. Hell, *I* hate me right now."

"I don't hate you."

"Thanks, but two against one says that I'm an asshole."

Kasabian pounds on the wall. "It's three to one. Shut up and let me get back to sleep."

I steer Vincent out of the storage room.

"Come upstairs for some coffee."

When the machine finishes, Candy wanders into the kitchen in a Killer BOB wanted-poster T-shirt.

She pours herself some coffee and hands the pot to Vincent. He pours himself half a cup and fills the rest with milk and five sugars. He sniffs it, smiles, and washes the brew down with another pill.

I wash up and go back to the kitchen. Candy sips her coffee, not looking any more awake than when she came in.

"Do you know where we're going?" I ask her.

"I'm not supposed to tell."

"That doesn't fill me with confidence, especially if we're supposed to go in armed."

"You're always armed."

"Yeah, but Julie *wants* it this time. That makes it different."

"Whatever you say, Deputy Dawg. I'm getting dressed."

It's almost nine when she's ready. Everyone piles in the Crown Vic and I drive us to Julie's office. I don't bother getting out. I just call her and tell her we're downstairs. She comes down with a big USGS map under her arm. I look at her in the rearview mirror.

"Which way?"

"Take Sunset all the way to Pacific Palisades," she says.

I pull out into traffic.

"Where are we going?"

"Will Rogers State Historic Park."

"Goody. A picnic."

"Not even close," she says, studying the map.

When we get to the park entrance, Julie pays the entrance fee for everyone.

I say, "Don't forget the receipt."

"Thank you," she says like a tired substitute teacher.

I park the car and Julie pulls out a map of the park, studies it for a minute. Parts of it are marked in yellow highlighter.

"This way," she says.

We follow her as she looks around for landmarks. The park is green and boring, just like all parks. At least Griffith Park has an observatory and an abandoned zoo. Those are kind of fun.

In a few minutes, we come to a polo field and Julie walks us around it to the east side. She pockets the Will Rogers map, pulls out the USGS map and a GPS device about the size of a cell phone. There's a trail leading from the side of the field. She starts down it and we follow. Candy has on her round welding-glass dark shades. In the sun, her pink hair is as bright as a flare. Vincent looks around like one of those immuno-fucked-up bubble kids who's never been outside before. I trudge along at the rear.

The trail winds down into the canyon. When we come to a creek, we follow the trail up farther into the canyon.

It's not long before the trail fades out into a one-lane dirt rut. I look around.

"Are we still in the park?"

Julie doesn't look up from the map.

Candy says, "We're heading into Rustic Canyon. It might be where Vincent came from."

"I'm guessing they don't have polo fields there."

"Just trees and snakes."

Oh hell. I check my gun.

We follow the rut made by other hiking idiots, through

trees and vines, crisscrossing the creek for half an hour. I was already annoyed when we got off the trail. Now I'm annoyed and sweaty.

Eventually, we come to a dam and a man-made waterfall.

I look at Vincent. He's squinting, swiveling his head around.

I say, "Does any of this look familiar?"

He looks around.

"I'm not sure. It was night and I was disoriented."

We head up a steep dirt trail and I take off my coat, toss it over my shoulder. My Colt is exposed now, but it's not like we're going to run across a Boy Scout jamboree in this shit-forsaken wilderness.

"How much farther?"

Julie looks back at me, frowning.

"Another mile or so."

"Fuck me. Now I know why you didn't want me to know where we were going."

"The fresh air will do you good," says Candy just to torment me.

"Un-huh. No fresh air is going to pollute my lungs."

I shake the Maledictions from my coat pocket.

Julie stops.

"Put those away. This is fire country. One spark and you could burn the whole canyon."

I stick the cigarettes back in my coat.

"I'd say I was back Downtown, but at least in Hell I could smoke."

"I like it here," says Vincent.

"I can't go on. Leave me here and save yourselves."

"Hush," says Julie.

"Yes, boss."

It's another solid hour of climbing over, well, nature. Fucking trees, and fucking vines, and across fucking creeks, until we come to an old wooden ranch house that's held together with nothing but cobwebs and dry rot. Soon the trail opens up out of the trees. We bear left.

"A quarter mile more," says Julie, studying her GPS.

Vincent looks back at a stable.

I say, "It looks familiar?"

"I'm not sure. Maybe. I'm sorry."

"Don't sweat it. I can't tell one goddamn thing from another out here in broad daylight. They ought to tear down this place and put up a mall. Pizza and a pedicure sound good about now."

Candy looks over Julie's shoulder at the map, then jogs ahead of us around a bend.

"We're here," she yells.

The rest of us follow her around the corner. When we do, I stop.

Ahead of us is a concrete building, a broken-down two-story freak-show hovel that's been tagged by every hippie, goth kid, skate rat, art twerp, and metal head in Southern California. Spray-paint eyeballs, monsters, naked ladies, gang signs, and names cover the front of the place. It's such a shit shack that if I didn't know better, I'd think it was a Sub Rosa mansion.

"Where the hell did you drag us to?"

Julie doesn't turn around. Candy runs up and grabs my arm.

"Isn't it a charmer? And for just a small down payment, it could all be ours."

"What the hell is it?"

"Welcome to Murphy Ranch."

Julie says, "We think this is where Vincent walked from."

I look at him.

"Is she right?"

He walks to the front of the building. The entrance is up a few steps from the ground. He grabs the metal handrail and slowly pulls himself up the stairs. He's moving slow. I can't tell if he's being careful or if the sight of the place is frying his brain.

When he gets to the building's entrance—a wide black gullet where double doors used to stand—he hesitates, then steps inside. Julie walks up after him, and Candy and I follow.

When we get inside, Vincent is facing us, standing over a magic circle laid out in black paint. Someone covered the graffiti and piss stains on the floor in white so that the black would stand out against it. In the very center of the white is rust-colored splatter. A lot of splatter, like someone emptied a kiddie pool of color on the floor.

"Is that dried blood?" says Candy.

Julie says, "I think so."

"This is it. Here," says Vincent. "This is where I woke up."

I walk into the center of the circle, stand in the old blood.

"You sure?"

He nods.

"I'm absolutely certain. It was night, but warm. I was naked. I found my coat and clothes over by the door."

"You remember anything else? Anything you haven't told us?"

He shakes his head, holds up his hands.

"I don't know."

I turn three hundred and sixty degrees. Whoever set up the room knew what they were doing. The paint created a binding circle, and a good one. Whatever someone drew down here, maybe even an angel, would have a hard time getting out. And if there was, say, a body at the center of the circle, a clever necromancer Dead Head could drive the entity right down into the meat and there's nothing it could do about it.

Vincent gets on his knees and touches the circle, looks up at the ceiling. There's black there, but it's not paint. It's a scorch mark. I crook a finger at it.

"Something came down hard from up there. It would have gone right through the floor and out again if it hadn't been caught in the circle."

Vincent lies down on his back in the middle of the circle and rubs his chest. He points at the back wall.

"It was here. I woke up facing that way."

There's a symbol painted on the back wall.

"Do you recognize it?" says Julie.

"No."

Candy takes out a pocket camera and snaps a few pictures. She shoots a few more of the circle. Vincent gets up and dusts himself off. Julie points to a spot near the door. A White Light Legion emblem. Candy shoots it.

I look at Julie.

"What the hell is this place?"

"I told you. Murphy Ranch," says Candy. "Hitler's American love shack. Sort of."

I look from her to Julie. Julie looks around appraisingly.

"She's right. Remember the Silver Legion, the precursor to the White Lights? Like them, the compound was started around the same time they did. It cost four million dollars. That's in 1930s dollars, and was entirely financed by one couple: Winona and Norman Stephens."

"A couple of Silver Legion groupies," says Candy. "This is just one building. The whole compound covered over fifty acres and had its own water system, a diesel generator for power, and a bomb shelter."

"Everything a self-sustaining Nazi community would need to ride out the war," says Julie.

"I guess history didn't go their way. What happened to the place?"

"It was raided by local police and shut down in '41," Candy says. "And that was the end of der Führer's Hollywood penthouse."

I look at the walls and floor, hoping to find a clue, an explanation for Vincent and this place.

"You think the White Lights did the ritual to grab Death and stick him in a body. Why? What do they get out of it?"

"That's what we need to find out," says Julie. "Edison Elijah McCarthy spent his life studying the supernatural and higher states of consciousness. If we could find him, we'd know."

I go over to the entrance, take out a cigarette, and light it. No one objects this time.

"He'd be an old man by now."

"Yes," Julie says. "An old man with a powerful and ruthless organization behind him."

"A bunch of assholes, if you ask me," says Candy. "We

shouldn't have let that bunch on Wonderland get away."

She's right. And if I'd had my gun the other night, we would have had them then too.

"We'll get 'em next time, cowgirl."

Vincent looks around.

"If we found the right person and brought them here, could they put me back where I belong?"

"Probably," I say. "The trick is finding the right one. My money is still on Tamerlan."

Julie looks at me.

"I'm not saying he's a goose-stepper. I'm saying he likes money. He'd do the ritual, take the cash, and never ask a single question."

"Has Brigitte reported anything yet?" says Candy.

"We're meeting tomorrow," Julie says. "I'll know more then."

"Can we come along?" says Candy.

"I was going to suggest it."

"You'll see," I say.

"I prefer not to jump to conclusions," says Julie.

Over the stink of the Malediction, I smell something else. Something sweeter. I drop the smoke and crush it out with my boot. Step to the side of the door. A few seconds later, a kid wanders in smoking a blunt the size of a chimichanga.

He has long, dirty blond hair halfway down his back. He's wearing battered boots, a thrift-store leather jacket covered in patches for different metal bands, and a Pantera T-shirt.

He's staring at his feet on the way in and doesn't spot Candy and Julie until he stops to knock some ash off his joint. He steps back when he sees them, then pulls his shit together.

"How's it hanging, ladies?"

Then he sees Vincent.

The kid yells "Fuck!" and bolts for the door. I step in his way with the Colt in my hand. He pulls up short and puts his hands over his head. Looks back over his shoulder.

He's about twenty. His red eyes are not those of an Einstein. He has a scraggly mustache and a faint scattering of acne scars on one cheek. He looks from me to Vincent and back again.

"Okay, Megadeth, tell me what you see."

"That guy over there," he whispers like no one else can hear.

I take a step toward the kid.

"I know. They cut his heart out. You were one of the assholes partying here that night, weren't you? Did you see what happened?"

He nods.

"Part of it."

"Want to elaborate?"

"Mostly it was over. They took his heart and put it in some kind of jar with a bunch of writing on it, then stuck the knife back in his chest. After that, they took the other guy and left."

"What other guy?" says Julie.

The kid stares at her, then Vincent.

I come up behind him and drape an arm over his shoulder.

"What's your name, kid?"

"Varg."

"Sure it is. Varg, that lady is my boss. If you don't answer her, I'll be obligated to stir-fry your balls for her pet piranhas."

Varg looks over at where he dropped his joint. He's either regretting being high or wishing he was a lot higher. He moves his head in two jerking nods.

"Okay."

He points at Vincent.

"But keep him away from me."

I wave Vincent off. "Why don't you grab some wall?"

He goes to the back of the room and stands in the corner watching us.

"Time to answer the lady, Varg. What other guy did you see?"

"The other stiff. They wrapped him up with the heart and took him away. They were a lot nicer to him than to that guy," he says, nodding his chin at Vincent.

"What did the other people look like?" says Julie.

"I don't know. I couldn't see too good. They had some flashlights is all. I didn't get a look at their faces. Except for the chick."

"What chick?" says Candy. "What did she look like?"

"She was hot. Like you," he says, trying to be charming.

Candy raises her eyebrows. "What did you fucking say?"

Varg squirms. I tighten my arm across his shoulder.

"Sorry," he says. "But, I mean, she really was hot. A blonde. Pretty like a model."

"Wow. It's like she's here with us right now," says Candy. "What else did she look like?"

"I don't know. One of the dudes called her Sigrun."

"That's a funny name," I say. "Are you sure you heard it right?"

"I thought it was funny too. But the dude said it again. Sigrun."

"Tell us about the other body," says Julie. "They killed two people that night?"

Varg shrugs.

"I don't know. But they both looked dead to me."

He whispers to me as he stares at Vincent. "How's he walking around?"

"Well, Varg, that's the Angel of Death. Want to meet him?"

"No way."

"Smart boy."

"Which way did they go when they left?" says Candy.

He points outside opposite of the way we came.

I say, "Was one of the men here that night dressed like a used car salesman?"

"What do you mean?"

"You know, flashy. Not normal flashy like in a magazine. Old flashy like you'd see on *Starsky & Hutch*."

"Yeah, I know them. But no. I didn't see anyone like that. They were all wearing robes or some shit. I couldn't see anyone's regular clothes."

"You took the knife from his chest," says Julie, pointing to Vincent. "Why?"

"Did you see it? It was cool."

"And it came out of a real live dead guy, right? Your friends would love that."

Varg nods.

"None of those pussies would touch it. But I did."

"Thanks, Varg," I say. "If you hadn't done that, Vincent over there might not have woken up."

"I thought you said he was the Angel of Death."

"He is."

"The Angel of Death's name is Vincent?"

"Your name sounds like a dog fart, Varg, so don't get pushy."

"Sorry."

"Anyone have any other questions for Lemmy?"

Candy comes over.

"Let me see your driver's license."

Varg gets out his wallet and gives her the license.

She photographs it, then reads it over.

"Now we know your real name, Danny, and where you live. Don't tell anyone you talked to us and don't try to run away or we'll send Vincent after you."

I feel Varg tense.

"I won't. Can I have my license back?"

Candy hands it to him.

Varg puts his wallet away. He looks at me.

"You know what this place is, right?"

"Yeah. Hitler's bachelor pad. What of it?"

"Well, some of the people, including Sigrun, they were speaking German."

"Too bad. I don't suppose you're bilingual, Varg."

"Yeah. I am. My grandma's from Düsseldorf. That's why I remember what they said."

Julie comes over.

"What did they say?"

"When they were wrapping the one guy up, the one they liked, one of them said, 'Get wormwood' or 'Get the wormwood.' I figured they were going to go and get high."

I'm guessing pretty much everything means getting high to Varg. I'm surprised he remembered as much as he did. If

I let Vincent loose on him, I bet he'd remember all the state capitals and the names of Santa's reindeers, but Julie would never let me do that.

"We done here?" I say to Julie.

"Yes. Let him go," she says.

I take my arm from Varg's shoulder.

"You're free to go. We're releasing you back into the wild."

"For real?"

"Scoot, Varg."

He hesitates.

"Can I have my weed back?"

The joint is still lying where he dropped it.

"Sure."

Varg runs over, scoops the joint into his pocket, heads for the entrance. He stops and points back at Vincent.

"That guy's a freak, man."

"It's not smart to be mean to Death. He has a long memory."

"That asshole's not Death," says Varg. "The other guy is. That's what the blond chick said. *Er ist der Todeskönig.* 'He is the death king.'"

I turn to him.

"Why didn't you mention that before?"

"'Cause fuck you, that's why," says Varg. He holds up his hands, flipping us double birds, and runs off into the trees.

Candy starts after him.

"Let him go," says Julie. "We're not going to get anything more out of a frightened stoner right now. Besides, we can find him if we need more later."

Vincent is by the entrance, staring in the direction where Varg ran. He goes down the stairs and follows the kid's trail.

We follow him a few yards past more buildings. Beyond a stand of thirsty trees is a set of steep concrete stairs going a couple of hundred feet, all the way up the canyon wall. Varg is already a quarter of the way up.

"That's the way I left," says Vincent. "I remember climbing and climbing."

I look at him. Vincent isn't a big guy. I try to imagine anyone climbing all those steps with a hole the size of a shotgun blast in their chest. I couldn't do it. But this scrawny bastard did. And fucked up as he was, he tracked me down all the way in Hollywood. Vincent has more brains and bigger balls than I imagined. Damn. Now I actually want to help the prick. But it's nice that I'm being paid to do it.

I wave a bee away from my face. Goddamn nature. All it wants to do is hitch a ride, kill you, or sting you. Sometimes all at once.

"Are we done here?" I say to Julie. "I need a drink and a tick bath."

"Yes. We're done."

She keeps looking at Varg and the stairs. I start back the way we came.

"If you want to go after him, be my guest, but I'm not climbing that. Fire me if you want, but I'm going this way and cranking the air conditioner in the Crown Vic all the way to Ice Age."

Julie nods.

"Let's head back," she says, coming after me.

As we walk, she turns to me.

"Good job back there, Stark. You were menacing, but didn't try to shoot anyone. A big step up for you."

"Thanks. I'm happy to just be part of the team."

"That's why it pains me to tell you."

"What?"

"The air-conditioning in the Crown Vic doesn't work."

I really hate this job.

CANDY AND I go to Bamboo House for a few drinks after work and have a couple of more at home. Kasabian is binge-watching *Mulholland Drive,* transfixed by Naomi Watts's cheekbones. Vincent went to his room after we got back from Murphy Ranch and I haven't seen him since. My guess is he popped a couple of pills and passed out. Can't say I blame him. Still, I might have to steal the pill bottle from him sometime when he's not looking.

I fall asleep early, still bruised and battered by my encounter with trees and grass. Now I remember why I don't like to leave Hollywood. The closest thing to nature we have here are the tofu joints out past La Brea Avenue, and I can get over the trauma of seeing them with a plate of *carnitas* and frijoles.

In my dreams, I'm back at Murphy Ranch lying, like Vincent, in the bloody center of the circle. When Mason Faim sent me to Hell, it was through a magic circle. I use them all the time when I'm doing high-level hoodoo.

My life is full of circles. For all the batshit craziness of my first trip back from Hell—the Drifters, ghosts, ghouls, cops, Hellions, and gods—it was really about finally getting clear of Mason. Now Mason is dead for good, a sacrifice to a mob of angry old deities. Maybe I'm starting a new circle. If this is the beginning, I'm not sure I want to see where it ends.

I used to dream about being back in the arena in Hell.

Now I dream about being stuck in traffic in the Crown Vic, my new Hell on Earth. Even when I was a Hellion slave, I never felt as trapped as I do now that I've lost the Room of Thirteen Doors. I keep trying to find angles. Ways to get it back. Ways to convince myself that it's okay to open it and go inside. That another universe won't rush out to devour this one, and that the old gods, the Angra Om Ya, are dead and gone forever. But I know it's not going to happen. I can't ever open the door again. The Room is gone for good. But I can't live without it. I can't stay planted on the ground like a goddamn beet farmer, shuffling my way through the dirt and mud forever. There has to be an angle I haven't figured out yet. Something I can steal or buy or trade for what will let me shadow-walk again. The price will be high, but I'll pay it. I need to know I can walk the universe again and that, in the end, there's one safe refuge that's mine and mine alone. Even Candy would be safe and she could wear her own face again. But I don't even know where to begin looking. Well, I do. But I don't want to go there. There are parts of L.A. stained enough with blood, bile, and misery that even I don't want to deal with them.

Just keep cool. See where you land. If you work shit out for Vincent, he's going to owe you. Death can go anywhere at any time he wants. Maybe he knows a trick or two he can pass on, right?

No. That's not the kind of luck I have.

I dream about the White Light Legion and a blond Valkyrie ripping my heart out. It almost means something and I can almost see Sigrun's face. They put my heart in a jar and carry it home. Is it a trophy? An offering? Or just Rover's dinner?

My chest hurts. I'm sweating. I'm back on Wonderland Avenue. Every door to every home is open. Blood trails smear across the welcome mats and driveways, down the street, and into the dark. I see the brand on Vincent's arm and his knife in my chest. I want to choke Tamerlan until all this madness makes sense. I want the Room, but never to have gone to Hell. It's mostly childish noise, I know, but pieces of it are worthwhile. If I get one or two more, maybe things will start falling into place.

I wake up and get out of bed. In the kitchen I start to pour myself a drink. Instead, I go and wash the sweat off my face and sit on the couch. Someone left the Blu-ray player on pause. I hit the play button and *Nightbreed* starts playing. It's a strangely comforting movie. Monsters living with monsters in a world built just for monsters. Of course, civilians eventually come along and fuck it all up, the way they fuck everything up. I watch for a few minutes, until the cops head out to hammer Jesus and good clean American living into the monsters. Then it gets depressing, so I turn it off. I go to the window and smoke a cigarette. I wish I hadn't given Vincent's knife to Julie. I'd like to see it and feel it in my hand. Now that I've seen where it was used, maybe it would mean more.

I finish the cigarette and go back to bed.

Things are going to get weirder and worse before they get better. I can feel it. Goddamn skinheads are bad enough, but smart skinheads mixed up with hoodoo? That's bad news.

I go back to bed. Candy rolls over and drapes her arm over me, only it's not her arm. It's Chihiro's arm. Things can't stay like this. Things have got to change.

WHEN I GO downstairs in the morning, I have a headache. Vincent's door is closed, but Kasabian's is open. However, the store is closed and there's nothing playing on the big screen. I go to Kasabian's door and knock. He looks up at me, holding a piece of paper in his metal mitts.

I say, "You have some aspirin? I can't find any upstairs."

He shakes his head.

"No. What I have is this."

He hands me the paper. It's on L.A. County Court letterhead. It reads, *Dear Mr. Kasabian, As you may be aware, L.A. County has conducted several studies that will eventually lead to an extension of the 101 Freeway to serve the region and assist our county with economic development. The site portion of the study has recently been concluded, and this letter is to notify you that your property may have to be purchased for the freeway extension.*

The rest of it is all a lot of property parcel codes and legal noise. I hand the note back to Kasabian.

"What does that mean?"

He drops the letter on his bed.

"It's called eminent domain. It means that the county can come in and take Max Overdrive and there's not a goddamn thing we can do about it."

"How is that even legal?"

He shrugs.

"It's the government. They've got more money and lawyers than regular people, so they can do pretty much anything they want."

"It doesn't even make sense. The 101 is like a mile down

the road. To bring it out here, they'd have to knock down half of Hollywood."

"Someone's got a theory," he says.

Candy comes downstairs.

"What's going on? What's all the whispering?"

"Remember when we got tossed out of Chateau Marmont?" says Kasabian. "Well, it's going to happen again."

Candy looks at me.

"What's he talking about?"

"We got a letter, and according to Atticus Finch here, it means that the county can come in and take Max Overdrive out from under us."

"What? What about the store? Where are we going to live?"

Kasabian picks up the letter again, stares at it. I try to read it over his shoulder, but it still doesn't make much sense to me.

"Can't we get a lawyer and fight it?" I say. "This is bullshit."

Kasabian laughs.

"Look around the room. We're three dead people in a store full of movies that doesn't exist. Plus, we're broke. What lawyer is going to work for us?"

"Maybe a Sub Rosa one," says Candy.

"As I recall, the Sub Rosa like to eat, just like regular people," Kasabian says. "We don't have the money to pay a civilian, a Sub Rosa, a Lurker, or your aunt Sadie."

I reach over and take the letter out of his hands.

"I know what this is. It's the fucking White Lights. They've been around long enough they probably have all kinds of connections to crooked county pricks and lawyers. If they can't kill us, they're going to ruin us."

Candy says, "Let's show the letter to Julie. She'll know what to do."

"What if you're wrong?" says Kasabian.

"How am I wrong?"

"You talked to the Augur, right? Told him you didn't want to work for him."

"Yeah. So?"

"What if you pissed him off and this is his way of getting back at you."

That little rat bastard. I hadn't thought of that.

"It doesn't matter. We still have to show the letter to Julie. We can worry about who sent it later."

I give Candy the letter.

"I don't want to leave," she says. "The only other home I had around here was Doc Kinski's clinic, and they burned that down. Now someone wants to burn us out of here."

Kasabian looks past us at the storage room.

"Too bad we can't let Vincent loose on these people. We have the Angel of Death in our pocket and we can't even keep the doors open."

"No one is going anywhere," I say. "First, we show the letter to Julie and see what she has to say. After that, I'm going to clean my guns."

"Can't you just talk to the Augur and apologize?" says Kasabian.

"We don't even know it's him. And if it is, caving without a fight doesn't give us anything to bargain with."

"I'm getting dressed. You get dressed too. We're going to the office," says Candy, tapping me on the shoulder with the letter.

"Yeah. We can hear what Brigitte found out too."

Vincent opens his door and comes out.

"Good morning. Is there something wrong? You all sound tense."

I start back upstairs.

"Nothing's wrong. Someone's just looking for a fight is all. Stay here with Kasabian and open the store. Act normal."

"I don't know what acting normal means," says Vincent.

I stop on the stairs.

"None of us do, so just keeping doing whatever it is you do."

"Maria called," says Vincent. "She asked if you'd found Dash."

"Fuck Maria's ghost. Unless he went to Harvard Law School he can fucking hang until we get this shit sorted."

"I'll just tell her that you're still looking."

"You do that."

Upstairs, Candy is already half dressed. She stops when I come in.

"Things are going to be okay, right? We're going to work this out?"

"We're going to be fine," I say. "But this is what happens when I try to be reasonable. I should be out shooting people right now. And you should be next to me tearing up the people I don't shoot."

She comes over and puts her arms around my neck.

"Let's try things this way first, okay? If they don't work out, there's always time to run amok."

"I'm glad you see it my way. You sure you don't want to tell me where the White Light Legion hangs out?"

Candy gives me a peck on the lips, then goes back to putting on her clothes.

"Reasonable now. Decapitation later. That's the deal," she says.

"I love it when you talk dirty."

WHEN WE GET to the office, Julie isn't exactly surprised to see us or the letter. She reads over ours, takes an envelope out of a drawer, and drops an almost identical letter on the desk.

"It came yesterday," she says. "Someone has it in for us. In a way, this is good news."

"Exactly how is getting evicted good news?" I say.

"Because it means we're making someone nervous and that only happens when you're getting near the truth. We're close to a breakthrough. I guarantee you, we'll know why someone wanted to bind Vincent in a few days."

"In the meantime, what do we do about these?" says Candy, holding up the letters.

"Sit tight. I'll have some lawyers in the Vigil's legal unit look them over. There's always something to be done."

I sit down.

"Are you sure? I mean these letters are obviously bullshit. No one is running the freeway through your place or ours. That means these aren't legit and that means whoever sent them might not be in the mood to be reasoned with."

"It's still a legal proceeding," Julie says. "Let me handle things."

I get up and go to her coffeemaker, pour three cups.

"You're the adult in the room. But if legal doesn't work, I'm going to throw a big, bloody tantrum."

I bring the cups to the desk. Julie takes one and says, "If legal doesn't work, I might join you."

Someone presses the buzzer on the street. Julie checks the little security cam over the door on her laptop and presses a button to unlock the door. A few seconds later, Brigitte comes into the office. She's wearing a smart, navy-blue dress with a longer skirt than usual. Conservative business wear for a meeting with the boss. She sets her bag on Julie's desk. There are no more chairs, so she perches gracefully on the edge of the desk like a femme fatale in an old gangster movie.

"Thanks for coming in," says Julie.

"It's lovely to see you all. How was your walk in the woods?"

"Very interesting."

"Hot," I say. "I almost got stung by a bee."

"You poor dear," Brigitte says. "How did ever you survive?"

"It was touch and go for a while," says Candy. "But we poured him into a cold martini and managed to revive him."

"And they all lived happily ever after," says Brigitte.

Julie coughs.

"If you three are done."

"Of course," says Brigitte.

"How did it go out there? How many of Tamerlan's people did you get to?"

"Six in all. It was interesting interacting with real people in real places who had no idea they were in my little play."

I say, "Did anyone give you any trouble?"

She raises a hand to say no. "I was much too charming and needy for that."

"What did you tell them?" says Julie.

"That I needed to speak to my poor dead mother and get some advice from her."

"How did they respond?"

"The first two told me to go to an ordinary medium. The rest were all too happy to take my money."

"Did you convince the others to help you?" I say.

"Of course. I told them that my mother was a bitch, but she knew the whereabouts of a small family fortune. I told them I'd give them a cut if they could contact her spirit and extract the information."

"Is any of that true?" says Candy.

"Not a word. My mother is a lovely woman, living happily in Prague."

"What did you find out from Tamerlan's people?" says Julie.

"That a smile makes an impression, but a gun and a smile makes even more. I also learned this: that the necromancers who work through Tamerlan's franchises are more afraid of him than a pistol."

Julie shakes her head, sips her coffee.

"You people and your guns."

"You learn a lot about someone when you show them a gun," I say. "Like that the ones who still won't talk are worried about something worse than dying."

Brigitte says, "That's what Tamerlan's people are like. Every one is afraid of him."

"Did you find out why?" says Julie.

"On the surface, Tamerlan appears to be a simple—though ruthless—businessman, but there is something else. His lackeys are afraid of him, but none will say why."

"Did you learn anything useful about his business dealings?"

"He is obsessive when it comes to money. He is bleeding dry the necromancers that work through him. He demands not only money, but favors, though I don't know what kind."

"So, he's shaking his franchisees down."

"Not exactly. He never touches the money himself. According to the people I interviewed, he seems to have no connection to payments. They all go through a company called Wormwood."

Julie, Candy, and I look at each other.

"Did I say something interesting?" says Brigitte.

"We heard the name yesterday," Julie says. "Did they say what Wormwood is or how to find them?"

"Or him or her," says Candy. "It could be a person."

"Good point."

Brigitte shakes her head, picks up my coffee.

"Is this yours?"

"Yes."

"May I?"

"Of course."

She takes a sip and sets down the cup.

"What was most interesting," she says, "is that even when I became quite physically insistent that they tell me about the money, no one would. They are all quite afraid of *both* Wormwood and Tamerlan."

Julie writes something down on a pad.

"I'll do some research on Wormwood. If they're operating in California, they must at least have a business license."

"I can help with that," says Candy.

"Thank you."

Brigitte says, "By the way, I showed each of them the photo you sent me of the brand on your guest's arm."

"And?"

"No one was able to identify it. Some seemed quite certain they could, and consulted various grimoires and books of arcana. It was all futile."

"Are any of those Dead Heads going to remember your face?" I say.

"The ones not staring at my chest."

"I mean will they be able to identify you if Tamerlan or someone asks?"

"They might know my face, but not my name. And I wore gloves, so there will be no fingerprints or any aetheric residue they can use to find me."

"You're the best," says Candy.

Brigitte winks at her.

I look at Julie.

"Any chance I could get Vincent's knife back?"

Julie frowns.

"Why?"

"It's not a very good reason."

"Then why should I give it to you?"

"Because maybe it will look different after our trip to Murphy Ranch."

"Is that all?"

"Also, I had a funny dream about it."

"He has these dreams sometimes," says Candy. "Sometimes they mean he should have taken an aspirin before bed, but sometimes they mean something."

Julie goes to a file cabinet, takes out a key, and unlocks it. From the bottom drawer, she removes the knife and brings it back to the desk. I pick it up, turn it over in my hands.

"Well?" she says. "Any vibrations from the spirit realm?"

"Not yet. Can I keep it for a couple of days?"

Julie sighs.

"Just be careful with it. Besides Vincent's clothes, it's our only piece of physical evidence."

"What did the Vigil techs tell you about it?" says Candy.

Julie picks up her coffee cup, sets it down again in a gesture of exasperation.

"Nothing. No one would touch it. They know I'm working with Stark on the case and that makes it too hot for them to handle."

"You always make an impression, Jimmy," says Brigitte.

"That's what my mom said."

I put the knife in my coat pocket.

"I have a question about Tamerlan," I say. "If he's involved with this Wormwood thing, doesn't it make sense that I was right and he's working with the White Light Legion? It makes sense. He's the brains and they're the muscle. The enforcers."

Julie says, "Then why wasn't he at the ceremony at Murphy Ranch? From what Varg said, it sounds like the woman, Sigrun, could have been performing the ritual."

"And he specifically said he didn't see anyone who looked like Tamerlan at the ceremony," says Candy.

"He's deeper in this thing than we know yet, I'm sure of it. And he's part of what happened on Wonderland Avenue. What if those people owed him money, or owed Wormwood, and he sent his thugs to get them? Maybe it doesn't relate directly to this case, but it's something we could use as pressure against him to get some answers."

Brigitte takes a piece of paper from her purse and sets it on the desk.

"One of the gentlemen I chatted with was good enough to give me Tamerlan's contact information."

Julie snatches the paper off the desk before I can get near it. Too late, though. I already saw the address. She puts the paper in a drawer.

"I have an assignment for you, Stark," she says. "Starting tomorrow, I want you to shadow each of Brigitte's necromancer contacts. Maybe one of them will reveal something without meaning to."

"Stake out six people? How am I supposed to do that?"

"One at a time," she says.

I sit back in my chair.

"This is just busywork, while you and Candy do the big-brain stuff."

"We need to keep you from playing in traffic," says Candy.

"Or getting stung by a bee," says Brigitte.

"You know, you two should do a ventriloquist act. You can take turns being the dummy."

Julie says, "It's only busywork if that's what you make it. Real investigative work isn't always exciting, but seeing people at unguarded moments can be key to finding out what they're really up to."

"I suppose you want reports on everyone. Write down everything I see."

"That would be nice."

"What if all I see is the idiots reading palms and going to McDonald's for Shamrock Shakes?"

"Then write that down. The smallest thing might be helpful as the case progresses."

"If I'm right and Tamerlan is at the center of this, you owe me a drink," I say.

Julie considers it.

"All right. And if you're wrong?"

"I'm not. But if I am, you get free rentals at Max Overdrive."

"I'm not really a movie person. I'm more of an ESPN person."

"I used to run Hell and now I'm working for a jock."

"I used to be a U.S. marshal and now I'm working with a felon."

Candy raises a couple of fingers and says, "Two felons."

"Two felons."

Julie looks at Brigitte.

"I don't suppose you're a felon too?"

"No. Merely an ex-pornographer."

Julie looks into the distance and sips her coffee.

"It could be worse," I say.

"How?"

I think for a minute.

"Actually, I'm not sure. But I'll think of something and put it in my report."

"I can't wait to read it."

"I can't wait to make it up."

STARTING TOMORROW I'LL be a potted plant. Humpty-Dumpty sitting in a car, making notes, eating donuts, watching my gut get big, and wanting to blow my brains out. But until then, no one told me what to do.

I leave Candy at home, happily pecking away at the laptop. This is the first time I haven't missed her since we started this case and she decided she liked data better than kicking in doors. She doesn't need to go where I'm going. It's not the worst place in L.A. It just smells the worst.

I drive out to Echo Park and leave the Crown Vic by the arboretum in Elysian Park, a sprawling patch of green near the 5 Freeway. On the east side of the park, just about under the freeway, is a greasy-spoon diner called Lupe's. Supposedly Lupe Vélez used to eat there in the thirties, back when it was a chic spot for movie stars to slum. They say she ate her last meal here just before she took eighty Seconal and lay down for one last long nap.

Next to Lupe's is an auto wrecking yard with no name I've ever been able to find. Out front is a hand-painted sign that says WRECKERS, and that's it. No hours. No phone number or address. Above the razor-wire-topped fences you can see piles of dead, rusting car bodies. Through the fence are wooden bins full of greasy axles, dusty brake drums, carburetors, and a hundred other parts. Everything you'd need to fix or assemble a car. But I've never seen anyone inside, and don't know anyone who's seen a sign of life from the place. No one even knows how long it's been there. As far as anyone can remember, it's always been in this spot, even when they were originally building the freeway. But I'm not here for Lupe's or Wreckers. I'm here for what lies between them.

Piss Alley.

It's exactly as fragrant as its name, but the smell doesn't

seep into the street or bother the diners at Lupe's. You have to go into Piss Alley to get a hit of the pure product, and, man, what a product it is. It's like all the toilets in L.A. take a detour through the alley on the way to Piss Heaven. It smells like ammonia and rotten meat. It doesn't matter how many times you go into Piss Alley, it's always a shock. Your eyes water, your nose runs, and your stomach says, "You weren't planning on ever eating again, were you?"

I hold my breath and take a step between Lupe's and Wreckers. I'm nauseous for a second. This is why people used to think that smells—miasmas—caused disease. If smells could kill, Piss Alley would make a nuke seem like a car backfire on the Fourth of July. There's only one reason Piss Alley is allowed to exist and why morons like me come here.

It grants wishes.

The way I look at it is this: I can't shadow-walk anymore, but I need to go places, get past doors, guards, and alarms. Even Mustang Sally, the highway sylph who knows every road, turn, and shortcut on the continent, can't help me with that. I need something more direct and desperate. I need Piss Alley.

Asking for a wish is easy. Getting it granted isn't. The Alley has to be in the right mood and you have to ask the right way. But the basic process is easy.

The walls of Piss Alley are covered with scrawls in paint, chalk, pencil, even blood. You just write your wish on the wall and hope for the best. Of course, just like the rest of the world, a bribe helps. There's a '32 black Duesenberg halfway down the alley. The front end is crushed like it was in a head-on collision, but the passenger compartment and rear are still somewhat intact. The trunk lock is long gone. It's held closed by a loop of rusting wire. I twist it and get the trunk open.

If anything, the trunk smells worse than the alley. A swarm of flies rushes by my head, taking a break from feasting on old food offerings and the animals that dined on them and died in the trunk. I set a bottle of Aqua Regia in a clear spot by a tire well and wire the trunk closed again. Then I start on the wall.

There isn't a clear inch on the bricks to ask for a new favor. No problem. I get out the black blade and carve my message over the old ones.

*I want to Shadow-Walk.*

*There's a present on the altar.*

*I saved the world. You fucking owe me.*

Not exactly Walt Whitman, but I think Piss Alley will get the gist. There's nothing to do now but wait and see if it wants what I'm selling.

I go back to the car at the arboretum and drive back home with the windows open, letting my bruised sinuses fill with healing L.A. smog. I stop by Donut Universe to pick up a bag of greasy death. Every time I come here, I think about Cindil. She worked at the place until she was murdered. I rescued her from Hell and I need to give her a call. Adjusting to life back on Earth can be a little . . . well, look at me.

Back at Max Overdrive, I give Candy first crack at the donuts. I take an apple fritter, and Kasabian and Vincent descend on the rest like cruise missiles. They're watching a weird version of *Spider-Man* I've never seen before.

"It's the version James Cameron was supposed to direct," Kasabian says.

I watch for a few minutes, but I've never given much of a damn about poor, pitiful me Peter Parker, so I go upstairs to have a drink with my fritter.

"Aren't you supposed to be off playing *I Spy* with Tamerlan's flunkies?" says Candy.

"Not until tomorrow. My job today is to wait."

"For what?"

"I'll know tonight."

"What are you doing until then?"

"Eating this donut and drinking this drink."

She closes the laptop and pinches off a piece of her donut between thumb and forefinger. She chews and swallows it.

"I was thinking of taking a break too. Why don't you pour me a drink and take off your clothes? We can wait on your whatever together."

"Don't you have work to do?"

"Why do you think I want your clothes off?"

She doesn't have to ask twice.

AFTER I'M SURE everyone is asleep, I grab my coat, go downstairs, and head out.

I get halfway through the sales floor when Vincent's door opens.

"It's nearly three," he says. "Where are you going?"

"I just have to check on something."

"Do you need help? I could come along."

"Aren't you tired?"

He shakes his head.

"Not much these days. At night, I mostly lie in bed trying to remember the way things used to be."

"I know the feeling. Look, I'm not going to a nice place. This might be dangerous."

He cocks his head.

"You mean I might die?"

"Okay, not that. But it's still dangerous."

"I'll get my coat."

His coat is a sweatshirt Kasabian loaned him. It doesn't matter. This is L.A., where, if the temperature dips below sixty, we call in the National Guard.

I head out to the car and Vincent follows. When he gets in, he takes out the bottle and pops a pill.

"You should take it easy on those."

He swallows hard, getting the dry pill down his gullet.

"It doesn't matter. That was my last one."

"You went through that whole bottle?"

"Yes. Do you think you can get more?"

"We'll let the doctor decide that. I'm sure she'd love to meet you."

"It would be nice to meet some new people."

I steer the Crown Vic into the light middle-of-the-night traffic and head east. Vincent looks out the window, watching the city roll by.

"I didn't often get to look at places in my work," he says. "I like it."

"Enjoy it while you can. We'll have you back with a scythe in your hand in no time."

"I hate that image. It makes me look like a monster."

"If they painted you in pink taffeta with fairy wings, you'd still be a monster to ninety-nine-point-nine percent of the human race."

"I know."

"The pills make that easy to deal with, don't they?"

"I feel the pull of life. The rejection of limbo and nothingness, and that's what death, unexamined, feels like. Even though I know otherwise, it feels as if my body itself rejected the idea of its end."

"Survival instinct. I suppose you immortal types don't worry about that much. We deal with it every day."

"You're part angel, but you still worry about death?"

"Not the death part so much as the stuff I'll leave behind. I lost a lot of years Downtown. I've barely started making up the time."

"And your friends?"

"What about them?"

"You're afraid of leaving them behind."

"Sure. Why wouldn't I be?"

"We're friends now. I'll make sure their transmogrification is an easy one."

We're almost to Elysian Park. I look at Vincent.

"Thanks . . . I guess."

"You don't want them to die at all."

"No one wants people they care about to die."

Vincent stares out the window and starts to hum. It takes me a minute to get the song. "Chim Chim Cher-ee" from *Mary Poppins.* I imagine him in his room, humming all the songs from all the movies he's watched with Kasabian.

"Things were easy before, less frightening when came back from Hell and knew you could go back when you wanted, weren't they?"

"A lot easier."

"We're the same, then. I can't go home and neither can you."

I never thought of Hell as home before, but in a twisted way he might be right. It's the place I always think of running to when things get bad here. Maybe home isn't the place you love, just the place you know best.

I say, "Maybe tonight will change that. Maybe I'll be able to walk to Hell and back again, and if that happens, maybe you can too."

Vincent settles back into his seat.

"Going home won't make me *me* again."

"One step at a time, man."

I stop under the 5 Freeway near Lupe's and get out with my na'at in my hand. If things go sideways I don't want to attract any cops with gunfire.

Vincent follows me out of the car, looks around.

"What are we afraid of?"

"Lions, and tigers, and bears. And shitheads who want our cash."

"I don't have any money."

"If you explain that to them, I'm sure they'll understand."

When I'm sure there's no one on the street, I grab Vincent's sleeve and pull him behind me into Piss Alley. I see his face change when the smell hits him.

"Oh my," he says.

"Not so great having senses now, is it?"

"Why are we here?"

"To see if I'm getting wings. Stand over there," I tell him.

He goes to where I'm pointing, a trash can well away from the Duesenberg. I extend the na'at to the length of a sword and twist the grip to shape it into a blade. Holding the na'at up, ready to gut anything waiting for me in the car, I use one hand to twist the wires holding the trunk closed.

It pops opens and nothing attacks me. A few rats scatter down through the exposed undercarriage, but they mostly head off in the direction of Lupe's to party in the Dumpster out back.

I lean to the side to let street light fall into the trunk. A small brown bottle glitters in the middle of all the garbage in the trunk. I pocket the bottle and wire the trunk closed again. Vincent follows me back out to the street. I collapse the na'at and put it in my coat.

"What is it?" he says.

"A bottle. There's a note attached."

Paper dangles from a red ribbon around the bottle's neck. In florid script, the note says *Drink me.* I hold it up to the light to make sure I'm reading it right.

"They think I'm goddamn Alice in Wonderland."

"Who?" says Vincent.

"Them. Whoever runs Piss Alley. The bottle wants me to drink it."

"Is that all?"

I turn the paper over. There's more writing on the back. *Sidestep for one week.*

Vincent moves around, trying to stay clear of rats and bugs. "What does it say?"

"It wants to me to dance a jig. Or something. I don't know what the hell this is."

"Drink it and find out."

I look at him.

"You know how to drive?"

"No," he says.

"Too bad. If this kills me, you're shit out of luck. Cabs don't come here."

"Then good luck."

I hold the bottle up to the light. There's nothing special about it.

"Fuck it."

I take out the cork and upend the bottle, swallowing the slimy stuff in one go.

It doesn't really taste that bad. Sort of like cherry cough syrup with a whiskey bite. I put the bottle back in my pocket and wait. Nothing happens. A minute later, nothing is still happening.

"Did you do it wrong?" says Vincent.

"It said 'drink me.' How can you fuck that up? Maybe the stuff went bad sitting in the trunk. I should have come earlier."

"Maybe you should have," says a man holding a gun to Vincent's head.

I was so wrapped up in my *Alice in Wonderland* bottle that I didn't hear the crackhead creeping up on us. I'm going to be very embarrassed if I get shot because I was waiting for the Queen of Hearts' tarts.

"Don't look at me," says the creep.

Vincent's eyes are wide.

"Be cool, Vincent. This will be over soon."

I shouldn't have put the na'at away. The fucker has his finger on the trigger of a snub-nose .357 pressed behind Vincent's left ear. I'm fast, but I'm not fast enough to stop the gun from firing. The extra good news is that while I still have a lot of the $500 Julie paid me, it's back at Max Overdrive on the bedroom dresser.

"You, talker, give me your cash," says Mr. 357.

"I don't have any."

I hold up the keys to the Crown Vic.

"Want a car?"

The crackhead shifts his stance nervously, pressing the gun hard enough into Vincent's skull he might be tunneling for gold.

"Don't fuck with me," he says. "Give me the money."

I speak slowly, like I'm trying to explain differential equations to a Chihuahua.

"I'd like to, but I don't have any."

Mr. 357 keeps hold of Vincent, but points the gun at me.

"Last chance, cocksucker," he says.

"Really, man, I want to help."

I measure the distance between us. It's too far to grab him before he fires.

"Fuck it," he says in a tone that I recognize.

As the gun goes off, Vincent screams and I jump to the right, hoping to slip past the bullet.

And I come down in a hurricane. Grit stings my eyes. I put up an arm to keep the wind from blinding me. Overhead, the sky swirls like oil in black water. Things blow by around my ankles. Trash it looks like, but trash that's alive. The street is still the street, but time seems to be moving very slowly or I'm moving very fast. The slug from the .357 emerges from the barrel like a snail out for an evening stroll. Things boom in the distance. L.A. disappears. Crumbles to the ground. Things like swarms of insects land on the rubble and build the city again. Then it falls apart. And is rebuilt. Ants up the block use the living garbage to assemble other things. Horses. Rivers. Air.

This is it. The note really meant to take a sidestep, right out of reality and into the machinery that keeps the show running. This is the world, just from a different vantage point. Behind the scenes, where you aren't supposed to peek.

I lean into the wind, struggle a few steps until I'm behind Vincent. I get out the na'at, and this time I take a step to the left. The wind lets up. The sound of the gun going off deafens me. I swing the na'at like a cosh at Mr. 357's head. His skull makes a satisfying cracking sound and he falls like a hippo with the bends.

Vincent whirls around and looks at me.

"Where did you go?"

"Into the wings. Did you miss me?"

I push Vincent to the car and kick the crackhead's pistol into Piss Alley. Let's see if he or the cops have the balls to go in and pick it up. My guess is no.

Jamming the key in the ignition, I start the Crown Vic and head back through Echo Park. Somewhere in the distance, I can hear sirens. When the crackhead tells the cops about the guy who disappeared right before his eyes, they're as likely to 5150 him as arrest him. Maybe vacationing for a few days in the loony bin will do him some good. The food can't be worse than any other lockup and I bet the beds are better than jail. Hell, if the county throws us out of Max Overdrive, maybe I can get us all locked up together. It ain't the Chateau Marmont, but it's better than trying to live in the car.

And it will have a/c.

I DROP VINCENT back at Max Overdrive and head for Tamerlan Radescu's place. I need to get as much done tonight as I can, before I turn into a bump on a log tomorrow.

The address on the slip Brigitte gave Julie was on Elrita Drive, near Mulholland. Of course Tamerlan lives in Laurel Canyon. Where else would the prick be?

I head down the winding roads through the hills, past gated palaces with circular drives and fences out back to keep the coyotes from eating the pets. Dump the car on Laurel Canyon Boulevard and go the rest of the way on foot.

The driveway is so long that I can't see Tamerlan's house from the road. I'd hop the Spanish tile fence out front, but there will be surveillance and alarms, and maybe even armed security. Instead, I hide in a shadow and take one step to the right.

The hurricane hits me again and I'm backstage. The sky is a whirlpool of glistening oil. The living garbage blows by. Some piles at my feet, tossed by the wind to land on my ankles. They touch me, run their smashed and crumpled bodies up my legs, trying to figure out what I am. Insects destroy and reconstruct the mansion as I watch. The fence disintegrates and I step past it before the insects have a chance to rebuild it.

It's a long, stumbling walk up the drive. Each step feels like falling, a nauseating sensation. The hurricane blows down the hill, harder than it did on the flatlands. Off to my left lies L.A. Despite the storm, the backstage view of the city is bright and clear and beautiful. Between gusts, I can see all the way to the ocean. Between whitecaps, the water too dries up and is rebuilt by the insects.

Then the house comes into view. It's a white Italian villa hugging a stone hillside. There are marble lions flanking the entrance. The villa seems more substantial than the fence, more solid than much of what I've seen tonight. The walls are translucent, but they stay in place and don't crumble like so much of the architecture I've been seeing. I touch the front door. It stretches like a thin latex membrane. Pressing my face to the thin skin, I push. The wall membrane stretches, and curls, enveloping me. In a few seconds, it peels open and I'm through.

A step to the left, and the wind stops. The world goes back to normal.

I'm in the foyer. A checkered marble floor. Grand piano. Flashy paintings as memorable as motel art on the walls, but probably costing more than a black-market kidney. A staircase to my left. The kitchen to my right.

I stay put, listening for anything that means people are awake.

From upstairs comes laughter. Several people. Men's voices. I take out the Colt and head up the steps.

A few doors down the second floor is a large room. A desk and laptop to one side. Pricey chairs and sofa around a carved coffee table in the center of the room. Tamerlan sits on a leather recliner at one end of the group, his men scattered on the sofa and chairs. Six of them. I put the Colt away. If I could shadow-walk, I could come through the dark patches on the walls and floor and take the men out. But I can't figure out how sidestepping will help me do that. So, I go with a different, much dumber strategy. I put the Colt back under my coat and walk into the room unarmed.

Tamerlan sees me first. He holds up a forefinger like he was expecting me.

"That's close enough," he says.

His men turn in my direction, then scramble to pull out guns. They're clearly Sub Rosa and able to throw hoodoo. The fact they went for their guns means they might use the same trick I do: dipping their bullets in Spiritus Dei, a rare and expensive potion that when coated on a bullet will kill fucking anything. I'm not about to put up my hands for these pricks, but I hold them out at waist level so they can see I'm unarmed.

"Do you know who I am?"

Tamerlan nods. The room is full of smoke. Foreign cigars the size of brown burritos sit in crystal ashtrays. Tamerlan still holds his.

"Everyone knows who you are."

"You don't seem surprised to see me."

Tamerlan shrugs. He's wearing a dark red tracksuit with brown loafers and white socks. It's a strange look. Part CEO of a software start-up and part Russian gangster, but his voice doesn't sound like either. More like an East River tugboat captain than a crooked Dr. Moriarty.

"I knew someone was going to show up, though not you in particular. Why've you been you harassing my business partners?"

"Partners? They hate your guts."

"People don't need to be best buddies to do business."

"No, but it makes for better New Year's parties."

"You missed the holidays. But Valentine's Day is coming

soon. I'll buy you one of those boxes of chocolates shaped like a heart before I have my men kill you."

"Speaking of hearts, I want to talk to you about the guy whose heart you had cut out."

He puffs his cigar, blows smoke. It hangs blue over his head.

"How did you get in here?" he says.

"I walked through the wall."

"Yeah. I heard you could do shit like that, but I wasn't sure I believed it."

He turns to his men.

"Shoot this asshole."

Before he actually gets near the word *asshole*, I've dropped to my knees, pressed my hands to the dark wood floor. A shot tears out a piece of the doorframe over my head as I shout Hellion hoodoo. The rest of the shots go up into the ceiling as Tamerlan's men fall where I made the floor disappear. I shout more hoodoo and the floor reappears. Tamerlan sits up straight in his chair. His is the only part of the floor I left untouched. He puts down his cigar, tries to play it cool and not show shock, but the microtremors in his hands give him away. I close the door and speak a little more hoodoo. The door and windows fade away and are replaced by a smooth surface of walls. Tamerlan looks around at his redecorated room.

"You know you're going to die, right? I'm tight with the Augur, and Abbot takes care of important people."

I go to his desk. His phone is lying on top. I throw it against the wall and it shatters into a thousand pieces.

"You're going to have to shout pretty loud for the Augur to hear you in here."

"My men will be up here in a minute."

"Maybe. But the ones without broken legs will take a while to get inside. In the meantime, we're going to talk."

"About what?"

"The dead man. Well, two dead men. One you took away from Murphy Ranch and one you left to rot."

"I never heard of Murphy Ranch."

He picks up his cigar and sticks it in his mouth.

I go over to him and pull Vincent's knife from my pocket. Tamerlan freezes. I stick the tip of the knife into the glowing end of his cigar and push it through the full length of the stogie until it bumps into Tamerlan's teeth.

"You remember anything now? Or do I keep pushing?"

He lets go of the cigar. I shake the knife so the smoke falls on the floor. Tamerlan picks up the cigar and tosses it into an ashtray so it won't burn the pretty rug.

"What exactly is it you think I did?" he says.

"You and the White Light Legion—which is where I'm guessing your pet poodles downstairs came from—you did a ritual to corral and bind Death into a human body."

"Why would I do that?"

"I've been thinking about that. Once you control Death, I figure that you were planning on making a fortune selling life-extension policies to people who don't want to die."

Tamerlan leans back in his chair again, a little more relaxed now that he knows I'm not just here to kill him. He shakes his head.

"That's cute, but it's not much of a business model. I'm a

necromancer. Death is my bread and butter. Anyway, the life-extension idea wouldn't work."

"Why not?"

"It's too obvious. A bunch of rich jerks stick around too long and people start getting suspicious. And tampering with death itself? That's heavy baleful magic. We both know that if the Augur or his people find out, you can get put in a box in the ground for that kind of thing. It's not worth the risk."

I watch his eyes as he talks, waiting for a change in his pupils. They dilate a little with tension, but that's it. He's not lying.

Time to shift gears.

"Are you Wormwood? Admit it. Wormwood is a front for your Dead Head business and any other shit you're into. It's a way to launder all your money so it can't be traced to you."

He chuckles and shakes his head, briefly putting a hand over his face.

"Oh man, you don't know anything about anything, do you? I don't have to launder money because, whatever opinion you might happen to have about my business, I'm legit. I make plenty of money from spirit conjurations for a few select clients and from my franchises. That's it. It's not that I have anything against being crooked, it's just that I don't have to be."

"But you know people who need money laundered."

"That's neither here nor there. Sure, I work with Wormwood, but I'm not them."

"What exactly is Wormwood, then? Do the White Lights launder their money? They have enough muscle they could run it."

"Now you're just guessing."

"Okay. Let's back up a little: What is Wormwood?"

Tamerlan sits back and squares his shoulders.

"Pal, if you needed to know about Wormwood, trust me, they'd make sure you did."

"What if I broke your arms and legs and burned down your house if you don't tell me more?"

He laughs again.

"You're not going to do that. You're dumb, but not that dumb."

"What makes you think that?"

"You want something. Killing me won't get it, but maybe I can be useful when you find it. But I can't be if I'm dead. Plus, the Augur wouldn't like it."

I think for a minute.

Tamerlan takes a new cigar from a wooden humidor by his chair.

"Your problem is that you've got a Jesse James complex. You're an outlaw. That's how you think and that's how you think everybody else thinks. You don't think like a businessman. In business, the trick is maximizing profit and longevity. I go playing with baleful magic and talking out of school about Wormwood, I'm going against both of those principles."

"Let's try something else. A business deal."

"I'm listening."

"Someone bound Death in a human body and he can't get out."

"If you say so."

"I want to hire you to do an exorcism. You can do those,

right? I want you to pull Death out of the body of this Townsend guy so he can be himself again."

Tamerlan shakes his head.

"This human body you're talking about, was this Townsend still in it when someone corked Death inside?"

"No. They killed Townsend and bound Death to the body."

Tamerlan holds up his hands.

"Then you're shit out of luck. Exorcisms only work when a spirit takes hold of an inhabited body. Your body was empty when Death entered it. He's the animus now. The life force. You don't exorcize that."

Fucking hell. I don't know enough about death magic to make any headway with this guy and he knows it. I should have studied up. This whole thing is like an anxiety dream where you show up without pants for a final exam in a class you never went to.

Then I get it.

"I know you're involved."

"How?"

"Because there's a brand on the body Death's inhabiting. It's a necromancer's mark."

"Bullshit. You got a picture?"

I take out my phone and show him the photo.

Tamerlan bursts out laughing, hands me the phone.

"Oh my God, you're so much stupider than I thought. How do you remember to zip your fly, you fucking idiot?"

"You're saying that's not a Dead Head mark?"

"No, asshole. It's the logo for a talent agency."

That's not the answer I was expecting.

"Come here," he says.

We go to his desk. He touches the space bar on his laptop to wake it up, and types a URL into the browser. A second later, a page appears. It's for the Evermore Creatives Group. The logo, the exact shape of Death's brand, is at the top of the page with the agency's name. I stare at the page, trying to figure it out. Trying to find Tamerlan's angle. How he's tricking me.

I type in a few more URLs and they all come up on real pages that I recognize. I put the agency's name into a search engine. When I check the results, they take me back to the page Tamerlan showed me. Death's mark and Townsend's body's big secret is that he was probably some kind of small-time actor.

I say, "What kind of talent agency brands its clients?"

"Why don't you go break into *their* fucking place and leave me alone?"

This is bad. Was I this wrong the whole time? Is he really just a Mr. Moneybags creep and not the secret boss of the White Lights? He won't tell me about Wormwood, so he could be lying. Or maybe there's something about Wormwood that scares him the way he scares his minions. I think I just wasted a lot of time and hoodoo on nothing. I haven't been this wrong about anything since I bought a Genesis album because I was drunk and I thought the lady with the fox head on the cover was kind of hot.

Tamerlan claps me on the shoulder and sits down behind the desk.

"Holy shit, thanks for coming tonight, Stark. With people not dying and business being off, I needed a good laugh."

I look at him.

"Aren't you worried about what's going to happen to you when you die? You must have pissed off a lot of dead people in your time. Some of them will be waiting for you in Hell."

"I'm not worried," he says. "A little bird told me that some do-gooder changed Hell all around. Made it nice for people. He even opened the door so souls can go to Heaven. The way I figure it, anyone who might have been waiting for my ass won't be there to give me grief. And who knows? I might like Hell with all the riffraff cleared out. I could set up business there. Cut deals with necromancers back here to get souls and information for them."

He aims a finger at me.

"That's what I mean about you not thinking like a businessman. What you think of as death and damnation, I see as another capital opportunity."

I'm having trouble taking in all the ways I've fucked up in the last few days. Am I missing something? Is Tamerlan dancing around me, hiding his White Light connections? If he is, I'm goddamn sure not going to find them right now. I need to get clear and think.

I go to his humidor and take one of his cigars, put it in my pocket. I could kill Tamerlan right now and no one would weep for the bastard. But I'm not going to do that, on the off chance that he really isn't involved in the case. Besides, I don't have to. People like Tamerlan, sharp guys who think they have all the angles covered, eventually end up playing fast and loose with the wrong people. All I have to do is sit back and wait and watch. He'll dig his own grave.

"Thanks for the cigar," I say.

"Thanks for the good time tonight. I can't wait to tell the boys all about it."

"You do that."

I sidestep to the right and go back into the storm. Walk through a wall and back outside, leaving Tamerlan stuck in his doorless, windowless office. Fuck him and his mansion. Let his dog boys chisel him out.

I go back to the car and drive home. The only thing worse than having Tamerlan laugh in my face is knowing I'm going to have to tell Julie about it without making myself sound too stupid.

I toss his cigar out the window.


"YOU DID WHAT?"

Julie is shouting. I've never heard her shout before. It isn't a pleasant sound, especially when the shouting is aimed at me.

"I talked to Tamerlan last night."

"He just let you into his home in the middle of the night?"

"Eventually."

"You mean you broke in."

"Technically, I walked in."

"But you weren't invited, so it's still breaking and entering."

"He let me have one of his cigars, so he couldn't have been too mad."

She's at her desk. She drops her head into her hands.

"Did he recognize you?"

"Our kind of people pretty much know who I am by now."

"*Our* kind? You mean people who break into other people's homes and threaten them?"

"No. I meant people who deal in hoodoo."

She brings her head back up and looks at me.

"I can't begin to tell you how many ways I'm angry right now."

"Sorry."

"That's all you have to say?"

Candy crosses and uncrosses her legs nervously.

"What he means is this will never happen again. Isn't that right?"

She turns to me.

"Yes. What she said. Never again."

Julie blows out a long stream of air.

"Do you think this is going to come back at us? I mean, should I be talking to a lawyer?"

I shake my head.

"I don't think Tamerlan wants everyone knowing how easy it was to get into his place. Plus, I kind of rearranged the architecture. He has that to take care of."

Julie stares at me. I'm not explaining myself well.

"He laughed in my face. I don't think he's coming after you or anyone else 'cause he had too good a time with me. And he'll have a better time telling his friends what a fuckup I am. Your agency is safe."

"You better hope so. I'm not losing everything I've worked for because you can't help playing cowboy."

Candy says, "You have to admit, though, that he came back with some good information. We were still going page by page through old magic texts. How long would it have taken us to figure out the mark came from a talent agency?"

Julie purses her lips and looks away.

"That doesn't get him off the hook for anything."

She turns back to me. I nod, trying to look sorrier than I feel, part of my indentured servitude.

"I understand. But shouldn't we follow up on this lead? The Evermore Creatives Group is right down on Wilshire."

"What I should do is cut you loose right now, just to protect myself. You understand that, right?"

"If you want me gone, just say the word."

"I didn't say I was going to, just that I should. You still know things about the magic world that we need."

She sits back, thinking.

"Consider yourself on probation," she says.

"That sounds fair," says Candy.

I nod.

"Thanks."

Julie says, "Remember that I went out on a limb for you two. All I'm asking is that you consider your actions in the future."

She's right. She saved Candy. Okay, now I feel bad.

"I'll clear things with you in the future."

"Thank you."

"What are we going to do about Evermore Creatives?" says Candy.

"We do need to check it out. But I should do some research before we approach them directly. Find out who they are."

"They peddle B actors and dancing girls to the movies," I say. "What else do we need to know?"

"Thank you for that succinct description, but I prefer to go in with facts," says Julie.

"Stark could keep an eye on the place while we go into the background. See who goes in and out," says Candy.

"That's something we could do, or you could go with Stark. He keeps an eye on the agency and you keep an eye on him."

"I'd really rather do computer stuff with you."

"This is the way it has to be. Stark needs a babysitter and it's not going to be me."

"Okay," says Candy, and gives me a look I don't want to see again.

"I promise to be good," I say.

"See that you are. Now both of you get out of here. I have a lot of work to do. I have to give my lawyer a call just to let him know what might be coming."

Julie turns to her computer in such a way that I know it's time to leave. I start down the stairs and Candy follows.

Outside, she walks fast, heading away from me. It takes a few steps for me to catch up.

"I'm sorry," I say. "I didn't mean for you to get caught up in my shit."

She stops, looks at me, and puts on her black sunglasses.

"But you did. I'm not ready to sit in a car with you all day. I need to walk for a little while. Follow me in the car. Drive around the block. I don't care, but don't talk to me for a while."

She walks away. I light a cigarette and watch her. I thought today might go something like this, but I didn't want Candy to end up as collateral damage. I don't think even finding her brass knuckles right now would get me back in good with her. And she'd punch me if I bought her flowers or something stupid like that. Better just to keep my head down and my mouth shut. I get in the Crown Vic and follow her down Sunset.

She crosses over to my side of the street at Fountain Avenue and gets into the backseat. I look at her through the rearview mirror. If she's less angry, I can't see it.

"Don't talk," she says. "Just drive."

"Yes, ma'am."

"Shut up."

Heading to Wilshire, I'm careful to obey all traffic laws and stoplights. This would be a lousy day to get a ticket.

A lousier day, I mean.

I PARK THE car down the block from the Evermore Creatives Group. Far enough away not to be noticed, but close enough to see the main entrance. It's an ordinary office building. A concrete, steel, and glass shoe box tipped on its side along a quiet section of the boulevard. Mostly hotels, drugstores, and lunch joints down here for the tourists who can't afford thirty dollars for a room-service burrito.

Candy moved up to the front seat when we parked, but hasn't said much since. She's just been screwing around with her phone. I roll down the window and have a smoke. Couriers with packages and snappily dressed men and women go in and out of the building. A lousy actress from a C-minus caper movie I saw a while back comes outside, walking a husky on a leash. A FedEx truck pulls up. The driver unloads packages and takes them inside. A couple walks by holding hands, eating tacos.

"I don't know if I can do this much longer. The excitement is killing me."

Candy shushes me.

She likes to play a game on her phone called Mecha Disco.

It's sort of like Dance Dance Revolution, but with robots and lasers that blow up the dancers when they can't follow the beat. But she isn't wearing her headphones and her phone isn't beeping and shaking like a Martian vibrator. I lean back in my seat, trying to see what she's doing.

"Stop that," she says.

"What are you doing?"

"Just 'cause I'm away from the computer doesn't mean I can't do background research on Evermore Creatives."

"Find anything interesting?"

"Not especially. They've been around since the thirties. They used to handle a lot of musical acts, but couldn't compete with the big agencies, so they went small and boutique."

"Who do they handle now?"

"Mostly ghosts. A lot of famous ones too. The big agencies worked with them when they were living—"

"And ECG got them when they kicked. It's a smart deal. People are dead a lot longer than they're alive."

"But they still represent some regular acts too," she says.

"Probably to keep up appearances. No one wants to be pigeonholed in this town."

"Get this. They make a lot of money selling wild-blue-yonder contracts."

"Of course. Every star needs one."

"No. They sell to civilians. It's almost as big as their ghost business. Isn't that a little weird?"

She's right. I puff the Malediction. A guy walking by with a yoga mat under his arm makes a face when he passes through a cloud of my fumes.

"Excuse you," he says.

I wave to him.

"Have a blessed day."

"There's something I don't understand," says Candy.

"Why does a talent agency brand its clients?"

"Exactly. That doesn't sound like a business–client relationship. That's more like . . ." She searches for the right word. "Ownership."

"Maybe they owned Eric Townsend. I want to know why a talent agency is doing business with the White Light Legion."

Candy stares at her phone. She's still mad, but at least she's talking.

"We don't know that they are," she says. "It could just be the one guy."

"I wonder if that one guy lived with the other zoo animals in Laurel Canyon?"

"Julie might know. I'll e-mail her."

"Send her my love."

"See me typing? That means I'm ignoring you."

I drop the rest of the Malediction out the window, look around for somewhere to get coffee. If I can't have Aqua Regia, maybe caffeine will help me get my brain around all that's happened in the last few days.

I say, "What do we have? Someone killed Eric Townsend and dragged him and another stiff out to a Nazi condo in the woods."

Candy sets down her phone.

"One that's not easy to get to. That would be a hard hike carrying two corpses."

"Right. The White Lights performed a ritual to bind

Death to one of the bodies, dumped it, and then went to all the trouble of hauling the first body out of there."

"Why leave a body behind when you just bound an angel inside?" she says.

"Maybe those kids partying spooked them. Remember, Death was locked in a rotting corpse. He wasn't going anywhere until Varg took the knife out of his chest. What I want to know is why the White Lights were so in love with one body that they dragged it to the ranch, then humped it all the way back out again."

"And assuming it was magicians from the Silver Legion that did the ritual," says Candy, "why talk about Wormwood? What does Tamerlan's bank have to do with Death?"

"I'd like to see that other body. I bet it had an ECG brand on it too."

"There's a lot more we don't know. Who is Sigrun?"

"And who or what is the new Death?"

"I've been looking for actors, singers—anyone in L.A. involved in show business named Sigrun. I haven't found anything."

I point at the ECG building.

"I'll bet you a dozen donuts she has a blue-yonder contract with those creeps."

"Or she could work there. Or just be a freelancer they brought in for the job, which will make it harder to track her down."

A seagull circles overhead and shits on the Crown Vic's hood. The bird was probably aiming for me and missed.

"It's no fun going over things if you aren't going to jump to conclusions with me."

"That's exactly what I'm trying to avoid doing," Candy says.

I look at her.

"I haven't seen you so latched on to something since Doc Kinski died."

She flips through screens on her phone, looks up at me.

"I'm liking this private-eye thing. I like learning things and doing smart work."

"So, does that makes the work we did before dumb stuff?"

"That's not what I mean. I liked kicking in doors and punching bad guys with you. But sometimes I missed working with Doc. I learned things working at the clinic with Allegra, but it wasn't the same. Now there's this new thing and I think I could get pretty good at it. What do you think?"

"I think you can do whatever you set your mind to."

"But do you think I'm wasting my time with Julie?"

"You're doing a lot better than I am. And if brainwork is what you want, I think you can handle anything she throws at you."

"Thanks."

She smiles.

"Now let's see if you can get me out of the doghouse with her."

"I'm not sure anyone's that smart."

She holds up her phone and takes a photo.

"What are you shooting?"

"I'm Instagramming the seagull shit."

"Good idea. It could be a Nazi seagull."

"Please. Seagulls are anarchists," Candy says. "They don't play by anybody's rules but their own."

I open my mouth to argue with her, but what comes out is, "Oh shit."

She turns where I'm looking.

"What is it?"

"Lock the back door on the passenger side. I'll be back in a second."

I get out and walk as fast as I can without attracting attention.

Outside the ECG office, David Moore is having a friendly chat with his phone. I wait until he's facing away, come up behind him, and put the black blade to his back.

"Hang up," I whisper. "Tell them you'll call back later."

Without missing a beat he says, "Babe, I've got to call you back. Something's come up."

I turn off the phone for him and put it in his pocket.

"Let's take a ride."

"Why can't we talk here? I won't run away."

"I don't like the sun. My scars don't tan. I end up with freaky white railroad tracks all over my face."

"Where are we going?"

"Back here for now. Later, who knows?"

I walk him to the Crown Vic. Candy leans over the seats and opens the rear passenger-side door. I shove Moore inside and get in next to him.

He looks at Candy in her big black shades, black lipstick, and pink hair.

"This is Chihiro," I say. "She has a gun and a phone, so it's fifty-fifty whether she'll shoot you or Instagram you."

"I told you, I'm not going to run."

"You got that right," she says.

She crooks her finger at me.

"Can we talk a minute?"

I keep the knife against Moore's ribs and lean up where I can talk to Candy.

She whispers, "This is kidnapping, exactly the kind of thing Julie doesn't want us doing."

"I suppose you're right. Maybe you should leave that part out of your report."

"This once, but we seriously need to work on your bedside manner."

"Good plan. But I already have Moore, so let's see what we can get out him."

"Fine."

I swivel around so I'm facing Moore again. He's pressed up against the door, as far from me as he can get.

I say, "You wanted to sell me a wild-blue-yonder contract a few days ago. Actually, you lied to me—said you were with the *L.A. Times*—then you tried to sell me a contract."

"So? I embellished a little. Welcome to show business."

"Why come to me?"

"I told you before, the agency wants A-listers. You'd fit right into our Smoking Gun department."

"What's a Smoking Gun department?"

"I think he means crooks," says Candy.

"Is that what you mean? Who else do you have in there?"

"Client names and affiliations are confidential."

"But basically you want me to do a dog and pony show with Johnny Stompanato for some rich idiot's sweet sixteen party?"

Moore frowns.

"I don't have to tell you anything."

"What else do you do for ECG?"

"I just look for clients."

"For wild-blue-yonder contracts."

"Yes."

"You must have a lot."

"Not as many as you might think. We have high standards. Only the right backgrounds get an offer."

"What's the right background?"

"That's also confidential."

"Show me your left arm."

I grab his arm and pull it straight so Candy can hold him by the wrist.

He wiggles and pulls, but she's got him tight.

"Don't hurt me," he says.

I hold up the knife.

"It'll only hurt if you move."

Digging the knife into a seam, I slit the sleeve of his jacket and shirt all the way up to his shoulder. Up near his armpit is a brand in the shape of the ECG logo.

"What does the brand mean?" I say.

"That's confidential."

"You're talking to a bored man with a knife. What will I cut next?"

Moore looks from me to Candy. She shrugs.

"Don't look at me. There's no reasoning when he gets this way."

I say, "Let me get things rolling. I bet you have a blue-yonder contract. Is that what the tattoo means?"

He nods.

"Why mark people?" says Candy. "Is it to scare off other agencies?"

"Partly," Moore says. "But it's to let paramedics and morticians know, anyone who might work with dead bodies, about the contract."

"A blue yonder is about the spirit," I say. "Why does the body matter?"

"Each brand is a little different."

"Like a serial number," says Candy.

"Yeah. They use it to confirm you're dead so the necromancers can collect your soul."

I tap his leg with the knife, thinking.

"How long does a contract last?"

"Indefinitely," he says.

"So, basically ECG owns you forever. Who told you to come to me?"

"No one. I'm a salesman. Getting you to sign would have been a big deal for my career."

I look at his eyes, trying to read him, but he's too scared for me to get anything useful.

"You know you're talking to someone with a history of erratic behavior, right? And I'm holding a knife."

He looks at the ceiling for a minute. Candy lets go of his arm and he snatches it back.

"It was my boss," he says.

"Who's your boss?"

"Mr. Burgess."

"And who told *him*?"

"I don't know."

"Someone from the White Light Legion? Wormwood?"

"How do you know about Wormwood?"

With all the conviction of a good liar, Candy says, "We know all about Wormwood. They own your agency."

Moore narrows his eyes, but his face relaxes a little.

"No, they don't. The Burgess family owns it. You don't know anything about Wormwood, do you?"

I prod him with the knife.

"Why don't you enlighten us?"

Candy's phone rings.

In the split second she and I look at the phone, Moore pulls the door handle and stumbles out onto Wilshire. He sprints across the street, dodging traffic like a goddamn ballet dancer. He almost makes it to the other side when a van pulls out of a parking space down the block, peels rubber, and mows him down. I get out of the car, ready to go after it.

Candy tackles me and pulls me out of the street just as a blue Honda Civic sideswipes the Crown Vic and takes off. I don't have to run after it this time. I recognize the car from the other night when it shot up the front of Max Overdrive. That means the van that took out Moore was another White Light vehicle.

"Where'd he go?" says Candy.

I look up and down the street. There's no evidence left of Moore's collision but some skid marks and blood.

"They must have grabbed his body. Let's get out of here."

We jump in the car. It starts and drives just fine. All the damage the Civic did to it was cosmetic.

"Why are we running?" says Candy. "Somebody back there must have gotten our license plate. The cops will find us at home. Or find Julie."

"Not necessarily," I say. "After the other night, when the White Lights got our number, I switched plates."

"With who?"

"A Porsche by Bamboo House. I took them while the owner was inside drinking mai tais."

"So, besides kidnapping, we've been riding around in a car with stolen plates."

"Yeah. Are going to rat me out?"

"Are you kidding? If I told Julie this shit, she wouldn't fire us. She'd have us arrested."

"Was she the one who called?"

Candy looks at her phone.

"Yes. I'll call her back when we get home."

"That'll give us time to get our stories straight."

"You're going to change the plates back to the real ones. And throw the damned Porsche plates away."

"What are we going to tell Julie about the car?"

Candy thinks a minute.

"We didn't see it happen. We went for chicken and waffles, and when we came out, we found it this way."

"That's good. I'd buy that."

No one talks for a while, then Candy says, "I don't want to have to lie for you again."

"You won't. And thanks for saving me back there."

"I had to. You still owe me brass knuckles."

"I'm working on it."

"You better be."

"You've got to admit, though. The thing with the cars. That was a rush back there."

"Yeah, it was," she says. "Poor stupid Moore."

"Poor? An ECG employee is going to get priority treat-ment. They're probably processing his blue yonder right now. He's going to be fine."

"I wonder what he'll end up doing?"

"Probably babysitting his Smoking Gun goons. Once a company man . . ."

"Always a company man."

WHEN WE GET back to Max Overdrive, Kasabian and Vin-cent are sitting on the step by the front door. Kasabian is eating a donut and Vincent is sniffing the bag like a starving dog.

I park and we go over.

"Knock it off," I tell Vincent. "You look like my grandma huffing paint."

"Sorry," he says, and sets the bag on the step. "It just smells nice."

"What's going on?" says Candy.

Kasabian hooks a thumb over his shoulder. There's a piece of paper glued to the door and chains on the lock. Candy shades her eyes so she can read the notice.

"It's from the county," she says. "It has something to do with the eminent domain, but I can't understand anything past that."

"Take a picture and send it to Julie," I say. "It's another message. More harassment from the White Lights."

Vincent studies the dents and scrapes along the Crown Vic's side.

"What happened to your car?" he says.

"A Nazi tried to run me down."

He looks at the locked door, then to me.

"I think the Nazis are winning."

"He's right," says Kasabian.

He gets up and clanks over to me.

"You can do something, right? Just break the door down."

"I wouldn't try," says Candy.

"Why?"

She holds up her phone.

"This is a Vigil app, kind of an augmented reality thing. It detects and displays traces of magic."

I look at the screen. Max Overdrive is rimmed in pulsing neon green.

"That's cool. Good for the Vigil."

"Fuck the Vigil," says Kasabian. "Can you break the door down?"

I shake my head.

"Whatever kind of hoodoo they're using, it looks powerful. If I knocked the door down the blowback would probably wreck the whole store."

"That's what someone wants," says Candy. "For you to break in. The county calls in the sheriff's department, and they seize the property out from under us."

"We get thrown out of the Chateau Marmont and now we can't even go home," says Kasabian. "Vincent and me, we don't have any clothes but what we're wearing. We were out getting food."

I haven't eaten all day. I take a donut out of the bag. Chocolate glaze. It's pretty good.

"They were probably waiting for you to leave."

"Screw your clothes," says Candy. "I don't have my laptop."

I go around to the side of the building.

"Hang on, all of you. We can't live here, but maybe I can get some of our things."

"How?" says Kasabian.

"Are you going to do that trick again?" says Vincent.

"I'm going to try."

"What trick?" says Candy.

"Something I learned the other night. It's a little like shadow walking, but it's going to wear off in a few days, so don't go asking me to steal the crown jewels."

"Where do you pick up this new talent?"

"At Piss Alley."

"Really. And what did you give them?"

"Just a bottle of Aqua Regia."

"It's going to cost you more than that, you know," she says.

"I know."

"If you can do something, then do it," says Kasabian. "I'm feeling a little exposed out here."

"Relax. I'll know in a minute if it works."

I step to the right and the hurricane hits me. The outside of the store glows the same neon green I saw on Candy's phone. I put out my hand and touch the side of the building. Nothing happens. No alarms and no counter-hoodoo. So far, so good. I press my weight against the wall. It bends a little, but holds. The hoodoo is powerful, even against sidestepping. I back up a back a few paces, then run at the wall. And end up on my ass, thrown back to where I started. I'm not going to try that twice.

I walk around to the front of the store. Candy, Kasabian,

and Vincent still stare at the place where I disappeared, moving so slowly they look like ants in amber.

The front of the store looks as solid as the side. There's only one place the hoodoo doesn't glow, over where the angel painted KILL. I touch the spot and don't feel any kind of resistance. It must not be ordinary paint, but something the angel brought with him from Heaven.

I put a finger on the side bar of the K and push. My hand goes right through the wall. Slipping my other hand into the K, I pull as hard as I can, and a small gap appears in the hoodoo. If I duck down and pull my shoulders in, I can just slip through the breach.

Inside, I go upstairs and grab some garbage bags from under the kitchen sink. Toss clothes from Candy's and my closet, then Kasabian and Vincent's room. Before I come down, I grab Candy's laptop and stuff it in our bag so the clothes will cushion it.

My one worry about being inside is that I won't be able to get out again. But there's a crack in the hoodoo at the point where I came in the front. I drag the K open again and shove the bags through, then climb out. Passersby on the street are just as frozen as Candy and the others. I grab the bags, go back to the side of the store, and step left.

The three of them stare at me and the bags.

"How did you do that?" says Candy. "You were only gone a second."

"It felt a lot longer than that. Time is funny when I'm backstage."

"Backstage?" Kasabian says.

"I'll tell you about it later."

I hand everyone a bag and we head for the car.

"Where are we going to go?" says Candy.

"Have a donut and give me a minute. I need to make some calls."

It takes twenty minutes, but on the fifth call I get hold of the right person who understands the subtle art of the bribe. Back in the car, I gun it and pull a U-turn, getting us back onto Hollywood Boulevard.

Kasabian leans up over the seats.

"I don't suppose you have a secret suite at the Beverly Wilshire?"

"Better," I say. "We're going back to the Beat Hotel."

He puts a metal hand to his face and slumps into the back.

"Somebody, kill me now."

If Kasabian wasn't such a drama queen he'd remember that things weren't so bad at the Beat Hotel. We stayed there a few weeks after an ill-behaved zombie horde overran L.A. and trashed Max Overdrive early last year.

The hotel is near the glamorous strip mall and parking lot by the corner of Hollywood Boulevard and Gower, and right across from the Museum of Death. The front of the hotel is painted a shade of green no one asks for, but just sort of happens. The place is a dump, but I love it. The rooms are reasonably sized and the decor is sort of a cross between seventies swinger and halfway house. The kitchens are the best rooms, explosions of reds, yellows, and glitter, like someone's bell-bottoms exploded on the way to a Ziggy Stardust concert.

Candy and I get settled into our room and Kasabian and Vincent settle into theirs. None of us are on the hotel's register because we don't know how long we're going to have to crash here and we don't want anyone knowing where we are. While I put away our clothes on the crooked wire hangers in the closet, Candy calls Julie back.

I can only hear one side of the conversation, but I can tell when Julie asks about the stakeout because Candy turns a little white and changes the subject.

"Max Overdrive was padlocked shut and the county put a spell on the place to keep people out. Be careful to take your work with you whenever you leave and back up everything else off-site."

There's a pause as Candy listens. Then she says, "I'll get you a report in the morning."

Another pause and she says, "What? Are you sure?"

She goes to the little kitchen and opens her laptop on the plastic table, types in a URL.

"Oh shit."

I sit down beside her.

"What's wrong?"

She turns the laptop so I can see the screen.

"Julie just told me about it."

It's a headline on the *New York Times* site. Two people have died. A young boy in Tulsa and an old woman in São Paulo.

It's starting.

The new Death is finally getting the hang of things. How soon will it be before he takes the thousands in comas all around the world? And then what does he want?

Candy cruises around the Web, looking at other sites to confirm the *Times*'s story. It's all over the place, the first story on every news site on the planet. Naturally, my favorites are the lunatics. Fundamentalist Christians claiming it's the Tribulation. Other, even crazier groups claiming that somehow it's the fault of gays and unwed mothers. Techno-hippies recalculating the Mayan calendar to prove that the 2012ers got it all wrong. Conspiracy freaks linking the situation to everything from the Kennedy assassination to 9/11 to lizardmen flying-saucer bases in the center of the earth. And then there's the hucksters, selling everything from magnetic prayer beads that cure your arthritis while mainlining your prayers to God to homeopathic cures for "the death virus released by global warming." There's even a black metal band in Norway that committed mass suicide so they can be the first group to play a concert together in Valhalla.

Humanity's best and brightest step up to the plate again. You've got to love 'em.

An hour later, Kasabian and Vincent come in. Kasabian is in a wrinkled tracksuit and Vincent is in an ancient Resident Evil T-shirt three sizes too big. Maybe I should have taken a little more time when I was grabbing clothes at Max Overdrive.

Kasabian drops onto the threadbare sofa and fires up the TV, scowling as he zips through the station listings.

He says, "I'd forgotten how much hotel on-demand movies suck. It's like we're stuck in a mall in Iowa still showing *Lethal Weapon 3*."

He wads up a Chinese-restaurant menu on the table and throws it at me.

"You couldn't have taken a few discs when you came out of the store?"

I toss the menu in the kitchen trash.

" 'Do not be surprised at the fiery trial when it comes upon you, but rejoice insofar as you share Christ's sufferings.' "

"What?" he says.

"It's from the Bible. I read it in one of those *Twenty Thousand Unbelievable Facts* books I found in Lucifer's toilet in Hell."

"Want to end the world's suffering? Give out HiDef boxes and decent surround sound systems."

"You're the thirteenth disciple, Kas."

"No, I'm Job. Reduced to an analog picture, one shitty speaker, and a cheap remote the size of a car battery."

"You're just spoiled," says Candy.

"Damn right. And proud of it. These primitives don't even letterbox their movies."

I shake my head.

"There's a special place in Hell for whoever invented pan and scan."

"I think it's nice here," says Vincent.

"So do I," says Candy, I think less because she likes the hotel and more out of solidarity with Vincent.

Kasabian continues to angrily flip through TV stations.

"Turn on CNN," I tell him.

He shoots me a look, but does it.

Vincent sits up when he sees the report on the dead boy and the old woman.

"I'm being replaced," he says. "I no longer have a purpose."

"Of course you do," says Candy. "Whatever that thing in the Tenebrae is, it's not Death. It's a monster."

"Monster or not, if it can transport the living to the land of the dead, then it's the true Death and I'm nothing."

"It's done it twice. That's not a great track record," I say. "What we need to do isn't get our feathers ruffled, but figure out a way to get you back home so you can kick that guy's ass."

From the kitchen, Candy says, "I think I found something."

I go in and sit down with her again.

"What is it?"

"Remember how I was looking for Sigrun under 'actresses' and 'singers'? Well, I started adding new search terms like 'fascist,' 'death,' and 'magic.' This is what came up."

She pulls up a picture of a beautiful young blond woman. I swear I've seen the picture somewhere before, but I can't place it.

Candy sees me trying to place her.

"Imagine her as a brunette," she says.

I look again.

"Are you kidding me?"

"I found a couple of more like it. They all look like her."

"When was the picture taken?"

"Sometime in the early twenties."

"Fuck me."

"Later. Should I call Julie?"

I go to the living room. Grab my coat and check for the Colt, the black blade, and na'at.

"Make the call if you want. I'm going out and I'm taking Vincent."

"Are you going to do something stupid?"

"Probably. Want to come with us?"

She has to think about it for a minute. Finally she gets up.

"I'm only going along to keep you from being too stupid."

"I'm never too stupid. I'm just stupid enough."

"That right there is the kind of stupid that worries me."

"What am I supposed to do?" says Kasabian.

I get the Chinese menu from the trash can.

"Order me some pork ribs in sauce and fried rice."

"And egg rolls," says Candy.

"I've never had Chinese food," says Vincent. "Order me anything."

Kasabian waves as we go out.

"Have a nice night. Fuck you all."

VINCENT SITS IN the back and Candy rides shotgun. I drive us out to a West Hollywood club called Death Rides a Horse. Back when John Wayne still walked the earth, it was an upscale cowboy bar. Now it's a cowboy bar, crossed with a rave and a fetish club, and populated mostly with dead people. If Death Rides a Horse was in a tourist brochure, it would say that the club is the biggest, baddest, and priciest vampire club in the city. And day and night, human groupies and suckers line up on the boulevard hoping to walk on the wild side and to taste a little bit of eternity.

I've been here before, so the bouncers all know me, which means they don't like me.

I nod to the guy working the door. He's bearded, balding, and a little pudgy for a vampire. That sometimes happens when you get bitten past a certain age. The ones who get bit young stay pretty forever, but get bitten past fifty and you're probably going to carry your middle-age gut and bad knees with you for the next billion years. Welcome to the glamorous world of bloodsuckers.

The doorman shakes his head when he sees me.

"Forget it, Stark. It's a private party."

"Not tonight."

I put my boot into his solar plexus and he flies through the front door like a chunky torpedo.

Candy grabs one of Vincent's arms and I grab the other. We shove and shoulder our way through the dancing, biting mob inside, all the way to the back, where there's a roped-off private table.

When a guard by the table tries to brace me, I break his jaw and toss him onto the dance floor.

The owner of Death Rides a Horse, the grande dame of all of So Cal's vampires, looks us over with her tombstone eyes.

"Not tonight, Stark. Whatever it is."

"Are you sure, Sigrun?"

Tykho's brows come down and she pulls back her lips, reflexively showing her fangs.

"What did you call me?"

I put my arm around Vincent's shoulder and pull him forward.

"Vincent, meet Tykho. Tykho, meet Vincent."

Vincent looks at me, then her.

"Tykho Mond?" he says.

"Who are you?" says Tykho.

"We met once," he says. "In Munich."

"I don't know you and I've never been to Munich."

"Yes, you have. It's where you escaped me."

She turns her dead eyes back to me.

"I know you'll cause a scene if I have you thrown out, so tell me what it is you want, Stark."

"Nothing. I just wanted you two kids to meet. Sigrun, Tykho Mond, whatever the hell your real name is—meet Vincent. Of course, Vincent is just what we call him around the store. What's your real name, Vincent?"

"Death," he says. And his voice carries the feeling of power and danger that I only heard from him once before.

"Very cute, Stark. Now go away or I'll make your beating part of tonight's entertainment."

Vincent grabs the velvet rope surrounding Tykho's table and starts babbling to her in German. Her eyes widen as he shouts.

One of Tykho's bodyguards grabs me, and I split open his face with the black blade. It starts healing immediately, but the pain leaves him rolling around on the floor for the duration. Vincent has crashed his way through the velvet rope and is practically climbing across the table to Tykho. They're still screaming at each other in German. Candy and I are dancing around with a dozen of the club's bouncers. Candy has already gone Jade. Her eyes, red pinpoints in black ice. Her hands are claws. She rips into the guards with her needle-sharp shark teeth. Hoping to settle things down, I manifest my Gladius, a flaming angelic sword, and hold it up high, where no one can miss it. Most of the bloodsuckers back off, but one of them grabs a fire axe and rushes me with it. Since it would be rude to kill him in his own club, I just cut off his arm. It goes spinning off across the room. The partiers all think it's part of the act, and toss the arm around the room like a beach ball at a concert.

I turn just in time to see Vincent grab Tykho's head so that they're eye to eye. Tykho begins to scream. She screams for a long time. Long enough that the crowd finally understands this isn't show biz. It's a panic attack. The lights still crawl the walls and strobe wildly, but the music stops.

"Everybody out!" Tykho screams. "Now!"

Security, even the one missing an arm, swoop into the crowd, shoving the bloodsucking jet-setters and immortal hipsters out onto the street, just like any bunch of punks and drunks getting the bum's rush. When the goons come for us, Tykho waves them off.

"Leave them. Wait here. I'll be in my office."

She holds up a finger for silence. I put out the Gladius.

"Not a word here," says Tykho. "Come with me."

She looks at Vincent, grabs my arm.

"And keep that creature away from me."

"Whatever you say, Sigrun. It's your house."

She walks away and we follow.

IF IT'S POSSIBLE for someone as pale as Tykho to turn white, that's just how she looks when we reach her office.

The door is plush leather on the inside, but made of heavy-gauge steel and secured with a keypad.

The room is Art Deco, polished wood in contrasting shades on the floor and walls forming elaborate patterns. The red leather chairs around the desk have rounded backs and arms, not quite shaped for human bodies. The wooden desk looks like something a Caesar would have, but constructed with graceful lines.

Tykho takes her seat behind the desk and the rest of us drop down into chairs around the room. Candy has her phone out, probably recording the conversation.

I say, "Tell us a story, Tykho."

She pours and downs a glass of thick vampire booze, blood with red wine and sometimes a little cocaine. She ignores us, running a thumb around her lips and sucking the last of the wine off.

When she's done she says, "First off, stop calling me 'Teye-ko' all the time. My name is French. It's pronounced 'Tee-ko.' Fucking Americans."

"But your last name, Mond, is German," says Vincent.

"Yes. My mother was French, my father German. Not that it matters."

"You're right. It doesn't matter. What matters is that you cheated me. You cheated Heaven and Hell. You aren't supposed to be in this world. Not for more than ninety years."

She smiles.

"And here you are, *Todesengel,* powerless to do anything about it. I think that means I won."

"I am not powerless. I'm not much of an angel these days, but I have an angel on my side."

He holds out a hand indicating me.

"He, I believe, can finish what I couldn't."

She flashes me a look.

"You wouldn't dare. Not on my own territory. You'd start a war."

I take out a Malediction, light it. Take a long drag and tap ash onto her million-dollar floor.

"Right now, *Tee-ko,* all I want is a story. We know you were part of the ritual that bound Death to this body. How are you connected to a bunch of supernatural skinheads and what do they want?"

Tykho looks off into space. She doesn't want to answer the question, so Candy jumps in.

"Why disguise yourself, Sigrun?" says Candy.

"Sure—you can start with that."

"Back in the day, a lot of us in the *völkisch* groups used noms de plume."

I say, "What does your nom mean?"

"It's the name of a Valkyrie."

"So you were a Nazi."

She shakes her head.

"I never cared about politics. I only cared about the real world that lay behind the veil we call the ordinary world."

"How did you cheat me? What did you do?" says Vincent. She looks through him like he's not there.

"I'm a medium. I was. I lost most of my power when I gave up a mortal life. There were several of us in the groups with the gift back then."

"What groups?" says Candy.

"The two in which I was involved were the Thule-Gesellschaft and the Vril Society. There were two main mediums in those days. Myself and Maria. Maria Orsic. We worked with other women who claimed to have the gift. I don't know if they were telling the truth, but what I do know is that one day I saw Death coming for me. So I did something about it."

"You went out and found yourself a vampire," I say.

She pours herself more wine.

"We knew many vampires in Munich. All the occult groups did. When I saw Death's shadow, I wasn't ready to go, so it was a simple matter to offer myself to a willing *vampir*."

Vincent stands up.

"You unbalanced the universe by what you did. The whole line of life and death was disrupted. Innocent people died before their time because of you."

"I don't care," she says. "I just knew that *I* wasn't ready to go."

"Tell us about the groups," says Candy. "What did Thule and Vril do?"

"They were merely occult study groups. Very esoteric stuff. You wouldn't be interested."

"I am if it has to do with the Murphy Ranch ritual," I say. "What if I say no?"

"Then I'll kill you. And you'll be gone and this little empire you've built will fall apart because—you're right—there will be a war. But not between shroud eaters and civilians. The bloodsucker factions will all want to take your place and all the world will have to do is sit back and let you rip each other apart. There won't be enough left of your kind to knock over a taco stand."

"You're more right than you probably know," she says. "All right—I joined the Thule-Gesellschaft in 1919, the Vril Society a year or two later."

"Tell us about Thule," says Candy.

"The Thule Society was simply an occult study group, looking into the origins of the Aryan race. The name Thule comes from a region far to the north. The top of the world.

The capital of ancient Hyperborea. Many in the society believed that this was the origin of the Aryan people."

Candy types furiously on her phone.

I say, "Bullshit. Thule was into all kinds of baleful magic. Demonology. Murder hexes. Possessions."

Candy studies her phone.

"The Thule Society had a lot of connections to the early Nazi Party. How does that square with an innocent study group?"

"Baleful magic never interested me. I was curious about history. When I joined the group it was believed that the Hyperborean race was a peaceful, enlightened people of advanced philosophy and technology. As for the other point, sadly some in the group became involved in right-wing politics. Like baleful magic, I found it all a bore."

"Let me get this straight," I say. "You weren't into magic. You weren't into politics. All you wanted to do was exercise your library card. Those must have been some short fucking meetings."

Tykho sips her wine, ignoring the comment.

"What is Vril?" says Candy.

Tykho sets down her glass.

"Members of Thule and Vril had known each other for some time. When a handful of Vril members joined Thule, we formed an inner circle for more serious and intense study."

"Studying what?"

Tykho takes her time getting a cigarette from a drawer, tapping it on the desk. I lean across and spark the smoke with Mason's lighter.

"Studying what?"

Tykho takes a puff and blows smoke my way. I'm used to Maledictions, so her puny smog barely registers.

"There was a theory that some catastrophe destroyed Hyperborea and that the ancient Aryans took refuge underground. They lost most of their culture and technology in the disaster, but in their caverns they developed tremendous mental powers."

"Like a 'May the Force be with you' kind of thing?"

"That's how an idiot would describe it. Vril was and is believed to be a kind of mental energy that can be directed to create or destroy, sicken or heal, with a thought."

"What does that have to do with the ritual that bound me to this body?" says Vincent.

"Let her talk," I say. "I want to hear the whole tall tale. So, you're trying to find a Nazi Obi-Wan Kenobi at the center of the earth. What next? How does this hook you up with the White Light Legion?"

"When the more insufferably right-wing members of the society turned our work increasingly into propaganda for the National Socialist German Workers' Party, some of us broke away and formed a smaller study group. But things became harder for organizations like ours to function as the Nazis came to power. Hitler was always paranoid about the influence of the occult and all so-called secret societies and began dissolving them."

"Wait," says Candy. "Did the people in your group know you're a vampire?"

"Of course," says Tykho. "That's why it was easy to form our own study group. Many believed that my vampiric powers were a crude example of Vril energy."

"What happened next?"

"Even before Hitler became chancellor, it was clear that the group could no longer function. Several high-ranking members were arrested and thrown in prison. By 1934, many of us were emigrating to France and Switzerland."

"Get to the White Lights," I say.

"The White Light Legion wouldn't exist for many years. Have you heard of William Dudley?"

"Yes," Candy says. "Julie gave me some background on him. He was a California fascist back in the twenties. He had some kind of supernatural experience that convinced him he had super mental powers."

"That sounds kind of like Vril," I say.

Tykho smiles, puffs her smoke.

"And that's why in 1935, when members of the society came to the States using forged French passports, they eventually came into contact with like-minded members of the Pelley's Silver Legion in New York. One of the Legion members they met was Edison Elijah McCarthy, the man who would go on to found the White Light Legion, based on the occult principles he learned at the feet of William Pelley."

"How did you end up in California?" says Candy.

"The group wanted to meet Pelley and to get as far away from Europe and the stink of the continent as possible. So they went west."

I say, "But you weren't with them, were you?"

"No. They didn't know that I'd made it to America. When the SA began attacking Lurkers right along with Jews and communists, I left the group and eventually Germany, wanting nothing to do with either ever again."

"Where were you?"

"I was already in L.A. I ran all the way across America for the same reason they did. I'd been taking elocution lessons, trying to lose my accent and erase my past. I kept my distance from the local German expatriate community, but when I heard about a powerful occult group coming west, I knew who it was."

"When did you meet them again?" I say.

She taps her cigarette ash into her wineglass. I keep dropping mine on the floor.

"It was in the summer of 1935. Shuna, another medium from back in the Thule-Gesellschaft days, came with them. She sensed me nearby in the city. Back then, I had enough of my gift left that I sensed it when she found me, so I came out of hiding and contacted her."

"What happened to them? Are they how you brought the vampire groups together?"

Tykho laughs.

"Hell no. I was done with their fascist nonsense. No, I met Shuna and the rest at the home of one of the Silver Legion's inner circle."

"Was it in Laurel Canyon?" I say.

She cocks her head.

"How did you guess? It's a hell of a power spot. Of course, none of the other members of the group knew I was coming. I was to be a great surprise. A present from Shuna to the group. I suppose I *was* a surprise in the end. I came through an upstairs window instead of the door and slaughtered every single one of them."

I crush out my cigarette on the bottom of my boot and

drop it with the ashes, pull out Vincent's knife, and bury it deep in the top of Tykho's desk.

"Did you use this?"

She looks at it like she's checking out an antique butter dish.

"Not that one in particular, but there was a knife. I mostly used my hands and teeth. That's always more fun, isn't it, dear?"

She looks at Candy. Candy doesn't take the bait.

"What kind of knife is that?" Candy says.

"You haven't figured it out?" Tykho says. "I'm disappointed."

She plucks the knife from her desktop and removes a smaller one from her boot. Setting the big knife on its side, she scrapes away some of the tarry grit on the grip. Underneath is an eagle and an SS thunderbolt.

"It's an SS officer's dagger," she says, "fitted with a witch's athame blade, to create a National Socialist sacred object. Himmler loved these things. You could get a hell of a price for it on eBay."

I snatch the knife out of her hand and point it at her.

"You cut up Vincent with this one and I bet you had another for the second body. Who the hell was it and why did you do it?"

Tykho pushes off from the desk and spins around in her office chair like a kid.

"Isn't it clear by now? Who was the one man still alive with even more will and occult desire than William Pelley?"

She stops the chair and looks at us.

"And who now was old enough to fear death just like I did

years ago in Munich? It was the head of the White Lights, Edison Elijah McCarthy. That's who I killed at Murphy Ranch. McCarthy is the new Death."

Vincent stares at her. I can't read his expression. Is it shock and anger, wonder and loss, maybe a mix of all of them? What I know is if I don't say something, he'll go on staring at Tykho forever.

So I say, "Here's what I don't understand. You say you don't like these Nazi fucks, or the White Lights, or any other occult bullshit artists, and yet there you were. Out in the sticks with a knife in your hand helping with the ceremony like Suzie Sauerkraut. Why would you do that?"

She looks straight at Vincent.

"What lady doesn't want Death to owe her a favor?"

Vincent slumps in his chair, his hands clasped together, letting his hands drop between his knees.

"The fascist movement had some power in L.A. in the thirties and early forties, but we're long past that," says Candy. "How does the White Light Legion keep going?"

But I know the answer. "Like any other crooks, right, Tykho? Protection. Loans. Easy cash crimes. We know from Wonderland Avenue that they shake down people and kill the ones who can't pay. But with this occult angle there has to be more to it than that."

"There is," she says. "A lot more."

"Want to let us in on some of it?"

"Why should I? You bring me this husk and call him Death? Yes, he was a powerful angel, but look at him now. Why should I say anything more than I've already said?"

"Because I'm going to kill the new Death, and when I

do, Vincent is getting his old job back. Maybe Edison Elijah McFuckall owes you, but Vincent doesn't. You might be a vampire now, but even vampires die, and Vincent can wait a long time. Plan all kinds of special surprises for you."

Tykho spins around once in her chair.

"Fine. Why not? If it will get you out of here for good."

"No promises. Tell us something charming."

"How about wild-blue-yonder contracts?"

"I know all about those. I've been offered one more than once."

"But do you know where they come from?"

"Where?"

"Right here."

She throws out her arms.

"Sunny California. You see, a group of necromancers developed the original method after World War One, when death was on everyone's mind. They sold a few, just enough to finance their own studies and research into deeper, darker arts. Later, other, more ambitious magicians, seeing the potential of the contracts, began working with the necromancers as brokers. This being L.A., they went to where the money and power lay. Hollywood. They started selling them to celebrities, who brought in other celebrities. And the money rolled in. Who do you think runs the blue-yonder racket now?"

"The White Light Legion," says Candy.

Tykho nods.

"Through some of the more open-minded talent agencies around town."

"Like Evermore Creatives?" I say.

"They're one of the biggest," says Tykho. "There's one more thing I'll tell you and then you have to go."

"Make it something good."

"The people you say you saw killed on Wonderland, and others who've died in the canyon, what do you think happens to them?"

"The nonfamous blue-yonders? They become flunkies for the big-name ghosts. Valets and butlers."

"Not as many as you might think," Tykho says. "Think bigger. There's no profit in maid service for ghosts."

I look at Candy and Vincent, but get nothing from them.

"I'm sick of smelling your shit wine. It reminds me of Hell and I don't need that tonight. What else do the White Lights do with the dead?"

"Entertainment. Spectacle," she says. "In a show-business town, the big money is in show business. What can ordinary people, with no singing or acting talent, no name and/or status do when they're dead?"

"Ask me a lot of stupid questions?"

Tykho leans across the desk and speaks quietly.

"Did you hear of an online phenomenon years ago on the Web? It was called bum fights."

Candy says, "Sure. Frat-boy assholes would pay homeless people to fight. They'd video it and put it online and charge to watch it."

"Well, imagine what dead souls can do to each other in a dog pit," Tykho says. "It's quite a thing to see."

I say, "Where? I want to see for myself. How do we get in?"

She opens a drawer and tosses an envelope on the desk.

"Here are some passes. They were supposed to be a raffle

prize tonight, but you spoiled the party, so you might as well take them."

I take the envelope and put it in my pocket with Vincent's knife.

For a minute, I think very hard about killing Tykho. Candy puts a hand on mine.

"Let's go home. Tykho is more useful with her head on her shoulders," she says.

"Yes. I really am."

I have to give it to Candy for keeping her cool. I was two seconds away from putting my Gladius through Tykho's throat. But like she said, the new Death owes her a favor. How would killing her now hurt her?

I say, "Is there anything else you haven't told us?"

"Lots," says Tykho. "But that's all you get now. You ruined my party and it will take days cleaning and ass-kissing to fix it. Go now and play save the world like you always do. But when you go to the fights and see the slaughter, remember that those people *asked* to be there. They volunteered their souls."

"I doubt that," I say. "No one is going to buy into something like that."

"You've been to Hell. What horrors do you think ordinary people will endure on Earth so that they don't have to go into the Abyss? Go see the fights. Educate yourself."

We leave Tykho's office. Candy and I have our guns out, but none of the guards bother us. Vincent doesn't say a word. Not on the drive back to the Beat Hotel or when we drop him off at his room.

"Good night," Candy says.

He just stares at her with the thousand-yard stare of someone who's been through Hell and knows that whatever happens, he's never going home again.

CANDY CALLS JULIE and tells her what we found out at Tykho's club, without going into details of how we got it. I think. I can only hear Candy's side of the conversation, so I guess it depends on what questions Julie asks. Not much I can do about it either way. Candy tells her we're going to check out the bum fights and asks if she wants to come with us. We could use the backup. While they're talking, Candy looks at me and shakes her head. The last thing she says to Julie is "Okay. We'll call when we get back. Be careful."

I'm drinking coffee spiked with Aqua Regia.

"Be careful about what?"

"She says there was a car parked across the street all day, and when she left the office, it followed her."

I hand Candy a nonspiked coffee.

"Should we go after her?"

"She says she's got it under control. She took a couple of turns to lose the tail, then got behind the car. Now she's following them."

"Good for her. I hope she doesn't do anything stupid."

"So says the man who went into Death Rides a Horse like it was Omaha Beach. I might be able to cover you on what happened outside of Evermore Creatives, but the club? That's going to be all over town."

"It was a lot of noise, but no one got hurt."

"You cut a guy's arm off."

"He's a vampire. It'll grow back. And we got a lot of useful information. Plus these." I hold up the tickets.

"I agree. All I'm saying is that Julie might question the approach."

"I'll send Tykho roses and a pint of O negative. She'll get over it."

Candy blows on her coffee, sips it.

"Do you think it's a good idea for us to use those fight tickets without backup?"

"Probably. But that's half the fun."

"Seriously, what are we going to do?"

"Vidocq and Allegra looked bored last time I saw them. Maybe they'd like a night out."

"Goody. I'll call them."

"Tell Vidocq to bring some potions. I don't know what the crowd is going to be like tonight. We might need to leave quickly."

"No arm cutting, please."

"I'm on my best behavior."

"Be better than best. Be super best."

"I'm going to need another drink for that."


I PICK ALLEGRA and Vidocq up and we head out to the address on the tickets.

Turns out the space is in the old Warehouse District, which L.A. now insists on calling the Art District. I've never seen any art this way, but it makes perfect sense that the city would shove whatever artists it has left out to the land of hauling companies, cold-storage facilities, and train depots.

The address is a two-story warehouse with several out-buildings off Sixth Street, across the L.A. River, near the via-duct on South Mission Road. There are railroad tracks on one side and a wasteland of faceless storage companies and trucks on the other. If there are any artists around, they're keeping a low profile—like subterranean.

The warehouse has a large parking lot, but cars spill out all up and down the length of Mission Road. The cars are a mix of old numbers like the Crown Vic and spit-and-polished Caddys and Porsches. There's even a Rolls-Royce Silver Cloud, being babysat by a chauffeur with a bulge under his jacket like he's got a grenade launcher in there.

Outside the warehouse is a mix of methed-up bikers and street punks with L.A.'s young, beautiful, and stupidly wealthy. The kind of people who open Fair Trade cupcake shops and art galleries with names like Paradigm. There are Sub Rosas in both the biker and artisanal asshole groups. I keep my head down and don't meet anyone's eye. Last thing I want tonight is to be recognized before I even get inside.

My instincts were right about one thing: it was smart to leave my weapons in the trunk of the Crown Vic. Everyone going into the warehouse gets a pat-down. A guy with tattoos on his face and a graying jarhead crew cut frisks Vidocq. When he hears something clink, he opens the Frenchman's coat. Sewn inside are dozens of small pockets for the potions he always carries.

"What the hell are those?" says the crew cut.

"I have allergies," Vidocq says.

Crew Cut gives him a look, grabs a bottle at random, and sniffs it. He makes a face like a baboon just shit in his mouth.

"What is that stuff?" he says.

"Cobra bile," says Vidocq. "Very good for digestion."

The crew cut gives him back the bottle and waves him through, saying, "You want to use that stuff tonight, you take it outside."

"Of course," Vidocq says.

Crew Cut has a good time giving Candy and Allegra a thorough going-over. They deal with his bullshit without a word, but it's obvious they'd like to pull out the guy's guts with a boathook. I keep my eyes away from his while he gives me the once-over. The fucker reminds me of someone, but I can't quite place him. On the wall above the door is the White Light Legion sigil. The crew cut isn't in uniform, but he has the Legion's tattoo on his right arm. It makes sense. Hold the fights at the Legion's compound. Let them work security and keep all the cash in-house. They'll skim from the profits, but letting them handle the muscle work leaves Evermore Creatives to deal with the talent and the public.

It's stiflingly hot inside. I don't think the warehouse's old air-conditioning unit was meant to deal with a crowd this size. We're on the top floor. There's a walkway all around that looks down onto a large ring in the center. Down there, close to the ring action, the crowd is really packed in. There are good seats, up front, close to the ring, and cheaper ones behind, separated from each other by a tall barbed-wire fence. Uniformed Legion members patrol the area. They keep the peace just by staring people down.

They're packed two deep against the guardrails up here. It's hard to see anything, so we go around the walkway to check if we can get a better view. There's a bar in the corner where the well-heeled smart set can rub elbows with colorful ruffians and share a glass of watered-down Jack. It's a real meeting of the minds in here. The UN if it was run by sadistic morons.

I get next to Vidocq and say, "What do you think?"

"I don't think they're observing the fire codes," he says.

"Anything else? Come on. You've been around and seen some shit."

"We had places like this in Paris in the old days. There were dog fights. Men would fight. Even women. I once saw an exhibition where a disreputable sideshow impresario set his charges against one another. Men with no legs fighting men with no arms. Bearded ladies and . . . what's the word? Pinheads? It seemed like a vision from Hell."

"Did you do anything about it? Tell the cops?"

"Who do you think kept the peace during the exhibitions?"

Allegra stays close to Vidocq, her arms wrapped around one of his. When we find an open spot along the rail, I let Candy get in front.

There are three ghosts in the ring downstairs. Two of them are working over a third. I recognize the duo act from some old books. Manny King and Joey Franco. A couple of enforcers back when Bugsy Siegel was still big man on campus in the forties. They're going at the other guy with heavy wrenches and baseball bats. I suppose it could be worse. One side of the ring is like a murder wholesale house. It's full of heavy tools like you'd find in a garage—chains, crowbars, and even some torches. Kitchen knives and cleavers in another area. Old weapons like something from the Crusades. Swords, morningstars, bell hooks behind them. With all the blood in the ring, it's hard to remember that all three of these guys are already dead. Yeah, ghosts have a kind of ectoplasmic blood. You cut them just right and they gush like anyone alive. They can even die. Blip out of existence like they were never even here.

It seems like the fight has been going on for a while. The crowd is getting restless. The guy on the floor won't die and the two bully boys can't or won't finish him. The loser is flat on his stomach. Manny, with the pipe wrench, stands over the guy's back with the weapon over his head, going for a kill shot. Before he makes him move, the guy on the floor finds a small cleaver and swings it back into Manny's leg. Manny lets go of the wrench and falls over. Now he's the one screaming. Joey laughs at him and kicks the guy on the floor over on his back.

It's Dash, Maria the witch's lost ghost. His face is a pulpy mess, but I still recognize him. So does Candy. She grabs my hand, pulls it down to her side so that no one will see her reacting.

I still dream about the arena Downtown, though not as much as I used to. But I don't go for more than a day or two without recovering some tasty bit of memory in which I'm either slaughtering or being slaughtered. Unfortunately, it's usually the second thing. I don't twitch and punch the air like I used to, but I remember what every blow felt like. That kind of thing never leaves you. But I made it out alive and sane, more or less.

I don't give Dash such good odds.

The kid has shed more than a few pints of ectoplasm all

over the ring. His eyes are almost swollen shut and one of his legs is bent like something that would look better on a flamingo. He punches and grabs at Joey's legs as he stands above him. But the blows are marshmallows. Joey lets him punch himself out. When Dash gets so tired he can't lift his arms anymore, he drops them. He doesn't move or make a sound. He's a man who's seen the future and can't wait for it to come. Joey doesn't make him wait long.

He lifts the bat over his head and brings it down hard. It only takes one shot from the Louisville Slugger to crack Dash's skull. They crowd goes wild. They can't get enough of this shit. I'm not sure even Hellions enjoyed watching us beat each other bloody as much as these assholes.

Joey raises the bloody bat in the ring—King Arthur pulling the sword out of some poor slob's brains. He does a turn while Manny struggles to his feet. Him stumbling around gets big laughs, but the big cheers go to Dash as his spirit goes transparent and fades away, like an image on a dying TV set. A lot of cash changes hands when he's gone. Joey helps Manny to his feet. There are necromantic physicians backstage who'll patch him up so he can do it all again tonight or tomorrow, whenever Evermore Creatives and the White Lights want to see those particular monkeys dance again.

I won't be telling Maria the witch about any of this. She doesn't seem the type to take it well. Honesty can be very overrated, while a good lie can give someone peace of mind when there isn't a goddamn thing they can do about the awful shit at the center of the truth.

"What did you bring us to, Stark?" says Allegra.

"I told you what it was."

"Yes, but I didn't think it would be so . . . this."

"Neither did I. How do you feel about being in the field again?"

"I'd be more comfortable going after Drifters, but I guess beggars can't be choosers."

"No, they can't. Did I tell you that Julie's building has a downstairs no one is using?"

She looks at me.

"Really? Do you think she'd rent it out?"

"It wouldn't be too bad an idea, a PI firm with a clinic right downstairs to take care of paper cuts and stubbed toes. Maybe Candy can ask her for you."

"Why Candy?"

"Because she'll listen to me," says Candy. "If Stark recommends you, she'll think you're running bootleg organs or a cut-rate asylum."

"Thanks. I'd appreciate it."

"I'll ask her when we report in."

Down in the ring, a ghost cleanup crew is swabbing the ectoplasm off the floor and putting the weapons back. I recognize a game-show host and a one-hit-wonder singer in the cleanup crew. I guess even show-biz ghosts can end up on the broom if enough people forget about them. They should have read the fine print.

When the ring is clean again, a pretty ring girl in a bikini made of less material than a cocktail napkin comes out. She waves to the crowd, blows kisses. They love her. She must be a regular at the scene, Miss Texas Chain Saw Massacre, beauty queen of the cannibal set. Soon she waves the crowd to quiet down and someone hands her a microphone. When she speaks it's with a full-on Texas twang.

"I want to thank y'all for coming out tonight. And, as

always, we'd like to thank the White Light Legion for their hospitality and lovely facilities."

That gets a polite round of applause and whistles.

"And, of course, Evermore Creatives for the super-exciting ring action. Remember their motto, 'Death is no reason to lie down and die.'"

That gets big laughs. The beauty queen eats it up.

"Anyone who wants information on wild-blue-yonder contracts, there are some lovely young ladies circulating through the crowd with brochures and preregistration forms."

She manages to split the word *forms* into two syllables.

"And now we have an announcement from the Evermore itself, Mr. Lucius Burgess."

Burgess gets some serious noise. The crowd knows the guy. He must be the Burgess David Moore talked about before he took a runner. The beauty queen hands him the mic.

"Thank you all for coming. Good evening to our first-timers and to our longtime fans. A few of you veterans for our friendly neighborhood fight club have probably noticed a lot of old faces coming through the ring lately. I want to thank you for putting up with that. With no new dead to bring into the stable, I know there have been a lot of reruns lately. But I have good news. Many of you have heard about the boy in Tulsa and the woman in Brazil who finally shuffled off this mortal coil? Well, you'll be happy to know that six more people have passed over today alone. And we expect that number to increase every day from now on, so very soon we should see a lot of new talent coming through the door. Thanks again for indulging us during these reruns, and here's to the good times to come."

Between the screaming and brain-dead yahoos stamping their idiot feet, the walkway sways under us a little.

Vidocq says something to me, but I can't hear it over the shouting. He points to the other side of the walkway. I look, and who's there but Brigitte Bardo and an older guy with a suit sharp enough to cut your throat. The older guy chatters away. Brigitte smiles and nods at his patter, but the smiles look forced and tense. She glances away from him for a moment and our eyes lock. Without missing a beat she turns back to the guy in the suit. When he shuts up long enough to catch his breath, Brigitte leans over and says something him, then kisses him on the cheek. He scurries away like a rat to the bar. I push through the crowd, trying to get to her before Hugo Boss comes back with their drinks.

She turns when she sees me.

"What are you doing here?" she says.

"Why the fuck are *you* here?"

"I hate this place, but I can't talk now."

She looks past me in the direction her date went, then across the way to nod to Candy and the others.

"We're going to Bamboo House of Dolls. Meet us there later," I say.

"I can't just leave."

"Tell Daddy Warbucks you have a toothache, whatever, just get there."

"I'll try. Now you have to go."

I shove my way back into the crowd and go all the way around the walkway to hook back up with the others.

"Everyone seen enough?" I say.

"Much too much," says Vidocq. Candy and Allegra agree.

We leave the same way we came. I keep my head down on the way out.

Cars come and go from the parking lot and the sides of the road. When I see the chauffeur with the gun under his jacket, I whisper some Hellion hoodoo. A trash can nearby explodes in flames. When he runs over to investigate, I key the Rolls-Royce.

CANDY CALLS JULIE in the car. She makes it to Bamboo House an hour after we do. The four of us have been doing more drinking than talking.

The funny thing about the ghost killing was that you couldn't smell anything until the fight was over. Then we all got a stinging whiff of ozone as Dash's spectral body dissolved into nothing. The smells of the arena downtown were intense and maybe that's why I can't get the warehouse scene out of my head. It feels like a scene from Hell, not a recent memory but one that's been sitting in the back of my brain so that the details start to fray. Like the lack of smell. It makes the fight feel more real, like I'm down there, part of it. With each drink, the sensation lets up a little. But I know I won't be sleeping much tonight.

"I followed the car out to a warehouse off Sixth. There was a party or some kind of gathering going on inside. I got photos of some of the guests. Not a savory crowd," Julie says.

"That's hysterical. That's a goddamn Hallmark card," I say. "We were inside. We probably just missed each other."

"Too bad. I wish I'd been able to get in there."

"You're better off using your imagination. You don't need that shit in your head for the rest of your life."

Julie quietly grunts, not convinced.

Candy says, "It's the White Light Legion's headquarters. There was a show going on. A kind of fight club, only it wasn't people fighting. It was ghosts."

"Those were the tickets Tykho gave you?"

"Yes."

Julie takes a sip of her martini. On the jukebox, Esquivel is doing "Limehouse Blues."

"Did it occur to you that if Tykho is mixed up with these people, she might have called ahead and had God knows what waiting for you? And your friends."

Candy looks at me, then at Allegra and Vidocq.

"No. It didn't occur to us."

"Tykho is smart and doesn't let things slide," I say. "If she didn't sell us out, it was for a reason."

"What?" says Julie.

"Maybe she's as sick of the White Lights as I am. What are they into? Money crimes to keep their white-power playpen stocked. Maybe they're into Tykho for something. Like protection money? Aiming us at them might have been her way of trying to get them off her back."

"The Legion does have a reputation for extortion. Tell me what else you saw and heard."

We run down the whole thing. The crowd. The fight. The bets. Mr. Burgess talking about new deaths and promising fresh blood soon.

Julie turns her glass around with the tips of her fingers.

"Burgess was telling the truth. There are reports coming in of deaths all over the world. It was up well over a hundred by the time I got here. It's causing as much chaos in Washington as when the deaths stopped. People at the top still think it's all terrorism related. The craziness is even hitting the world stock markets."

"Wall Street doesn't like a mess," says Allegra.

"People in power never do. They feel insecure. It reminds them of their own mortality," Vidocq says.

Julie sighs.

"People exhaust me sometimes."

I finish the Aqua Regia and wave my glass at Carlos for another round. He gives me a thumbs-up.

"Does Evermore Creatives have overseas offices?" I say.

"Yes," Julie says. "Europe. Russia. Asia. What's your point?"

"There could be fight clubs all over the world. Tykho says this thing has been going on since World War One. Get out your calculators and count how many disappearances, John Does, Black Dahlias, and gangster hits there have been since then. That just covers the D-list ghosts. What about the ones like Dash tonight? Now throw in every high-profile disappearance and murder. Look at a guy like Bugsy Siegel. Technically, he was killed because of how he handled the Mob's money in Vegas. But what happened to him afterward? He'd be a headline act. Tickets would go for a fortune if he was part of the show. Or Johnny Stomp. He and Lana Turner's daughter could replay his murder every night. How many blue-yonder contracts have been sold since the war? Between crooks like Eddie Nash, who set up the original Wonderland murders, and psychos like Manson and the Hillside Strangler, you've got a ghost factory ready-made for pricks like Mr. Burgess."

"Consider also that seeing what happens to errant citizens

would help keep discipline among the White Light Legion's members," says Vidocq.

"You think that's why they chose Townsend for the ritual? He wanted out of the group, so they used him for a sacrifice?" Julie says.

"It makes sense."

"I wonder if his spirit is in their murder stable?"

"Wouldn't surprise me," I say. "He was probably the last guy on the planet to die before Vincent lost his job."

"I keep coming back to one thing," Julie says. "What does the White Light Legion want with Death? Yes, he's a powerful entity and you could use him as your own personal killer, but that seems like a lot of work when they were killing people so efficiently before."

Candy says, "There's something missing. Something we haven't figured out yet."

Allegra stares at her drink, then blurts out, "I thought I'd seen enough blood and violence at the clinic, but this is on a whole new scale."

Everyone looks at her. She shrugs and looks at Julie.

"Stark told me about your new office."

"Yes, it's coming together slowly, but nicely."

"I heard you have a downstairs you're not using."

Julie nods.

"For now. I might rent it out to help with the mortgage."

"Why not rent it to a new clinic? I could give you a good rate on any medical services you need."

Allegra gives Julie her brightest smile.

"Allegra would be a great choice," says Candy so that I don't say anything and maybe jinx the deal.

Candy continues. "She's worked on humans and Lurkers. She can fix anything."

Julie gets up to get another drink.

"I'll give it serious consideration," she says.

"Thank you," says Allegra.

As Julie walks to the bar, Brigitte comes in. Julie sees her and points her in the direction of our table.

Brigitte comes over and sits down, still decked out in the evening dress she had on at the fights.

"Good evening for the second time," she says.

No one says anything. I lean across the table at her.

"What the fuck were you doing tonight? Have you been to that slaughterhouse before?"

She shakes her head.

"No. And I hope to never go again."

"Who was that guy and how did he talk you into going?"

"Someone from the old country. A producer acquaintance wanted me to show him the sights. It sounded like fun. I haven't been home in a year. I don't often get to speak my own language."

"How did you end up at the fight?" says Candy.

"He knew about them. He'd been to something like it in Vienna."

"Did he tell you what you were going to see?" I say.

"No."

"Why didn't you just leave when you saw what was going on?"

"He's a financier of some kind. A powerful man with powerful friends. He could make trouble for me with my visa if I didn't stay with him."

"He said that? He flat-out threatened you?"

"He didn't even say it as a threat. It was a game to him. He wanted me to sleep with him, but I left. You have to draw a line somewhere, isn't that right?"

"Yes," says Allegra.

Candy says, "Damn straight."

"Give me his name and hotel and I'll have him on the first plane out of town tomorrow," I say.

"Don't bother," says Brigitte. "There was another reason he took me to see the fight."

"What?"

"Do you remember Simon Ritchie? The friend who helped me come to America last year?"

"Yeah, you were supposed to be in his Lucifer movie."

"Yes. That's him. He did something else for me. He said that all of his wealthy friends had done it. That it was common practice in Los Angeles."

"Shit. Please don't tell me."

She wipes a finger under her nose, stifling tears.

"Yes. I have a wild-blue-yonder contract. That man tonight. He wanted to show me where I'd end up if I didn't let him do what he wanted to me."

"Okay, then. He's dead. Tell me where he is. I'll go right now."

"I left him at the fight."

Candy squeezes my hand, trying to calm me down. It doesn't work.

"Are you going somewhere, Stark?" says Julie, coming back. She heard my tone and her question has the ring of a warning. I stay put.

"I was thinking about it," I say.

She sets a glass of Aqua Regia in front of me and sips a new martini.

"Don't," Julie says. "Have your drink and stay with us for a while."

I take a gulp of my drink.

"Sure. Why not?"

We drink in silence for a couple of minutes, then Vidocq says, "You should let him go. There are things that can only be settled a certain way."

"I have a better idea of what to do about the Legion," says Julie.

"We weren't really talking about the White Lights, but what is your idea?"

"If not the case, what were you talking about?"

"A tourist. I'm going to show him Hollywood Forever cemetery."

If Julie gets what I mean, she doesn't show it.

"That can wait," she says. "I have an idea of what to do about the White Lights and the fight club."

"What?"

"I owe friends in the Vigil a favor. Shutting down the Legion and getting proof about what they and Burgess have been doing would be quite a feather in their cap."

"A raid? Tell them I'll go along."

Julie laughs.

"Yes, they'd love that. No. They're done with you."

"They've seen what I can do. They need me."

"They don't need trouble, and that's what you always bring with you. Forget about it."

"I promise to play nice."

"It's not going to happen."

"If you say so, boss."

She starts to say something, but gives it up.

"Do you really think there's a way out of my contract?" says Brigitte.

"There's a way out of anything," I say. "Let us handle it."

I look at Julie.

"When do you think the Vigil can move?"

"They don't like to waste time. If there's another fight tomorrow night, they'll probably go then."

"Okay."

"Stark, I'm telling you to stay away from this."

"I understand. I won't interfere with the Vigil or the raid."

"Thank you."

"Who wants another drink?"

"You haven't finished that one," says Allegra.

I swallow the rest. Odds are I can drink these lightweights under the table, go back to the club, and peel the skin off one sharp-dressed dead man.


IT TAKES NINETY minutes, but people start fading, one by one. Brigitte is the first to go, looking exhausted after her lousy evening. Allegra and Vidocq are next. Arms around each other, they head outside to find a cab. Julie is the last holdout. I don't think she wants to leave because she knows I'm going to do something she won't approve of. But even she succumbs after half a dozen martinis. Candy and I pour her into a taxi and walk home.

I put Candy to bed, go the kitchen, and drink some coffee. By the second cup, I'm wide-awake. No one figured it out, not even Candy, but once it was my turn to pick up a round of drinks, I'd gotten Carlos to water down my Aqua Regia. My hands are steady enough to do surgery. Maybe that's what I'll do to Brigitte's pal. A heart bypass. Or his head staked out on a parking meter.

I drive back out to the warehouse, park, and try to blend into the crowd milling around outside. I can't just stroll back in through the front door. Crew Cut already took our tickets. So I go around the back of the warehouse like I'm looking for somewhere to piss.

It's like old times for a second. Around back, I head straight for a shadow. I can't walk through it, but it's a good place to launch from. I step right and enter the hurricane. Then back around front, I squeeze past the shit heels with their tickets, past the crew cut, and back into the crowd, where no one is going to notice me as I step left.

And I'm back in the steam room heat and humidity of the fight club. The crowd whoops and cheers as some stupid son of a bitch pummels another stupid son of a bitch. The sounds of meat slamming into meat is old and familiar, but I don't bother looking at the fight. There's nothing I can do about it, and considering what I'm here for, it's an unnecessary distraction.

Keeping to the edges of the place, I make a circuit of the second floor walkway where I first saw Brigitte and her friend, but I don't see him. Downstairs, I wade into the tightly packed crowd. No way a guy in a sharp suit like his would allow himself to be steam-pressed by these troglodytes, so I push my way up front to the barbed-wire fence separating the good seats from the cheap. I spend several minutes up there, scanning the crowd. The bettors. The touts. A body hits the floor. I look at the fight long enough to see an old MTV reality-show contestant with a machete bearing down on a D-list game-show host swinging a motorcycle chain. Neither is long dead, but they're both already forgotten enough to end up as ghost chum.

I give the killing floor one more look. Forget it. If Brigitte's friend is with the crowd past the barbed wire, I can't see him.

Back upstairs, I take one more look around. Nothing. I head for the bar in the corner and order a whiskey. The bartender pours something brown from a plastic bottle and I taste it. It's quite memorable. Like someone melted a G.I. Joe into a bottle of rubbing alcohol. I drink half to be polite and toss the rest in a trash can held together with "Caution" tape.

Just past the bar is a curtained room. A White Light in uniform takes money from men and women and lets them inside one or two at a time.

I head over and get in line. When I make it to the front, I fake it.

"This the special show?"

The White Light grunts either yes or no. Who can tell?

"I lost my ticket."

He shakes his head.

"Doesn't matter. It's an extra fifty to get in."

I reach in my pocket for some of Julie's advance money, peel off three twenties. The White Light gives me change and stamps the back of my right hand with the number eighty-eight. I've seen it before. It's not a head count. It's skinhead shorthand for *Heil Hitler*. I nod and push through the curtain.

A White Light on the other side opens a heavy door. When I get through, he closes it and the whooping from the front of the club disappears. The room is soundproofed.

It's as silent as a library back here, and dark. The only lights are focused on whatever is happening down below us. The air is thick with cigarette and weed smoke. Moans here and there as couples play grab ass and guys on their own hold a joint in one hand and the crotch of their jeans in the other. A couple move away, deeper into the dark, and I slip up to where they were standing. The scene below is awful, but it isn't surprising.

There's a couple on a dais, both ghosts. The man is tied to a chair bolted to the floor and the woman is strung up on a set of bare metal box springs. The man is bleeding ectoplasm onto the floor. One of his hands is missing. Two assholes, also ghosts, in crude homemade devil masks are behind him. Devil one is sawing off the guy's other hand while devil two is browning the guy's first hand on a hibachi. I recognize these fucking freaks. I bet they've been having fun in town a long time.

Back in the early 1900s, way before Bugsy and his bunch rolled into town, one of the first L.A. crime syndicates was run by the Matranga family, big shots in the New Orleans Mob. When word got back to the Big Easy about the sweet pickings in sunny Southern California, it brought out more gangsters and even a few semilegit business types. It also attracted some of Louisiana's more colorful swamp crazies, including Les Enfants du Diable. Take a shot of backwoods Catholicism, a twisted, survivalist version of Santeria, add a dash of good old-fashioned inbred devil worship, and you get

Les Enfants. Their cannibalism was a sacrament. Even their shit was sacred, considered the temporary resting point before their victims' souls eventually joined them in Hell. I guess it's easier hiding a lifetime's worth of shit in a swamp, but it's harder in a city, even one as rural as turn-of-the-century L.A. The smell gave them away and street justice did the rest. But here the clan is, star of their own variety spectacular.

It makes sense that lowlifes like the White Lights would end up running snuff shows. Bread and circuses keep the money flowing, but when the crowd gets tired of the slap and tickle show in the front room, some of them are going to look for a rougher scene. And the White Lights wouldn't consider any of the victims in their cannibal melodrama clean enough, pure enough, lily white enough, or simply strong enough to care about, so why not make some coin?

None of what's happening onstage particularly shocks me. There's isn't much left regular people can do to make me think less of them. Plus, I've seen similar scenes Downtown. What I can't get out of my head is an image of Cherry Moon. I know she's back safe at Lollipop Dolls. She never had a blue-yonder contract, maybe the one smart thing she ever did in her ridiculous life. The thing is, I know there's someone like her here. Just as dumb and desperate and afraid of death as she was. Someone as pretty. Someone who'd put on a hell of a show for these blood-hungry corpse fuckers. I don't want to kill them. I want to slash their hamstrings and set the place on fire. Let them be the meat on Les Enfants' grill. But none of that is why I'm here, and if Julie is right, I won't have to lift a pinkie because the Vigil is going to ride in on white stallions and carry all these theater lovers off to Jesus jail, hallelujah.

Now that my eyes have adjusted to the dark room, I look around again. But I get the feeling Brigitte's friend is long gone. I'm wasting my time and I don't even know if I should tell Julie about the snuff since she didn't want me coming back here. Still, I'll have to chance it. Who knows what the Vigil is into these days? They might need prodding to go after the White Lights. This should do it.

Before I split, I take one last quick look at the scene. Over in the corner of the room, smoking a spliff and looking slightly bored, is the crew-cut doorman. I was so busy trying not to be seen when I first came in that I never got a real look at him. He has tattoos all over his face, including curving devil horns where his eyebrows should be. What did Vincent say about one of the men at the ritual? That he had horns. And a number in a circle.

I edge around the room, moving to where I can see the other side of Crew Cut's face. The crowd gets restless as the action onstage builds. It's a good thing humans can't smell ghost smoke, or the stink of cooking human flesh would have this bunch knee-deep in their own puke by now.

As the crowd creeps in closer to the action, so does the crew cut. As he edges in close enough, I can see it. A circle of letters that reads PROPERTY OF SAN QUENTIN. Inside the circle is a number fourteen, skinhead code for "We must secure the existence of our people and the future of white children."

The crew cut is so wrapped up in the action onstage that he doesn't feel me come up behind him until I have the Colt against his back. He starts to say something, but I pull him back into the dark and sidestep.

Here's the funny thing. I have no idea if I can sidestep

with another person. For all I know, I'm going to kill this cheesesteak instantly or leave half of him back in the regular world. Lucky for me, Hermann Göring comes along just fine. The hurricane kind of surprises him. He doesn't fight or try to run away. He falls right down on his ass and stays there, looking around like a lost dog instead of getting up. Some people just don't like surprise parties. I pull him to his feet and shove him into the storm. It feels like a couple of hundred years trudging from the club back to the Crown Vic. My Nazi new best friend can't wrap his brain around what's happening. He keeps reaching out to touch the barely moving people around us. I have to swat his hand like a kid trying to steal cookies before dinner.

Finally, we make it to the car. I step left, bringing us back into the regular world, and slam my knee into the crew cut's lower spine. He collapses beautifully, falling headfirst into the Crown Vic's spacious trunk. I slam the top down and get behind the wheel. He doesn't make a sound the whole drive.

BEFORE RETURNING TO the Beat Hotel, I stop at a bodega and buy a roll of duct tape.

The asshole is waiting for me when I open the trunk, but being an asshole myself, I'm waiting for him.

When the trunk is half open, he kicks out with both boots, aiming for my head. He's fast, I'll give him that. So fast he doesn't see the black blade in my hand. I step back as he kicks and stick the knife through the sole of his right boot until he can feel it, but not so far it cripples him. He howls and thrashes around like a wolf on acid, so I pop him on the chin to bring his temperature down. While he's lying there stunned, I wrap duct tape around his head, from nose to scalp. Ball up my fist and make like I'm going to punch him again, and he doesn't flinch, so I know he's blindfolded enough to take inside. While he's still loopy, I flip him over and tape his wrists together behind his back. Before finally hauling his ass out of the trunk, I wrap more tape around his mouth. Give him a couple of slaps and all he can do is *mmmm* and *rrrrr* through the gag. One more loop of tape goes around the foot I stabbed so he won't bleed all over all the hotel's theoretically clean carpets. I wrap Crew Cut in my coat, toss him over my shoulder like a sack of Nazi potatoes, and head inside to our room fast. Even at the Beat Hotel, which is used to some weird sights, people might think twice about me carrying a body inside.

Vincent and Kasabian are in their room, so I head straight in and dump Crew Cut on the floor. Candy wanders out of the kitchen. When she sees the lump on the floor, she mouths a silent *What the fuck?*

I put a finger to my lips to let her know to stay quiet. Lean in and say, "He was with Tykho at the Murphy Ranch ritual. You go Jade and I'll ask questions."

She grins and does it, her eyes going black, her teeth going to points.

I rip Himmler's gag off, taking some skin off with it. He blurts "Shit!" and tries to get up. I grab him and plant his ass in a chair.

"You're dead," he says. "Do you fucking know who I am? My people, they're going to find you, cut you up, and feed your soul to those crazy French cannibals."

"You're really that important?" I say.

He smiles big and wide. One of his canine teeth is gold.

"I'm core, man. Inner circle. You made a big mistake."

"You're one of the White Light's magic men? Use your Vril power and Pelley superbrain tricks to deal with the dead?"

He nods.

"That's right, fuck heel. I know the teachings. I've seen the sights. I'm fucking Gandalf, motherfucker. What are you? Some little bitch thinks he's going to get a ransom?"

"Well, Gandalf, just how good is your kung fu if you can get snatched by a little bitch?"

"Fuck you. I'm going to kill you myself."

"We'll get back to that later. Right now tell me more about your magical, mystical tricks. You a necromancer? You Sub Rosa?"

"Hell no, I'm not one of those Sub Rosa faggots. And I'm not any goddamn Dead Head. I'm a lightning rod. A strange attractor. The mystic loves my shiny ass."

"I get it. You're a channel. Like a human wand. A necromancer or whoever can use you to concentrate their hoodoo in one spot."

He leans back a little.

"How come you know so much about it?" he says.

"I'm one of those Sub Rosa faggots."

"Bullshit. Sub Rosa would have hexed my ass on the spot, not thrown me in the trunk like his bitch laundry."

Candy goes back to human.

"Stop saying that," she says.

"Who the fuck is that?" says Crew Cut, craning his head around trying to zero in on her voice.

"Never mind," Candy yells. "Stop saying it."

"Saying what?"

I say, "I think she wants you to stop saying 'bitch' all the time."

"Fuck you," says Crew Cut. "Fuck both you bitches. I'll say 'bitch' anytime I want, bitch."

Candy goes Jade again. Curls one of her claws under the edge of Crew Cut's blindfold and rips it off.

He blinks a couple of times before getting Candy in focus.

"Fuck me. What the fuck are you?" he says.

"Say 'bitch' again," I say. "I double dog dare you."

Crew Cut looks at me and back to Candy. Her lips are pulled back from her razor teeth.

"Shit," he says.

"Good. Now that that's settled, let's get to work. You're not a Dead Head, but you work with them for the Legion. You ever work with a vampire?"

"What do you fucking care . . . ?"

He's about to say "bitch" again, but catches himself.

"What was the necromancer's name?"

Crew Cut squirms around on the chair.

"I don't know. What do I care about Dead Heads and vampires? I don't know nothing about them."

"Really? Because I hear a necromancer, a vampire, and a dumb fuck who looks a lot like you had a party in the woods not too long ago."

He shakes his head.

"Don't know anything about that."

"You sure?"

He plants his feet on the floor and looks at me.

"Why don't you untie me and we'll work this out like men, okay?"

"Two minutes ago I was your bitch. What's changed?"

He struggles with the tape on his wrists long enough to figure out it's not coming off.

Candy moves around behind him and runs her claws up his arms, his neck, and over his face. He freezes while she plays with him.

"You know a place called Murphy Ranch?" I say.

"Nope," says Crew Cut.

Candy flicks a claw against his cheek. Draws blood.

"Fuck," he says, and tries to shake her hands off his shoulders.

I go over and whisper to Candy. She turns human again and goes next door.

"I'm tired," I say. "And you're boring. I've dealt with shit sacks like you my whole life. Tinhorn tough guys afraid their daddy has a bigger dick than them, so you prove you're a man by taking your bullshit out on the world. Now, your particular flavor of bullshit is this white-power game. First you invent an enemy, which gives you and your little friends an excuse to get together and stomp people. Then, because you wrapped it all up in a political bow, you're not a bunch of zero-future losers, you're big-balled soldiers saving the Fatherland from the godless hordes. Am I getting close, Chuck? Am I in the ballpark?"

"You don't know shit about shit, bitch," he says, drawing out the last syllable nice and long so I'm sure not to miss it.

Candy comes back in just as he's running out of steam. She's not alone.

"Okay, so we've established that you and some of your friends used your Wonder Twins Vril powers to help out a Dead Head ritual."

Crew Cut laughs.

"We haven't established shit, motherfucker."

"What was the ritual for?"

"Don't know. Wasn't there."

"You and your friends have a real hard-on for death magic, don't you?"

He shrugs.

"The warehouse shows?" he says. "Pays more than meth and it's easier than whores. Dead people aren't whining all the time about rough trade and who came where."

"Did you know any dead people in particular?"

"Why should I? I told you. It's business."

I go behind him and pull Candy's companion over into the light. Vincent has no idea what's going on. He looks as blank as a person can be and remain upright. I shove him in front of Crew Cut.

"Do you remember this dead guy?"

When Crew Cut lays eyes on Vincent, I'm a contented man. The look on his face is like Christmas all over again. He kicks out with the foot I stabbed. I pull Vincent out of the way and slap Crew Cut's injured foot. He curses and tries to get up, but Candy holds him in the chair.

"Keep that fuck away from me," Crew Cut yells.

"So, you do know him."

"No. Goddammit. I don't. Just . . . fucking keep him back."

"Is it because you're afraid of Eric Townsend or because you're afraid of what's inside him?"

"Fuck you. I don't know shit about shit."

I get the SS dagger out of my coat and put it in Vincent's hand.

"Cut him," I say.

"What? I can't do that," says Vincent.

"He's one of the assholes who ripped your heart out. He owes you."

Vincent looks at the knife, at me, then shakes his head.

"I can't."

I grab the dagger out of his hand.

"If you won't take his heart, I will."

I slice the front of Crew Cut's shirt. He pushes back on his heels, but Candy wraps her arms around him and holds him tight.

I hold the tip of the blade to his chest, just hard enough to draw a bead of blood. The way he looks at me, the dope thinks I might really do it.

"What are you doing?" he says.

"Any last words, Gandalf?"

Crew Cut looks past me at Vincent.

He says, "How is he up and walking around?"

"How is who?" I say. "Tell me his name."

"Death," says Crew Cut. "How is he alive?"

"What does it matter? He is. We know you were at the Murphy Ranch ritual with Tykho and at least one necromancer—"

"Three," he says. "It took three to get it right."

"Get what right?"

"To bind him in that body."

"What happened to the other body you killed? Where is it?"

Crew Cut's eyes move to meet mine.

"Somewhere safe. A place of reverence."

"Hell, with you geniuses, that could be a mayonnaise jar next to the chunk-style Skippy."

"What does it matter where his body lies in state? He's the real Death now. Not this prick. Yesterday's garbage."

I lean on the dagger a little to remind him to be polite.

"We know Edison Elijah McCarthy has replaced Death. I guess he didn't read the handbook before he went over. It's taking him a while to figure out the job."

"But he's doing it," says Crew Cut. "More people are dying all the time. Soon it's going to be a tsunami. All the mongrels and mud people, faggots and assholes like you."

"Is that it? You went to all this trouble for a hit man? You could have gone to any of the old Sub Rosa families still practicing baleful magic and cut a deal with them."

"I told you," he says. "We're men. White human men. We don't cut deals with pixies and fairies."

"Owning Death, you can reach out and kill anyone you like anywhere in the world."

"Goddamn right," he says.

"You won't even need blue-yonder contracts after that, will you? Death's the one who takes the souls away. He can hand the choice ones over to you."

Crew Cut smiles.

"Maybe. Let me go and I'll tell you."

"I'd rather cut you up."

He laughs.

"Go ahead, asshole. Do it. I dare you. Edison'll reach down and pluck your bitch soul like a daisy and blow you away."

"I've been dead before."

"Not like this you haven't."

Candy reaches over Crew Cut and uses a fingernail to draw a Valentine around the swastika tattoo over his heart.

He can't take his eyes off her hand as she works, like she's tattooing him with a blowtorch.

"None of this'll matter come tomorrow anyway," he says, trying to sound like feral women sketch on him every day. "A few hours and it's all over. We'll own Death, the whole soul trade, and there's nothing anyone can do about it."

"What's tomorrow?" I say.

"That's when you suck my dick and pray for mercy."

He's so fucking dumb I want to hurt him, but that's even dumber. I can't kill this idiot no matter how much of my time he wastes because he knows something I don't.

"It's a new moon," says Candy.

She's holding Crew Cut with one hand and thumbing her phone with the other. Holds it up to show me an app with the phases of the moon. Tomorrow is going to be a dark night.

"That's it, isn't it?" I say. "So, what happens tomorrow?"

"Nothing. That's the beauty of it. That's why I'm Gandalf and you're an ant. Ain't nothing is going to stop what's coming. The sun rises tomorrow. The sun sets. And when it comes up the next day, we own the whole fucking afterlife. Who dies and when you die is up to us. How much will you pay for that kind of protection? How much you willing to pay for Death to even let your soul pass on to Heaven or Hell and not end up doing shows for us? How much?"

I look at Candy.

"We've got what we need."

I look at Crew Cut.

"You know, as soon as we stop your plan, your friends are going to wonder what happened and they're going to look at you. The one who disappeared and came back slapped around and cut up. It won't take them long to figure out that you're the one who talked. Ask me nicely and I'll kill you quick before your friends deliver you to a pissed-off McCarthy."

For a couple of seconds I think he actually considers it. He's smart enough to know I'm right about him getting blamed, but stupid enough to think that when the time comes, he'll be able to talk his way out of it.

"I'm not asking you anything," he says.

I get out the duct tape, blindfold and gag him again.

"Let's take a ride," I say.

CANDY HELPS ME manhandle him back into the trunk. We get in the car and drive north on the 101 to the 5 and over the steep five-mile grade of the Grapevine. Along a dark stretch of road between nowhere and nothing, we dump Crew Cut into a ditch. Maybe a trucker will find him. Maybe the coyotes. Who cares which?

It's an hour back to L.A. Plenty of time to smoke and think.

"Is this all there is?"

"Isn't it enough?" says Candy.

"I mean, for these White Light knuckleheads to come up with a plan like this. To put all the pieces together. They had help from someone. I swear, there's something we're missing."

"Worry about that later, Sherlock. We have to figure out what's happening tomorrow night."

"I know who can help us."

"Who are we kidnapping next?"

"No one. I'm talking about civilized people."

Candy doesn't say anything for a while.

"What am I suppose to tell Julie about tonight? I want to be like her, but . . ."

"But you keep ending up more like me?"

"Yeah."

"Maybe that's more my fault than yours. I keep bringing you into these things."

"And I keep letting you. I'm a big girl. I make my own choices."

"It won't always be like this."

"How do you know it won't be like this again? How many knives are you carrying these days? Plus a gun and a na'at."

"This case is kind of a big deal. Later, we'll probably do a lot of divorces and guard celebrities when they go kale shopping."

"Just drive. I need to think."

In the end, Candy stays home. No need for her to get caught up in more trouble if things go sideways for me.

I drive to West Hollywood and dump the car, walking the last few blocks to Death Rides a Horse.

The usual eager, desperate crowd is waiting outside, dressed to the nines, tens, and elevens.

When the doorman sees me he takes a step back. I hold up my hands to show him I'm in friendly mode. He looks me over, not quite convinced. He's a slight guy in a dark suit and white shirt. Hasidic *payot* curls hang down near his ears.

"What do you want, Stark?" he says.

"Tell Tykho I'm here, and for the last time."

He stares for a second more, then says something into his

walkie. Touches his earpiece like he's having trouble hearing over the street noise. He nods.

"Wait here," he says.

While I wait, he checks IDs and looks over the crowd, deciding who's worthy enough to get inside the club. A couple of minutes go by, long enough that I'm rethinking my peace and love approach to the situation. I don't want to ambush Tykho by sidestepping into her office, but I'm not standing here all night while apple-cheeked tourists and drunk bachelorettes get past the velvet rope.

About the time I'm thinking of getting physical, the doorman waves me over.

"Go in," he says. "But wait for your escort."

The music hits me when I open the door, the bass like a Munchkin beating on my solar plexus with a rolling pin. A phalanx of bruisers rolls up before I can take two steps inside. Big beefy boys with necks as big as manhole covers. Do vampires need some kind of fang extensions to drain a few drops from guys like this? Before I can ask, they surround me and hustle me through the packed crowd like a troop of bulldozers plowing through a field of bunnies.

When we reach Tykho's office, the lead bulldozer opens her door and the rest shove me through. The door closes behind me. Tykho is behind her desk, making a big show of not looking up. She's signing papers with a gold Montblanc pen.

She says, "I'm only seeing you because you said it was for the last time. Can I hold you to that?"

"If you tell me the truth."

"About what?"

"What happens at the new moon?"

She stops writing, puts down the pen, and holds a hand out to a chair for me to sit down. I do it and pull the chair up close to her desk.

She thinks for a minute and says, "Do you know a book called *Germania*? It's sometimes called the *Codex Aesinas*."

"Never heard of it."

Tykho puts her hands flat on the desk.

"On the surface it's nothing. Just a brief Roman account of the history and customs of ancient Germanic tribes they encountered while they were busy trying to rule the world."

"What's the big deal about it?"

"There have been a few slightly differing translations of *Germania* over the years. We had several in the Thule group. Himmler was mad for the thing. He, and some in his circle, saw the book as final proof of the superiority of a pure German Aryan race."

"Like you fucking Nazis needed more propaganda."

"I told you. I wasn't political."

"Yeah. You said. What does a fascist tourist brochure have to do with what went down at Murphy Ranch?"

"I told you there were several translations, but the thing is, none of them was complete."

"What was missing?"

She picks up the Montblanc and doodles something on a pad. I can't quite see it.

"Why, the chapter on ancient Aryan magic, of course. That's why Himmler wanted any of the few surviving complete manuscripts. He sent a whole squad of his pretty SS boys to a villa in Italy for it. He missed that one, but the Ahnenerbe eventually found another."

"What kind of hoodoo are we talking about?"

"How to become the Lord of Death."

Now we're getting somewhere.

"If those *übermensches* running around the woods had that kind of power, how is it the Romans kicked their asses?"

"The Romans didn't conquer all the tribes, but your basic point is right. They never did make proper use of the power."

"Why not?"

She pushes the pad across the table to me. It's covered with alchemical symbols and runes. I wish I'd brought Vidocq along.

"Because back then they couldn't put all the pieces together," says Tykho. "The magic described in the book called for certain kinds of metals and potions, things they couldn't produce at the right purity, so they could never complete the death ceremony."

"And maybe they needed a nonpolitical vampire for the ceremony?"

"Maybe. The point is that it took the believers two thousand years to create everything the ritual required."

"But they haven't finished it, have they?"

"That's right. Until the new Death reigns through a new moon, the ritual isn't complete."

"How do we stop them?"

She takes the pad and sits back in her chair.

"Why should I tell you? You keep showing up uninvited. What's in it for me if I tell you anything?"

I lean my elbows on her desk.

"Let me ask you something: Why did you help me the last time I was here? Why did you hand us those tickets? You wanted me pissed off, didn't you? You want us to take down the White Lights. What do they have on you?"

"I don't like people knowing about my past. It makes them feel like they have power over me and they're prone to take liberties."

"What kind?"

"Some things are private, even from you."

"I know about your past now. You coming after me next?"

She makes a face at that.

"Please. Everyone knows you're insane. Tell them I'm Sigrun. Tell them I'm Catherine the Great or Wonder Woman. No one is going to believe you."

She has a point.

"How do I stop the ritual?"

"Don't be so dense, Stark. When we cut Townsend open, what did we take?"

"His heart."

"Right. Restore the body. Put the heart back where it belongs."

"And that will kill McCarthy?"

"No. But he'll be weak enough that he can be destroyed. Of course, you'll have to go to the Tenebrae to do it."

"How the hell do I get to the Tenebrae? And more important, how do I get back?"

She picks up her pen.

"I've given you enough. You're on your own from here. Run along, little angel."

"Where's the heart?"

"In a canopic jar in the *Gruppenführer*'s office in the Legion's warehouse. It's on a high shelf, next to lovely framed photo of Adolf and Eva and some other party nonsense."

"Where's the office?"

"You found the special room upstairs?"

"Unfortunately."

"Straight through there."

"Just one more thing: Is Burgess in on this?"

"I have no idea."

"What about Wormwood?"

"Wormwood Investments? It wouldn't surprise me. They have their fingers in a lot of interesting pies."

"What does a bank have to do with Death?"

"Good-bye, Stark. You know the way out."

Tykho's door doesn't budge when I push it. I have to bang on it a couple of times before it swings open. The bruisers crowd the way out, looking over one another's shoulders, checking on their boss, and keeping an eye on me. As soon as Tykho nods the all clear to them, they do their bulldozer thing again, and shove me out the front door without slowing down. I almost trip on the pavement, Charlie Chaplin with a gun. The meat puppets in line get a nice chuckle out of that.

The guy with *payot* is still working the door. For a second I'm tempted to go over and tell him who his boss is. But she was right. I might as well say she's Hello Kitty. He'd believe me about as much.

I get in the Crown Vic and head home.


MY BRAIN SPINS in circles as I drive.

Bugsy Siegel first came to California in '33, the same year

Hitler became chancellor of Germany and William Pelley formed the Silver Legion. When Bugsy settled in Beverly Hills in '37 he looked up his old pal, movie star George Raft, best known for his roles as gangsters and tough guys. Both men were sharp dressers and there were a lot of arguments around town over whether Bugsy was copying George or it was the other way around.

Hollywood has always loved a good crook and Bugsy palled around with big-name actors, studio heads, and millionaires. Any L.A. luminary who wanted to get a whiff of the wild side. The closest thing America had left to Wild West outlaws, Jesse James or Cole Younger.

Here's the funny thing: Bugsy was a hood and a creep, but he hated Nazis. In '38, the lovely Countess Dorothy Dendice Taylor DiFrasso took him to Europe and introduced him to Göring and Goebbels. Bugsy couldn't fucking stand them. He even offered to put a hit out on them, but that went nowhere fast.

Which brings me all the way back to Murphy Ranch. If he'd won the war, would Hitler have loved that concrete Eagle's Nest? And would Hollywood have embraced Europe's wild man the way they did Bugsy? Der Führer was a vegetarian who loved animals, so two points in his favor right there. And he had a hard-on for art. He was also a painter, though a lousy one. Of course, that sure never stopped any Hollywood celebrities who liked to dabble in watercolors from getting shows in tony L.A. galleries looking to make a splash off the star's name. With the right connections, would Hitler have eventually hung next to Hollywood art-world luminaries like Sylvester Stallone and Stevie Nicks?

Part of me feels very far from home. I'm sure as hell a long way from where this case started. From Vincent finding me at Bamboo House of Dolls, I've skated from Laurel Canyon to the world of old-school mobsters right into a necromancer dead end. All the way to Himmler's book club and séance rooms in twenties Munich, then back further to pelt-wearing Teutonic horsemen, all the way to the Thule group's Hyperborea. But the thing is, throughout this weird ramble, I never really left Hollywood. Once I make it through all the craziness, where do I track the source of and solution to this whole mess? To a fucking playhouse off Sixth Street where entrepreneurial Nazi shitheads are staging nightly pageants, like Andy Hardy and Betsy Booth doing a musical in a barn.

This might be the end of the world as we know it, but it's still show biz.

SAMAEL IS WAITING for me outside the Beat Hotel eating a Pink's chili dog. If anyone ever wondered if he used to be the Devil, all they'd have to do is watch him down that dog. The sloppiest food in the known universe, and he devours it without dropping so much as a molecule of grease or chili on his suit. That's hoodoo of the highest order. When he's done, he wads up the foil wrapper and tosses it into the gutter. I point to it as I come over.

"You're messing up my city. Would you dirty up Hell like that?"

"Of course," he says. "I invented littering. Before I was thrown out, the streets of Heaven were strewn with ambrosia containers and empty six-packs of divine mineral water."

"You must have been an annoying kid."

"No worse than you."

"I'm not a litterbug."

"No. You just run around shanghaiing innocent citizens."

"There aren't any innocent citizens in L.A., especially the ones I grab."

He smiles.

"It's always good to be back, Jimmy. Seen any good movies lately? Anything to recommend?"

"A few, though the thing is, we're kind of out of the movie business at the moment. The county padlocked the store."

"Why don't you unpadlock it?"

I take out a Malediction, offer him one. He waves me off. I light mine.

"Because it might bring down more trouble than we need right now, what with this strange case I'm helping with."

"Look at you, a responsible civilian. Restrained and refined. The Jimmy I knew a year ago would have torn the doors off City Hall and driven a police car through the mayor's office."

"You have no idea how strange this feels, thinking things through before I do them. But I'm sort of responsible for other people these days. Don't want them getting hit with the shit I kick up."

"I know what you mean," he says. "Working as father's right-hand man, it gives me pause. Father wants to make peace with the angels denying humans entry into Heaven, while I think the whole thing could be solved by cutting off a few heads."

I take a pull on the cigarette.

"When did things get so complicated?"

"They didn't. We did. Men like us, with intemperate natures, we're not supposed to consider our actions. We just *do* and clean up the mess later."

"In other words, thinking hurts."

"You hit the nail on the head."

We stroll down Hollywood Boulevard, past the Museum of Death.

"I've never been in," he says. "Is it worth it?"

"You'd love it. It's like a mortuary textbook crossed with an old Hollywood scandal sheet."

"Sold. The next time you're taking friends, count me in."

"Sure thing. I guess things aren't going so well up in Heaven."

"Not especially."

We walked in silence for a bit. Finally, I say, "I've learned a few things about the new Death. Who he is. What he wants."

"Will any of it kill him?"

"Maybe. Someone gave me a clue. I think I can trust her, but I'm not a hundred percent sure."

"These aren't one hundred percent times. Go with your gut, I say."

"Might as well. My brain isn't helping."

"How is your guest doing?"

"It's hard to tell with him. He went through his pain pills pretty fast and he wants more, but I don't think it's for the pain."

"Give an angel a body and they go mad, each and every one."

I nod.

"Hey, you know anything about breaking a blue-yonder contract?"

He shakes his head.

"It can't be done. They're as binding as mine were."

"So, back in the day you wouldn't ever give someone a break? Not even a friend?"

"Well," he says.

We walk a little farther, past empty clubs and car lots.

"There are exceptions to everything," he says.

"So, it could be done."

"You'd have to make a deal with Death and I have the feeling this particular one isn't in a dealing mood."

"Shit."

"Yes."

"Someone told me that if I could get to the Tenebrae in the next twenty-four hours, I might be able to take out McCarthy."

"Who?"

"The new Death."

"What an evocative name for Death. 'What happened to old Frank?' 'It looks like he's McCarthyed.'"

"Hilarious. I keep saying you should do stand-up."

"And I keep telling you that you're the comedian, not me."

"I'm not feeling so funny right now. I can't shadow-walk anymore, so I don't know how to get to the Tenebrae."

Samael looks at me.

"Is that what's bothering you?"

He reaches into his pocket and drops a small, gnarled red thing in my hand.

"What the hell is this?"

"Do you remember the story of Persephone?" he says.

"Not really."

"I forgot. You're illiterate. Just eat the pomegranate seed and it will take you to the Tenebrae."

"You walk around with a pomegranate seed in your pocket?"

"It brings back old times."

I put it in my coat.

"Thanks. Just one more thing."

"You want to know how you're getting back."

"That would be swell."

"Getting you back is trickier than sending you. Do you still have the key to the Room of Thirteen Doors in your chest?"

"I can't use the Room."

"No, but if you can make it back to Tenebrae Station, I'm sure the key will let me bring you the rest of the way home."

"Sure? You've done something like this before, right?"

"Of course."

"You're lying."

"I'm being reassuring."

I stop and head back toward the hotel. It takes him a second to catch up.

I say, "You're not supposed to admit it when you're telling someone a comforting lie. You're the Prince of Lies. You should know these things."

"I can bring you back with one hand tied behind my back. We can even stop for ice cream if you're a good boy."

"That's better."

"Well," he says. "I should be getting back. I'll look for you tomorrow in the Tenebrae."

"I'll wear a rose in my lapel so you know it's me."

A Lincoln limo pulls up and a chauffeur opens the door for him.

"A rose? Funny, I always pictured you as a prickly-pear man."

"I'm whatever will get me rescued."

He waves and steps into the car. It takes off, disappears around the corner. The worst thing about knowing I might be stuck forever in the land of the dead tomorrow? Now I want a hot dog, but Pink's is all the way across town and I'm goddamn exhausted. I head inside. Maybe we'll order pizza for a last meal.

CANDY IS WATCHING *Girls und Panzer* and eating tamales when I come in.

"Where did you get those?"

"I went to Bamboo House of Dolls. Carlos gave me a plate."

"Did you leave any for me?"

"You don't get to eat yet. Julie wants you to call her."

"Am I in trouble?"

"When aren't you?"

"Did you tell her the car was dented?"

"I did."

"And?"

"She wasn't happy, but at least you hadn't totaled it."

I go into the kitchen, where the rest of the tamales are on the table, wrapped in foil. The hotel keeps garage-sale-grade plates and forks in the cupboards. I grab a plate, pile on a couple of tamales, and go back to the living room. Candy has turned down the sound on the show. When I set my plate on the table, Candy pushes it away.

"Bad dog. No food for you until you call Julie."

"I'll call her after."

"Your tamales are getting colder by the second."

"I hate having a job."

"You had a job before."

"Running Max Overdrive wasn't the same. I was boss."

"Really? Tell that to Kasabian."

"I'd rather argue with Julie."

"Now would be a perfect time."

I get out my phone and hit Julie's number.

She picks up on the second ring. She's been waiting.

"Stark, Candy called and told me that you have new information about the Legion and their plans. I'm not even going to ask how you found it out because I don't imagine I want to know."

"Probably not. But I have something else."

Julie sighs.

"No. It's okay," I say. "We just talked. Tykho told me where Vincent's heart is hidden. If we get it, I think we can put him back the way he was."

"Where is it?"

"At the White Lights warehouse."

"Good. The Vigil raid is set for tomorrow night. They'll take possession and keep it safe."

"You want to give the heart to the feds? We need it right away. Before dawn, or Vincent is fucked."

"I'll speak to my contacts. We'll get it in time."

"And you trust the fucking feds to just hand it over? How many forms do we need to get notarized?"

"We'll make it work. Where's the heart?"

"They're going to screw this up, and if you complain they'll make it your fault and there goes your agency."

"Stark, where is the heart?"

One room over, Vincent is watching TV with Kasabian. If things go wrong, that's all he's ever going to do until Townsend's body wears out and he floats off to where McCarthy is waiting for him.

"Beneath the fight ring on the main floor. Buried under the floorboards."

"Good. I'll pass that along."

"I want to go in with the raid."

"You know that's not possible. I want you staking out the necromancers working with Tamerlan. Something you should have been doing all along, I might add."

"More busywork."

"Not if you do it right. We still want to know which necromancers helped at the Murphy Ranch ritual."

"The Vigil will get that from those clowns ten minutes after they arrest them."

"Candy has the list of necromancers you're to check out."

I look at Candy and she holds up a sheet torn from the hotel memo pad.

"Remember our deal," says Julie.

"I know I owe you, but you're playing this all wrong."

"It's the way it has to be."

"Okay, then. Is there anything else?"

"Stay home. Eat something. Go to bed and get an early start in the morning. We'll meet with the Vigil after the raid and go from there."

"Sure. Good night."

"Good night."

I put down the phone and Candy turns up the sound on the TV. I reach across her and retrieve my tamales.

"What does she have you doing tomorrow?"

"Same as you," says Candy. "Babysitting Dead Heads. We divvied the list in half."

"You know she's making a big mistake."

"Maybe. But I don't want to go to jail, so she calls the shots."

"She wouldn't rat you out."

"I don't think she would either, but I just want to be an employee with a job who does what she's told for a while, you know?"

"Yeah. I know."

"So, do what you're told. We can talk on the phone. If you're lucky, I'll get bored and sext you."

"Just as long as you don't mind Kasabian getting a copy. He can hack my phone."

"I'm the only one with a laptop. He'll have to make do with hotel spanktrovision."

I take a bite of my tamale. It's great. I used to mooch off Carlos's kitchen all the time. I might have to start again.

I say, "Life is funny, isn't it? Look at us. We're private dicks."

"It's not where I thought I'd end up. But it's not bad."

"We're going to have to do something about getting the store back."

"I kind of like the place, but we can't live here forever," she says.

"We can't afford it."

"Yeah."

We eat our tamales and Candy brings the rest out of the kitchen. We gnaw on a couple more while Candy turns on the news. Crew Cut was right. More people are dying all over the world. It's still just a few at a time, but more than a hundred have checked out in the last twenty-four hours. Vincent needs to get back in the saddle.

I look at Candy.

"That thing you said the other day, about missing women. I meant it when I said I'm not getting in the way of anyone you want to be with."

"Not now. I'm busy eating."

"Okay. I just wanted you to know."

She sits for a minute.

"I miss the Jades sometimes. Rinko came by with a message that one of the Ommahs is coming to town. I should go see her. And the rest of the girls."

"The Ommahs are kind of your den mothers, right? The matriarchs?"

"That's right."

"Going sounds like a good idea."

"You think so?"

"Absolutely."

"I'll think about it."

"You do that."

Candy turns back to the other channel. *Cowboy Bebop* is on. She hums along with the closing theme music, sounding almost happy. Like maybe she hadn't hooked up with a complete idiot after all.

IN THE MORNING, she leaves first. Julie loaned Candy her Prius and she wants to get to her Dead Head's place before opening, but without rushing. No scratches on the boss's wheels.

I'm supposed to keep an eye on a guy named Sabbath Wakefield. He runs his necromancer office out of a shop on Venice Beach. He doesn't have a necromancer sign in the front window or anything. He's set up as a fortune-teller. Cards. Palm reading. Crap for the tourist trade. It says in the file Julie texted me that he makes sure the local authorities know it's all in good fun, and he greases the palms of the local cops so they spend their time hassling boardwalk weed vendors and leave him alone.

He runs the actual necromancy trade out of a back room, like a speakeasy. Only the right customers with the right passwords get past the counter to the inner sanctum. In other words, he's utterly boring. If he conjured Fatty Arbuckle and sent him down the beach on a mammoth's back, he'd still be boring.

I get there a few minutes before he opens, when I can get a parking space with a decent view of the shop. The camera Julie gave us to work with is pretty idiot proof, so I get some shots of him opening up. Checking out a few lady joggers who run by. Feeding a piece of his morning donut to a local mutt who trots away to hustle other handouts. I write it all down in my notebook. Julie is going to get a record of every person who goes in, every tarot reading, every pigeon who shits on his awning. It will all end up in my report.

Ten people wander in and then quickly out of Wakefield's shop in the first hour. I take photos of all of them. The mailman comes by. I get a shot of him. In another hour, six more people go in and out of the place. I get shots. Wakefield comes out for a smoke. *Click. Click. Click.*

Two hours in and I can't stand it anymore. I dial Candy, but she doesn't answer and the call goes to voice mail. Even with the windows down, it starts getting hot in the Crown Vic. I smoke a Malediction, then another. Wonder if I could sneak away to get a cup of coffee, and curse myself for not buying a cup on the way over.

Around one Wakefield locks up and wanders down the boardwalk to a burrito place and has one with a beer. I get some discreet shots of him with his mouth full. Sexy stuff. Helmut Newton would be jealous.

Another dozen people go in and out of his shop. No one stays very long. Either his business is on its last legs, or he charges enough for the stuff he does in the back that he doesn't need much tourist trade and he just likes being at the beach. My guess is it's the second. He looks like a man who truly does not give one single fuck.

It's a sunny January day in L.A., but still technically winter. The sun starts going down around five. By five thirty, the sky is dark and Wakefield hasn't had a customer in an hour.

At six thirty on the dot, Tamerlan Radescu and his crew arrive at the shop. Wakefield meets them outside and ushers them in. I put the camera on infrared and snap away.

Tamerlan is inside for all of twenty minutes. Then he's out again. He and Wakefield shake hands warmly at the door. Tamerlan's men scan the crowd like nervous meerkats in case a vicious skateboarder or some bikini girls decide to race up wearing dynamite vests.

After Tamerlan and his men leave, Wakefield starts to lock up. Faced with a choice between watching Wakefield have another cigarette or following Tamerlan, I go for door number two.

Just as I pull out of the parking lot, my phone goes off. It's Candy.

"How was your day?" she says.

"I longed for Gojira to rise from the sea and put me out of my misery. But things are looking up. Tamerlan Radescu just showed up and I'm following him."

"Aren't you supposed to stay with the other guy?"

"He's a stiff and Tamerlan was in and out of his place real quick. Just long enough for a shakedown. I want to see if he hits any other Dead Head shops."

"I guess that's a good idea. You should call Julie."

"Why don't you call her for me? I don't want to lose him."

"Don't spook him. Stay cool."

"Don't worry about my cool. I'm Steve McQueen riding a polar bear."

"Okay. I'll call Julie."

"How was your guy?"

"Boring too. He went to a bar down the street like ten times during the day. I kind of felt sorry for him after a while."

"Weren't you going to send me smut if you were bored?"

"Yeah, but I got depressed watching him. I'll mail you dirty pictures from the kitchen when I get home."

"Then I'll make this quick."

"You do that."

I hang up and concentrate on Tamerlan's limo. It heads onto the San Diego Freeway, then over to the 10. The fucker gets off in Boyle Heights and I have the strangest feeling I know what's going on. The limo pulls over, one of Tamerlan's men ducks into a coffee shop and comes out with a whole tray of cups. They head back on Whittier Boulevard, then turn north, straight toward the Sixth Street viaduct and the goddamn White Light Legion.

I let Tamerlan go on ahead of me. The street at the railroad yard near the Sixth Street bridge is dark, so that's where I park the Crown Vic. The dirt by the side of the road is loose and easy to pick up. I use it to draw a protective ward—a mean one—on the car's roof. Anyone who comes calling will go home sad, but wiser.

Over on Mission Road, I hunker down behind a lamp-post and wait. I've been waiting all day. What's a little more wasted time between friends?

It's seven thirty when I sit down with a Malediction. It's nine when I spot the first Golden Vigil vans and Humvees coming across the bridge. I even have a cigarette left. That has to be a good omen.

There's a slight breeze blowing down off the river channel. It smells like exhaust and ashes. A couple of rats run ahead of me down the road. I'm still a football field away from the warehouse, but don't want to be seen by White Light shit-heads or the Vigil, so I take a step to the right, into the hurricane, and make the walk backstage the whole way.

The smell coming off the river is more intense in the storm wind. Strange tattered things blow by, grab at my legs. The walk down the road feels like I'm climbing a mountain with a pickup truck on my back. I swear the hurricane is stronger out here, maybe because of all the baleful magic at the warehouse. By the time I get to the White Light's parking lot, I'm exhausted. My chest hurts and it's hard to breathe. But I still have a long way to go.

It took me longer than I thought to get up the road. The first Vigil cops are already in the fight club and more pour in ultra–slow motion from the vans, moving like ants in liquid amber. Civilians sprint out of the club—couples, bikers, mean-eyed blue bloods. They scramble out the door, frozen in place like snapshots of pants-wetting fear. Getting inside the club is like swimming upstream through human-size salmon, all going the other way.

Guns are going off all over the place. Skinheads pop off shots at the Vigil; each muzzle flash is an orchid of fire. The Vigil's nonlethal rounds move almost imperceptibly. Flashbang grenades explode like glacial fireworks. Beanbag rounds hang in the air, turning slowly like fat fist-size wasps. Looking over at the fight ring, I wonder if the ghosts can see me. The current bout features two men with barbed-wire-wrapped ax handles. Both ghosts are covered in bloody ectoplasm. One of the fighters wears a Lucha Libre mask. I swear his eyes follow me as I move around the frozen patrons.

The stairs are completely blocked by more White Light bully boys and panicked civilians. It's too packed to push through them. I have to climb on the outside of the stairs, holding on to the handrail, moving up one toehold at a time. It feels like forever getting up there. My legs shake and I'm sweating more than I should be. This backstage world feels like it's getting harder on me each time I enter it. Maybe I should have hung back and let the Vigil do the heavy lifting. But I can't risk them stumbling across Vincent's heart. It won't take them long to figure out that I lied about its location, but by then I'll be long gone.

When I make it up the stairs, I climb over the railing and head into the snuff room. I'm not careful with people anymore. I shove goddamn civilians and White Lights out of my way. Their legs tangle and heads butt against each other, or they will eventually. They fall and smash into each other a millimeter at a time.

The scene on the killing floor is the usual horror. A muscled guy in tighty whities I recognize from a series of forgettable straight-to-video martial-arts movies is running with a chain saw aimed at the head of a singer I can't quite recall. From his hair and clothes, he might be a one-hit-wonder hippie from the sixties who sang a song about flying horses. Maybe. They're both ghosts and I can't move them around like I can the civilians, but I can change the fight. The chair the singer is tied to is real enough, so I drag it a few feet to the side. If Mr. Martial Arts isn't hexed into staying on the fighting floor, he might just stumble out of the ring and into the crowd. I'm not exactly looking for him to saw anyone's head off, just maybe give a few patrons a taste of what they've been getting off on.

I go around the room testing the curtains that cover the walls, looking for the *Gruppenführer*'s office. The curtain fabric feels both stiff and gelatinous. My hand finally lands on a doorknob. I push the curtain aside and try to go in, but the door is locked. I get out the na'at and extend it into a sword, slice the lock off the door. When I kick the pieces out of the way they hang in the air like slow confetti.

The light is on inside the office. Cheap, dark paneling, like the inside of a trailer. A gray metal desk. An enormous Nazi flag that covers one wall, with a bookcase right across from it. There's a glass-front gun cabinet against one wall. I'll have to inspect that before leaving. I'm feeling pretty nauseous now. I close the office door and step left, coming out of the hurricane.

Tykho was right. There's a canopic jar covered in Nordic runes on a top shelf of the bookcase right next to a shot of their mustached dear leader and his squeeze. Another photo sits right below them. A battered, faded photo of Sigrun back in her Thule Society prime. Young blond Aryan perfection. Is this what Tykho was talking about? Is this trailer-park Colonel Klink trying to muscle her into some kind of liaison? Blackmailing a vampire is a questionable move, but blackmailing Tykho seems like an idea sure to get you drawn and quartered. I guess having Death on your side gave the Nazi fuck giraffe-size balls. I smash the frame and take out Tykho's photo, stuff it in my pocket. I also grab a Luger with an ivory grip off another shelf and a Bowie knife, stuff them all in my pockets too.

Another wave of nausea hits. I need to sit down, so I set the jar on the desk and drop in the *Gruppenführer*'s chair. And start going through his drawers. Jackpot in the first one. I stuff more baubles in my pockets.

I take a bronze bust of Adolf's head from his desk and toss it through the front of the gun cabinet. Push away the glass and start piling weapons on the desk.

The door slams open and shut behind me. I turn around and lock eyes with a guy in a bloody White Light uniform. It isn't like the others I've seen. His is cut better and has some kind of insignia on the shoulders and breast pocket. We stare at each other for a second, Colonel Klink is as surprised to see me as I am to see him. He sees the guns and the canopic jar on the desk and pulls a pistol from its holster.

I don't have time to go for the Colt, so I grab a Benelli shotgun from the pile of guns on the desk and hope it's loaded.

It is. The sound of the gun going off in such a small space is like getting whacked with hammers on both sides of your head. But I miss and it only stops Klink for a second. He blasts away with his 9mm and a shot catches my upper right arm. My right side goes instantly numb, but I fire away as another slug grazes my leg. I fall back against the wall as Klink's chest explodes, a couple of loads of double-ought buckshot catching him just below his throat.

I lean against the wall and slide down, leaving a red streak behind me. Nausea mixes with the numbness, trying to convince my body to lie down and not move for a couple of weeks. But my brain is on high alert. There's a better than even chance someone outside heard the shots. I don't want the Vigil catching me here, especially with a ventilated Nazi and my pockets stuffed with his bric-a-brac. I get up and step right.

The hurricane hits and blows my dumb ass down again. Getting hold of the desk, I pull myself up. The canopic jar goes under my good arm. I look at the pile of guns. What a waste. Some stupid feds are going to get most of them when they'd look so much nicer decorating my hotel room. I try to pick up a few with my injured arm, but it refuses to work right. Using my left arm and a lot of wiggling, I get the Benelli's sling over my shoulders so I can haul it out without holding it.

Strange light shines through the shot-up Nazi flag. I go over and look through the holes. And can see the river and railroad yard. I put down the jar and pull the flag down. There's a door in the wall, Klink's private emergency exit. It's probably what he was going for when he came in. I can't quite swing the Benelli around, so I bark some Hellion hoodoo. Part of the door explodes, splinters and metal spinning away languidly into the dark.

Getting down the stairs with a jar, a shotgun, a bad arm, and a goddamn bleeding leg isn't easy, but it's better than navigating the rat trap back in the club.

When I get around the front of the warehouse, more Vigil vans have pulled up. It's D-Day over here. Have a fun night, boys and girls. Bust everyone and don't be too mad when you don't find anything under the fight ring. It's nothing personal. It's just that I don't trust anything you say or do. I'd rather be shot up with the heart under my arm than Schwarzenegger-perfect beefcake without it.

The walk back to the Crown Vic is longer than it took to build the Pyramids. I stop at one point, lean against a stalled Mercedes and tear off part of my shirt, wrap it around my bleeding leg. That takes another century since I'm working with one good arm and another that's as numb as bologna. When I start off again, I'm no longer leaving a trail of blood behind me so the Vigil can follow, maybe get some DNA samples. With luck, all the traffic tearing along the road will rub out most of the blood I already left behind.

When I make it to the car, I'm shaking, ready to puke up the entire menu of the Last Supper. The tightness in my chest is back, but at least something interesting happened. There's a nice scorch mark around the Crown Vic where someone tried to break in and got a hotfoot for their trouble. That puts a smile on my face.

Stepping left, I come out of the hurricane. And almost fall over again.

I get the Crown Vic's passenger door open and wrap the canopic jar in a seat belt. Don't want Vincent's heart slip-sliding around the car if we hit any red lights. I wrestle my coat off and toss it on top of the shotgun in the backseat. Then I drag my ass behind the wheel of the car.

Usually getting shot doesn't take this much out of me. I don't ever want to go backstage with a bullet in my arm again. I have to start the car with my left hand and mostly drive home to Hollywood that way. I take surface streets. It's longer getting back, but there's less chance of me taking a gimpy turn and driving off an overpass.

There's a parking space near the Museum of Death, so I take it. It's a metered spot, but all my change is in my right pocket. Looks like Julie is going to get a parking ticket in the mail. Fuck it. Let her take it out of my next paycheck.

I hump the jar and the rest of the loot, still wrapped in my coat, across to the hotel. I can't reach my keys, so I kick the door to our room a few times. Candy opens up and turns sideways. Or maybe it's me turning sideways. Someone is definitely moving at a funny angle. I decide it's me when something slams into my nose and I get a faceful of hotel carpet. I want to explain what happened, but when I open my mouth, all that comes out is "Who was the guy who sang the flying horse song?"

WHEN I COME to, I'm in bed and everyone is staring at me strangely, like I'm the Fiji mermaid in spats.

My right arm and leg are wrapped in fresh bandages. I can smell one of Allegra's healing potions through the bandages. She's taking my pulse. Vidocq is behind her. Kasabian and Vincent are behind him and Candy is at the foot of the bed.

"I had the strangest dream," I say. "And you and you and you were there."

"Shut up, Dorothy," says Candy. "You weren't supposed to get shot tonight. You were supposed to watch Tamerlan and come home."

"I *was* watching him. Then some crazy Nazi started shooting at me."

"No wonder, with all the junk we found in your pockets. What, you couldn't fit his refrigerator in there?"

"Did you find the present I got you? Brass knuckles."

"Did you look at them? The knuckles have swastikas on them. I don't want them."

"Damn. I missed that."

"What's in that big jar?"

I look around for Vincent. He's next to Kasabian.

"I found your heart."

"You did? You mean Townsend's heart."

"It doesn't matter whose heart it is. It's how they bound you. If we put it back, you'll be your old self again."

"How do we put it back?"

"How did they take it out?"

"Oh," he says.

"You can't be serious," says Allegra. "You can't just cut him open and start shoving organs inside."

"I can't. But you can."

"Forget it."

"Listen, if we don't get rid of McCarthy by dawn, the White Lights will own death. They'll decide who lives and who dies and when. It's the ultimate racket."

"Are you sure about this?" says Vidocq.

"Yes. We don't have long to fix things. What time is it?"

"A little after three," says Candy.

"Dawn is only a few hours off. We can't fuck around arguing. Vincent, are you ready for this?"

He has a hand on his chest.

"Yes. I want to go back."

Allegra shakes her head.

"This is ridiculous. I won't do it."

I sit up. The room spins, but I don't fall over. I'm pretty hard to kill, and heal quicker than a civilian. I test my right arm. It straightens out about three-quarters of the way. It hurts, but I don't pass out. I try raising it and get it as far as my shoulder.

I say, "If you won't do it, I will. Come on, Vincent. This is probably going to be messy. Why don't you get in the bathtub?"

He sighs.

"All right. Will it hurt?"

"The bathtub? No. It'll be cold."

"No. The cutting."

"Did it hurt when you woke up with your heart gone?"

"No. I simply felt . . . disembodied. As if I was in Townsend and somewhere else at the same time."

"There you go. This is going to be a breeze."

"Stop it. Both of you," says Allegra.

She looks at Vincent.

"You can't let this idiot hack you open."

She turns to me.

"And you can't just slice people up like an Easter ham."

"Then who's going to do it?"

She looks at Vidocq. He leans down and they whisper to each other. Allegra looks back at me.

"I'll do it," she says. "But you should stay in bed and heal."

"I'll heal later. Just give me something that will get me through the night so Vincent and I can finish this."

"Wait. What happens after you put Vincent's heart back?" says Candy. "I thought you said he'd be Death again."

"He will. But that means there will be two Deaths. We have to kill the other."

"Why do you have to go with him?"

"In case something goes wrong. Because something always goes wrong."

"I don't want you to go," she says.

"I don't have any choice."

I look at the others.

"Are you going to go? Or you? Or you? No. I'm the only one who's faced anything like this."

"You're a wreck. Please don't do this," Candy says.

"You said it yourself, people always get hurt around me. That includes me. I made it back from Hell twice. The second time just to see you. I can make it back from this. Besides, Vincent will look out for me. Right?"

He nods.

"Right," he says in the least reassuring tone possible.

Candy shakes her head.

"Fine. And when Julie calls to get our reports I'll tell her she can't have yours because you took our client to the land of the dead."

"You can tell her I'm solving the fucking case. That's what she wants."

"She doesn't want you dead."

"Maybe not, but let's be honest. What she really wants is the credit for saving Death. Tell me I'm wrong."

Candy doesn't say anything.

"Let's get going," I say. "Vincent, you strip and get in the tub. Allegra will get her tools and I'll get the heart."

Candy might be mad at me, but she looks more like I'm on my way to the gallows. She helps me up and I have to lean on her for support until I get my balance. I look at Vidocq.

"What do you have for a man who needs to keep moving no matter what for a few hours?"

He reaches into his coat and pulls out a small clear bottle full of a red liquid.

"Malefic baneberry. It doesn't taste good, but one teaspoon and a skeleton would dance a jig."

He takes out the cork and hands me the bottle.

"To the Führer's mustache," I say, and down it all.

*Malefic* is a nice word for what it tastes like. I want to spit it out, but it feels like my mouth and throat have sealed shut. The room spins. I sway. Candy grabs my good shoulder. Then I'm enveloped in warmth and the room stops moving. My mouth works and I can breathe again. I feel great, ready to run a marathon and wrestle Rodan.

"How do you feel?"

I lean over and kiss Candy.

"Not bad at all."

Candy pushes me away and spits.

"It tastes like you gargled vinegar and ammonia."

"Sorry. I just feel good."

"You better pray you come back, and when you do, hit the toothpaste before you get near me."

I look at Vincent.

"You ready?"

He's standing in the middle of the room naked. Turns and heads for the bathroom. Allegra gets her medical bag and I get the jar. Everyone follows us.

Vincent lies down in the tub as Allegra lays out her surgical tools. She swabs Vincent's chest with antiseptic, running her hand over the ugly scar where his heart was cut out. She selects a small scalpel from her kit.

"Are you ready?" she says to Vincent.

He nods.

She takes out a potion and rubs it on his chest.

"This will numb the area. You won't feel anything," Allegra says.

He nods. She gives me a dirty look.

"You better be right about all this."

"I am."

She turns back to Vincent and makes a straight incision across the scar.

"Does that hurt?" she says.

"I barely feel it," says Vincent.

Her medical kit used to belong to Doc Kinski, an archangel. It isn't exactly a regular kit. I don't recognize half the instruments. She uses things that look like knitting needles and an astrolabe to open Vincent's chest and hold it open.

And there it is. The same broken ribs and his sternum over the deep red hole. Vincent cranes his head down to see the opening. He doesn't like what he sees and lies back in the tub.

"You have my heart?" he says.

I open the jar. Until this moment, it hasn't occurred to me to make sure it's inside. I reach in and touch something wet. Pull out a big fistful of long, thin leaves. Graveyard tree, a common poison in old Eastern European Sub Rosa families. I peel back the leaves to reveal a thick mass of gray muscle. Townsend's heart does not look in tip-top shape. While I peel off the rest of the leaves, Vincent sings quietly. "Mack the Knife" from *The Threepenny Opera*. Kasabian hums along.

"I don't exactly know what's going to happen when I do this. You ready?" I say.

He nods, still singing.

I lean over his open chest with the heart.

"Stark," says Allegra.

"Yeah?"

"You're putting it in backward."

I turn the heart around.

"Thanks."

With one hand on the edge of the tub, I push Townsend's gray, dead heart into Vincent's chest.

Instantly, it begins to beat. Blood vessels, arteries, and ventricles stretch to meet each other. Blood begins to flow. The heart turns red. Vincent doesn't move.

"How do you feel?" I say.

Vincent turns to look at me. The whites of his eyes gradually fill with blood, turning a burning red.

"Fine," he says. "Better by the second."

His voice is different. Lower. It sort of ripples, deep and slow, like he's speaking through heavy sluggish water.

Allegra looks at me like she's saying, *Is that normal?*

I shrug.

Vincent sits up in the tub, pulls Allegra's tools off. The skin on his chest knits itself shut.

"Thank you," he says. "All of you."

"You okay to travel?" I say.

He stands.

"Can we go now?"

"Give me a minute."

I find my coat and go through the pockets.

Back with Vincent, I pop the pomegranate seed in my mouth. I nod. Vincent, still naked, starts to fade away. Candy comes over and hugs me. I put my good arm around her. Then bite down on the seed.

My vision shifts like someone jerked my head all the way around. I'm in L.A., but it's a junked, almost nuked place. Trash and burned-out cars in the streets. Empty storefronts. The dead city just beyond Tenebrae Station. Vincent is waiting for me.

"This way," says.

We walk through the pagoda-like Chinatown gate, go a few blocks through town and across the twisted, useless metro line tracks. In regular L.A., this would be the Los Angeles State Historic Park. Here, it's the beginning of the desert. The real land of the dead. Tenebrae city is for the spirits that don't want to pass over. A literal ghost town. The desert is where the other souls are divided up and sent—let's face it—mainly to Hell.

A half mile across the dry, cracked plain, a dust devil reaches into the sky. I stop for a minute, but Vincent keeps walking. I have to trot a few steps to catch up.

"You ready for this?"

He doesn't say anything for a full minute.

"This Death has taken my place, but he has no idea what he's doing," Vincent says.

"What do you mean?"

"He handles souls like a butcher handling sausages. You don't *pull* them from life. You escort them, giving them their dignity and easing their fears."

"I don't think dignity and good vibes are high on McCarthy's agenda."

Vincent looks at me like he's never seen me before.

"Yes" is all he says.

As we get closer, I see what he means about manhandling the dead. Souls hang in the sky. Row upon row of them, as far as I can see, a whole nation of uncollected spirits. The dust devil sends out whirling tendrils to the souls, yanks them out of the sky, and drops them, like a drunk picking apples. The stunned souls wake up on the ground having no idea what's going on. With no one to guide them, most of them probably don't even know they're dead. There are thousands of them, wandering the desert. Fucking McCarthy has figured out how to get the dead out of their comas, but not what to do with them yet. He's just collecting them like porcelain thimbles.

The dust devil plucks a few more souls from the sky and

drops them. Then it stops moving. It just swirls, kicking up the dry Tenebrae soil high into the sky. I have a feeling it knows we're here. I look at Vincent.

"He'll move soon. Get ready."

He looks at the whirlwind.

A moment later he says, "I've never had a fight."

He turns to me.

"I've argued, but in all the universes I've lived through, I've never had to fight anyone."

"It's easy. You just make a fist and put it in the other guy's face as fast as you can before he can do it to you."

He looks at me like I'm suddenly speaking Urdu.

"I don't know how. This was a mistake. I'm useless."

"Calm down, man."

The dust devil lurches and the sky fades to moonless dark. It whirls faster and skims across the desert in our direction. Lightning flashes. I swear I can see the vague outline of Edison Elijah McCarthy's stupid face in the flashes.

Vincent says, "I don't know what to do."

I move my right arm, testing my right shoulder. It's stiff but moves.

"That's okay. I do."

I take the black blade from my boot, start cutting a magic circle in the dusty plain. The vacant souls have seen us and are following the dust devil as it skims forward.

I work fast, cutting runes, spells, and sigils into the ground.

The dust devil bears down on us, a Mack truck of whirling crystal dust that will cut skin—my skin in this case—to beef jerky. When it's still fifty yards away I pull Vincent into the circle and shout Hellion hoodoo as loud as I can.

The dust devil convulses, like I kneed it in the balls. Lightning goes mad, cuts across the sky, explodes into the ground. Panicked souls scatter. The dust devil recovers, whirls in place, puffing itself up bigger than ever, and heads for us again.

Vincent takes a step back.

"What do we do?"

"First off, we don't step outside the circle."

Vincent quickly gets back inside the circle.

"What else?"

"We'll figure that out as we go along."

He sings quietly to himself, but the wind is too loud for me to make out what the tune is.

I bark more hoodoo, a mix of hexes I learned Downtown, and shit, I'm just improvising.

A wall of fire explodes before the whirlwind. It stops and shrinks back. Lightning smashes up the ground. Cuts deep black gashes in the desert floor until the bolts plunge into the fire itself. And sucks them up like a goddamn thousand-foot-tall shop vac. The flames swirl inside the dust devil. It glows like neon, and this time there's no question. It illuminates McCarthy's face.

The bastard is smiling.

He throws lightning bolts down at us. They explode around the edges of the circle, turning the air to ozone and making my skin tingle. Vincent flinches. He isn't singing anymore.

McCarthy rushes across the desert floor, moving over and around and completely surrounding us in his whirling, choking body. Desert dust clogs my nose and burns my eyes. Vincent has his hands over his face. He turns in a circle like he wants to run, but doesn't know where to go. He stumbles and falls. I pull him to his feet.

"Don't let this guy get to you," I say. "You're Death and you're as powerful as he is and you've been around longer. You know more tricks than him."

"I still don't know how to fight."

"Everybody knows how to fight. It's called survival instinct. I have it and so do you or you would have given up by now."

Vincent looks up at the whirlwind that engulfs us, not impressed with my pep talk.

"Go get him," I say. "This is all tricks. You're the real Death. Reach up and pull his fucking heart out."

Vincent wipes dirt from his eyes and walks to the edge of the circle.

"I am Death," he says in a booming voice I never knew he had inside him. "Leave this place and these souls, liar. Usurper. You belong here as just another ordinary soul, nothing more."

Vincent reaches into the whirlwind. And gets thrown backward like a crash-test dummy. I try to catch him, but we both land in a heap.

He looks up at me.

"I'm sorry."

I help him up.

"It's okay."

"I know I can do more, but I can't remember how. My powers feel like they've been gone for a million years. This flesh has me trapped."

"Let me do this," I say, and take off running.

I manifest my Gladius and run to the edge of the circle, plunge it into the dust devil. The blowing sand feels like I shoved my hand into a garbage disposal. My skin feels like it's peeling off in layers. Lightning bursts above my head. But McCarthy roils and convulses. Parts of the whirlwind shear off, man-size whirlwinds that blow across the plain and scatter to dust. The wind howls, like a man screaming in pain. I pull out the Gladius and shove it into the wind again, deeper. In a second, I feel McCarthy begin to pull back. The whirlwind shrinks around the circle and moves away in a slow retreat. I keep the Gladius buried deep in its gut, feeling good, knowing I have McCarthy on the ropes.

Until I realize that the situation is the exact opposite.

A gust of wind and dust hits me. I look down. McCarthy retreated and I took the bait. Moved straight out of the circle. I'm ten feet into the open desert. Lightning flashes and I catch a glimpse of McCarthy's face. I've used the Gladius to kill humans, Hellbeasts, and angels, but even an idiot like me knows that a burning sword isn't going to take out Death.

A swirling coil of wind reaches down and knocks me over the packed earth. When I get up I feel something scraping in my injured shoulder. I run for the circle. McCarthy reaches down again, but I see him coming and shout some hoodoo, shattering the coil with an air burst of fire. McCarthy bellows and I keep running.

I don't know if he's playing games or if I get almost lucky, but I'm right on the edge of the circle when he comes at me again, throwing down a bolt of lightning that knocks me over. Then a cone of wind settles over me, crushing me into the desert floor. I can't get up. Can't breathe or see. All I can do is lie there while McCarthy grinds me down to my bones.

Then I'm moving again, dragged across the packed ground. The wind lets up enough for me to open my mouth and shout a stream of black Hellion magic at the sky. Old arena stuff, each phrase a killing curse.

I don't know which one did it, but McCarthy rears a little. I open my eyes and see Vincent, covered in grime, his skin cut and bleeding from the blowing desert grit. He's pulled me back into the edge of the circle.

He helps me up and there's blood on his hands. I turn him around, checking for where he's hurt.

"It's not my blood," he says. "It's yours."

I look down at myself.

Yeah, it's mine all right. My plugged shoulder has opened up, along with a thousand little cuts on my arms and face. Fuck it. I want to tell Vincent it's all right, that I've bled before, but he's too scared to listen. He's never had someone else's blood on his hands before. The poor slob is getting hit with a whole lot of firsts these days, but I can't exactly buy him a drink and talk it over. McCarthy has surrounded the circle again and we can't stay like this forever. I manifest my Gladius, figuring that if I sliced off a little piece of his form before, maybe I can take off enough to hurt him. I start back to the edge of the circle when Vincent runs around in front of me.

"You'll die if he pulls you out there again."

"Me? I'm fine. I was just playing possum."

"You're lying. Help *me* fight him."

"How?"

He holds up his bloody hands.

"I can't do anything. You gave me my heart, but I'm still trapped in this flesh."

"What do you want me to do about that?"

"Free me from this body. Kill me."

"How do you know that won't destroy you?"

"Neither one of us has a choice. You can't go back out there and I can't fight him like this. Please. I can't watch you die and I can't live like this."

"This could be a really bad idea."

"What alternative is there?"

I look up. The sky is bottom-of-the-ocean black. When McCarthy sends out lightning bolts, the thousands of dead in the sky glow like ornaments on a Hellion Christmas tree. Vincent is right. We might be in the land of the dead, but the two of us are still meat. McCarthy can starve us and stomp us if we try to leave.

"What if this doesn't work?" I say.

"Then no one is worse off than they were before. McCarthy already controls life and death. I'm the only thing that can stop him, but not like this."

I picture Alice, the girlfriend I came back from Hell to avenge. Cindil, the donut-shop girl who was murdered to teach me a lesson. Father Traven, who died saving our lives in Kill City. All the people who, one way or another, died for me or who I let die. Even Johnny Thunders, the sweetest zombie you could ever hope to meet. I got revenge for some of them and did what I could for the others, but they still went through hell because of me. Am I going to add one more name to the list?

"Stark, we need to act. Don't die to protect someone who isn't afraid to die because he is Death. Free me."

I look at Vincent one last time.

"Vincent, I don't say this very often, but you're an okay guy for an angel."

"Don't worry about me. We'll see each other again someday."

"Not for a while, I hope."

"So do I."

Vincent closes his eyes.

I swing high and fast so maybe he won't feel it, and catch him at the base of the throat. Vincent's head rolls away across the packed ground. His body falls. There's no blood. The Gladius cauterized the wound. He's just in two dead pieces of useless skin. It's as simple as that. I let the Gladius go out.

The wind pauses for a second, as if McCarthy is trying to figure out what he just saw. When the gusts pick up again, moving even faster and wilder than before, I swear I can hear the fucker laughing over the din.

I sit down on the hard ground, lie back, and stare up into the sky. The earth is warm against my back. My shoulder hurts and I'm starting to lose energy. Guess the fight took a little more out of me than I thought. I wish Vidocq had left me more of that baneberry juice. That or a line of coke. I could use a pick-me-up right now.

The wind blows and there's nothing else.

I get the black blade out of my boot and crawl to the edge of the circle, cutting into the ground, repairing the place where Vincent dragged me back inside. I wonder how long I can keep this up. The wind wears away the perimeter of the circle and I repair it. In theory I can stay safe and cozy in my dust pied-à-terre indefinitely. But I'm going to fall asleep sometime. Soon probably. How much damage will it take for McCarthy to snake an arm through a crack in the circle and drag me back into the open desert? Doesn't really matter. There's nothing else I can do. Vincent is gone. There's no one to spell me. I look over at his corpse. There's nothing left of him. It's just Townsend's dead meat now. The worthless skin of a Nazi coward who thought he could buy his way out of the party with a blue yonder and got trapped like everybody else.

So long, Vincent.

As I lie down again, a roar thunders down at me. The kind of sound you feel in your bones as much as hear. McCarthy is still perched above me, but the perfect cone of his body begins to distort. It stretches and pulls thin around the middle.

He howls again as a hand the size of a Sherman tank punches through the stretched spot. As it pulls out, it rips some of McCarthy's swirling body out with it.

The dust devil shoots away from me, out into the open desert. McCarthy isn't alone now. Vincent is there too. He's almost as tall as McCarthy, his head scraping the bottoms of the black, rolling clouds. His eyes are blood and silver. His body is a bluish white, like polished stone. His arms are buried deep in McCarthy's whirling body, and he rears back, ripping out pieces of it. They fall, tiny tornadoes that skid across the ground and fall to dust. McCarthy howls and Vincent rips him apart.

Lightning flashes into Vincent's eyes. He stumbles back, blinded. McCarthy lunges for him, tearing away chunks of his skin. Vincent's bones glow from the open places, but he charges back into the storm, ripping at McCarthy's face. The storm returns the favor, slashing at Vincent's belly, ripping him open. His glowing blue flesh blows away like sheets of burning canvas into the distance.

It goes on and on like that. Two Deaths slicing each other apart. They fly to pieces. Small tornadoes skittering across the sand. Huge sheets of angel flesh lifted into the air and disappearing.

They begin to shrink. No longer as high as the sky. They drop below the clouds. Then the mountains. Wind and flesh fly in every direction. Roars like thunder shake the ground.

Vincent and McCarthy lose form faster and faster. Become transparent. A thin wisp of swirling sand and a glowing collection of bones, shredded skin, and muscles. They beat and howl until all at once they stop.

Neither moves for a few seconds. McCarthy comes apart first. The big bag of wind blows away like dust on the breeze, scattering to nothing. The black sky begins to clear to a purple twilight.

Vincent's glow fades. His torn body takes a few painful steps backward. He goes dark and falls to his knees. His body sways, then falls, shattering like glass. And it's dead quiet for a long time. I sit on the ground and look at what I've done.

We've gone from two Deaths to exactly zero.

The souls hanging in the sky are going to hang there forever. How many million more will join them because I couldn't think of anything better to do than kill my friend?

After a while I drag myself to my feet and start walking. I need a drink and a smoke and a shave and a three-hour shower to get this grit off me.

I'm moving slow. It takes maybe an hour to get back to the city, then another half hour through it to get to Tenebrae Station. I sit on the edge of the platform and wait. Soon I lie back and go to sleep.

I wake with a sharp pain in my side. I open my eyes and see Samael. He's poking me with a stick.

"Oh good. You're alive," he says.

"What's with the stick?"

"You're a bit . . . well, filthy and as bloody a mess as I've ever seen you—and I've seen you in bad shape."

"You here to take me home?"

"That was the deal."

"Do you know what happened?"

"Yes. So does Father. He's not happy."

"If he was so concerned, why didn't he do anything about it?"

"You know how he is. Standing up for noninterventionist deities everywhere. Hip hip hooray."

"So, what happens now?"

"I have no idea. We've never been without a Death before. I guess we'll play it by ear."

"That's a great idea. I'm sure all those semidead people won't mind while you get your shit together."

"Don't get snippy with me. I'm not the one who broke the universe . . . Again."

I nod.

"Can you take me home?"

"Of course."

"Great. I have more good news for you."

He tosses the stick away onto the tracks.

"And what's that?"

"I don't think I can walk. You're going to have to carry me."

He raises his eyebrows.

"You're going to ruin my suit."

"I'll get you a new one."

"You can't afford my tailor."

"I'll buy him off with a bottle of Aqua Regia."

"What makes you think he'll accept it?"

"It's all I have. Unless he wants a set of Nazi brass knuckles."

Samael looks down at me.

"No. I don't think that's quite his style. Can you at least get on your feet?"

I struggle up onto my knees and Samael pulls me the rest of the way.

"You're sure you can't walk? I love this suit."

"Sorry."

Samael isn't a huge man, but he picks me up like I'm a toddler and walks like I weigh nothing at all. I guess even ex-devils have secrets.

"Don't ever tell anyone I agreed to this."

"My lips are sealed."

It's a long walk down the tracks and through the station.

"What kind of aftershave is that?" I say.

"What? I don't wear aftershave."

"You smell nice."

He stops for a second.

"Say that again and I'll throw you in a ditch."

"Some people can't take a compliment."

I have him leave me off in front of the hotel. As usual, one of his endless number of limos appears from nowhere and a driver opens the door for him.

"I assume you can make it the vast expanse of twenty feet from here?" he says.

"Yeah. I'm good. Thanks."

He goes to the car. Takes his dirty jacket off, folds it, and hands it to the limo driver.

Before he gets in he says, "This is going to end badly, you know. There not being an Angel of Death and all."

"Any ideas what kind of bad?"

"Yes, but nothing I can talk about now. I'll be in touch."

"Take it easy."

He smiles.

"You might want to consider the same."

"That's the plan."

I go across the parking lot and knock on our door.

It opens and everyone else is still there. I look at Candy.

"Is that pizza I smell?"

"Kasabian got hungry," she says.

"I got hungry," says Kasabian.

Candy pulls me inside and I drop down onto the couch. I must look bad. Candy is the only one who wants to get near me.

"You're bleeding, you bastard," she says.

"I missed you too."

"What happened over there?"

What the hell can I say to them?

"McCarthy is dead."

"Did you kill him or Vincent?"

"Vincent."

"Good for him."

"Yeah. Good for him."

Allegra dive-bombs for my bleeding arm. I get her to hold off on the Dr. Kildare scene until after I take a shower.

The sun is coming up outside and I wish I could say that everything is right with the world, but it isn't. It severely isn't. But I'm not about to tell anyone. They'll just freak out and I won't get any pizza.

I SLEEP MOST of the next day, waking only for the occasional Malediction and shot of Aqua Regia—soothing Hellion Bactine for all your wounds.

In the afternoon, I turn on the TV for a few minutes. It comes on to CNN. No surprise that the lead story is how people have stopped dying again. The fucked part is that a lot of usually solid citizens are taking it worse than before. Riots. A stock-market dive. Prime ministers, potentates, and other assorted high-and-mighties deposed. It's an old story. Taking people's candy away is always worse than there being no candy at all.

Julie calls around four. Wants to know what's going on, if Vincent won the rumble in the desert. I tell her that, after being trapped in a body, Vincent is still getting his sea legs back. I'll have to come up with a better excuse soon, but right now I can't think of anything else and, really, I just want to go back to sleep.

Allegra comes by in the evening, changes my bandages, and gives me lovely, mind-numbing drugs. I can see how Vincent might fall in love with his pills. If Aqua Regia didn't burn so good going down, I might get a crush on the stuff too.

Vincent. What the fuck happened there? McCarthy was stronger than either of us thought. Or maybe it's just the nature of Death itself. Like the difference between big-name whiskey and some of the better no-name stuff. The off-brand might not taste quite as good, but it will fuck you up just as well as the expensive. McCarthy might not have been Angel's Envy or Gentleman Jack, but he was high enough proof to stand up to an angel. Best-case scenario, my lie isn't such a lie after all. Maybe Vincent really is hurt and just lying low until he's his old self again. Yeah. Let's go with that for now.

Candy takes pity on me. Brings me more tamales and donuts. Of course, Kasabian, nervous little fuck that he is, comes over and gobbles most of the grub, then heads back to his room to see if he can break the hotel's pay-per-view codes.

I fall asleep soon after that. I'm healing slower than usual from a couple of lousy gunshots. Normally, I'd be up and walking by now, but I still feel like shit. I should check the slugs in the Luger. Maybe Colonel Klink spiked his shells with poison, the clever little fuck.

When I wake up the next morning Candy is gone, but I actually feel a little better. My right arm is still stiff as hell, but my leg is mostly healed. I shuffle into the kitchen and turn on the coffeemaker, then go back to the other room to get dressed for the first time since I got back from the Tenebrae.

There's something white across the room. I go over and find an envelope someone shoved under the door. It's addressed to Mr. James Stark in fancy, florid handwriting, so it's not a kick-out notice from the hotel. I open the envelope. Inside is an invitation about the size of an index card.

It's from Wormwood Investments. There's no address or phone number, just a message scrawled in the same ornate hand.

*The presence of Mr. James Stark is requested at
3 P.M. today at the La Cienega oil field. This invitation
does not come with a plus-one. Come alone.
Lunch will
be provided.*

> *Regards,*
> *Geoffrey Burgess*

Just like the Augur's invitation, the card feels like it was
written on the kind of paper you'd print million-dollar bills
with. Rich people sure love their precious invites. Maybe it's
to disguise the fuck-you nature of the so-called request. Like
someone wouldn't show up to drag my ass out to La Cienega
if I didn't show? Is this Burgess part of the talent-agency family? It would be a big coincidence if he wasn't. And his first
name. Jeffrey spelled Geoffrey. Never trust a Geoffrey. Either
they're pretentious pricks or bitter that the family spelled
their name funny.

This has trouble written all over it.

I check the clock. It's already after two. In my current
shape, I'm not driving anywhere fast. It takes a couple of minutes of struggling to get my coat on. I leave the SS dagger on
the table. Don't want that on me if someone digs up my body
in a few weeks. But I keep the Colt, the black blade, and my
na'at. I'm tempted to take the Benelli, but they might consider
that rude and I'm not sure I want to start out on the wrong
foot with the kind of people I'll probably be meeting today.

As I'm locking up, Kasabian comes out of his room with
an ice bucket.

"Where are you going? You look like shit," he says.

"Just making a run to Donut Universe."

He looks me up and down.

"You always go out strapped to buy fritters?"

"You never know. I might have to wrestle someone's granny for the last one."

"Okay. You told your lie and we got that out of the way. Where are you really going?"

For a minute I consider telling him.

"I can't say. But if I'm not back by six, have Chihiro give this to Julie."

I hand Kasabian the envelope. I sealed it, which was pointless. Kasabian will steam it open the moment I'm out of sight. But at this point, I can't worry about that.

"I don't know what you're up to, but if you expect me to give Candy your suicide note, fuck you."

"I don't know what's going on either. I'm just trying to cover all the bases."

"You're going off to get killed and leaving me and Chihiro to fend for ourselves. We don't even have the store to go back to."

I head across the parking lot.

"I'll try to be back by dark. Just give her the note if I'm not."

The Crown Vic is still parked by the Museum of Death. I forgot I left it in a metered spot. There are about fifty tickets and a tow-away notice on the windshield. I throw them all in the gutter.

My right arm is still pretty useless, so I have to lean over and start the car with my left. I didn't take any of Allegra's pills because they'd make me too loopy to drive, which already makes me dislike Wormwood goddamn Investments.

I drive south, left-handed all the way. Am I nervous or just on autopilot? The oil fields seemed to appear out of nowhere just a few minutes after I left the hotel, but I know I've been driving for at least half an hour.

I turn on Stocker Street and see an open gate to the fields. I'm not that stupid. I park on the shoulder of the road around the corner and go through the gate on foot.

Inside are a few sheet-metal buildings, a couple of trailer offices, breaker boxes, and a scattering of porta-potties. All around me, the oil pumps rise and fall like those stupid drinking-bird toys. People don't think of L.A. as an oil town, but they've been sucking crude out of the ground for over a hundred years. More people have died for these fields than in all the gangland gunfights and hits in L.A. The Mob tried briefly to make a move on them. Oil was the only money game that managed to completely and utterly shut them out. That's how much muscle petroleum has always had in this town.

I come around a corner and into a scene I'd expect only Samael could pull off.

Food trucks are lined up in a semicircle. Mexican, Korean, southern, and a few others. At the end of the line are a couple of trucks that look like they're handing out desserts.

In the middle of the semicircle, on the packed dirt ground, is a long dining table set with crystal glasses, and expensive-looking china and cutlery. Eight people, four men and four women, move between the trucks and the table. They're in suits and evening gowns. They all stare at me when I come around the corner.

A bald man with his jacket off and sleeves rolled up heads in my direction. Right behind him is a dark-skinned woman pretty enough to make Salma Hayek blush. It's all plastic surgery, of course. The tightness of her face is a dead giveaway. The man has had work too. When he smiles, enough of his face doesn't move that I bet he has his own in-house Botox Dr. Feelgood. Still, this is no time to get judgmental. With my limp, gimpy arm and dirty boots, what do I look like to them? A Victorian street urchin with his nose pressed against the window, hoping for some scraps of their Christmas goose.

"Stark," says the man, extending his hand. "Thanks for coming. I'm Geoff Burgess. And this is Eva Sandoval."

He's not the same Burgess I saw at the fight club, but there's a decent enough resemblance. I shake both of their hands and look around.

"This is quite a spread. You always eat like this?"

"Not at all," says Burgess.

"Geoffrey is just showing off because we're having such an important guest," says Sandoval. She takes my good arm and walks me over to the food trucks. I wonder if Sandoval got on my left out of old-world charm or to make sure I can't reach the Colt. Burgess walks on my right. I'm surrounded. Politely, but still surrounded.

"I hope you're hungry," says Sandoval.

"What do you recommend?"

She smiles at me.

"I hear you've developed a taste for Japanese. Maybe some sushi?"

A Chihiro joke. Great. We're already starting with the veiled threats. Or was that just a little rich-people humor to remind me that no one has secrets from shits with enough money?

I look over at the southern truck.

"How's the fried chicken?"

Burgess says, "Outstanding. That's what I had. Beer batter with enough cayenne to wake you up, but not send you to the emergency room."

"That's for me, then."

Burgess raises a hand, and when we get to the truck a leg and thigh are waiting for me in a paper tray. I take it and some napkins and follow my hosts to the far end of the dining table. Before I can sit down, the other lunch guests get to their feet and applaud something. I look around and realize it's me. The applause doesn't last long, but it's still unnerving. The last time anyone gave me a standing ovation was in the arena in Hell.

"Don't mind them," says Sandoval. "They want you to know how happy we all are to finally meet you."

I nod, spread out a napkin on my lap.

"About that. You said something about me being an important guest. You want to explain that?"

"Try the chicken first," Sandoval says.

"You're a whiskey man, right?" says Burgess. He goes to one of the trucks and comes back with a couple of glasses of amber liquid. I sniff mine.

"Don't bother," Burgess says. "You won't recognize it. We have our own distillery and bottle it ourselves. Just for family and friends, you understand. Let me know what you think."

I take a sip.

Holy shit.

"How did you come up with this recipe?"

"Why do you ask?"

"This is the best thing I've tasted next to Aqua Regia and I've never met anyone up here who even knows about the stuff."

"I suppose that means we're not just anyone," says Burgess.

"I suppose so."

"Try the chicken and then ask your questions," says Sandoval. "I suspect that you have a few."

I take a bite of the bird.

"What do you think?"

"It's as good as the whiskey."

"It is, isn't it?" she says. "Now, what's the first thing you'd like to know?"

"What are you people? What's Wormwood? Some kind of bank?"

Burgess nods.

"To some people. But really we're an overall investment entity."

"What kind of investments?"

"Money, of course. That's what most freshman investors with us want."

Sandoval sips her whiskey, then says, "For more discriminating clients, we handle specialized products. Physical commodities. Oil, obviously. Land too. In more exotic departments, human organs. People."

Burgess wipes away a water ring on the table with his thumb.

"And there are our ephemeral departments. They handle

items such as souls. Damnation. Salvation. Those are some of our biggest markets."

I wipe the chicken grease off my fingers and push it away.

"I don't understand a single thing you just said. How do you invest in damnation?"

"Let me explain it to you," Sandoval says.

"In as small words as possible."

"Of course. When we said you were an important person, we were being quite sincere. Our investments in afterlife products were minuscule until you came along."

"Try this," says Burgess. "You're a profit center for us. We've backed a lot of your exploits."

"Through direct investments and working the margins," says Sandoval.

"I don't know what you're talking about. I don't even have a checking account."

"Simply put," says Burgess, "everything you've done since escaping from Hell has generated profits for us, both tangible and intangible. And everything you do in the future will continue to generate profits."

I look at the two of them, then the others.

"The White Lights didn't want Death," I say. "You did."

Burgess brightens.

"Well, the Legion wanted Death for their reason and we wanted him for our own. Their blackmail operation was going to bring in some revenue, but we had bigger things in mind."

Sandoval says, "Death can kill, but he can choose not to kill too. That was our first concern. We planned to live forever. We still do."

"With Death on our side, we could nudge the ephemeral

division in any direction we wanted," Burgess says. "Some chaos is all right. Even useful. But too much randomness is bad for business. Unregulated deaths are too wet and messy. But with Death on our side, we can manipulate markets on Earth, as well as our Heaven and Hell departments."

"Are we talking about money?" I say.

"Money, sure. But it's more than that. Those Cold Case merchants you dislike so much? Where do you think they get the majority of their souls? We collect all kinds of collateral and forfeited assets."

"In the end, it's not about wealth, but about power," says Sandoval.

"Why do you want that kind of power?"

"Only people with no power ever ask that question."

"Have you ever read *Nineteen Eighty-Four*?" says Burgess.

"I haven't even seen the movie."

"There's a passage in there, a small monologue by a character named O'Brien. I'll try to paraphrase it for you. Wormwood isn't interested in the good or even bad of others. We don't have a political ideology. We're interested in power, pure power, because the object of power is more power."

"For what?"

"It doesn't matter. For whatever we want," says Sandoval. "Here or in other places of existence."

Burgess chuckles.

"You know, we lost a lot of money in the damnation market when you convinced God to allow damned souls access to Heaven. I'll admit it. We didn't see that coming."

"But we made it back when the angels barred the souls from entering," Sandoval says.

"Exactly," says Burgess.

"You see? In the end, anything you do enriches us."

She looks at my plate.

"Your chicken is getting cold."

"Fuck my chicken. Is Abbot, the Augur, part of Wormwood?"

They both laugh.

"No," says Sandoval. "Wormwood is only for important people."

I remember a man I once met. They said he was the richest man in California.

"I bet Norris Quay was part."

Burgess picks up his whiskey and sniffs it.

"He still is. Our man in Hell, scouting for new investment opportunities."

I copy Burgess and finish the rest of my drink.

"So, all the White Lights killing people, Vincent and McCarthy, Tykho's crazy Nazi past, the battle for death, all those poor semidead slobs caught in limbo, all the ghosts destroyed in the club—all that meant nothing?"

Sandoval picks pieces off my chicken with her fingernails. Swallows them.

"Not nothing," she says. "They were each a factor in an investment decision. Think of it this way. There is war in the Middle East and there are pirates in Somali that seize oil tankers. They both affect the price of oil, but that's all. There's always been war and there will always be pirates. No one particular thing is special. But if you understand the markets, there's always profit and power to be had no matter who wins."

"The simple point is, Stark, there's nothing you can do or not do that won't benefit us," says Burgess. "Live. Die. Fight for truth, justice, and the American way, put down a zombie hullabaloo, or drown in a bottle. Your actions since your return have made you an investment factor. Even showing up here today made me a few shekels. Kominsky over there thought we'd have to send a riot squad after you."

Burgess shouts to someone down the table.

"Here he is, Pieter. Don't forget to pay up."

Pieter, a fat young man in a Caesar haircut, looks up.

"Don't bother me. I'm eating."

The crowd laughs quietly. I don't.

I say, "But Vincent killed McCarthy. You're not going to live forever."

"Please," says Sandoval. "We're not naive. We hedged the hell out of that fight and came out fine."

"Because we always do," say Burgess. "And there are other roads to immortality that we're exploring."

"Why are you telling me all these things? Did you bring me out here to kill me?"

"Of course not. You're much too valuable. We just thought it was time for you to know who you've really been working for all this time."

"You're not part of the Golden Vigil, are you?"

"Who knows?" he says.

"No. You'd tell me if you were. You're fucking with me to see what will happen."

"We just want you motivated and interesting."

"Did you have anything to do with Mason killing Alice or sending me to Hell?"

"I wish we'd seen that one coming."

"When you lived . . . well, it's our job to spot a good investment," says Sandoval. "We've had our eyes on you for almost twelve years now. Your exploits in the arena did well for us."

Burgess says, "Of course, we had to adjust our strategy when you kept winning."

"I hope you don't mind that we rigged a few of your fights. I mean, you had to lose sometimes to keep people betting. But don't be too mad. We were the ones who suggested to Azazel that he give you the key to the Room of Thirteen Doors. You weren't his first choice."

"So really, you owe us," Burgess says.

"You sicced the county on us, didn't you? The fucking eminent domain."

Burgess holds up his hands.

"Guilty as charged."

"You were getting too comfortable. The market was slumping," says Sandoval.

"And we're the ones rescinding county's order, so calm down. You did enough for us getting Vincent and McCarthy together."

"Rescind Julie's order too."

"Of course."

My head hurts. I wonder for a second if they put something in my drink. No. They said they weren't out to get me, and as insane as they are, what profit would there be for them?

"Do either of you have an aspirin?"

Burgess calls down the table, "Does anyone have an aspirin?"

Lots of shrugs and shaking heads.

"Sorry," he says. "We don't really get sick."

Sandoval says, "Technically, we do. But we have people who do it for us."

"A sort of Dorian Gray situation," says Burgess. "Surely you know that story."

"That's a movie I've seen."

"Excellent."

I look around at Geoffrey Burgess and Eva Sandoval, at their friends, the food, and oil pumps. All the miserable trappings of their astonishing power and wealth. I haven't eaten much today. The whiskey is dancing around in my stomach.

"Thanks for lunch. Can I go now?"

"Of course. No one is keeping you here," says Sandoval.

"Okay. Then I'm going."

I get up and start walking.

"Safe driving," she calls.

"Yes. Remember to take your vitamins," Burgess yells. "We want you bright-eyed and bushy-tailed."

Before I go around the first set of oil pumps, I turn and give them all the finger. More laughter and applause.

Black smoke coils up into the sky and blows down Stocker Street. I walk to the shoulder of the road.

The Crown Vic is on fire. Fully engulfed. Don't bother calling an ambulance. The patient cannot be resuscitated. I stare at it for a couple of minutes.

It's a mild day. In the midsixties. My head and my arm hurt. I wish I'd brought some of Allegra's pills along. I start walking to Hollywood.

I'm not more than a few hundred feet down the road when some genius starts honking at me. I flip him off and keep walking. He honks again. I reach under my coat. Maybe I can scare him away with the Colt.

I turn and sitting a few feet away in a red 1960 Ferrari 250 GT is Thomas Abbot. He's as young and handsome and posh as ever. I want to hate him, but I'm too tired.

He rolls down his window.

"Need a lift?"

"How did you know where I'd be?"

"Wormwood isn't the only one keeping tabs on you. Get in."

I consider it and decide that if Abbot wanted me dead too, he could have just run me over.

I go around to the passenger side of the Ferrari and get in.

"Nice wheels."

"Awesome wheels," he says.

He rolls up his window and hits the accelerator. The car takes off like a rocket and he pilots it like someone who's been doing it for a while.

"Did you burn my car so you could give me a ride back?"

"No. But I saw who did it."

"Who?"

"Audsley Isshii."

Some people seriously need to get a new hobby.

"I wonder why he didn't wait till I was in the car before he lit it up."

"Because I told him I'd be upset if he did that."

"Thanks. Why?"

"You did a good job with Death."

"You think?"

"Of course. People have started dying in droves. They estimate almost a hundred thousand since last night."

"I haven't watched the news since yesterday."

"You ought to."

"That's what my boss says."

"Speaking of bosses, have you had a chance to reconsider my job offer?"

"Honestly, no. It's been an eventful few days."

"I can match and beat any offer anyone else makes you."

"Why do you want me so much?"

"I just told you. You handled the Death case so deftly."

"And because Wormwood is so hot for me."

"That too."

I think about it as we drive.

"How's Tamerlan Radescu doing?" I say.

Abbot glances at me.

"All right, I suppose. Why do you ask?"

"What I mean is, is Radescu on your payroll?"

"No. He came around offering his services, but I don't have any use for a Dead Head. How did you know about that?"

"He was heading to your boat when I was leaving."

"Ah, right. He and my father were close, but we're not. He's turned into a mean old bastard. I don't need that around."

I nod, wishing I could see his eyes so it would be easier to tell if he was lying.

My arm throbs.

"If you were right there, why did you let Isshii burn my car?"

"I wouldn't have if you'd been one of my employees. It would have been my obligation to step in."

We drive for a while longer.

"Do you have any aspirin?"

"In the glove compartment."

I find the bottle and dry-swallow four pills.

"Give me twenty-four hours," I say.

"That's fair. Where should I drop you?"

"My boss's place so I can tell her about the car. It's in Silver Lake."

"Let's go."

I spend the rest of the drive wondering who's started killing people again.

ABBOT DROPS ME outside of Julie's building and heads off to do important Augur stuff, like sipping drinks on his yacht.

I head upstairs. Julie must have the security cams on because Candy meets me at the top of the stairs.

"You look terrible. What are you doing out of bed?" she says.

"I'm fine. I just need to sit down."

She pulls a chair over by Julie's desk and I drop down into it.

Julie pushes her coffee my way. I drink some and nod thanks.

"She's right, Stark. You don't look good. What do you need that we couldn't talk about on the phone?"

I take the keys to the Crown Vic out of my pocket and slide them across the desk.

"Here are your keys. You'll probably be getting a notice from city impound. Maybe a junkyard."

She takes the keys and drops them in a drawer.

"Where's the car?"

"What's left of it is out on La Cienega. I had to get a ride back with a friend."

"Who?" says Candy.

"Thomas Abbot."

That gets Julie's attention. She writes something down on a yellow legal pad.

"I'm torn here, Stark. Despite all the time you didn't listen to my orders and went off on your own, you did a lot of the heavy lifting when it came to solving this case. You handled some very dangerous people and helped reinstate Death to his rightful place. And your information helped to shut down the White Light Legion. Congratulations. You really put the agency on the map."

Candy reaches over and squeezes my hand.

"Thanks. Just happy to be part of the team, boss."

"With that in mind, I have a couple of announcements. First, Chihiro isn't an intern anymore. I'm hiring her full-time."

I look over at Candy. She's practically beaming.

"That's great news, babe. You deserve it."

"Also, Stark, you're fired."

"What?" says Candy. "Why?"

"For all the reasons I listed before. You never listen to any-body. You lost me a perfectly good car. You lied about where Vincent's heart was and you interfered with a Vigil raid. Plus, I'm sure there are a dozen other things I don't know about."

"At least a dozen," I say. "Two things, though. First, what did you think was going to happen when you saddled me with a cop car? Second, don't take any of this out on Allegra. If you give her a chance, she'll be a great tenant."

"It's all right," says Candy.

"Yes, we talked the other day while you were out," says Julie. "She's moving in at the end of the month."

I get up and take out a Malediction.

"By the way, I got your eminent domain called off."

"How?"

"Don't worry about it."

I walk to the stairs, turn back to her.

"There's just one more thing."

"What?" says Julie.

"Vincent is dead."

"Then who's Death?"

"I have no idea. See you around."

WE SPEND THE night at the Beat Hotel and move back into Max Overdrive the next morning. I'm still walking wounded for a couple more days, so we schedule the reopening and Candy's new-job party for the weekend.

Carlos gets there first and sets up a sound system. I thought he was just bringing a boom box with some Martin Denny and Les Baxter. Candy is thrilled. I'm happy she's happy, but plan to spend a fair amount of time outside smoking.

A little after six, Allegra and Vidocq are the next to arrive. They have Brigitte with them.

"Let me see your arm," says Allegra.

I flex a few times as she pokes, prods, and does generally uncomfortable doctor stuff to me. After a few minutes she seems satisfied.

"You're almost back to your old self. I'm just concerned

about you healing so slowly. Have you taken any drugs? Eaten anything different? Changed any habits?"

I think about the chicken and whiskey with Wormwood, but that can't be it. I was already fucked up when I got there.

"The week is up. I can't sidestep anymore. Maybe that's it?"

"I'm glad it's gone," says Candy.

She yanks a hair out of my scalp, shows it to Allegra. It's gray. She looks at me.

"Piss Alley always charges you more than you think it will. I think sidestepping was eating my life force or something. Anyway, it's over now."

"Good thing too," says Allegra.

"I just missed shadow walking so much. I guess it's really gone for good."

"You're stuck here with us groundlings."

"Sounds like it."

"You realize what this means?" says Candy. "We're going to have to get a car. You can't steal them forever and I have a respectable job these days."

"You stick to the respectable stuff. As long as I have the black blade, I can get any car I want. Besides, how are we going to register a car? We don't exist."

"Maybe the Augur can help?"

"Why would the Augur help you?" says Vidocq.

"You didn't tell them?" Candy says.

"I was going to do it tonight."

"Tell us what?" says Brigitte.

"Stark is respectable too, whether he likes it or not," says Candy. "He's going to work for Thomas Abbot."

"It's not like I'm going to be shining his shoes. I'll just be on the Sub Rosa advisory council."

"Congratulations," says Vidocq.

He and Allegra hug me. Brigitte does too, but laughs while she does it.

"Oh, Jimmy, don't become too housebroken."

"I don't think that's going to be a problem," Candy says. "He used my computer to find Audsley Isshii's license plate and drove his car off a pier."

"He's insured, so fuck him."

A few of our regular customers come by. Courtney, the Lyph, and her boyfriend. Cindil and Fairuza arrive together. Turns out that Cindil is apprenticing to Allegra at the clinic. Manimal Mike, the Tick Tock Man, pulls me aside and slips me something. I thank him and put it in my pocket.

I watch Candy talking excitedly with Fairuza about getting their band back together. Technically it will be a new band. Candy is gone, so it will be Chihiro on guitar. She pulls Cindil over.

"Can you play bass?" she says.

"No. I used to play clarinet in the school band."

"Perfect. We only know three chords. You're our new bass player."

"Cool," says Cindil.

I go outside with a cigarette and an Aqua Regia.

Guess this is how things are going to be for a while. Me stuck in the dirt not shadow walking and Candy pretending to be someone else. We can handle it. Other people deal with worse, right? And as long as Wormwood doesn't get directly in my face, I can handle that too. Besides, maybe me and the

Augur together can do something about them. I know I'm lying to myself, of course. Things like Wormwood don't go away. With their wealth and power they're dug too deep into L.A.'s hide. Maybe going respectable is my one way of beating them. If you can't murder them your only option might be to bore them to death. Maybe I'll get a car after all. A used brown Volvo. Let them try to figure that one out.

Samael comes in around seven. He has a flunky with him, carrying a chilled bottle of champagne in a silver ice bucket. The flunky leaves it on the front counter and excuses himself. I don't bother looking at the bottle's label. I won't recognize the name and Samael will probably tell me how he snatched it from the pope's private reserve.

He pours us each a glass and we head outside, where it's quieter.

"You look a lot better than the last time we saw each other."

"Yeah. I'm about back together."

"The tailor was able to save my suit, so all you owe me is the cleaning bill."

"Good. Send it to me."

"It might be a bit more than you're expecting."

"I'd be disappointed if it wasn't."

I try the champagne. It's not my favorite poison, but this stuff is better than most I've had.

"You heard?" I say. "People are dying again."

"Of course."

"You know who's responsible?"

"Sadly, yes."

"It's you, isn't it?"

He nods, stares into his drink.

"Father appointed me a few days ago. He says I should consider it a great honor to be the Angel of Death. I don't know. I'm not used to being in the same guise, doing the same thing day after day."

"Wait. If you're Death, how can you be here? Shouldn't you be off collecting souls?"

"I am. Death, like Santa Claus, can be many places at once. Me, I'm here with you. I'm also in Detroit, Nairobi, Vienna, Buenos Aires. Everywhere."

"Doesn't that get a little confusing?"

"It takes some getting used to, yes. I was constantly dizzy for the first couple of days. But it's getting better."

"Well, I'm sure you'll do a bang-up job."

"What about you? You're almost as acquainted with Death as I am. Would you like the job? It's a great honor. You're loved and feared around the world."

"Thanks. I'll pass. Besides, I already have a new job."

"How about one of your friends? The Frenchman seems like a smart fellow. How do you think he would do?"

"No. No one I know wants the job. We're all irresponsible and we all drink too much."

"I wish I could still drink too much."

"Since you've got the inside story, let me ask you something. One of my friends was stupid enough to get a wild-blue-yonder contract. What's going to happen to her now?"

"May I have one of your cigarettes?" he says.

I hand him a Malediction and light it for him. He blows out a long, satisfied stream of smoke.

"What about Brigitte?" I say.

"Don't worry about lovely Ms. Bardo. When the two previous Deaths died, all blue-yonder contracts became null and void. She's like the rest of you now. Someday she'll see me again and we'll take a final walk together."

"What about Tykho? Is she on the menu?"

"Tykho. Yes. She is a special case, isn't she? Maybe I should pay her a visit while I'm here. Let her know there's a new sheriff in town."

"Take me along if you do."

He takes another puff of the cigarette.

"No. I won't be seeing her on this trip. But she's on my naughty list."

He looks over my shoulder into the store.

"What's that music? It's lovely."

"It's Martin Denny. Carlos can tell you more than you ever wanted to know about him. I'll introduce you."

"Please do."

"But don't tell him you're an angel, especially not the Angel of Death. I don't have that many friends. I need to keep them all."

"Of course."

I go inside. Candy has her red Danelectro guitar out and is showing it to Cindil. They're plotting how to get her a bass cheap.

Candy spots me across the room and I signal for her to come over. She hands the guitar to Fairuza and heads over my way.

"Cool party, huh?" she says.

"The coolest. I have something for you."

"Yeah? Gimme. I'm drunk and going to get drunker, so show me now while I can see straight."

I take out a dirty handkerchief and hand it to her.

She gives me a funny, what-the-fuck look.

"This is a heavy hanky."

"Open it."

She smiles the moment she sees the brass knuckles with hearts on the tip of each finger loop. Slips them on and play-punches me in the jaw. Then kisses me on the spot where she clocked me.

"Thank you! Where did you get them?"

"Manimal Mike did them. He melted down the Nazi knuckles and made these. I figured it was good revenge on the fuckers."

"What every fashionable lady needs," she says. "I love them."

"Good. That's what they're for."

"Come on. Let's show them around."

She pulls me with her and starts pretend cold-cocking everybody in the room. I really should have given them to her when we were alone. She's going to be doing this all night.

When she tries it on Samael, he catches her fist. They smile at each other. A couple of killers on the prowl. He lets her loose and looks over the new knuckles. Gives her an approving nod.

"They suit you."

"Damn right they do," she says, glancing around for more people to punch.

Samael looks at me.

"You once told me about a place called the Museum of Death."

"Yeah. It's a little ways down on Hollywood Boulevard."

"You fancy a wander through? I thought with my new job, I might as well do some homework while I'm in town."

"Yes!" says Candy. "They're still open. Let's go right now."

Samael cocks an eyebrow.

"My car is right outside."

"Can I ask a few more people?"

"Whomever you like. It's my treat."

I grab Vidocq, Allegra, and Brigitte. Take them to the waiting limo and we head out, riding with Death to one of the few places he's never been. A museum dedicated to him. It's not how I expected to spend our first night back in the store, but that's okay. What's life without a few surprises along the way? It's death, and we're not having any of that tonight.

# ABOUT THE AUTHOR

*New York Times* bestselling author Richard Kadrey has published ten novels, including *Sandman Slim, Kill the Dead, Aloha from Hell, Devil Said Bang, Kill City Blues, The Getaway God, Butcher Bird,* and *Metrophage,* and more than fifty stories. He has been immortalized as an action figure and his novel *Butcher Bird* was nominated for the Prix Elbakin in France. The bestselling and acclaimed writer and photographer lives in San Francisco, California.

*People are dying again, only to
find that the war between Heaven and Hell
means souls are now trapped in Limbo.*

*Which is kind of how Sandman Slim
feels all the time . . .*

With a nefarious new drug sweeping through every realm, Stark might finally have something to give him focus once more. And if he has to kill a few people along the way, at least it's something to do, right?

READ AN EXCERPT FROM

# THE PERDITION SCORE

The next Sandman Slim novel
Coming Summer 2016 from Harper Voyager

THOMAS ABBOT IS talking about the end of the world, but I can't keep my eyes open. The inside of my head is all Disney dancing hippos and gators going at each other with knives like candy-colored Droogs.

Ever notice how the more pain you're in, the funnier the world gets? Sometimes it's peculiar funny. Sometimes it's "ha ha" funny, but it's always funny. I remember almost bleeding to death in Hellion arenas and all I could do was laugh. I understand if that seems a little strange. That's what I mean about peculiar funny versus ha ha funny. It's all a matter of perspective. The more totally fucked you are, the funnier everything gets. Right now, the world is hilarious.

What was I talking about? Right. Abbot. The end of the world. At least, I think it's the end of the world he's going on about. Maybe someone just keyed his Ferrari. Whatever it is, I'm not listening. It's not that I'm bored. I'm tired, my head aches, and my eyes hurt like someone's tunneling out with dynamite. It's been a month since I've slept right. At night, my dreams keep me awake. Awake, the daylight feels like someone scouring my skin off with steel wool. I laugh once and everybody looks at me because they're not in on the joke. I'm squinting at the light too hard to explain it to them.

"You have something to add, Stark?" says Abbot.

"Not a thing. I'm hanging on every word. But I might have missed some of the last part."

"I was saying the meeting was over. We've voted on everything on the agenda. I had to put you down as an abstention on, well, everything since you didn't feel like joining in."

The other ten members of the Sub Rosa council—the den of thieves, high rollers, and important families that run most of our little world—stare or shake their heads in my direction.

"I was with you in spirit, boss."

"That's what makes it all worthwhile."

He turns from me and back to the room. People are getting up, gathering briefcases, purses, and jackets. You could feed every refugee in Europe with what these people have in their pockets.

"Thank you all for coming. It was a good meeting. I'll see you next week," says Abbot.

Goodbyes to Abbot and general chitchat in the room. It's like my brain is an open sore and their voices are salt. I don't ever remember feeling this way, even Downtown.

"Hang around for a few minutes, Stark."

I nod to Abbot. With my head like this, I wasn't planning on going anywhere soon anyway.

When everyone leaves, Abbot comes over and sits down next to me. He's a handsome fucker and that's always bugged me. All-American boyish looks with all the power of the Sub Rosa at his disposal. We're on his houseboat in Marina del Rey. The meeting room is trimmed in gold and exotic woods. There's enough video monitors and other electronic gear along the back wall to launch a nuclear war. Abbot's floating pad is like a comic book supervillian's orbiting death lair. Yet, I kind of like the prick. He seems honest. He gave me a seat on the Sub Rosa council. And he hasn't thrown me out for doing a lousy job. But I can't help wondering if I'm about to get a Dear John letter. "Things aren't working out. It's not you. It's me." You know the routine.

Abbot laces his fingers together and gives leans back in his chair.

"You don't look so good," he says. "Please don't tell me you're missing meetings because you're hungover."

I shake my head and immediately regret it.

"If only. Then, at least, I'd have had a good time. This though. It's a Trotsky icepick."

"Have you ever been checked out for migraines?"

"I don't get migraines. I leap tall buildings in a single bound."

Abbot gets up and looks through an expensive leather messenger bag.

"Let me give you my doctor's name. He does great work. You're aware, aren't you, that as a council member you get health insurance?"

"I do?"

"It was in the packet I gave you when you started."

"You gave me a packet?"

He comes back over with something in his hand.

"Maybe you lost it at home. Look for it. You even have a small expense account."

He puts a business card on the table. It has a doctor's name on it.

"Free money? I'll find it. And thanks for the advice, but I have my own doctor."

"Then go see him or her. Doctors are like aspirin. They don't work if you don't use them."

"Speaking of aspirin, you have any?"

There's something else in his hand. He sets down a small yellow prescription bottle.

"Aspirin won't do much for a migraine. But you should try these. I get headaches myself and these clear them right up."

"Your doctor's Sub Rosa?"

"Of course. Why do you ask?"

"I don't know. You're one of the moneyed chosen. I always pictured you with your own hospital or something."

He smiles.

"Just the wing of one. It's all dad could afford."

I look at him.

"I'm kidding," he says.

"Just give me the pills, Groucho."

He hands me the bottle and points to the glass of water that's been in front of me the whole meeting. If it had been a snake, I'd be taking a venom nap by now.

I pop the pills in my mouth. They taste like flowers. Like one of those goddamn violet candy bars my mother used to gnaw on with her whiskey. Very classy. Very sophisticated. I want to spit them out, then remember they're medicine, so I don't. Abbot pushes the water to me and I take a long gulp.

"How was that?"

I finish the glass.

"It tastes like the wreathes at a mobster's funeral."

He puts the cap back on the prescription bottle.

"It does, doesn't it? Anyway, you should feel better in a few minutes. I can give you a few extra if you'd like to take them with you."

"Thanks. But I'll bug my doctor for something that doesn't taste like a Hobbit's lunch."

"Suit yourself. But if you change your mind . . . "

"Thanks. But I won't."

Listen to yourself. Stop whining. This is your boss you're talking to. He's given you free drugs and is offering more. That's what people do when they see someone in pain. Shut up. Be a person.

"I feel better already."

Abbot gets up, tosses the bottle in the messenger bag, and brings it back to the table.

"I doubt that," he says, "but you will. Is your head clear enough to talk? I want to discuss something with you."

"Is this the part where you chew me out for being bad in class?"

"No. I understand how awful migraines can be. But tell me next time and maybe we can do something about it. No, I wanted to talk to you about the real agenda for the meeting."

"Going to dish about your rich friends? What do you tell them about me?"

He sits back down.

"Nothing. But, trust me, they ask. What I want to talk about is the real reason for the meeting. Did you hear anything I said tonight?"

"Something about charities. Climate change. The end of the world."

"You're right about the charities part. What I wanted to

see was who was pushing for which charities. I think some of the board members are in bed with Wormwood."

Wormwood Investments. What can I say about that bunch? They're into money and power. And they have a good time getting and keeping both.

Charity doesn't really seem to be their thing, though, so I try to get my mind wrapped around that.

"You think that dicking around with charities will tell you which ones are on the take?"

Wormwood is like a mob run bank if the mob was a Hellion horde and the bank was the world. They make money when the market goes up and currencies collapse. They make money on where and when famines kill the most people. They make money on who is or isn't damned.

And they make money on me.

Who I kill. Who I don't. Whether I'm a good boy or a bad boy, they make a profit and it pisses me off.

"Wormwood has a lot of front groups," says Abbot.

It clicks. "And the council can funnel to them through the charity fronts."

"Exactly."

"So, you want to see who recommends which ones."

"You've got it."

Another wave of pain gets me just behind my left eye. I close it and squint at Abbot through the right like I'm doing my best Popeye impression.

"Did you find out anything?" I ask.

"Maybe. I made sure everyone knew there was money to be spent. We batted around the names of a few groups, including two that I know have Wormwood connections. The next meeting we'll vote and see who pushes for which groups."

"How diabolical of you."

"Thanks. I'm flattered."

The wave of pain passes and I can use both eyes again. I get up and go around the table to where there's another full glass of water and drink most of it.

"Listen. I know a guy—Manimal Mike—with a lot of power tools. Why don't you point me at some of the shifty types on the council and I'll show them Mike's saws?"

Abbot raises an eyebrow before saying, "I'd need some proof before I'd let someone called Manimal Mike loose on anyone."

"Point me at the Wormwood creeps and I'll make them sing La fucking Traviata."

"I hope it won't come to that."

"If it's Wormwood, it will."

"You might be right."

I sit back down again and the light in the room stops strobing.

"Hey. I think your hamster food is starting to do something."

"See? I told you so." He pauses. "There's one more thing I wanted to talk to you about."

He reaches into his bag and pulls out a white folder. He opens it on the table. There's a photo of a young boy.

"A friend's son has gone missing. His name is Nicholas. He's run away before. Mostly to his father's house in San Diego. Everyone was assuming that's what had happened this time, but my friend hasn't heard anything and is worried. I remember that your lady friend, Chihiro, works for a detective agency. Do you think she could look into it for me?"

Abbot knows damn well that Chihiro is really Candy living with a new name and a new face courtesy of a powerful glamour. I have to give Abbot points for being discreet enough, even though we're alone, to use her cover name.

"I was heading to her office after the meeting. I'll give it to her then."

Abbot's face relaxes. I hadn't registered the worry until it wasn't there anymore. I also notice that he's gone far out of his way to not say who his friend is.

"Thank you. That means a lot to us."

Okay. The friend is someone close, not just one of the council members trying to hide a family scandal. So, who is it? A childhood pal? A lover? Is Abbot married? I can't see his ring finger, but that's also a pretty Judeo-Christian tradition—not so much among the Sub Rosa types.

I focus back on the missing child.

"How many times has this kid run off? He looks like he's maybe twelve."

Abbot picks up the picture, looks at it, and sets it down again.

"Yes. He's always been precocious. With luck, this is nothing. But there's some worry that his father might have abducted him."

I flip the picture over. There's information on the back. Eye color. Hair color. Height. The only contact number is Abbot's. I close the folder and put it in my coat pocket.

"I'll give it to Julie. She runs the agency and decides who gets what cases."

"That's great."

"So, what time are we doing this charity vote thing tomorrow?"

Abbot laughs.

"Stark, it's Friday. We don't meet again until Monday. Take the weekend. Get your head fixed."

"Right. Friday. How about that?"

Where the hell did this week go? I swear, it was Tuesday just yesterday.

"Okay then. I'll see you next week, boss."

"See you Monday," says Abbot.

I leave and walk back to the dock as sunset comes down over the docks. From here, Abbot's floating Xanadu looks like a burned out garbage scow. Sub Rosa chic. They love their mansions to look like ten-week-old shit from the outside.

One okay thing about being on the council is that I get a stipend (and apparently an expense account—really need to look at that packet Abbot talked about). Since I can't use the Room of Thirteen Doors anymore, and since the last car I borrowed got burned by a psycho named Audsley Ishii, I got one of my own. A black '68 Pontiac Catalina fastback. Actually bought it. Inside, the previous owner put a rebuilt 455 V8 under the hood. Outside, it looks like a hearse and a cruise missile had a bullet-nosed baby. I get in, turn the key, and make the monster roar.

THE DRIVE FROM Marina Del Rey to Hollywood isn't as hideous as it could be. The 405 tonight is a plodding lava flow instead of a graveyard. Abbot's gerbil food pill tuned down my headache, but the headlights on other cars still hurt my eyes. I can't believe I almost missed Friday. My head will be shaken back into place soon enough. I swear, having a job is half of what's wrong with me.

I never liked being an employee. I tried it before. Signed on with the Golden Vigil—basically, a government anti-hoodoo spook force. It didn't work out. The bosses—Larson Wells in particular—and I didn't exactly get along (I fought the law and the law won). Then they threw Candy in jail and would have shipped her to a Lurker Alcatraz in the desert if I didn't get help from a friend. Then they screwed me out of my paycheck. Then I tried playing private detective.

Don't bother asking how that worked out.

Even though the council gig is a pretty cushy job, being a salaryman grates on me in a very basic way. It reminds me of working for Azazel, a Hellion bigwig Downtown. The relationship was simple: He was the boss and I was his slave. Pull the plow or get sent to the glue factory. This job isn't as bad as that by a long shot, but being under the thumb of anyone who can burn down your life with a phone call makes me, let's say, uneasy. Maybe that's why my sleep has been shit.

I can't help wondering what Abbot does and who he talks to when I'm not there. Does he discuss me with whoever his personal friends and advisors are? No, that's not really in doubt—of course he does. The questions is what he says and why. I mean, he's the Augur. He'll play whatever angles he needs to stay who he is. That means he'll use me against the blue bloods, the blue bloods against me, then he'll turn around and use us all against each other. None of this automatically makes him a bad guy, just a politician. For now, I'm going to assume he's on the level with me. But if I get one

whiff of nefarious unpleasantness, I'll dump him in one of the open graves in Teddy Osterberg's cemetery collection in Malibu and bury him alive.

Right now, though, I need to get off the road as soon as possible. The headache wants to come back down on me. It tightens the back of my skull like an anaconda wrapped around my head. But Abbot's flower power pills keep it at bay. I just need it to work for another hour or so. Then, depending on how things shape up, I'll go to Allegra's clinic or the other place.

The one I really want to get to.